DARK BLACK

For Chris,
Thanks for your
support.
Hope you enjoy!
Jessica

Jessica GERMAINE

Jessica GERMAINE

DARK BLACK

An Urban Street Novel

THIS BOOK ALSO COMES WITH A SOULFUL RAP AND R&B MUSIC CD ALL LYRICS WRITTEN AND PERFORMED BY Jessica GERMAINE. IF YOU DO NOT RECEIVE A COPY OF THE CD WITH THE BOOK, YOU CAN ALSO DOWNLOAD IT FOR FREE AT DATPIFF.COM: KEYWORDS JESSICA GERMAINE/ DARK BLACK.

ISBN: 978-0985594503

ISBN-13:0985594500

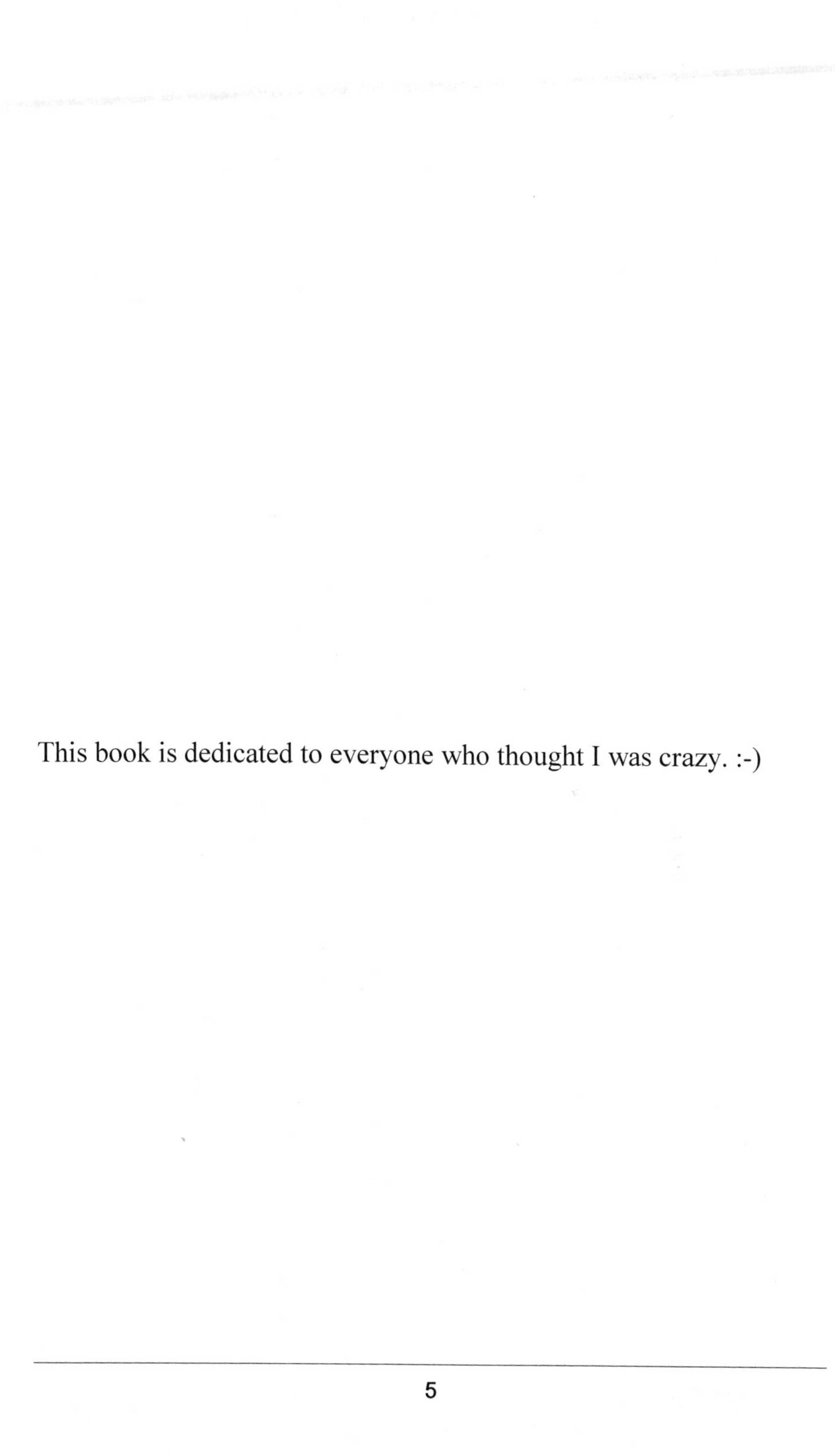

This book is dedicated to everyone who thought I was crazy. :-)

IN LOVING MEMORY OF

LARRY D. SMITH

JAMIE FLEMING

DONTAE GARY

DARTANYA BENTLEY

Before you get into the contents of this book, I would like to take some time to share with you the meaning behind it. I want you to keep in mind that this is flowing directly from my heart. I told myself that- unlike the book- when I write this particular passage, I would focus less on being grammatically and 'formally' correct, and focus more on just sending a message. In fact, besides any major errors, most of it I won't even dare to change.

You see, this foreword is more than just a 'Word to the Readers' column that authors commonly display at the beginning of their books, it is my testimony. Some of you may not understand, some may judge, some may take what I say as personal business and turn it into gossip, some may even read this and decide that you are no longer interested in DARK BLACK. But I pray that you will put any negative thoughts or feelings aside, and in turn, open your hearts and minds to less judgmental way of thinking.

FIRST, I WOULD LIKE TO GIVE SOME BACKGROUND INFO ABOUT MYSELF. I AM JESSICA SMITH. GERMAINE IS MY MIDDLE NAME. ACCORDING TO 2013, I AM TWENTY-FIVE YEARS OLD AND THE MOTHER OF A BEAUTIFUL FOUR-YEAR-OLD GIRL NAMED ALOURIE. I GREW UP IN SAVANNAH, GEORGIA TO A SINGLE PARENT MOTHER. I REMEMBER BEING THE TYPICAL CHILD- NAÏVE, SENSITIVE, RESPECTFUL, SMART, AND WAS NOT A SECOND BEFORE MY TIME, JUST THE WAY A LITTLE GIRL WAS SUPPOSED TO BE. GROWING UP, I CAN VIVIDLY REMEMBER BEING VERY BASHFUL, BUT IT WASN'T UNTIL I GOT TO COLLEGE THAT I SAW JUST HOW BAD MY SHYNESS WAS. I REALIZED THAT I COULDN'T DO THE MAIN THINGS I NEEDED TO DO TO SURVIVE IT, WHICH WAS TO ADJUST, ADAPT, AND ASSOCIATE MYSELF WITH OTHER PEOPLE. AND EVENTUALLY, I NOTICED THAT THE WAY I WAS BEHAVING JUST WASN'T WHAT THE VAST MAJORITY OF US WOULD CALLED "NORMAL."

FOR EXAMPLE, DURING THE FIRST WEEK OF SCHOOL, IF THE PROFESSOR MENTIONED ANYTHING ABOUT A GROUP ASSIGNMENT OR A CLASS PRESENTATION, I WOULD IMMEDIATELY GET UP AND WALK OUT OF THE

ROOM, EVEN IF THE COURSE WAS MANDATORY. I WOULD WALK TO A CLASS THAT WAS THIRTY MINUTES AWAY- INSTEAD OF CATCHING A BUS THAT WOULD GET ME THERE IN THREE MINUTES- BECAUSE I DIDN'T WANT TO RISK THE CHANCE OF PEOPLE STARING AT ME WHEN I GOT ABOARD. MY COLLEGE MAJOR WENT FROM SOMETHING I REALLY WANTED TO DO, TO "WHICH MAJOR DIDN'T REQUIRE I TAKE PUBLIC SPEAKING?"

SADLY, MY GROWING FEARS AND TROUBLES WEREN'T JUST WITH SCHOOL; IT ALSO AFFECTED MY PERSONAL LIFE. SIMPLE DAILY ACTIVITIES, LIKE WALKING THROUGH THE AISLES AT THE LOCAL WAL-MART, OR GOING THROUGH A LINE AT THE MCDONALDS DRIVE-THRU, BECAME A SOURCE OF WORRIATION AND STRESS FOR ME. I KNEW IT WAS ODD THE WAY MY BODY RESPONDED TO THOSE SITUATIONS, BUT I NEVER SEEK HELPED. INSTEAD, I TRIED TO CURE MYSELF BY ACTING LIKE I WAS PERFECTLY FINE. ALTHOUGH IN REALITY, CONSTANT SATURDAY NIGHTS ALONE DIDN'T EXACTLY MAKE ME FEEL GOOD ABOUT MYSELF. SEEING MY ROOMMATES GETTING DRESSED UP TO GO OUT WITH THEIR FRIENDS WHILE I JUST SAT HOME MADE ME FEEL DEPRESSED AND LONELY. BEING M.I.A FROM BIRTHDAY PARTIES, SOCIAL EVENTS, AND GOING INTO PERIODIC DEPRESSIVE 'SHELLS' CAUSED ME TO LOSE FRIENDS, AND IN SOME CASES, GAIN ENEMIES. I HAVE A GREAT MUSICAL GIFT AND WAS A PART OF GREAT TEAM WHO BELIEVED IN ME, BUT I WAS EVENTUALLY LABELED AS A NON-SUPPORTER AND A DEAD TALENT BECAUSE I WAS TOO AFRAID TO GO TO SHOWCASES OR PERFORM MY OWN MATERIAL.

ALL THOSE THINGS I JUST MENTIONED, ALONG WITH MANY OTHERS THAT I DON'T EVEN HAVE THE TIME NOR SPACE TO GET INTO, MADE ME FEEL HORRIBLE AS A PERSON. SO HORRIBLE, THAT I BEGAN TO FEEL CERTAIN TYPES OF NEGATIVE WAYS ABOUT MYSELF. I FELT LIKE A NOBODY. I FELT LIKE AN OUTCAST. I FELT LIKE A WEIRDO. A COWARD. AND I BEGAN TO CALL MYSELF THOSE NAMES, UNTIL ULTIMATELY, I BEGAN TO DO THE WORST THING A PERSON COULD EVER DO TO THEMSELVES- BRING DOWN THEIR SELF-WORTH.

I WONT GO INTO SPECIFIC DETAILS, BUT ANYBODY WHO HAS EVER BEEN DOWN, KNOWS EXACTLY WHAT I MEAN. WHEN YOUR SELF-ESTEEM IS LOW YOU BEGAN TO ACCEPT THINGS THAT YOU WOULDN'T NORMALLY ACCEPT, AND YOU BEGAN TO DO THINGS THAT YOU WOULDN'T NORMALLY DO. AS SOON AS I WAS LEGALLY ALLOWED TO DRINK, I DID SO, AND BY THE TIME I WAS TWENTY-THREE I CAN HONESTLY SAY THAT I HAD A SERIOUS ALCOHOL PROBLEM- AVERAGING ABOUT A BOTTLE OF WINE OR A PINT OF LIQUOR A DAY, AND MY SMOKING HABIT WASN'T FAR BEHIND.

THOSE THINGS DID TEMPORARY EASED MY PAIN, BUT AFTER THE HIGH WAS GONE, I FELT EVEN WORSE THAN I DID BEFORE. I COMTEMPLATED SUICIDE. I SLACKED AS A MOTHER. THERE WERE DAYS WHERE I LOOKED IN THE MIRROR AND LITERALLY HAD TO TOUCH MY FACE AND ASK MYSELF, "WHO I AM?" HELL, I WENT FROM BEING VOTED MOST LIKELY TO SUCCEED IN MY HIGH SCHOOL CLASS, TO DROPPING OUT OF COLLEGE AFTER TWO-AND-A-HALF YEARS, WITH NO INTENTIONS OF EVER GOING BACK. I SETTLED FOR A PART-TIME LIBRARY JOB BECAUSE I WAS TOO AFRAID TO GO ON INTERVIEWS, AND THE ONES I DID BUILT THE COURAGE TO GO ON, I FROZE UP AND ENDED UP MAKING MYSELF LOOK COMPLETELY DUMB. I COULDN'T AFFORD TO PAY MY BILLS SO I ENDED UP DEPENDING ON GUYS TO GIVE ME MONEY. NO I WASN'T A HOE, BUT I WOULD TOLERATE THINGS THAT I NORMALLY WOULD NOT HAVE JUST BECAUSE I NEEDED HIS HALF OF THE RENT. MY LIFE IN MY EYES WAS A TERRIBLE DISASTER.

BUT YOU KNOW HOW THE OLD SAYING GOES, SOMETIMES YOU JUST GET "SICK AND TIRED OF BEING SICK AND TIRED" AND THAT'S EXACTLY WHAT HAPPENED. I BELIEVE I CRIED MY LAST TEAR WHEN WALKED OUT OF CHURCH IN THE MIDDLE OF SERVICE BECAUSE I WAS TOO AFRAID TO USHER, AND I FINALLY DECIDED BEFORE **GOD,** THAT I DIDN'T WANT TO LIVE IN FEAR ANY LONGER.

I SOUGHT PROFESSIONAL HELP AND FOUND OUT THAT I SUFFERED A SEVERE CASE OF SOMETHING CALLED SOCIAL ANXIETY DISORDER, WHICH

IS BASICALLY A DEEP FEAR OF BEING SOCIALLY INVOLVED WITH PEOPLE. IN MY CASE, IT WASN'T HEREDITY BECAUSE MY MA, NOR MY PA, WAS LIKE THIS, NEITHER WERE MY BROTHERS. AND THE MORE I RESEARCHED THIS CONDITION, THE MORE I LEARNED THAT I WAS NOT THE ONLY ONE WHO SUFFERED FROM IT. THERE ARE MANY PEOPLE HIDING BEHIND THEMSELVES, AND WORSE, THE MAJORITY OF THEM WILL NEVER BUILD THE COURAGE TO SPEAK OUT ABOUT IT.

UPON HAVING A BETTER UNDERSTANDING OF WHAT WAS GOING ON WITH ME, I DECIDED TO TRY AND WEE MYSELF AWAY FROM MY BAD HABITS BY DOING MORE POSITIVE THINGS, SUCH AS STUDYING BIBLE SCRIPTURE DAILY, WRITING POEMS, READING BOOKS. AND ONE DAY, AFTER MY BINGE OF READING URBAN NOVELS, (AND IM NOT BASHING ANY OF THE URBAN AUTHORS) I CAME TO REALIZE THAT MANY OF THOSE TYPE OF BOOKS PRETTY MUCH HAD SIMILAR PLOTS- THE HOTGIRL-MEET-DRUG-DEALER THING. FOR ONCE, I WANTED TO PICK UP A BOOK THAT *I* COULD RELATE TO. MAYBE SOMETHING ABOUT AN ORDINARY GIRL WHO MAY NOT HAVE BEEN SO PRETTY, WHO COULDN'T AFFORD PRADA AND GUCCI, WHO WENT THROUGH LIFE JUST AS THE MAJORITY OF US "REGULAR FOLKS" DO. THEN I CAME ACROSS A QUOTE BY MAYA ANGELOU THAT SAID SOMETHING ALONG THE LINES OF, "IF THERE IS A BOOK YOU WANT TO READ THAT HASN'T BEEN WRITTEN, THEN YOU SHOULD WRITE IT." I READ THAT THING ABOUT TEN TIMES UNTIL A VOICE INSIDE OF ME SAID, "YOU CAN WRITE THAT BOOK." WITH NOTHING TO LOSE, I ATTEMPTED WHAT SEEMED TO ME TO BE IMPOSSIBLE, AND BEFORE I KNEW IT 'DARK BLACK' WAS BEING PUBLISHED.

WRITING 'DARK BLACK' BROUGHT ME SO MUCH JOY, BECAUSE I BEGAN TO UNDERSTAND THE *WHATS?* AND THE *WHYS?* OF MY LIFE. I BEGAN TO UNDERSTAND MY PERSONALITY AND STARTED TO REALIZE WHAT MY PURPOSED WAS. ALTHOUGH THIS BOOK IS FICTIONALLY, IF NOT FOR ME BEING 'A CERTAIN WAY' AND BEING IN CERTAIN SITUATIONS, SOME OF THE MOST VITAL EVENTS OF THIS STORY WOULD NOT HAVE EVEN BEEN THOUGHT OF. SEE, ALL THOSE THINGS, GOODS AND THE BADS, RIGHTS AND THE WRONGS, MADE ME A STRONG PERSON AND A GREAT AUTHOR.

I DON'T WANT TO LINGER ON, I JUST WANT TO SAY TO EVERYONE WHO IS GOING THROUGH A TRIBULATION, WHETHER IT BE ANXIETY, DEPRESSION, SICKNESS, GRIEF, LOW SELF-WORTH, FINANCIAL INSTABILITES, SUBSTANCE ABUSE, CHILDHOOD ABUSE, LONELINESS, WHATEVER. GOD SEES YOUR PAIN AND HE HEARS YOUR CRY. EVEN IN THE MIDDLE OF MY 'TROUBLING LIFE', HE USED ME TO MAKE A WONDERFUL STORY THAT WILL THE TOUCH LIVES OF ALL WHO CHOOSE TO RECEIVE IT. HE DID IT FOR ME, AND IT MAY NOT BE THROUGH A BOOK, BUT HE CAN DO THE SAME FOR YOU. YOU JUST HAVE TO STAY POSTIVE AND HAVE FAITH.

AND TO THOSE WHO SUFFER FROM SOCIAL ANXIETY, IT'S HARD TALKING ABOUT IT, LET ALONE GETTING PEOPLE TO UNDERSTAND WHAT YOU'RE GOING THROUGH. JUST KNOW THAT YOU ARE NOT ALONE. I AWARE THAT THIS IS NOT SOMETHING THAT CAN BE MAGICALLY BE CURED, BUT ASK GOD GIVE YOU THE STRENGTH TO SEEK HELP BECAUSE THERE ARE WAYS YOU CAN MAKE LIVING YOUR LIFE EASIER.

ALTHOUGH THIS BOOK HAS NOTHING TO DO WITH SOCIAL ANXIETY, I TOLD MYSELF THAT THE ULTIMATE PURPOSE OF WRITING IT WAS TO BRING AWARENESS TO THIS DISORDER BECAUSE IT IS DEFINITELY A SERIOUS ISSUE THAT HAS BEEN OVERLOOKED AND UNDERMINED IN AMERICA. EVERY DAY PEOPLE ARE KILLINGS THEMSELVES, AMONGST OTHER THINGS, BECAUSE THEY'RE LIVING IN FEAR. I COULD HAVE BEEN ONE OF THEM, BUT BY THE GRACE OF GOD, I WASN'T. I'M NOT LOOKING FOR ANYONES SYMPATHY, BECAUSE NO MATTER WHAT I GO THROUGH OR HAVE GONE THROUGH, I AM STILL TRULY BLESSED. ALL I ASK IS THAT YOU SUPPORT THIS BOOK AND BE A PART OF MY TESTIMONY. THANK YOU GUYS! I HOPE YOU ENJOY!!!! -JG

PART ONE

1: DARK BLACK

I killed my mama. I admit, it’s my fault she’s dead. But don't act all surprised; it happens all the time- kids killin’ dey parents and shit. Hell, Tiyana Arnold from around the corner, drove a screwdriver through her mama’s neck, all because she wouldn’t let her go to the movies with her friends. And I don’t know what po’ lil Tommy Kicklighter’s mama did to make him shoot her in the head when she was sleeping, but he did. Left her dead on the spot too.

So you see, it’s not unusual anymore. Although fortunately for my mama, I'm not the violent type. Stabbing and shooting and shit just ain't my style. But still, don’t get it twisted. I'm much worse than that Tiyana girl and that Tommy boy put together, ‘cause what I did to my mama was much worse and much more painful; I was born.

Yep, it was the birth of me that stole her last breath. I guess pushin' out seven pounds of pure hell was just too much for her to bear. I never got the chance to be smothered in the cushioning of her bosom. We never shared that special first moment, where I looked into her eyes and all my problems for the next couple decades were magically transferred over for her to endure. I missed the opportunity to be guided by her wisdom and loved by her nature. Most importantly, I never had anyone understand me- or at least try to understand me- the way my own mother would have.

Come to think about it, that probably explains why, at age fifteen, I was lost out in the world... with no family, no real place to call my home, and no sense of myself. And it could be the reason why I spent most of my life feeling so empty, that it almost seemed as if I didn't exist. In fact, the only thing that makes me even half sure that my birthday was really real, was the long scar I got across my face on that dreadful day.

I often find myself reminiscing back to the day I too died- internally that is. That's the day I realized I was the reason my mother was no longer living. I was just a kid then, seven years old to be exact.

You see, after mama died, I was picked up by my evil Aunt JoAnne. And I spent most of my childhood living with her and her three kids- Korey, Keisha, and Keyshawn. Because Auntie Jo, as I called her, constantly partied and ran the streets, Keisha- although was just a kid herself- was forced to care for me. And even though there was a ten year gap between us, she didn't mind me hanging around. In fact, she sort of liked the idea of feeling like I was her child. It made her feel older; that was right up her alley since she always wanted to be grown anyway.

To me, Keisha was my mom. She did everything a real parent would do. She'd dress me. She'd bathe me.

She'd fuss at me. She'd even spank me for little things. But I didn't mind, I was just happy someone cared enough to do that much.

Anyway, it was on a cold, winter night in mid-February. Keisha and her best friend Shannon were planning on ditching their high school's annual Valentine's Day Dance. They met two older guys one day we were all walking to the corner store, and they wanted to hook up with them. The three of us were hanging out in me and Keisha's bedroom, and I watched them both get dressed, and prepare for their big night out.

"Did you talk to them yet?" Keisha asked Shannon, as she pulled her red silk dress over her head. Then she began to comb her sandy, bob-length hair in the mirror above her dresser.

"Yeah bitch, I told them to pick us up from the school at 7:15." Shannon, who was also in the mirror, answered before sliding her plump, round hips over to allow more room for the both of them.

"I hope you told them to park across the street. I don't want nobody to see us leaving, especially Mrs. Holland, or Shameka's nosey ass," Keisha pouted.

"I'm two steps ahead of you girl. You know I'm a pro at getting away with doing slick shit," Shannon boasted. "I told them to scoop us from off the corner of Columbus and 32nd Street. That means we gotta walk through the neighborhood, but at least no one will see us."

"You mean I gotta walk in these heels!" Keisha yelled, as she pointed down to her black six-inch stilettos that strapped around her toes and ankles.

"Or would you rather have Mrs. Joanne stuff that heel up ya ass?" Shannon reminded her.

"I'd take the walk for 300!" Keisha joked. "Besides, I'd walk *all* the way to California to see their fine asses any day. Both of them niggas look good!"

They both giggled.

"Damn Keish," Shannon replied, after toning down her laughter. "You talkin' like you got yo' mind made up. I hope you not planning on giving Tre any. You know how easily persuaded you can be when it comes to a cute guy."

"*Easily persuaded*?" The expression on Keisha's face quickly changed from a happy to confused one. "I hope you're not trying to say that I'm easy, because I'm not. I'm just bolder than you."

"I didn't say you were *easy*," Shannon defended herself. "All I'm saying is that every time we meet guys at the same time, you the first one to give it up. I know I'm always right behind you, but at least I wait a little while."

"Oh, so now you better than me because you wait *a couple days* later," Keisha mocked her. "You mean to tell me that you ain't think about going all the way with Kevin, not once today?"

"I can't lie, I thought about it," Shannon confessed. "But that don't mean I'mma do it."

"But the point is... you want to. And from what my grandmama- God bless the dead- used to tell me, thinking about it is just as wrong as doing it."

"I know, I know. But can you blame me? That dude is *capital F* fine. Not only that, he's real cool too," Shannon said. Then she began to go into a daze, probably thinking about Kevin. "Keisha, I know I've said this about all the rest, but I think this is the one. To be honest, I want to do it with him, but I just don't know what he would think of me."

Listening to their every word from the corner of the bedroom where I was sitting, I peeped my head up from out of my coloring book, threw my crayon down to the floor, and butted head first into their conversation.

"Do what?" I said innocently.

Shocked, Keisha and Shannon looked to each other, then broke out into a heavy laughter.

"Little girl, stay out of grown folks conversation befo' I slap you in the mouth!" Keisha screamed. Then they both continued to laugh.

Crushed by being yelled at, and unaware of what I did wrong, my smile quickly turned upside down. Shannon rushed over to give me a big hug, letting me know that they were just playing. She always came to my aid whenever Keisha would hurt my feelings. For some reason, I believe she pitied me.

"We're just playing Charlytte," Shannon comforted me, then placed her hands over my ears before she continued talking. "I just don't know, Keish. I think I might give him some H-E-A-D, but the problem is, I'm not all that good at it. I mean damn, he might laugh at me if I don't do a good job. I don't wanna be known around town as the girl with the bad headache, if ya know what I mean," she winked.

"Well I ain't never had no complaints in that department, so I'mma just test my luck," Keisha said confidently.

Keisha must have never told Shannon that she had been down on a guy before, because Shannon looked like she saw a ghost when she heard those words come out of her mouth.

"*Ooooooh*...you did that before?" Shannon questioned her, right before we were all interrupted by the sound of a ringing phone. Hoping it was the guys, Keisha dashed to it like she was competing in the Olympics.

"Damn, this just ma," she yelled from the other room. "Hello."

While Keisha held her conversation in the kitchen, back in the room, Shannon began slipping into her clothing. She wore a long-sleeved, pink blouse with some black slacks, and some gold heels to compliment her gold accessories. Watching Shannon dress, I couldn't help but admire her beauty. She was just as pretty as Keisha was.

Once her clothes were on, Shannon stood up in the mirror and sung Faith Evans *'You Gets No Love'* to herself, while applying her make-up. After she was done with everything, she turned to me and asked, "How do I look?"

Not that she valued the opinion of a seven-year-old, she just wanted to have her ego boosted by hearing somebody, other than herself, tell her she looked good.

"Very nice," I answered timidly.

"Thanks babes. You have great taste. When you grow up, you gon' be just like us," she said, as if it was some type of compliment.

Shannon rewarded me by brushing some of her gold eyeshadow against my eyelids. I was just about to ask her to decorate my lips too, but we were interrupted by the sound of Keisha's loud flip-flops flapping swiftly towards the room. Before I could turn around to look at her, she barged in and pushed me so hard that I fell to the floor, knocking my head on the dresser on the way down.

"Why you do that!" I cried out, confused and hurting at the same time.

"You little bitch!" she yelled at me. "I hate you sometimes! Why did you have to be a part of this family? Why couldn't *you* have died instead of my Auntie?"

"Don't say that Keisha! That's mean. What the hell is wrong with you?" Shannon asked as she helped me up and comforted me by rubbing my head where I held it.

"Can you believe that mama is saying she's too drunk to drive over here and watch her! She said she's staying the night at Evelyn's house, but I know she's just going to lay up with that nigga. She makes me soooo fucking mad sometimes! I'm tired of babysitting and all these damn responsibilities! This ain't my damn child! She ain't giving me nothing out of the check she getting! And it ain't my fault she killed her mama! This shit ain't fair man! It's just not fair!"

Keisha was angry. Her eyes went from angel white to devil red, and her veins were literally about to pop out of her neck. I had never seen her so mad before. I mean, I've heard her curse her boyfriends, snap on her brothers, and she often said some pretty foul things to me, but never anything of that magnitude. Nothing could describe the pain I felt once those words left her lips and entered my tiny little innocent ears. And from that moment on, I blamed myself for my mother's death.

"Calm down Keisha," Shannon told her. "Plan B, that's all. We just gotta move to Plan B."

"What's Plan B?" Keisha asked, trying to figure out what the 'Queen of Mischief' had up her sleeves.

"Well...when ya mama stays out, she doesn't come home until early in the morning, right?"

"Yeah, so?"

“Sooo… if we can’t go to the guys, how about they come to us?"

"Bitch I ain’t never brought no man up in my mama house!" Keisha shouted. "You trying to get me kilt fa' real."

"Well fuck it. I'mma just call and tell them that we can’t come out, like we some lil’ damn girls. I know fa' sho they ain’t gon’ wanna fuck with us again. Shit, that’s better than going to the school and somebody seeing us anyway."

"You kinda right. Callin’ them would make us look bad," Keisha scratched her chin. Clearly she was beginning to re-think Shannon's proposal. "Just tell them they can come over, but they gotta be out by two, got that? And we can let little Miss Fuck-it-up be our look-out. She owes me that."

"Bet." Shannon said, sealing the deal.

A couple hours later, I was sitting in the living room watching an episode of The Berenstain Bears, when I heard a soft knock at the door. Keisha ran to the bathroom to check her hair and make-up, and Shannon went for the door.

"That’s them," Shannon whispered quietly to Keisha, while looking out of the peep hole.

"Well open it," Keisha whispered back.

When the door flung open, two handsome guys stood boldly on Auntie Jo's doorstep. One of them had smooth pecan-brown skin with a fresh low cut, and stood about six feet tall. He had on a brand new pair of white Nike Air Force Ones and a matching white collared shirt. The other guy wore all black. He was much darker and a lot shorter, but hands down, he was cuter. I may have only been seven, but I could recognize a good-looking guy when I saw one. I could now see why Keisha got so mad with me, but that still didn't change the fact that I didn’t like either one from the moment I saw them. Partially because they both looked like stone-cold players, but mainly because I knew I was going to lose the battle for Keisha and Shannon's attention to them.

The dark-skinned guy, who I assumed to be Tre, hugged Keisha. Mr. Pecan, Kevin, grabbed Shannon from behind and embraced her. After their quick lovey-dovey session, they walked deeper into the house, took their seats on the living room couch, and began looking around to get a feel of the place. Keisha and Shannon took their places beside them.

"Y’all beautiful ladies care to have a drink with us?" Tre asked, once they had gotten as comfortable as they were going to get. Then he took two midsize bottles out of a brown paper bag and placed them on Auntie Jo's glass coffee table.

"Yeah, most definitely," Keisha replied. "What's that you got there?"

"Some Absolut for y’all ladies, and some Hennessy for us big dawgs," he said, causing both him and his friend to laugh.

"What’s so funny?" Keisha asked. "Y’all don’t think we drink dark liquor? Shannon girl, they must not know us."

"I never said that,” Tre clarified. "I just want y’all to drink the white."

"It really don’t matter to me," Shannon said. "I’m down for whatever."

Keisha headed off to the kitchen to get some cups and ice, and with Shannon and Kevin beginning to flirt and play around a little bit, Tre, who was sitting all alone, turned his attention to me.

"Hey lil' girl. What's yo name?" he asked.

I didn't say a word. I just looked at him like he was speaking a foreign language or something. Then I rolled my eyes and continued to watch the television.

"Well *excuse me,* little lady," he snapped back, before yelling out to Keisha, "Hey Keish! Is this the lil' one you told me you have to look after?"

"Yeah, that's her!" Keisha hollered back.

"Oh, I figured," he chuckled. "She must get that sassy attitude from you."

Keisha stuck her head from out of the kitchen. "What? I know she ain't in there being grown. She still mad from earlier. I had to knock her up about something."

"Oh, that's why she got that mark across her face," he joked.

They all started laughing. But I didn't think anything was funny. I was sensitive about my scar. I thought it made me ugly. Sometimes I hated looking in the mirror, just because I knew it would appear, and I always prayed to God that he'd remove it. The kids at school laughed at me. The teachers even stared. And the questions people asked constantly reminded me of it. I was tired of making up stories about how I got it, especially since I didn't have the slightest clue myself.

And Keisha, of all people, knew how I felt about that scar, but instead of cursing them out like she did Korey and Keyshawn for laughing at it, she just joined in and laughed too. My poor heart was crushed.

"No. Some shit happened when she was born. I don't know the full story behind it," she informed them, then she looked to me. "Girl, go in the room and watch TV. I'mma call you back out here when I need you. And don't fall asleep because *I am* going to need you."

As I was told, I went into the bedroom, turned on the television, and found The Berenstain Bears again. That show reminded me of what my family should have been like. Sometimes I even dreamed that I was Sister Bear, and that my mother was Mama Bear. It's sad to say, but I learned more from that show than I did from my own family.

Another hour went by and I found myself still watching cartoons, but I couldn't concentrate on my show with the four of them talking so loudly. They were running off about everything from Court T.V. to sex on the rooftop. Then suddenly, their outbursts turned into a silence.

As a result of my curiosity, I slowly cracked opened the door to get a peep. From where I was standing, I could see Shannon on top of Kevin, kissing him on one couch, and Tre on top of Keisha, hunching her on the other. Both couples were going at it like it was none of each other's business. After I had seen enough, I slowly closed the bedroom door again. But not even a couple of seconds later, there was a hard knock on it.

"Charlytte Monique Black!" Keisha banged.

I jumped in fear and then my heart started pounding. I just knew Keisha saw me spying on them. And I knew I was about to get a good whooping for being nosey.

"Yes ma'am," I said innocently.

"Come here and look out this window until I tell you otherwise," Keisha yelled from the other end. "If mommy or anybody pulls up, hurry up and come get me. And *DO NOT* cut on the television because I don't need you getting sidetracked. I need you focused."

The only thing I wanted to focus on was the back of my eyelids. It was about eleven o'clock at night. I got up for school at six that morning. Instead of me being put to bed like any other seven-year-old, I was forced to sit at a window and be a lookout girl.

"Yes ma'am," I said slow and unwillingly. I knew better than to tell her 'no.'

"I'm telling you little girl, you better not fall asleep, or you're gonna wake up with my foot in ya ass! And don't disturb me, unless it's mama."

When Keisha opened the door, Tre was slouched behind her like she was a piece of meat and he was a carnivore. He had this wicked smile on his face as if he just knew he was about to get him some. Clearly he was feeling good, and it made me a little uncomfortable the way he was gazing at me. I quickly looked away as I passed them.

Keisha and Tre entered the room and fell straight on top of my Princess bedspread, even though Keisha's bed was just a couple of steps away. I closed the door behind them, leaving them to their privacy. Korey and Keyshawn's bedroom door was also closing, and the living room was empty, so I knew that Kevin and Shannon had just gone in there.

I walked back into the living room, grabbed me a fold-out chair, and took a seat by the window. As I stared out of it, I noticed that the night seemed extremely dark and still. I looked up at the dim sky to find no moon and no stars. The late night street animals were not out roaming. Even the wind and the trees were motionless. And I was feeling everything that a seven-year-old should not have been feeling- alone, betrayed, and crushed. On top of that, I was hearing sounds that I should not have been hearing. I didn't know if I was supposed to mind my business, or help those girls. I was indeed, only seven-years-old.

In attempt to take my mind off the strange sex noises and keep myself awake, I figured since I was up, I would work on my homework. Earlier at school, my art teacher asked us to draw a picture using the colors that describe our feelings. I grabbed my crayons out of my backpack, along with the Manila paper she had given to us, and then looked through the box for a color that best described me.

Scheming over different shades, I found one. I began to paint my entire paper this one color and when I finished, I still wasn't satisfied. I colored it some more, pressing down harder and harder on the canvas. When I was finally tired, I signed the back of my paper, because that was the only place my name would have shown. Pleased with what I had done, I held the project up with both my tiny little hands.

"Dark black," I said, before I shut my eyes and began to dream.

2: THE SWEETEST REVENGE

Enough with the sad and mushy stuff, allow to me properly introduce myself. I am Charlytte Black: the world's curse, and living proof that God does make mistakes. I'm forced to tell my own story because nobody cares enough to tell it for me. I got a juicy taste of reality at a very early age. By fifteen, I was making my own chips and taking care of my damn self. I worked at a hood grocery store called Mr. Chill's. It was owned by an old, black man who only gave me the job because he's a pervert and didn't mind looking at my ass from his office room while I worked.

The store was in the heart of the hood, and within the first month of working there, nothing was surprising to me. Sometimes my life didn't seem that bad when I saw some of the folks that came up in that place. I remember one time, this crackhead lady tried to pay for some meat with some damn Monopoly money, *and* had the nerve to get mad and try to fight me because I wouldn't take it. Then another time, this old man came in and walked up and down one of the aisles, just staring at me. Before I knew it, he was standing in the middle of aisle three with his pants down to his knees, jacking his you-know-what while staring deep into my eyes. I almost passed the hell out.

Whoever said that when you're at the bottom, the only place you could go from there was up, told a big fat ass lie, because things went from bad to worse after Keisha left Auntie Jo's house. She had been gone ever since the day Auntie Jo came home early one morning, found me sleeping up against the window and two strange guys passed out naked in each of her kids' bedrooms. Auntie Jo never officially kicked Keisha out, but the beating she put on her made her run away and never look back.

When Keisha ran off, she went to live with Shannon. Shannon's mama didn't care. She was always too high to care. But Keisha didn't stay there too long because Shannon eventually moved into the projects. Apparently she wasn't such a "pro" after all. She couldn't *professionally* make Kevin put on a rubber the night they snuck them into the house. Ten months later she had a baby girl and the rest of 'em just seemed to pop out each year after that. But fortunately, all four of her kids were from Kevin.

Keisha came to visit Auntie Jo every now and then, when she was looking her best. Only time we saw her was when she had a new car, a new outfit, or a new boyfriend. She had a lot of expensive things, but never once mentioned anything about where she worked. She tried so hard to prove to Auntie Jo that she was doing fine without the help of her, but I knew differently. I saw right through that phony smile, straight under those name brand clothes, and Keisha, my dear Keisha, was naked.

But although she hurt me, I was willing to forgive her. After all, she did take good care of me. I didn't want to see her leave. Besides, Auntie Jo didn't pay me half the attention that Keisha did, and me and the boys were never close anyway.

Korey, Auntie Jo's oldest son, was almost twice my age, so there was nothing we could of possibly had in common. As a matter of fact, I could never even remember him being around. When I was growing up, he was always sleeping over at his girlfriend's house. Eventually they married, moved to a small town an hour away, and had two kids together. But unlike Keisha, although Korey moved away, he came around regularly. Especially when Auntie Jo cooked big meals, because he said his wife couldn't fry bologna. Well, if food was the way to a man's heart, she must have been cooking up something wonderful in the bedroom because he was still crazy about that woman.

Keyshawn, on the other hand, was only a couple months younger than me, but we definitely couldn't hang out. He was so deep into that thug-life crap that he almost believed he actually was the young Tupac. Keyshawn started showin' out when he was about five, and the older he got, the worse he got. By the time he was fourteen, he had already got busted twice for breaking into someone's house, suspended six times for fighting, and got caught with some of the older guys riding around in a stolen Lincoln. He was enrolled in school, but was either always suspended, or just didn't care to go. His idea of an education was sneaking his homeboys into Auntie Jo's house to playing video games.

His little bad ass was selling drugs too. One time I was looking for the remote in his bedroom and found a ziplock bag full of weed. Good shit too! Auntie Jo knew how he got his money, but she was so wrapped up in her boyfriend Lewis's arms, that she pretended to be unaware of what was going on right under her nose. She even demanded that Keyshawn pay her fifty dollars a month, and he was always on time with her money. Never once did she question where he got it from, but with him not having a job, I'm sure she had a pretty good idea.

I stated it before, but I'll say it one more time… when Keisha left, nothing was the same. I spent most of my childhood crying at night and praying for my real mama. I only wished she could have rose from the dead and saved me from that terrible place I was supposed to call home. And constantly being in a state of sadness, caused me to create an imaginary shell and hide in it. I distanced myself from everyone, even my classmates. In school I had no friends, not so much because I couldn't make any, but because I didn't want any. Still, I was always my teacher's favorite because I was smart, never got into trouble, and always did exactly what was asked of me.

Some of the kids didn't like that, particularly because they were jealous. I remember back in the eighth grade, this girl named Samantha hated me, but it didn't have anything to do with my academic achievements. It was only because her boyfriend told one of his friends he had a secret crush on me and that he wanted us to have sex. Somehow the word got back to Samantha, and she told everyone in the entire school that she was going to beat my ass, like I was the one who said it.

Samantha was short and big-boned. She wasn't at all attractive, but she was well-known, particularly because her family was full of heavy drug dealers who sold major dope in the neighborhoods. Her older brother couldn't bust one rhyme, but he was living the rapstar dream. He had the money, the clothes, and the cars that already came with the hoes in them. They had the city on lock. Anybody who grew up in the small town of Ordale knew not to fuck with the Hutchinson family.

I spent the entire school year being threatened and bullied by Samantha. Every day she would find something new to do to humiliate me. She would say smart shit when I walked by, and she would really get under my skin by calling me 'Scarface' and 'Tiger'. She would even get physical, sometimes bumping into me intentionally when a teacher was nearby.

Although Samantha constantly made a fool out of me, I never said one word back to her or even attempted to defend myself. She thought she had me spooked, and let me tell ya, I may have been a lot of things, but scary was not one of them. If I didn't learn anything in Auntie Jo's house, I learnt how to survive on my own, and I learnt that fear would get you kilt. Every time Samantha would do something mean to me, inside it would only make me angrier. I couldn't just let her get away with treating me the way she did, so I created a plan for her, and I knew exactly when and how I was going to carry it out.

It was May 29th, the last day of school. I had been secretly talking to Samantha's boyfriend, Alex, on the phone for about two weeks. I knew the little dog really just wanted to have sex, because he only offered to come by my house when my folks weren't home. I never invited him though. I didn't like him like that. I just needed him to be a part of my revenge plot.

When the final bell of the schoolyear rang, Alex was to meet me at the bus ramp, where I knew Samantha and half the damn school would be. She stayed on the other side of town, so she caught the bus. I only lived a couple of blocks away: I walked home.

I yelled goodbye to my favorite teacher, exited through the double doors of the building, and headed straight out to meet him. Alex was sitting against a pole waiting for me; however, he was looking out for Samantha too.

"Why you make me come out here?" he asked nervously.

"Because, this is the way I walk home. Past the buses and cross the street there," I pointed.

"I thought you said you was cool with me having a girlfriend. What if Samantha sees me?"

"Look, you want this pussy or not?" I asked, trying my best to act how Keisha, or Shannon, would have. "It's the last day of school, you not gone see Samantha for another three months. Ya'll just gone break up anyway. If you too scared, then go back."

"I'm coming, but if she sees us, you better watch yo' back," he warned.

"We'll see about that."

I intentionally walked past Bus 519 and held Alex's hand, flirting with him a bit. He was uneasy, but still, he enjoyed the attention I was giving him. I slowly scrolled past the back of the bus where Samantha normally sat.

The farther I got away from the schoolyard, the more faith I loss because my plan seemed to be failing. But, as soon as I was about to completely give up, I heard a loud, obnoxious voice yell out from behind me, "HEY BITCH!"

Bingo. I knew it was Samantha.

I slowly turned around to see a whole stampede of kids rushing toward me. It must have been the entire Lee James Middle. I stopped in my tracks and purposely let fear show all over my face.

"What the fuck do you think you doing Alex?" Samantha asked him angrily, once she had caught up with us.

"I…I…I ain't doing shit," he lied. "*She's* the one who

asked *me* to walk with *her*. You know I don't want Scarface.""

No this punk ass nigga didn't. I thought.

"I don't care," she stopped him. "She's holding *your* hand."

Samantha turned back to me. "And you, lil' tiger face bitch..I should've whooped yo ass a long time ago, but now I don't give a fuck because it's the last day anyway."

"I don't want to fight you Samantha," I said as I slowly reached behind my back and grabbed something from out of my back pocket.

"WELL I-"

As soon as she opened her big mouth, I shot her in the face with a can of Auntie Jo's mace. Then I sprayed and sprayed and sprayed some more. Samantha grabbed her face and began to cry out, "My eye! My eye!"

Not even the least bit through with her, I grabbed the sharpened pencil from out of my other pocket and begin jabbing her with it. I didn't care about her face or that blood was seeping from her punctures. I felt no remorse for her. I wanted Samantha to feel the same pain and humiliation that she caused me throughout my whole eight-grade year. Shit, I wanted her to feel the pain I felt my whole life.

For a second, nobody did anything. None of her so-called friends jumped in to help her. Hell, Alex didn't even do a damn thing. He just sat there and looked stunned.

When I saw the administrators headed towards the crowd, I quickly took Alex's hand and made a run for it. "Come on," I told him.

We dashed like dogs were chasing us, and didn't slow down until we got a couple streets from my house. When we finally stopped, I looked around to see if the coast was clear. Thankfully, we had lost them.

"What the hell got into you girl?" Alex asked, still trying to catch his breath. I was tired too.

Looking over to Alex, I shot him a cute little smile. He was a wannabe player, so I knew he was slightly turned on by what I had just done.

"Nothing, just come here." I said, holding my arms out as if I was about to give him a hug.

Alex walked over to me excitedly. As soon as he got close, I grabbed the mace can and sprayed him in the face with the rest of it. He fell to his knees and grabbed his eyes too, just like Samantha had done.

"If you ever even think about doing it to me, you better think again!" I yelled. Then I picked my right foot up and kicked the crap out of him between his legs. "And that's for calling me Scarface!"

I didn't know if I got a good shot at his little raisins. He wore his jeans baggy. But I didn't stick around to find out either. I ran the rest of the way home.

And as I ran, I felt a lot of weight being lifted from me, and I'm not talking 'bout burning off no calories. For the first time in my life, I took a stand for myself. I felt a sense of identity. I felt respected. And I can't lie, I felt like I was one bad bitch.

I knew what I did was wrong. I knew it wasn't over. I knew I would eventually have to face the school administrators, and Samantha Hutchinson, again. But it was all worth it because best of all, I knew it was going to be a while before anyone decided to fuck with me again.

3: MISS FIESTY

Not only was the summer after the fight hot as hell, but it also changed my life. I went from being the little quiet girl, to being the little quiet girl who kicked Samantha Hutchinson's ass. A lot of girls who never even looked my way were not only talking to me, but also trying to befriend me. I didn't pay them any attention though. I kept all conversations short and simple. I may have been a lot of things, but never was I a fake. If I didn't like you, or know you, I didn't fuck with you. Period.

Even the guys started trying to holler at me too, like I had suddenly gotten beautiful. I wasn't a total knockout, but I was cute, even with the scar. I had medium-length brown hair with an average, brown-toned face to match. I took my figure after my mama. The small waist, thick hips, and thick thighs were definitely something I was proud to inherit from her. Some people even said that Keisha and I favored, but hands down, she was better looking.

I didn't see or hear anything from Samantha again. Word on the streets was, her mama made her move out of the state because she was tired of her getting into trouble. But I think she was just embarrassed. Her family, however, was still in Ordale, selling drugs and trying to take over the whole city.

A week after the fight, the school tracked me down and expelled me for an entire year. Thankfully I didn't have to go to court. Samantha's mom didn't press any charges, although I knew she wouldn't. Her family was in the drug business; the last place they wanted to be was in court.

Along with my suspension, the principal also convinced Auntie Jo to place me in an anger management class. The class and the expulsion was a disappointing setback, but instead of bullshitting around, I used that extra time to work. Auntie Jo said she'd be damned if I was going to sit up in her face all year long, and lucky for me she knew a guy who owned a store that was looking to pay someone under the table.

The rest of my time off, I spent with Marcus, my first love. I met him on my way home from my anger class one Thursday morning. I caught the city bus and so did he. On this particular day, the bus was unusually full. It was hot outside, so I wore my white halter-top shirt with my little plaid shorts that made my ass look even bigger than it already was.

I got on board and scanned the entire bus for a seat, as I usually did. Spotting a girl sitting alone, I made my way over to her. Then I asked, "Do you mind if I take a seat?"

"My friend behind you is sitting here," she responded. Respectfully, I might add.

I turned and looked behind me to find a dark-skinned, petite girl with long black dreadlocks, waiting for me to move forward so that she could take her seat.

"Oh, okay," I replied, then kept walking down the aisle and found another one towards the back of the bus.

Just when I got good and comfortable in my seat, someone sitting behind me yelled out, "Ha! Ha! You just got punked out!"

When I whipped my head around, I saw a young boy, surprisingly, talking to me.

"Excuse me?" I asked.

"You were supposed to tell her to move over," he said. "Don't nobody own any seats on this bus. What, you scared or something?"

I couldn't believe this random guy was frontin' on me in front of everybody. The nerve of him. I had no choice but to give him a piece of my mind.

"First of all," I started off, "a seat on the bus is not that big of a deal to me. Secondly, if you know N-E-thing about *Charlytte Black,* then you would know that ain't shit scary about her."

"Whoa little mama, calm down," he pleaded. "I was only kidding with you."

I didn't even respond back. I just rolled my eyes, put my earphones in my ear, and played my favorite song by Tony Toni Tone, *All I Ask of You.*

Music eased my mind. Whenever I was down or upset, I would listen to the smooth sounds Sade or Floetry and all my troubles would temporarily fade away. I loved this song and I got deep into the lyrics, only to be interrupted.

Making love is what I wanna do/ but I need a true friend to make it come together/ Just give me all your lovin'/ Girl I'll do all the rubbin'/ That all I ask of you/ I'll kiss you anywhere/ Yes love, anywhere/ That's all I ask of you.

"Excuse me little feisty," someone planted two gentle taps on my collarbone.

What now? I said to myself, after I looked up to see that same jerk standing over me. I couldn't believe he still wanted to talk to me after I had just told him off. And I was even more upset that he had the nerve to touch me.

"What do you want?" I said, making my nasty attitude clearly obvious.

"Calm down and take this," he demanded.

The guy handed me folded piece of paper. I hesitated before I took it, looked down at it, and then up at him. As much as I hated to admit it, he was cute, with his freshly cut fade and his schoolboy attire. I didn't know what he was handing me, but if it was what I thought it was, then I was going to have a lot to think about on my way home.

"Use it," he said, then walked off the bus.

I decided not to unravel the paper until I got home, yet I still couldn't help but wonder what was inside of it. I honestly thought I was being pranked, and that if I opened it, it just might say BITCH in big bold letters.

When I got off at my stop, I immediately took the paper from out of my back pocket and stared at it for a couple of seconds. It looked as if it had been ripped off of something important, homework perhaps. I contemplated on just tossing it, but after I thought about how my whole life was a big disappointment, and how much I needed something new to happen in it, I changed my mind.

Anxious and nervous all at once, I slowly unfolded the paper and smiled really big when I saw a number and the name MARCUS written up under it. I felt a sudden urge to start skipping the rest of way home, and when I got there, Auntie Jo was in her room talking on the telephone. I assumed she had gotten into a big fight with Lewis because she was blabbing about him awfully. They were arguing a lot more often and each fight was getting more intense.

Lewis was a pretty cool dude, but there was something fishy about him. I didn't like the way he looked at my ass when I walked by him, but I never mentioned it to Auntie. She barely even liked me, I just knew she wouldn't believe me. Ignoring her cursing, I ran straight into my room and slammed the door. Nothing was about to kill the unusually great mood I was in.

• • • • • •

For the next couple of days, all I thought about was Marcus. I kept picturing that face I saw when he handed me his number. I was already fantasizing about holding him and kissing him. I knew I was jumping way ahead of myself, but I didn't care. They were my private thoughts. I didn't call him right away because I didn't want to seem too eager. But after three days passed, I felt I had waited long enough.

It was on a Friday night. Keyshawn was somewhere in the streets, and as usual, Auntie Jo was out drinking with Evelyn.

Although no one was home with me, I took the phone and hid in my room. I had Marcus's number memorized, and after I built up enough courage to call him, I began dialing…

"Hello," a woman's voice answered, only after a couple of rings. I assumed it was his mother.

"Hello, how are you?" I replied. I always believed in manners. I picked them up from watching numerous episodes of Barney.

"Uhm…I'm okay. And you?" the woman replied, as if she was surprised that I asked.

"I'm fine, thank you. Is Marcus home?"

"Yes, hold please." She placed the phone down on something hard. "Marcus!"

There was a quick pause, but it seemed like forever. Then I heard a rattle on the phone. It was Marcus picking up.

"Hello little miss feisty," he greeted me. "What's up?"

"*Excuse me*, do you even know who you're talking to?" I asked.

"Yeah, I'm talking to the mean girl who cursed me out on the bus the other day."

"I didn't curse you out," I blushed, "I told you off. It's a difference. And how did you know it was me?"

"Who else is supposed to be calling here for me?" he asked.

"Well I'm pretty sure you have other girls," I tested him.

"Nope, I only want you," he replied.

"You don't even know me," I shot him down quickly. "You saw me once on the bus and tried to holler. If you're already that persuaded about a girl you just met, then I'm not so sure I wanna mess with you anyway."

"Hold up *miss feisty*," he stopped me. "I let you tell me off before, now it's my turn…I catch that same bus you do every day of the week, and I sit in the same seat you saw me in. I watch you on Tuesdays and Thursdays when you get on, and sometimes off, the bus. Just because you're in your own world, with your headphones and your blank stares out of the window, doesn't mean the outside world isn't still spinning around you…It's something about you that interests me, something mysterious. I haven't quite figured out what it is, but I'm seriously eager to find out."

Those words cut me like a sharp knife, but at the same time, soothed me like a soft pillow. I didn't know whether to be crept out by Marcus, or admire him. All I knew was that he actually paid me some attention, and that in itself, meant more to me than anything.

"Yeah, whateva," I replied, as if what I just heard meant nothing to me.

"Well now that we got that out of the way, *Charlytte*," he said emphasizing my name. "Tell me something about yourself."

What is there to tell? I thought. *My mom died. My life sucks. Sometimes I want to run away and never come back.*

"Well…," I started, "I just finished middle school. I'm fourteen years-"

"I'm sixteen going on seventeen," he proudly interrupted me. "Does that matter to you?"

"Well no, not really, but I've never talked to an older guy," I answered. Secretly, I had never talked to any guy.

"What school do you go to?" I purposely switched the topic.

"I go to Franklin High. I will be a senior this year.

Well…that's if I pass this summer school class."

Senior, I thought. *This is going to be interesting.*

I never liked any of the guys my age anyway. Most of them were childish to me. One minute they're with one girl, and the next they're with someone else. All they ever wanted was sex and never took anything serious. Charlytte wasn't the clueless type though. I may have been only fourteen, but I still wanted something that would last, maybe even for a lifetime.

"Must be nice," I joked. "Can't wait 'til I become a senior. I'm going to Franklin High too."

"Yeah, you're still a baby," he teased. "I'll be long gone by them…on to a better life, *college*."

"Really?" I was amused. "What school?"

"Southern Pulaski State. It's like a two-hour drive. Me and my friends are already planning it. I'm going to major in Sports Management."

"Wow. That sounds fun," I envied.

"What about you? What do you want to do once you graduate?" he asked me.

"I want to be a nurse," I said without thinking. Although really, that was something I never thought about. I knew I wanted to be something in life, but I didn't know exactly what. At that point, I just wanted to be happy. I was sure I was jumping ahead of myself by lying, but I knew one big turn-off for any guy, was a girl who didn't know what she wanted out of life.

"Oh, so you want to take care of me," he flirted a bit.

"I don't know about all that, but I do want to take care of my bills," I joked.

Marcus's loud laugh turned into a small chuckle. Then the chuckle eased into an awkward silence. I don't know what he was thinking in his distant mind, but when he came back, he suddenly changed the subject.

"Well hey miss feisty," he called out to me. "I don't wanna end this great convo we're having, but I'm about to go ride off with my brother and play some ball at Lakeside. You should come by. You'll have to walk there, but the ride home is on me."

"Hmmm…I'll think about it," I answered.

"Aight, cool. See you there," he replied, as if he was already certain I was going to show. "And another thing," he added before hanging up.

"What's up?"

"Leave your mace at home!"

"Aww…shut up!" I yelled, both ashamed and shocked that he had heard about that incident. We cracked up laughing before hanging up our phones.

4: I LEAD, U FOLLOW

Lakeside Community Park was a twenty-five minute walk from my house, but I didn't mind. That smile Marcus let off when he saw me entering the gate, and the wonderful time we spent together, was well worth it.

I spent the first hour watching him play ball. I didn't know much about the sport, but I did know he must have been good at it because every time he attempted a shot, he made it. Marcus would occasionally look my way and do something fancy to impressed me, and I would blush at his efforts. And after the sweat began to pour and his shirt came off, I found myself more interested in his good-looking body than his good game.

Marcus and I laughed, played, and flirted the remainder of our time together. He even tapped me on my butt once. And although he tried so hard to act like it was an accident, I knew it wasn't. If he was any other dude, I would have had a couple of four-letter words lined up for him, but because he was Marcus, all I could do was grin.

As the weeks and months passed, our relationship grew stronger. We didn't go a day without talking on the phone and we always made sure we saw each other

often. Marcus would sometimes get off at my bus stop and he'd walk me home. Then from my house we would head to Lakeside, where I would watch him murder his opponents on the court. On the days I didn't have to go work, we'd wander the streets all day, showing off our affection to the world.

I liked Marcus a lot and eventually started to feel like I loved him, even though I had no clue what love really was. All I knew was that, when I was with him, I didn't think about the problems I had at home. I didn't think about how much I missed Keisha and mama, nor did I dwell on Auntie Jo and her lack of concern for me. All I cared about was him and how happy he made me feel.

Although we never shared anything more physical than hugs, and a couple hits on the butt, I wanted more of him. I started having urges to touch and feel him inside of me. At night I would go to bed thinking about kissing his sexy lips. I would imagine him kissing mine too- moving down to my breasts, then on to my belly button, and as he got to my goodies, I would suddenly stop- ashamed of my own thoughts.

I didn't know much about sex. I didn't even know how to approach him with the idea. Auntie Jo never talked to me about things like that. All she ever said was, "if anybody's gonna be fuckin' in my house, it's gonna be me." Hell, when I got my first period, I hollered and screamed because I thought I had been cut down there. My sixth grade teacher had to explain to me what was happening, and even then I didn't fully understand. Most of that other stuff, like condoms and STDs, I knew from my eighth-grade health class. Of course eventually, my curiosity led to me wanting to experiment, and that led to Marcus and I making love for the very first time.

I had to work really late that night because Mr. Otis had an emergency at home with his wife.

"Charlytte," Auntie Jo called from her room, as soon as she heard me entering the house.

"Yes ma'am," I answered.

"It was your night to wash the dishes. You should've been home hours ago."

She didn't ask me where I was, who I was with, or how I had gotten home. She didn't even ask was I alright- all the questions most parents asked when their fourteen-year old came home at almost midnight. I only wished I had some of those concerns thrown up at me, especially living in the crime infested neighborhood that we lived in.

"Sorry, I had to work late. Mr. Otis had an emergency with his wife. I think she's sick or something."

"I don't care if she died," she bluntly stated. "You were supposed to be here. Next time you let him know you got responsibilities at home, got that?"

"Yes ma'am," I rolled my eyes.

I was too tired for her drama. Normally I would ponder on what she said. I would feel depressed. I would cry. I would think about my mama. But I didn't have the energy for any of that. All I could do was go straight into my room, collapse on my bed, and fall fast asleep. Only to find myself waking up a little past midnight to the sound of three taps on my window. At first I figured it was Keyshawn trying to sneak back into the house, but then I realized that Keyshawn didn't sneak around for nobody. He did what he wanted, and as long as Auntie Jo got that little change from him, she didn't say a thing about it.

A bit frightened, I sat up and quietly crawled down to the end of my twin-sized bed. That's where the window was. Then I slowly pulled my curtains aside to get a good look on the outside.

"Charlytte! Charlytte!" a male voice yelled out softly.

I knew immediately it was Marcus. In a room full of one hundred look-a-likes, I could pick my baby out.

"What fool!" I whispered as I quietly eased up the window and focused in on the white around his pupils. That was the only part of him I could see.

"Boy, are you ca-ray-zee coming here like this. If my auntie sees you, she will kill you. I'm not playing either."

"I know, I know. I'm sorry. I just haven't heard from you all day. You haven't even called," he whispered.

"Sorry Marcus. Blame it on the store. I've been working all day. You know I missed you though."

"I missed you too," he replied. "How bout we make up for some of that lost time. My brother let me hold his car. Come ride with me."

My exhaustion had suddenly been replaced with excitement. I didn't know where we were going, and honestly, I didn't even care. I was willing to go anywhere other than Auntie Jo's.

"Sure."

I locked my bedroom door at exactly 12:45 in the morning. Marcus helped me climb out the window and then we headed straight for the car. As I walked swiftly behind him, I found the time to check out how good he looked in his crisp white T-shirt and blue jean shorts. His head was freshly cut and his face was neatly trimmed, as usual. Marcus was always cute to me, but this night he was just stunning. Too bad I couldn't say the same for myself; all I wore was a tired face and my dingy work clothes.

When we got to the front of the house, I noticed Marcus's brother, Anthony's, car parked at the neighbor's house. It was a 1987 blue Buick Regal in desperate need of a new motor and a new paint job. Sometimes Anthony would let Marcus hold it, as long as he promised to be extra careful, and he always took advantage of the opportunity.

Marcus opened the car door for me and a warm feeling tickled my insides. He knew exactly how to make a girl feel special and I loved him for it.

We took off, and although I was anxious to know, I didn't ask him anything about where we were going. I felt that if he wanted to tell me, he would have. And besides, the suspense alone made the quick get-a-way even more exciting.

When we made it off my street, Marcus turned the radio on and the song, *Best of Me* by Mya and Jay Z, played out of the speakers. I closed my eyes and enjoyed the music.

"Let your seat back," Marcus said, throwing off my groove.

"Huh...why?" I asked

"Because you look tired. I'm just trying to make you comfortable."

"Okay."

Just as Marcus had told me, I let my seat back. I found myself staring out of the front window, looking up at the night sky, and I began to flood my brains with all kinds of thoughts. I wondered what made the stars shine so bright, especially when they were so far away. I wondered if my mama was really up there, and if she was, was she looking down at me?

"How do you think it would feel to sit up on the moon and look down at the Earth?" I asked Marcus, unexpectedly.

"Whoa…whoa…what?" he chuckled. "You went completely left field with that one."

"Because Marcus, I'm a left field type of person... I mean, I like to analyze things. I don't just look up at the sky; I try to figure out why it's blue. Is that weird to you?"

"Uhhh….yeah!" he teased. "But seriously, I never really thought about it. I think it would be kinda cool though. "

I deeply exhaled. "Yeah, me too."

"Anymore crazy questions?" he asked.

"Nope, that's it," I pushed his arm playfully.

"You don't wanna know where we're going?" he questioned. "That's what you should be asking."

"Naw, I trust you," I replied. "Surprise me."

"Well okay," he gave in. "I wasn't gonna tell you anyway."

"Whatever, Marcus," I sucked my teeth, and then sighed off to myself. I felt a little bad for asking him the silly question about the moon. I thought I might have scared him a bit. I didn't want him to think that I was a weirdo, as much as I thought I was. Marcus always intimidated me because he was much older. I tried to be very careful about what I said and did around him, although sometimes I felt like he was the one who needed to get on *my* level. Not knowing what he was thinking, I closed my eyes and didn't speak for the rest of the ride. I figured if I didn't know what to say, then I just shouldn't say anything. We rode for about thirty more minutes, and I found myself dozing off before we even made it to our destination.

"Wake up," he tapped me on my thigh. "We're here."

"I am up," I tried to convince him, although wiping the little bit of drool from off the side of my mouth didn't help my claim.

When we got out of the car, I didn't have the slightest clue where we were. All I knew was that I was hearing splash-like noises and the wind was blowing unusually harder than it was before. I also saw sand, trees, and a wooden ramp that led to something that I couldn't see on the other side. Marcus took my hand and guided me along the way.

"Now do you know where we are?" he said after we made it over the ramp.

That's when I saw it. And it was beautiful. Like nothing I'd ever seen before. The water was glowing from the reflection of the moon, the wind was singing, and the sound of the waves, as they washed up against the shore, was like the sweetest music I'd ever heard.

"WOOOW!" I yelled like a little kid in a candy store. "It's beautiful!"

"The beach. It's nice, ain't it?" he asked, then came up behind me and put his arms around my waist.

"Nice ain't even the word. I think this is my new home."

"Don't get too excited," he warned. "It only looks this way at night."

I told Marcus around the time we first met that I had never been to a beach before, but I didn't think he was actually going to take me there. Tybris Island was about forty-five minutes away from our town, and Auntie Jo wouldn't dare considered taking us that far. The money she would use for gas could have been money she bought a twenty-four pack of beer with.

We took our shoes off the second we got off the ramp. I felt the sand as it caressed my feet, and as much as I hated gritty toes, all I could do was dig them into the ground and enjoy the feeling. As we approached the ocean, the waves moved our way as if they were eager to meet us. I moved back, afraid of a little water.

"Come on Charlytte," Marcus quickly ran out to the water. "Don't be scared. At least get your feet wet.

"But it's cold," I cried.

Although I had no plans on going any further, I was extremely jealous that the water was already to up his knees, and I was still trying to get it pass my ankles.

"Stop making excuses chicken butt," he joked.

"I told you once before," I replied. "I'm not scary."

"We'll see about that," he said, then picked me up, placed me over his shoulder, and began walking me deeper into the ocean. In fear of my life, I started kicking and screaming.

"No! No! Put me down Marcus!" I demanded. "Put me down right now!"

"Ooooo-k," he said, and just as I had asked, he put me smack down in the water. Now I was knee deep. When I looked down I couldn't see a thing, not even my feet. I didn't know what could have been in that water, and I sure as hell wasn't about to find out. I ran out of there as

fast as I could, found a nearby bench swing, and sat down on it. Marcus came running behind me. He was laughing very hard, but I didn't think anything was funny.

"Ha! You should've seen the look on your face!" he cracked up. Then tried to stop the swing so that he could sit down too. I intentionally kept swinging.

"That's not funny," I pouted, trying my best to be serious. I knew I couldn't be mad at him though. No matter how bad I wanted to be.

"Oh, so you mad now?" he asked. "You ain't mad."

Marcus managed to scoop me up and place me on his lap. I tried to resist, but he was much stronger than me. I could now look dead into his eyes, but it was the hotel resorts behind him that caught my attention. It was kinda cool seeing the fancy buildings, but I would have much rather saw the ocean as he did. I just knew I would've appreciated it more.

For a good minute, we just sat in silence. I didn't know what was going on in his head, but I was thinking about how happy I was just to be there with him. I appreciated him for taking the time out to do something special for me. But still I was a little self-conscious. I wanted to know exactly why he cared enough about me to make one of my dreams come true.

"Marcus, why do you like me?" I asked.

"Oh boy," he sighed. "Here comes another one of *them* questions."

"Marcus, I'm serious this time. I want you to answer me... I mean, you brought me all the way out here. You spend lots of time with me, and you really do your best to make me happy. If you can do all of that, then you should at least have a reason, and I should know just what that reason is."

Marcus rubbed my back with both of his hands. He started with my shoulders, and then moved down towards my hips. A warm feeling came over me with every touch.

"Look, I like you because you're beautiful, in and out. I like that you're caring. I like the way you call and check up on me. I like how you're so unpredictable. The way you smile. The way you think. I mean yes, you're only fourteen, but you're not like those girls at my school. Most of them are dumb and easy, but you're not. I knew the minute you cursed me out on the bus, that I wanted you as my girl…" he paused and took a deep breath. "Charlytte, I don't just like you…I think I'm in love with you."

Wow. I thought to myself. I could've died in that moment, the way my heart melted. Marcus had never said those words to me before; nobody had said those words to me before. If I wasn't in love with him before, I was then. And I knew it was time for us to take the next step.

"Show me," I said to him. "Show me how much you really love me."

"What else can I do?" he asked. "I just told you I do."

"No," I started rubbing my fingers down his chest. "Show me."

Marcus took one hard glimpse at me, and suddenly realized what I was implying. Without speaking another word, he took me by the face and slowly brought his lips to mine. Just when he was about to kiss me, I got nervous and drew back.

"Wait," I said softly. "I gotta be honest, I've never kissed a guy before."

"I know. I will show you. Just relax," he said. "I lead, you follow."

He grabbed my face once more and his soft, warm lips touched mine. He smooched them over and over until I began to do the same and with each peck I started to feel more confident. But, as soon as I felt I had grasped the concept of smooching, he opened his mouth and hit me with some tongue. I drew back again.

"Don't be nervous," he said, "I lead, you follow."

"Okay," I surrendered, slowly opening my mouth to allow his tongue re-entrance. I began to feel it touch mine as he moved it around rhythmically.

Marcus had his kissing game down pack. He would go in for about two seconds, and then pull out for about the same. I studied his system and began to imitate. He took the lead and I followed. Before I knew it, we were pecking, smooching, and tongue wrestling like we both could read each other's minds.

After the kissing became a bit of a bore, Marcus decided to turn up the heat. He gripped my hips with both his hands and began to move them back and forth slowly. I guess that was his way of teaching me how to grind. Again, I followed his lead and began to rock my body. At first I felt stiff and stupid, but the more I moved, the more I got the hang of it. Once I got to the point where I didn't need his guidance, I pushed his hands from off of me and began to do it all by myself. The way he was groaning, I knew I had caught on pretty quickly.

We continued to kiss, rub, and hug until he stopped me.

"What's the problem?" I asked, hoping I didn't do anything wrong.

"Nothing's wrong," he smiled. " Just get up for a second."

Marcus allowed me to get off of him and he rose from the bench. Then stepped away and turned his back to me. I didn't wonder what he was doing, because I was too busy thinking about what had just happened.

After a brief departure, Marcus finally returned with his t-shirt in his hand.

"Here, put this on," he said, as the light from the moon bounced off his bare chest. I had seen it many times before at Lakeside, but never like this.

I grabbed the big white t-shirt and slipped it over my work clothes. Then I pulled my pants and panties down to the ground.

Standing before him while he sat on the bench and admired my body, I had the privilege of feeling his two fingers rub over my clit. He did this in a circular motion and I felt a sensation like no other. It was breathtaking, much different from when I would do it.

Taking it a step further, he took that same finger and slid it inside of me. At first I jumped back, but quickly regained my composure and allowed him to continue. He gently twirled it around inside of me and the more he did, the better it felt. I had to wrap my arms around his neck, just to stop myself from falling over in ecstasy.

"Damn you're soaked," he whispered, after feeling the heavy amount of moisture between my legs. Then he rubbed the juice on my left thigh, as if he just had to prove his claim. "Sit down," he told me.

I sat down on top of Marcus, facing the resorts again. He had taken off his jeans too, exposing the dark blue basketball shorts that he wore over his boxers. This time I could feel everything, and boy, did I feel a lot. Once he saw that I was impressed by his size, he smiled with pride and kissed me once more.

"You ready?" he asked.

I paused for a second, then looked back at the ocean. There I was facing the horizon- a line that separated the sky from the land- and I was about to cross the line that separated a girl from a woman. In those quick seconds, I thought about my innocence. I thought about how it might change me. I wondered if it was worth it. I wondered if he was worth it. I even wondered if my mama was looking down from the stars watching us. That made me even more uncertain. Believe me, I knew how important my virginity was, but at that moment, I didn't care.

I slowly turned back to Marcus.

"Yes," I answered him.

Feeling my body temperature rise and my heart swiftly began to beat, I knew there was no turning back. Marcus slid his basketball shorts and boxers halfway down his legs, then pulled himself out from under me.

I reached down to grab it, as if I wasn't afraid. Then I guided him inside of me. Feeling a little pain, my body stiffened. I immediately tried to get off of him, but he snatched me by my waist and pulled me back down.

"Just relax and loosen up," he whispered. "I promise I won't hurt you."

Marcus was my man and I trusted him. I took a deep breath and relaxed, just as he had asked me to. Once my body let him know that I was ready again, he began to move in and out of me slowly, pushing deeper inside with every stroke. At first it was uncomfortable, but the more he would move, the more the pain started to be replaced by pleasure. Soon it began to feel so good that I too started moaning.

"Ooooh Marcus," I cried.

"Yes?" he whispered softly.

"I love you baby. I really do."

"I love you too, Charlytte," he said, while kissing all

over my neck.

The way Marcus said my name made me even more excited. I started to take the lead and moved slowly back and forth on him like I did when we were grinding.

"Ooooh damn," Marcus moaned, surprised by my ability to catch on so quickly.

"Oh shit!" he yelled and squeezed me, just as I started to get into it. Then he held me tightly until I could no longer feel him cuming inside of me.

5: THE LAST TIME

Marcus and I had sex the next day, the day after that, and the day after that too. We did it a couple more times on the beach, twice at his house, and he even convinced his brother to get us a hotel room once. Sometimes he would come by the house very late at night and we would do it in his brother's car. We called those drive-bys.

I would fantasize about him daily- at home, in the shower, when I was working at the store- practically anywhere I had time to think. I even missed a couple days of work just to sneak off with him. I must admit, I was addicted to Marcus. He had my mind gone. So gone, that being with him was all I wanted to do. He made me feel brand new and brought out a different person in me, someone who was more confident and much happier.

The best part about of it all was that Marcus and I wasn't just physical, we had an emotional connection too. We'd talk about our personal problems and we'd shared many of our deepest secrets with one another. I began to open up to him about my mama's death, and how her not being there was affecting me. I told him about Auntie Jo and how she treated me, and I even told him about Keisha leaving.

Marcus would talk to me about some of the things he went through too. He told me about his mama almost dying of breast cancer and how he struggled to take care of her. He even broke down one day and told me how his daddy used to beat her senselessly.

Even Auntie Jo started to see that I was changing, and she didn't like it one bit. I didn't pay her any mind though. I knew it was because she was jealous and didn't want to see me happy. Miserable ass Auntie Jo hated to see anyone happy.

Marcus and I were going about nine months strong when he got his first car. It was a midnight blue old school Chevy Caprice with dark, tinted windows and eighteen inch rims on it. It was a pretty decent car for a high school senior.

I was just as excited as he was when he got it, because at first, he would pick me up from work every day and we'd cruise around Ordale, getting into whatever the night brought our way. But after about a month, things started to, of course, change. He stopped showing up to get me, we didn't have sex as often as we used to, and when I called his house for him, I rarely got an answer. Half the time, he was never even home.

One night, out of the blue, Marcus decided to pop up unexpectedly at my job. Mr. Otis was out and it was a slow day. I was the only person in the building and the only reason I was glad to see him was because I was bored.

"Hey, what's up?" he said to me, as he walked up to the rusted wooden checkout counter.

"Nothing much," I said nonchalantly. I wanted Marcus to know that I had an attitude with him. I had some issues to address and I wasn't going to be satisfied until I got answers.

"Marcus what happened to us?" I immediately asked him.

"Here you go with these questions again," he sighed. "Nothing. We're fine."

"You know damn well that's a lie. We're not as close as we used to be."

"Charlytte," he sighed. "Now you know I'm about to graduate. I'm trying to do this and that. I've just been busy. You know I've missed you."

I didn't believe him. There was something very different about his attitude, like he had suddenly gotten cocky.

"I don't know what has gotten into you, but I don't like it."

"Aint nothing got into me girl. That's for damn sure. I'll be waiting outside until ya boss gets back. I'm taking you home tonight."

After seeing Marcus storm out like that, I started to feel guilty because maybe he was right. Maybe he did have a lot of things going on. And maybe I could have just become so obsessed with him that I was being selfish and wanted him all to myself.

I called up Mr. Otis as soon as Marcus left, and asked him if it was okay to leave. We were going to be closing in an hour anyway, and since we were already slow, he said it was fine. Glad to be heading out of there, I

quickly locked up the front door, then the back, and hopped into Marcus's car.

I couldn’t deny, his ride was fly. He knew it too. That was why he was so protective of it. He had plastic covering all over his seats on the floors to keep his dark blue leather interior and freshly vacuumed carpet, free from damage. He had also bought a new stereo, new seat covers, and a jazzy new black-leather steering wheel coat.

"Lemme call you back," Marcus said quickly, before ending a call on a cell phone that was unfamiliar to me.

"I didn’t know you had a phone," I said. "When did you get that?"

"Just a couple days ago. It’s no big deal.”

"Ooooh, so I’m just finding out that *my boyfriend* has a cell phone. That sounds like a big deal to me Marcus."

"It ain’t even like that. Please don’t start that tripping shit."

"Well then what is it like? And where are you going?" I pointed the opposite direction out my window. "My house is that way."

"We bout to go somewhere real quick. That’s all."

"Where?"

"Damn, what happened to girl who likes surprises," he joked.

"She died when you stopped giving a fuck," I told him. "And plus, it’s been a long, drawn out day. I’m tired. I just want to take a shower and get in my damn bed."

"Yeah whatever,” he hissed. “You're comin’ with me."

That demanding stuff usually turned me on, but this time I wasn’t moved. I laid my seat back and closed my eyes. "Take me home Marcus."

We rode for about fifteen minutes and stopped.

"Get up," Marcus said, rubbing my thighs aggressively.

I sat up, looked out the passenger window, then quickly realized where we were. Conveniently for him, it was one of the places where we used to go fuck; a real low lake spot in the back of a rich neighborhood. I didn't know how he found it, and although he denied it, I was certain he had been there before with someone else.

"Marcus, what are you doing?" I asked him after I politely removed his hand.

"Trying to show you how much I missed you," he said before he leaned over and tried to kiss me.

"No Marcus. Get off!" I screamed.

"Stop playing girl," he forcefully started to pull down my khaki pants. "You just wanna play this hard to get role. Okay…I'll play it with you."

Marcus climbed over the front seat and placed himself on top of me. Although he was surely succeeding at pulling my pants down, I still kept trying to fight him off.

Once he was satisfied with just getting them down to my knees, he pulled his own down and started to put on a condom.

"Marcus move! I don't know what you putting that on for!" I tried to snatch it. "I'm not doin' nothin' with you!"

"Ha!" he laughed in my face. "I said stop playin'."

From on top of me, he tried to push himself in my insides. I locked my legs together and clinched my muscles really tight, attempting to stop him from entering.

“You know you want me,” he said, still not quittng.

"Marcus stop!" I cried. "Stop it right now!"

He kept trying his luck, and it wasn't until I started punching him and screaming to the top of my lungs, like a mad woman, that he realized just how serious I was.

"So you really gonna say no?" he finally surrendered.

"Yes Marcus, I’m saying no."

I pushed him away once more and began pulling up my pants. I was tired and panting from all the tussling we did. Marcus, who was also breathing hard, stood up and stared at me as if he was in a state of disbelief.

"Okay. So that’s how you wanna play it," he zipped his pants back up and crossed over to the driver side. "You fuckin' somebody else?"

"Marcus, don’t try to use that reverse shit on me. You think you can just ignore me for weeks at a time, then snap your fingers when you want some, and I’m supposed to just drop 'em for you!"

"Ummm….yeah," he laughed, still taking me and my feelings for a joke. By now, I was heated.

"YOU KNOW WHAT," I snapped, "YOU CAN JUST TAKE ME HOME BECAUSE CLEARLY YOU HAVE ME FUCKED UP! I’D RATHER BE BY MYSELF THAN TO LET YOU TAKE ADVANTAGE OF ME AND USE ME WHENEVA’ YOU PLEASE. FIND ANOTHER GIRL TO DO THAT TO, BECAUSE I’M NOT THE ONE. You know, ever since you got this damn car you been acting brand new, like you ain’t used to nothing. Well you know what…fuck you and this damn car!"

Those words, or the fact that Marcus desperately wanted some pussy, must have really got to him. He cranked up his car, looked me dead in my face, and said, "Get out."

"What? Come again?" I asked.

"Since it's fuck me, and my car, then get out." He repeated himself.

"So you really gonna put me out of your car...At ten o'clock at night? Are you serious Marcus?"

"Do you see a smile on my face?" he asked, sealing his jaws tightly together. "Get out or I will put your little ass out. You chose."

Although Marcus's words hurt me, I was stubborn and kissed no one's ass for nothing. If he didn't want me in his car, I wasn't about to stay there. If he was going to be that hateful and make me walk all the way home, just because he couldn't get some, then I didn't want to ride with him anyway. God knows it was dark and I was afraid, but I was willing to do what I had to do. I opened the passenger side door and took one long look at him.

"It's over," I said.

"Tell me something I don't know," he replied, then sped off quickly.

As the car disappeared in thin air, I could almost feel my heart breaking into tiny little pieces. Marcus made it halfway down the street, then slowed down and came to a complete stop. When I saw his red brake lights shining and the car moving in reverse, I started to smile because deep down I knew he wasn't going to let the girl he loved walk home alone. I knew he wasn't that heartless

Marcus backed all the way up until his car and I was side by side. Then he parked it and jumped out. His face leaked with anger as he walked swiftly in my direction. I just knew he was going to snatch me up, hold me tightly, and tell me how sorry he was. Or maybe even kiss me passionately. Hoping for the best, I closed my eyes, puckered my lips, and waited for him to take me.

"And give me back my damn earrings!" he shouted, catching me by complete surprise.

Marcus had brought me some gold hoop earrings for my fifteenth birthday. When he gave me the box, there was a keytag that hung from it which read, '*You hold the key to my heart*.' I wore those earrings every day and cherished them dearly. It was the only very valuable birthday gift that I had ever gotten from anyone. He had no idea how much they meant to me.

I tried to take them before he could, but he was just too quick. He yanked both pairs out of my ear, almost tearing my lobes. "Not my earrings!" I cried. "There mine!"

“Yours?” he disagreed. “That’s funny.”

"Marcus, there mine!" I cried once more. "Give them back! I’m serious!"

Marcus didn’t say another word. He just jumped back into his car and I watch the dust kick up behind his back tires. I saw my whole life drive away in that moment, and what hurt me the most was that I knew I couldn’t possibly go back to him after that. Maybe if I would have prepared myself, it could have been easier to deal with. But this was all too sudden. I didn’t know what to do next. I had secluded myself from everything and everybody except that boy. I wasn’t ready to be alone. Nope, I just wasn’t ready to feel that emptiness again.

6: MISS TOO-GOOD

Being with Marcus and then losing him, was like dreaming you're in heaven but waking up in hell. It was back to Auntie Jo and all her drama. Back to Mr. Otis and his perverted comments. Back to just complete loneliness and pain. Luckily, the end of his school year was near, and the beginning of mine would shortly be approaching. I was excited about going back, especially since all I did was work.

One Sunday, Korey and his family came over for dinner. Auntie Jo didn't cook big meals unless she knew they would be joining us. That day she baked a delicious honey-glazed ham. She also prepared macaroni, rice, and string beans to go with it. That was Korey's favorite.

Even though I never saw him much, I always looked up to him. He was the "sane" one in the family. He had a steady job working at UPS and supplied *legally* for his family. His wife, Patricia, was also pretty decent. She worked part-time at a daycare and was also working on a degree in Medical Billing. She was a homely girl- the complete opposite of how we were raised. She grew up with both parents in the household. You know, the type of family who eats dinner at the table together every night with the television off. She wasn't at all flamboyant and dramatic, like those hoochies Keyshawn liked. Just a pretty and plain big-boned, high-yellow woman with a real nice face and a cute shape. I would often tease her by telling her she looked like Faith Evans, and even she couldn't deny it.

Surely I was fond of them, but whenever they came over, for some reason, I would always stay in my room. And I only came out if I absolutely had to, like to use the bathroom or something. His daughters, Amari and America, always kept me company though. Unlike everyone else, they seemed to love me. And I loved the feeling of being loved by them, even if they were only six and eight years old.

As the girls lay quietly on Keisha's old bed, putting together a puzzle, I was entertaining myself reading a Triple Crown book. With my room door cracked open, I could hear Auntie Jo, Korey, and Patricia chatting it up in the living room.

“This food is really good mama,” Korey told Auntie Jo, as he sat freely on her all-black loveseat and devoured his huge plate of food.

“Thanks baby,” she replied. “You know mama tries.”

“Yeah, you always make sure my belly is full when I come to visit,” he rubbed his firm, muscular stomach. “Speaking of visiting…has Keisha been by here lately?"

"Nope, but she did call about a week ago. I don’t know what’s up with that girl. All I can do is pray for her."

"That’s true," Patricia joined in. She always tried to stay on Auntie Jo's good side. "That’s all you can do."

"Who knows what that girl is up to? She’s probably runnin' round with one of them old thugs she likes,"

Auntie Jo said. "What y'all call 'em now, cripples and blood?"

"You mean Crips!" Keyshawn corrected her from in the kitchen, probably because he wanted to be one.

“Whateva,” Auntie Jo replied.

"Don't be so hard on her," Korey defended his little sister. "She probably gets that from you. You know you used to have them thugs up in here too mama."

Auntie Jo chuckled to herself. "I had a few back in my day, and Lewis just swears he’s an OG. You’re right son. She probably does get some of her ways from me. That’s exactly why we don’t get along. Whateva the reason, I just hope she don’t have no babies any time soon. Lord knows she ain’t ready."

"Yeah, true dat," Korey agreed. "Keisha’s too stuck on herself to be trying to have a baby...And how about Charlytte? Is she okay? She seems distant."

"Chile, that gal’s been distant since the day she was born. You know she always acted like she was too good for this family. Like she don’t want to be here," Auntie Jo said. "You should have seen her a couple months ago, prancin’ all around, lookin’ silly, smilin’ for no damn reason."

"And what was she so happy about?" Patricia butted in again.

"Some lil' big head boy comin’ around here and callin’ for her. They must have broke up ‘cuz I don’t see him, and he don’t call no mo’. She just sit up in that room, probably crying her lil’ damn eyes out. Shit, niggas come a dime for two dozen nowadays. They gone fuck you and leave you. This ain’t gone be the last time. She gone have to get over that honey, moping around here. One thing about it, I don’t need no man to validate me."

I couldn’t believe what I was hearing. Auntie Jo never paid me even a nickel's worth of attention, and then she had the nerve to say that I acted like *I* didn’t want to be apart of the family. Then, she claimed she didn’t need a man around, but she's always ready to take somebody’s head off when one leaves her, and it isn’t too long before the next one is coming. I wanted so badly to come out of my room and give her a piece of my mind, but all I could do was sit there, pretend I was still reading, and act like I didn’t hear a word of it. Besides, no matter what she said or did to me, I told myself that I would never disrespect her.

No longer wanting to tune in to the devil’s radio, I tried to block them out of my head and went back to focusing on my book. They continued to talk for another half hour, until Korey decided that it was getting late. Then he hugged Auntie Jo, thanked her for the food, and even cracked on his wife by telling her she should come back and take lessons.

After the food jokes, Korey eventually made his way to my bedroom to get the girls. Even though the door was slightly opened, still, he tapped softly on it to make his presence known. By now, America, the youngest daughter, was sitting next to me asking me all types of questions, and Amari, the oldest, was letting me put pigtails in her hair for camp the next day.

"Come on in," I told him.

The handsome and nicely built Korey entered my room, putting the three of us at his attention.

"Come on girls. It’s time to go," he said with his very deep and distinctive voice.

"I was just finishing up," I said, then rushed to put the last white barrette in Amari’s thick, fluffy hair.

Once it was snapped on, they both got up and began to gather their things. Their father's hazel brown eyes followed them as they scrambled around in the room collecting everything they had brought with them. He had a look on his face as if he was saying to himself, "Look at my babies."

Korey watched his girls up until they left the room, but instead of leaving out behind them, he closed himself inside with me.

"Hey Charly, is it cool if I talk to you for a sec?" he asked me.

I immediately got nervous. *What could you possibly have to say to me?*

"Yeah, sure," I slid over on the bed to make room for him. "What's up?"

Korey sat down beside me. "I just wanted to ask.... uhmm.... is everything okay with you?"

I heard him clearly, but I had to blink twice to see if he was really sitting there showing concern for me. Korey never did that before. It made me feel good, but it crept me out just the same.

"Yeah, I'm fine," I told him. Saying I was okay when I wasn't became easy after doing it for so many years. I said it so much that even I started to believe it.

"You sure Charl? I know it's probably pretty rough growing up without ya mama," he said. "And I also know how my mama can get sometimes, but if you say you're okay then I will just have to take your word for it. Just know that if there is anything you ever need from me, I got you. All you have to do is ask."

"Ok," I answered, nonchalantly though.

"I'm serious Charlytte, even if you just need to talk, I'm here. And if you feel that it's something too personal to discuss with me, you can also call Patricia. I know she'd be glad to hear from you. You're like a little sister to me. I wanna be there for you in any way I can."

“I understand,” I said. “Thanks Korey."

"No prob sis."

Korey reached into his back pocket, then pulled out a business card and a twenty-dollar bill. “Here is my new cell number, I don't have that other one anymore. You would know that if you called more often," he winked.

Ignoring his comment, I took the card, along with money, and examined them both. Korey kissed me on my forehead, grabbed a purple hat that America left behind, and headed out the door. Before closing it, he turned back to me.

"Anytime Charlytte,” he reminded me. “Call me anytime."

"Okay, I will."

After Korey left, I sat up on the edge of my bed and stared down at the floor. I began to think long and hard, wondering what that little talk was all about. Why suddenly the concern? Maybe he felt sorry for me? Maybe it was a part of him maturing? Or going religious? I didn’t know what it was, but whatever the reason, I was glad for it.

7: A HOOCHIE AND A HOTDOG

The closer it got to the beginning of the summer, the more I was ready to get back in school. But although I was excited about it, I wasn't happy with being placed a whole year behind. And I definitely didn't like being put back with kids that were even more immature than the ones in the class that I was supposed to be in.

Before my arrival, the school board set up a meeting between me and the Franklin High School principal. As I was told, it was supposed to help determine whether I should be admitted back into the school system. It was scheduled two weeks before the school year ended- the one I wasn't allowed to attend. So, for the first time in a while, some of my classmates would get to see me.

As much as I hated dressing up, I decided it would be best that I presented myself well. Hoping to impress the principal, I went for a business-woman look, wearing my black dress pants and short-sleeved, white collared shirt that I had bought only a couple days prior. I also wrapped my hair the night before, so by morning it would be soft and silky, just the way I liked it. And I wasn't a make-up wearing type of chick, but I did make sure that my lips were glossy. I even polished my toenails.

The morning of the meeting, Auntie Jo drove me to the school herself. She said that if she left it up to me, she knew I would be late. I never rode in the car with her much when I got old enough to walk places, but whenever I did, we never said more than two words to each other. There were times when I wanted to ask her why she didn't like me, or why was she so mean, but I normally just stared out the window and wished I had the guts to do so.

Luckily for me, on that day, I was too busy admiring myself in the side-view mirror to be thinking about her. If I had to say so myself, I was looking really nice. I had to look my best, not only for the meeting, but just in case I ran into Marcus. I figured maybe if he saw me, he'd want me again, or possibly miss what we had.

"When you go in there, make sure you do more listenin' than talkin'." Auntie Jo said as we pulled up to the front of the school.

"Yes ma'am," I sighed.

"I'm not playing with you Charlytte Monique. Be respectful. You are reflection of me and I don't need you makin' me look bad."

"*YES MA'AM*," I repeated, but this time louder.

I stepped out of the car and Auntie Jo sped off before I could even shut the door all the way.

"You already look bad bitch," I mumbled to myself, and even though she was long gone, I looked around in fear that she still might've heard me.

A bit jittery, I walked up to the double doors of the school building and made my entrance. I knew exactly where to go because I was familiar with Franklin High. I had been there a couple times with Keisha.

The school was much bigger on the inside than it looked on the outside. The walls were all-white and a thick, navy blue strip of paint ran down the middle of every hall. There were two big china cabinets at the front door filled with trophies, certificates, and pictures of the school's major past achievements. I even saw one of Auntie Jo's ex-boyfriends on an old basketball picture. Apparently Franklin High had won the state championship some time ago.

Class must have been in session because the hallways were quiet. It was a little after nine so I knew everyone was still in their first periods. There were a couple of students wandering the halls. Some were in a rush, and some were talking their times. But no sign of Marcus.

The main office- my destination- was easy to find. I entered, took a seat in one of the blue cushion chairs, and rested my forearm on its' wooden frame. Two administrative clerks sat behind a long white desk. One was an elder white lady with blond, curly hair; the other was a tall, black lady with an old-fashion bun. I couldn't help but stare at the black chick because she looked very down to earth, like she could have been an Auntie of mine.

"Hello, may I help you?" the chocolate woman from behind the counter asked, almost catching me staring at her. Her tone was very powerful and direct. It made me nervous.

Fretfully, I rose from my chair and walked to the counter.

"Uhm...yes, my name is Charlytte Black. I am scheduled for a meeting with the principal at ten."

"I am the principal," she informed me. "You're early. That's good."

This is the principal? I thought. I wasn't expecting *her* to be the person runnin' shit. Not saying that the school couldn't have a black principal; there's just a big difference between being black and being a nigga. And this woman standing before me, with those two gold caps in her mouth and that whopped up bun, looked like she was straight out of the Ordale Heights projects.

"Step back here inside my office, Miss Black," she pointed to a closed door that I didn't see until I walked behind the counter. "I will be with you as soon as assistant principal Arnold arrives. Let me page him now."

"Yes ma'am" I answered.

I stepped inside the room she directed me to, and took a seat in the rocking chair that sat directly across from her desk. I was still very nervous, but the soft, blue colored walls, and the flowery wallpaper trimming that ran across the rim of her ceiling, seemed to be calming me down.

Her office was much smaller than I imagined it would be. Even her desk, that was filled with papers neatly stacked on top of one another, was little. The first thing that caught my attention was the three portraits hanging up side-by-side on her wall. One was of a man, I assumed to be her husband. The other was of what looked like it could have been her daughter. And the last one was of a toddler boy, who could have passed for her grandchild. I just knew they were related because they all had those Chinese eyes and wide noses.

As I sat in the silent room just looking around, I wondered what would become of the meeting. Although I was in no hurry for them to come back, I was ready to get it over with.

After about ten minutes of waiting, someone finally came through the door. It was the principal, along with an older white guy, who entered quietly after her and shut the door behind himself. Now he looked just the way I expected the head principal to look- tall, skinny, and bald.

"Hello Miss Black, I am Principal Green," she said, as if she had never spoken to me at the desk. "And this is Assistant Principal Arnold."

"You can just call me Mr. Arnold," he told me.

"Good morning and nice to meet you both," I said politely, then stood to my feet and shook their hands.

"Before we get started, Charlytte do you have the paperwork we requested you bring?" she asked. "You should have gotten something in the mail."

"Yes ma'am," I handed her a thin, black folder.

The principal took the folder from me, then passed it over to Mr. Arnold. He began to skim threw the papers inside.

"Alright Miss Black, I understand that you were involved in an incident on May 29th with another student in your class, Samantha Hutchinson," she dug her face into her paperwork to confirm Samantha's name. "And this Fall you will be allowed to return back to school. So, the purpose of this meeting is to collect and process all the necessary paperwork that we have received from you. And just to give you a heads up, because of the magnitude of your actions, I will also be evaluating you to determine whether you should be allowed back into the public school system."

Allowed back? They were making me feel like I was some crazy person. I was far from that. I barely ever stood up for myself, but the second I did, all of a sudden I became the threat. I didn't like that one bit and I could immediately feel myself beginning to get upset.

"I see you have completed an anger management course," she continued, then waved my completion certificate back and forth in the air. "That's a good start. And what did you learn from this?"

Not to fight on school property, I said to myself. Then I folded my arms, looked down to the floor and, ironically, tried not to look nervous.

"I learned that violence is not the way to handle your differences, it's best to confront your problems accordingly and handle them as such."

I didn't know what the hell I was talking about. I barely paid attention in that class. I just said some shit I thought I heard the counselor say. It sounded right at the time.

When I looked up at Principal Green, I could tell she wasn't convinced. Then I looked over to Mr. Arnold. He just buried his expressionless face down into his notebook and then began making marks on his paper.

"Elaborate Miss Black," she told me. "What exactly does that mean?"

"It means that...uhm...I know what I did was wrong, but she bullied me all year. She made hurtful jokes, threw food at me, and even bumped into me a couple times *in front* of the teachers. Nobody did anything to her, but as soon as I defend myself, all of a sudden I'm the bad guy."

"No excuses Miss Black, you could have told your teacher or even your principal," she said. Mr. Arnold nodded his head in her favor.

"With all due respect Mrs. Green, nobody wants to be the school snitch. They're the ones that get picked on the most. That's just the way it is."

I immediately looked over to her desk and pointed at one of her pictures. "Is that your grandson?" I asked.

"It's *Principal Green,*" she corrected me. "And yes, that is my little grandson, Aaron. He's seven years old now."

"Well," I smacked my lips, "when little Aaron comes to you and tells you that somebody from his class has hit him, honestly, do you tell him to tell his teacher or do you tell him to hit them back?"

The heat in the room rose quickly. I was completely out of line and I knew it, but I didn't care. If I believed something, I stood by it, and this time, I just knew I had a point.

Principal Green held her head down for a couple of seconds, as if she was in deep thought or thinking of a good comeback. That short period of silence felt so long because I didn't know what to expect her to say or do next. The last thing I wanted was to have to sit out another year all because I didn't know how to shut my smart mouth.

She finally lifted her head up and slowly turned to Mr. Arnold, who was staying out of it by keeping his own head buried in his notebook.

"Excuse me Principal Arnold, but I can take it from here now," she told him.

Mr. Arnold grabbed his things quickly, took one glance at me, then left. He didn't even say goodbye.

Once he was gone, Principal Green stood her tall body up over her desk and pointed her long index finger directly at me. Although her skin was dark, her face still managed to redden.

"Listen to me, and listen to me closely *miss smarty pants,*" she said, moving her finger to the rhythm of her words. I had definitely pissed her off. "When my grandson comes and tells me that someone has hit him, you damn right, I tell him to hit they ass back."

That ghetto side- the side that I recognized when I first saw her- came out real quick.

She continued. "But I also realize that I have mouths to feed and in order for me to keep this job, I have to tell these kids to come to me when they have a problem, because morally it is the right thing to do."

"Do you know that the hardest part of this job is watching young girls, such as yourself, throw their lives away over petty bullcrap, like boys who'll trade them all in for a hoochie and a hotdog, and whose outfit looks the best."

"Do you know how many young girls I catch creeping out of here with these fast boys, chasing some pee-pee and missing out on their lessons? One girl here in the tenth grade has HIV, and that's only the case we know about."

"Charlytte, it's a blessing for you just to be sitting here in my office today. Think about it. What if that pencil would have dug into that girl's skin a little too far? What if she died that day? You would have been in jail for what...NONSENSE that could have been avoided."

Principle Green walked from around her desk, took her glasses off, and moved in closer to me. "Sometimes in life, you must follow the rules, regardless of what people may say. You think I got in this position by doing things my way? Hell no. My way would've had me working in the kitchen with the cafeteria ladies- no offense to them. I had to kiss some crackers' ass and they still manage to hate that a successful black woman is in this position. I can even see the envy in Mr. Arnold's eyes."

"Charlytte, these white folks don't give a damn about us, but I won't let them break me. I will continue to try to encourage these young girls that they are more than what lies between their legs. I will continue to tell these young guys that selling drug ain't the only way to make good money. That's why I'm here. Because I care. Do you understand me?"

I honestly felt in my heart that Principal Green truly cared about me, as well as the other students. She wanted to teach us things that the Geometry and Science class teachers couldn't, and that was how to survive in this life, especially being young and black. I never looked at it the way she put it. And even though I marinated on her every word, like pepper on a steak, I wouldn't show it.

"Yes ma'am," I shrugged, then looked away as if all that she had just said went in one ear and came out the other.

"Good," she ignored it. "Now I'mma let you back in here because for some reason, I like you. I don't know why, but I do. And keep in mind, I wanna see you succeed. You may go now."

Principal Green placed her glasses back on, then pointed to the door. As I made my way out of her office, she paged Mr. Arnold back in.

I was halfway out of the teacher's parking lot when I heard the school bell ring. And instead of making my way home, like my first mind told me, I turned around and went back into the school. Many kids flooded the hallways and the Commons center. Some of them looked like elementary school students, but most of them looked like grown-ups. I even saw a couple kids that I recognized from Lee James Middle. Some spoke and some didn't.

As I walked through the crowds, I could sense a couple guys looking at me. They would stare at my butt, tap their homeboys, and tell them to look too. I also saw a few girls whispering to each other as I passed them by and even heard one of them say, “That's the girl Samantha stabbed up. You see that scar she put on her face." I just laughed to myself and kept it moving. I didn't care who they thought won. I knew the truth and that's all that mattered.

I continued to walk through the crowds and ended up in a hallway where a separate group of kids were standing up against the walls. These guys looked much older. It didn’t take long for me to figure out that I must have been where the popular, upper-class guys hung out because most of them wore sports jackets and all the pretty girls were surrounding them.

Marcus played varsity basketball, so I scoped out the area carefully, hoping to spot him. But still, no sign. And after giving up on looking, I quickly made a U-turn, passing all the wannabe jocks again. That’s when I heard a familiar voice call out from behind me, "Freshman!"

When I turned around, who did I see? none other than the loser himself, Marcus Anderson. He was posted up against the hallway wall with a couple of his boys, wearing a devilish smirk on his face as if he still thought I was some type of joke. On top of that, he had the nerve to greet me by throwing up two fingers. I didn't know which I should do first, curse him or slap him.

"Who’s that?" I heard the guy next to him ask. He wasn’t familiar to me.

"That's the lil’ chic I was telling you about. She nice ain't it?" he said, nudging his friend's elbow.

"Hell yeah nigga!" the friend replied. “Make me wanna holla.”

"Well she’s fair game now," Marcus told him.

"Aight, you playing nigga, but don't be mad when I'm hittin' that," the friend joked.

They both started laughing, while I just stood there looking stupid. I wanted to be upset, but at that moment, I decided to just take it as a lesson and move on. I was finally able to go a whole day without thinking about him and I wasn't going to let one little childish encounter bring me back down.

Without saying a word to Marcus, I turned to walk away, but was almost knocked down by a tall, red girl with cornrows. When I regained my balance, I got a side glimpse of her. The first thing I noticed were her earrings because they looked similar- I mean damn near identical- to the ones that Marcus had given me. And I was certain that they were mine when I saw her walk over and kiss him on the lips.

So this lil' dyke looking bitch is the reason Marcus flipped the script on me. I thought, then quickly turned away before giving him the satisfaction of knowing that I saw them.

Deep down I was hurt, and I hadn't felt that angry since the incident with Samantha. I thought about going up to that girl and snatching my earrings straight out of her ear, but I knew that wouldn't have been smart. Besides, she probably didn't know they were mine, just like I didn't know that they were some chick's before me. If I was going to check anybody, it was going to be Marcus.

Principal Green's speech couldn't have come at a better time, because all I could hear was her voice in my head. I knew acting a damn fool wasn't worth it and I definitely didn't want to disappoint her by getting into a fight before I even started school.

I snuck a look back at Marcus and his new chick one last time.

"A hoochie and a hotdog," I whispered softly to myself as I pushed open the double doors and made my final exit. "She ain't lied about that."

8: NO SHE DIDN'T!

The steamy rays from the sun, mixed with the dry humidity of the air, made getting through the summer alive almost impossible. Crime rate in the neighborhoods was rising, as usual, and it seemed like people were losing their damn minds. Yet, no matter how hot the weather got, I loved the season.

I especially enjoyed going to the park with Amari and America, and sometimes went there by myself to clear my head. It was just something about seeing the beautiful ducks enjoying nature without a care, watching the innocent children play, and laughing at the old men get all excited when they caught a huge fish, that made my day.

Sundresses and flip-flops were my choice of style for the summer. It just seemed to go well with the heat. And I always kept my hair micro-braided because the last thing I wanted to get frustrated about in the summer was my head. Even at work Mr. Otis always encouraged me to wear less clothing. I knew it was just because he wanted to see some skin, but I didn't care. It was win-win for the both of us.

The end of July swiftly came to pass, and the beginning of the school year would be approaching shortly in August. I had gotten my learner's permit that June and was going to drive around with it until I got my official license. I didn't care about ridin' dirty, because no matter what, I wasn't about to catch that school bus. I had worked too hard for that.

In a way, that year out of school really paid off because I managed to save up two thousand and seven hundred dollars. I had been talking to Mr. Simmons, a longtime friend of Mr. Otis, about buying his wife's car. He was going to sell it for to me twelve hundred bucks. He originally wanted fifteen for it, but he favored me.

It was dark green '90 Honda Prelude with beige-leather insides. The car was in fairly good condition, although there were a couple of tears in the seat. The passenger window didn't roll down either, but I didn't care about that. It wasn't like I was going to be having any accomplices anyway. Besides, the air conditioner was running and I was fine with that.

"Is Mr. Simmons here?" I asked Mr. Otis, after busting into the store one afternoon as soon as I saw that Mrs. Simmons's Honda was parked out back.

Mr. Simmons came in often. He was a smooth old man who was always trying to be funny. Sometimes he was, and sometimes he wasn't. But I always laughed at his jokes and never felt uneasy about being around him, like I did with Mr. Otis. I met his wife a couple of times too. She was a highly sanctified woman who was always smiling and encouraging others to do so too. Mr. Simmons loved that woman and no one could blame him for it. He always talked about buying her a new car for Valentine's Day, and that year, he did just that.

"No," he replied, checking out a customer and my small developing breast at the same time. "He brought the car here today. He said it's yours as soon as you bring him the money."

"Really!" I screamed. "Yes!…I'mma need to run to the bank though. They close in about an hour."

"Go on. You can start when you get back."

"Okay, thanks Mr. Otis!" I shouted, then picked up my backpack and raced out the door. "Be right back!"

Finally, I was getting my first car. I couldn't do anything but thank Jesus himself, and Mr. Otis, since he was the one who taught me a little about driving. Because he had the privilege of having me sit on his lap, he would take me to the cemetery and let me drive along the dirt roads. And when I mastered that, he let me go out in traffic a couple times. I knew I still wasn't quite ready to pass that driver's test, but I figured a little bit of practice back and forth to school and work would eventually make me better.

The entire walk to the bank was a cheerful one. All I could do was picture myself driving and how cool I would look doing it. Most of the kids didn't get their cars until the tenth or eleventh grade, so I would be one of the few freshmen's to already have one. I had even mentioned it to Auntie Jo. She said she didn't care what I did with my money, as long as I paid my own damn insurance. And if I agreed to pay her half of the bill, she would happily add me on to her plan.

It was a fifteen-minute walk from the store to the bank, but somehow I made it in ten. I entered the building and took my place in line. There were about six people in front of me, but before I knew it, the male teller was calling me next.

"Hello ma'am, how may I assist you?" he asked

politely, watching me very closely as I made my way up to him. He was a tall, white guy with extremely long hair, very cute in a rock- starish sort of way.

“Hi,” I cheerfully waved. “My name is Charlytte Black and I’m here to take out some money."

"Here, just fill out this withdrawal slip,” he passed me a small piece paper. “I’m also going to need some identification."

"Ok. Thanks," I replied.

I snatched the form out of his hand and quickly began to fill it out. He watched me carefully as I did so. When I was finished, I gave it back to him.

"Okay. One moment please," he said, and then began typing my information into his computer. I waited a couple minutes, just looking around while trying to keep a calm composure. Truthfully, I was so antsy about getting the cash, and the car, that my legs were starting to shiver beneath me.

"Miss Black," he began to scratch his forehead. "How much did you want to withdraw again?"

"Fourteen hundred dollars," I said proudly.

"I'm a little confused," he frowned, then took his hand from off his head and placed it underneath his chin. "Do you have any other accounts?"

"No sir, I only have one…But wait,” I remembered, “it's under my mom, Joanne Black's, name."

When it came to public matters, I always called Auntie Jo my mama. Probably so people wouldn’t have to wonder or ask questions about my real one. Besides, they didn’t personally know me. I guess it just sounded good to say that I had one.

"Yes, I see both names here, but you only have seven

hundred dollars in this account," he said. "Oh wait... there was a $2,000 withdrawal on the fourth of June."

"What! Are you sure about that?"

"Yes, I'm positive. Would you like for me to print you out a statement?"

"Yes please."

He happily printed out a slip from his personal printer and handed it to me. I immediately began to examine the information. Sure enough, two thousand dollars had been withdrawn from my account, on June 4 at 9:37a.m. to be exact.

"Has someone tampered with your account?" he questioned. "If so, we will be happy to run an investigation for you."

"Uhmm...no. Let me go home and check with my mom, I'm sure it's just a mistake. Then I will go from there."

"Okay, that's fine," he said. "You can also call our customer service number. Here's a card."

The guy pointed to a stack of business cards on the counter. I grabbed one, thanked him, and rushed out the door.

All the way back to Mr. Otis's store, I couldn't help but to keep asking myself, "*What the hell happened to all my money?*" I wanted to just forget about work and go straight home, but I knew Mr. Otis had to take his wife to her doctor's appointment. That's the reason he asked me to come in. Shedding all hopes that it could have been cancelled, unfortunately as soon as I got there, he was packing up to leave.

"Uhmmm....I'm going to have to get the car tomorrow," I said without giving him a chance to ask me anything first.

"Why? What happened?"

"I left my ID at home," I lied. I could have told Mr. Otis the truth, but he knew Auntie Jo personally and I didn't want the word to get out about it, especially since I didn't know much yet myself.

"I'm sho' that aint a problem. Just get it when you're ready," he said. "It's all yours. I'm outta here. You got your keys right?"

"Yeah, I got 'em," I jingled them in my pocket just to be certain.

"Okay, see ya tomorrow."

When Mr. Otis left the store, I hurried to the phone to call Auntie Jo. Disappointingly, I didn't get an answer. I called, and called, and called again, but all I kept hearing was:

HELLO AND GOD BLESS. YOU HAVE REACHED THE BLACK'S RESIDENCE. SORRY I WASN'T ABLE TO RECEIVE YOUR CALL, BUT IF YOU LEAVE YOUR NAME AND A DETAILED MESSAGE, I WILL BE SURE TO GET BACK WITH YOU. ...AND REMEMBER, A LIFE WITHOUT THE LORD IS NOT A LIFE AT ALL.

"She's so phony," I said as I hung the phone, hoping that the answering machine didn't pick up my words.

Work was a drag and time managed to go by very slowly. To make matters worse, it seemed like all the nagging customers came into the store. When I finally got fed up with them all, I took it upon myself to shut it down, a whole thirty minutes early I might add. I had more important shit to attend to, so anybody who was planning on doing some last minute shopping was just going to be shit out of luck.

Without bothering to call Mr. Otis, I locked up, made my exit, and instead of driving my own damn car that I worked so hard for, I was walking home again. I was tired of parading those streets at night, and I was even more tired of all the consequences that came with it. Those guys who would roll up on the side of me and try to holler made me sick to my stomach. Most of the time, I would just keep walking as if I didn't even see their thirsty asses. And if I didn't answer them, they didn't do anything more to me than just call me a stuck-up bitch and keep riding. I didn't care, as long as they got the hell away from me.

When I made it to the house, Auntie Jo was laying down watching TV, talking on the telephone. Her room door was open so I politely barged in, flopped down on her bed, and purposely disrupted her conversation.

"Did you take money out of my account?" I got straight to the point.

She cocked her heavy head sideways, and gave me a disturbing look.

"Hold up, let me call you back Evelyn," she said, then quickly hung up the phone.

"Excuse me, come again?"

Auntie Jo sat up on her bed. She was trying her best to look confused, but I could tell by that phony expression on her face that she knew exactly what I was talking about.

"I *SAID*...did you take any money from my account, two thousand dollars to be exact?"

Then she confessed to it, as if it was no big deal.

"Oh...yeah, I was behind on the mortgage. I meant to tell you."

No this bitch didn't just say she 'meant' to tell me. I said to myself.

"Lewis ain't around to help out like he normally does. I've just be en struggling. I needed it to catch back up with the house. Them collectors been on my ass lately."

"Okay, but why didn't you tell me…and when you gonna pay it back? I'm trynna to buy this-"

Auntie Jo raised one eyebrow, hopped straight out of her bed, and went completely nuts.

"*PAY IT BACK! PAY IT BACK*!" she shouted. "You little ungrateful bitch! I took ya' lil ass in and raised you for all these years. I put a roof over ya head, clothed you, fed you, accepted you as my own child, and you got the nerve to ask me to *PAY YOU BACK*! Ain't dat some shit?"

I knew my face was turning red because I could almost hear my blood boiling on the surface of my skin. I couldn't believe it. All those mornings I got up and worked my ass off at that damn store, and she got the nerve to just take my money. Then, she didn't even have the decency to tell me about it. Enough was enough. I don't know what got into me, but I just snapped.

"YOU ACCEPTED ME AS WHAT?" I asked. "Keisha did a better job of raising me than you did! You never accepted me as anything. You barely even speak to me. All these years I been sittin' round wondering what the hell I was doing wrong, now I'm startin' to realize that it's not me, IT'S YOU!"

"You must be losing your fucking mind," she got all up in my face. "My own damn chirn don't talk to me like that, so I'll be damn if I let some ungrateful, unappreciative, cripple-face orphanage-bastard child do it! I ain't never asked you for much since your ass been working, or better yet, since you been living here. Now the minute I start struggling, and need to get something from you, you can't even be generous enough to let me have it."

"And what the hell you need with that kind of money anyway? Shit, you don't need no car yet, you can catch the damn bus like every other child. You sit round here acting like you better than everybody. Like because your mama died, the world gone wait on you. This world ain't slowing down for nobody, so you better get with the program. If it wasn't for me, ya ass would have been in some orphanage, or tossed around from group home to group home. Your uncles surely didn't want ya, and never once have you thanked me Charlytte! Never once!"

By then I had completely boiled over. There was no way I was going to walk away from a wonderful opportunity to speak my mind. I closed my eyes really tight and took- not one, not two, but three- deep breaths, then opened them and let her have it.

"Thank you for what JOANNE," I intentionally stressed her first name to show what little respect I had for her.

"Okay, here it goes... THANK YOU FOR BEING SOOO MEAN AND NASTY TO ME ALL THESE YEARS! THANK YOU FOR MAKING ME FEEL MORE LIKE A BURDEN THAN A DAUGHTER! THANK YOU FOR TELLING YOUR KIDS THAT I WAS THE REASON THEY COULDN'T GET THAT OUTFIT THEY WANTED! AND THANK YOU FOR MAKING MY LIFE A LIVING HELL!!"

"YOU HOLLERIN' 'BOUT YOU DON'T NEED NO MAN TO VALIDATE YOU, BUT YOU CAN'T KEEP YOUR OWN MORTGAGE PAID UNLESS

YOU GOT ONE. YOU'RE SUCH A GOOD MOM, BUT YOU WALK AROUND HERE ACTIN' LIKE YOU DON'T KNOW LEWIS GIVING YOUR FOURTEEN-YEAR OLD SON DRUGS TO SELL. YOU DON'T CARE ABOUT US, ALL YOU CARE ABOUT IS MEN AND MONEY!"

I stopped to catch my breath, then calmed myself down before speaking again. "YOU'RE RIGHT, THANK YOU FOR BEING MORE OF A BITCH THAN A MOMMY."

Without hesitation, Auntie Jo jumped out of bed, stood directly over me, cocked her fat hand back, and slapped the shit out of me with it. It stung worse than alcohol to an open womb. I was too shock, let alone too hurt, to do anything about it. Then she placed that same hand around my neck, pushed me down on the bed, and crushed me with her body weight.

"Don't ever insult me as a mother. On my God, if you do that shit again I will kill you and turn myself in. I do what the fuck I gotta do to put food in y'all mouths. Get yo' little ass in that room before I do something I may just end up regrettin'."

I rose up, angry and pissed to its highest power. Auntie Jo couldn't be serious about keeping my money. I mean really, it was mine. I worked hard for it. She couldn't just take it like that, even if she did take me in. I didn't know if I had the right to be mad, but I did know that what she had done wasn't fair.

When I got to the door, I looked back at Auntie Jo. And still not wanting to give up that easily, I cried, "It's my money! I earned it!"

"Kiss my ass Charlytte!" she yelled back.

I paused for minute, and then thought very carefully about what I said next.

"No, you kiss *my ass*. Or better yet, tell Lewis to do it. It seems he can't get enough of looking at it anyway."

Those words must have cut Auntie Jo very deeply, because she ran full speed, charging right at me. My room was directly across the hall from hers. I quickly dashed into it and locked the door, closing it just in time to block the bull from entering.

"Open this door Charlytte!" she began to beat and kick on it. "You don't pay any bills around here! Open this damn door now! I just want to talk to you!"

Talk to me? Please. I wasn't no damn fool. I knew exactly what she was going to do if I let her in that room. She was going to kill me.

Auntie Jo continued pounding, and even though I could tell she was getting tired, I knew she wasn't backing down.

"Charlytte Monique Black, I want you out of my house right now!"

Hell, I was way ahead of her, already grabbing my clothes. I figured I would go out the window and come back the next day when she cooled off. I didn't know where I was going, but I knew I didn't want to die.

After my backpack was filled up with whatever I could grab, I jumped straight out of the window. Then I took off running, dashing through the driveway and on down the street. When I got far enough from the house, I turned around to see all my clothes flying out into the front yard. I must have gotten out of their just in time.

"She really is serious about putting me out?" I panicked.

Still keeping my distance, I began walking back towards the house to make sure I was seeing what I thought I was seeing. I didn't get too close though.

Auntie Jo may have been a big woman, but she was strong and fast.

"YOUR STUFF IS HERE WHEN YOU'RE READY TO PICK IT UP!" she yelled to me.

"SO YOU REALLY GONNA KICK ME OUT!" I cried out to her, as loud as I could. "WHERE AM I GONNA GO!

"YOU CAN GO LIVE WITH YOUR MAMA FOR ALL I CARE!" she screamed, right before she went back into the house and dramatically slammed the door.

And just like that, I was homeless. But not only was I homeless, I was afraid and alone too. The only thing that seemed to be moving around me was the few cars that passed by. And even though the streetlights were beaming, I still couldn't seem to find any light. A part of me wanted to go back and beg for forgiveness, but I had had enough. I didn't know where to turn, but I knew that standing in the middle of the street wasn't going to get me anywhere. I thought long and hard about where I was going to go, then headed to the only other place I knew…

9: ON MY OWN

Staring at the car that was supposed to be mine added that final touch of disappointment to my horrible night. Everything I had gone through to get it- the filthy customers, the long hours, Mr. Otis's perverted ass- was just a complete waste. I dug up the keys from out of my backpack, looked around to see if anyone was watching, and unlocked the backdoor to Mr. Otis's store. I felt terrible going into the place without his permission, especially after he bragged so much about me being the first and only person he trusted with his keys, but I had to do what I had to do.

Unable to see a single thing in the dark, run-down building, I let my hands guide me to the office room. Luckily, a glowing beam from a nearby streetlight was shining through the blinds, allowing me to see all the junk he had in it. Mr. Otis had just about anything you could name packed up into that small space, everything from a couch to an exercise bike.

As soon as I entered his office, the heat attacked me and convinced me to let in some night air. I decided to crack open the window, but was very careful when doing it because the room faced an alley. I could see the back of people houses when I looked out of it and I knew that if I could see them, they probably could see me. The last thing I wanted was for the police to come busting into the store and locking me up for breaking and entering, especially when I had no one I could depend on to bail me out.

There was no way I could manage to do anything in the dark, so I was very thankful to see the familiar antique lamp resting on Mr. Otis's desk. We never used it because no matter what size light bulb we put in it, it never would shine as bright as it was supposed to.

I fumbled up under the lampshade until I could feel the switch, flicked it, and then placed the lamp on the floor to dim the room furthermore.

"Perfect," I whispered.

Once I finally felt safe enough to make myself comfortable, I flopped down on the couch and didn't even mind the cigarette aroma that rose up as I landed on it. On a normal day, you couldn't catch me lying dead on that old thing. I even gave it a name, Raggedy Ann. All I ever did was joke on Mr. Otis about how stupid he was for buying it. He would always reply by simply saying, "ya never know sugah, this raggedy piece of shit might come in handy one day." In that moment, all I could think about was Mr. Otis's words. And he was right; that old thing *did* come in handy.

After resting up a bit, I released my backpack from my shoulders and started dumping out the few items that were inside of it. There was a t-shirt, a pair of Jean shorts, two pairs of underwear, a tube of lotion, a digital planner that Keisha had given to me, and most importantly, my mama's picture.

That picture was the only real thing that connected me to her. I kept it on the dresser in my bedroom, and didn't go a single day without looking at it. My Uncle Johnny, the military man, gave it to me when I was just five. We went to visit him while he was stationed in Augusta, Georgia. He pulled it out one night when he was showing off his photo album to the family. I remember him setting me aside from all the other children, personally handing it to me, and telling me to cherish it forever. And as long as I had breath in my body, I was going to do just that.

I appreciated my Uncle for sharing it. Hell, Auntie Jo surely didn't tell me anything about her. She never discussed my mama, and if it weren't for us taking that trip, I probably would have never known what she looked like. If I tried to ask her questions, she would immediately act as if she was too torn up to talk about it. But when I asked her about my dad, she did manage to say that my mother was a hoe. As she put it, "that man could be anybody."

But even if she was a hoe, she was still beautiful in my eyes. And as I saw her young, slender body sinking slowly to the floor, I swept the picture up quickly from out of the air. I valued it too much to let it touch the ground. To me, there was nothing in the world worth that picture. It was my American flag.

For a minute, I sat silently, just admiring her wide and graceful smile. She looked so beautiful in her big, red blouse that was tucked inside of her sky blue jeans. Her feet were cut out of the picture so I couldn't tell what kind of shoes she was wearing, but I expected them to be just as cute as she was. Even her hair was on point. The way it fell down in a bob and cuffed her cheekbones. Of course I couldn't rock a style like that, especially not in my day, but the way her face was leaking with confidence, I just knew she was killin' 'em back in hers. I only wish I could have gotten the chance to meet her.

Still admiring my mama, I began thinking about how much different my life would have been if she was still alive. I wondered if I would have had a little brother, or a sister, maybe both. Not ones who loved me only because they were forced to- but a real family who loved me genuinely, just because it came natural.

Just thinking about a real family got me all emotional and a teardrop rolled down one of my eyes. I was alone, hurting, and I felt as if my soul had become dark again. That same darkness I felt the night I stood looking out the window when I was seven. Everything in my life was out of place. Marcus was gone. I had no friends. No family. And the only person I had to talk to, my mother, was dead.

A school counselor once told me that it might help if I tried to reach out to her, ya know, by talking. I never did it because I wasn't ready to face that emptiness I would certainly feel when I didn't hear her reply back. I can't lie, when I was younger, I believed that if called out to her, she would magically appear to me in a ghostlike form. Shit, the fairy Godmother did it in Cinderella, so why couldn't it have happened to me. It wasn't until I got older that I realized I was no princess and life was no fairytale.

But that night, for some reason, I just went for it. I guess I needed her to hear me. I needed someone to hear me. I placed the picture up to my heart, closed my eyes, and began to speak.

"Hey ma. It's me, your daughter," the sound of my voice crackled under my lips, like it was trying to find the strength to speak out and be heard. "I don't know where you are right now, or if you can hear me, but I'm lost and I need some guidance. Mama, I know it's not your fault that you can't be here. I know it's not your fault that Auntie Jo treats me the way she does. And I know in my heart that you were nothing like her, but still, why mama, just tell me why?"

My eyes began to swell up. I closed them tightly, trying to trap the tears. Then continued on.

"Why can't I stop feeling like I'm the reason why you're dead!" No longer able to hold back, I busted out into tears. "Please don't be mad at me mama! I hope this isn't your way of punishing me for what I done to you!"

I cried and cried and cried, until my body was unable to produce any more tears. I remembered hearing someone say that shedding a few here and there was a good way to flush out your troubles. It must have been true, because after I wiped away my last one and pulled myself together, I could literally feel a piece of a burden being lifted from me.

Eventually, I picked my spirits up and regained some energy, then grabbed my t-shirt from off the floor and covered up as much of my body as I could with it. It was still hot and stuffy in the store, but I could never rest well if I didn't have some sort of covering over me. I felt more secure that way.

Staring up at the ceiling, I couldn't help but think about everything I just said. I never thought I'd be trying to reach out to my mama, and I definitely never thought I'd be blaming her for all my problems. The devil was surely busy working on me. He knew I was weak and vulnerable. But even though I didn't feel like I had much faith left in me, and even though I felt like I was hanging on to my dear life by a very thin thread, I wasn't quite ready to just give up and let go.

I glanced at my mama's picture one last time before putting it back in my backpack. The way my gut tangled every time I looked at her and the way she captivated me, I just knew somehow and somewhere, she had to have been with me.

"I love you mama. I know you're watching over me," I whispered, and then eventually fell asleep.

The morning after came quicker than I wanted it to. I found myself awake at five-thirty in the morning, staring at the ceiling again. It was Saturday, which meant that Mr. Otis would be arriving to the store around seven. I knew I had a little more time to rest, but decided to get up and be out by six, because with my luck, he probably would have come early.

With my tired eyes, I peeked around at Mr. Otis's office. And when it dawned on me that I was there, I immediately shut them really tight- hoping that if I opened them again, I would be lying in my bed at Auntie Jo's house, my money would have never been taken, and that whole night would have been nothing more than just a terrible nightmare. Unfortunately, I re-opened them only to find reality staring directly back at me. I knew by the rusty old furniture and the crook in my back that I surely wasn't home and I definitely wasn't dreaming.

After briefly plotting on what my next move would be, I figured I'd first to go over to Auntie Jo's house and get my clothes from out of the front yard. She cleaned some rich white women's house every Wednesday and Saturday morning so I knew she would be leaving home early. She depended on that little change to rack up on her week's supply of liquor, so I knew that she wouldn't miss it. Nothing came before her money and her drinking, not even the fact that her fifteen-year old niece was somewhere out in the streets.

I wasn't due to be to work until 3:30 that afternoon, but since it was Saturday, I decided I would come back to the store and ask Mr. Otis if I could start before my scheduled time. He never turned down extra help, especially on the weekends. Plus his wife, Clarice, was getting sicker and she was calling him home almost every day.

I placed the lamp back where I found it, then threw my old T-shirt and underwear in the space behind the cabinet. Mr. Otis never moved that thing so I knew he wouldn't find it there. Afterwards, I fluffed the dusty pillows on the couch and headed for the back door. Before I made my exit, I looked around one last time to be sure that I left no evidence of an intruder. When all was good, I left the building and made sure that I locked the doors behind me.

I still had about an hour and a half to kill before Auntie Jo would be leaving, so the first thing I did was walk straight to the ATM machine. It was in the opposite direction of Auntie Jo's house, but I knew that by the time I walked there, then walked back, I'd make it just in time to watch her hateful ass leave.

The morning was settling in and nature's little alarm clocks were chirping at their usual time. Even though I wasn't happy about walking, I would have much rather been doing it early in the morning than late at night. I didn't have to worry about all those perverted men and their whack ass pick-up lines. Mr. Otis was enough.

The short walk to the ATM seemed like forever, but thankfully, the rest of my money was still there. Unfortunately, I could only withdraw the maximum amount allowed to take out in a single day. I was mad as hell because I wanted every last penny. I knew given the opportunity, Auntie Jo would have cleaned me out with bleach and Pine Sol. I didn't complain too much though. I would have much rather had some of it than nothing.

I took a slow scroll back to Auntie Jo's and arrived on her street about ten minutes after seven. She normally left the house around 7:30, but strangely, her car was already gone. I walked swiftly down the street, looking around and listening out for the sound of her '88

Mustang's loud engine, in case she decided to swing back through. I knew Keyshawn was in the house sleeping so I wasn't worried about him. He had a terrible habit of waking up and going to bed late. One afternoon he came home and slept through the night, the entire next day, and didn't get up until the following morning. I didn't know what could have had him so tired, but it could have been anything being that he was gone for three whole days before.

As I got closer to the house, the first thing I noticed was that I didn't see any of my clothes out in the yard. That was strange given the fact that the night before the grass and porch was covered in jeans, shirts, and panties. I quickly began to wonder where my clothes went. People rarely walked our street at night, so it was less than likely that a junky stole them. And I knew damn well Keyshawn didn't move them. If she would have asked him, he would have straight up told her 'hell-to-the-naw'.

Still puzzled, I eased my way up the porch steps and slowly crept open the worn out screen door. Then I slid my key in the front door and turned the knob. Just as I pushed the door in, I heard a loud thump.

What the hell? I thought, as I looked up at the door and realized that someone had bolted a latch lock on the other side of it.

"This bitch really ain't playing," I whispered.

I tried sticking my fingers between the space in the door and lifting the latch, but I wasn't strong enough to do it. Not wanting to give up so easily, I tried a couple more times but the only thing I managed to do was hurt my fingers. Next, I took my ATM card from out of my pocket and attempted to pop it with that, but just as I began to stick the card through the crevice of the door, it flew open.

"What you doing 'round here?" Keyshawn yawned and rubbed his small, tight belly all at once.

"I live here. What you doing up?" I replied.

Keyshawn and I never argued, but we never talked much either. Auntie Jo was pregnant with him when she took me in. Growing up, she always used to say that the clothes she brought for me had to be passed down to him because she couldn't afford to buy for the both of us. She never bought me anything pink or girly because she knew that once I got finished with them, Keyshawn was next. Up until fifth grade I wore nothing but boys' clothes- plain white t-shirts and khakis. I never wore the jeans with the flowers or the pretty little purple tops that the other girls rocked. It got so bad that my teachers would sometimes mistake me for being a boy and all the kids would laugh and call me Charlie.

Keyshawn resented us having to share clothes. Every year when we got our school gear together, he would pout and scuff at me. It was bad enough he had to wear hand-me-downs, but it was even worse that he had to wear hand-me-downs from a girl. I always wanted to tell him that I was sorry and that I would buy him a billion dollars' worth of expensive clothes when I got rich, but the dirty looks he would give me made me stay as far away from him as possible.

There he was again standing before me, staring at me with that same look in his eyes.

"No, you don't live here. Mama kicked you out last night," he reminded me.

"Anyway," I dismissed him, "where are my clothes? That's all I came back for."

"They ain't here!" he shouted.

"Then where are they?" I shouted back. I couldn't believe the attitude he was giving me. He didn't have anything to do with the situation. And I prayed that he would just stay out of it and move out of my way.

"Mama got them up this morning," he informed me. "She said she was selling them to that 'Jeans for Green' spot on the west side."

I didn't want to believe Keyshawn, but he didn't crack one smile when giving me that info. It confirmed to me that what he was saying was true.

"Why you think I'm up so early?" he asked, as if I was really supposed to know. "She been stompin' around here all morning, fussin' and hammering on this damn door. I never seen her dis mad befo.' You betta leave before she comes back. She will really hurt you if she sees you."

Finding out that Auntie Jo was really serious about putting me out, and to know that she'd rather sell my clothes than to let me have them, truly hurt me to my heart. I honestly thought that what happened the night before was just a phase. That we both were upset, and once we calmed down everything would be okay again. Just thinking about it, tears began to swell up in my eyes. I didn't want Keyshawn to see me cry, so I tried to play tough and get away from him.

"Move out my way!" I yelled, and then pushed him aside. He tried to grab my arm but I snatched loose and headed straight to my room. I could hear him coming behind me so I quickly wiped my cheekbone before he had the chance to see the teardrop rolling down on it.

When I opened my room door, everything looked the same as I left it. Nothing was moved off my dressers, my pictures were still hanging up on the wall, and my bed was still covered with stuff I couldn't fit into my backpack. Keyshawn followed me there and stood in the doorway, watching me as I scrambled threw drawers and dresser tops taking what little I could. Because I was afraid of Auntie Jo coming home, I was in too much of a hurry to pay him any attention.

"So where you gone go? You ain't got nobody," Keyshawn teased. I could tell he was purposely trying to discourage me, but I wasn't going to let him make me feel any worse than I already did.

"I don't need nobody," I said, confident but clearly uncertain. "I'll be fine."

"Fine? How you gone be fine Charlytte? You ain't got no place to go. Instead of coming up in here taking shit to leave, you need to be trying to apologize to my mama so that you can come back."

"Apologize?" I asked, starting to feel insulted. I stared him directly in his face. I wanted him to see in my eyes, how I felt in my heart. Besides, no matter how grown he thought he was, he was still something like my baby brother and the whole attitude he had with me was working on my last little nerve. I stopped stuffing my backpack, then gave him my full attention.

"Apologize for what Keyshawn, for being stuck in this *hellhole* y'all call a home?"

"You really are an ungrateful lil' *BITCH*," he stressed. "Mama ain't lied about that. Whether you like it or not, she raised you in this hellhole."

That last little nerve was I holding on to was now officially plucked. I was used to guys on the streets calling me a bitch, but it actually hurt when someone in my own family disrespected me like that.

"*Bitch*?" I asked, making sure I had heard him correctly. "So what you think you a gangsta now 'cause Teon let you hang wit' him."

Teon was an older thug who lived at the top of our

street. He was a twenty-year old high school dropout who sold drugs, was good at basketball, and had the flyest ride in the hood. Not to mention, he was cute and his long, black dreadlocks was definitely a plus. I had a crush on him growing up, but I knew he was too old and way too thuggish for me.

"The only reason you think yo' mama is *soooo* cool is because she let's you do anything you want. You come home whenever you please and stay out for days at a time." I continued filling my bag. "That ain't raising nobody, that's triflin'. You just having too much fun to understand that."

"I'm a grown ass man Charlytte," he shot back. "I work and help pay bills. So you damn right, I do what the fuck I wanna do. You just *too dumb* to understand that."

I couldn't believe Keyshawn was walking around thinking that he was a grown man. I admit, he was cut like one and he was very mature for his age, but he surely wasn't grown. We all grew up fast. In Auntie Jo's house, everyone pretty much had to fend for themselves.

"Spell dumb," I said childishly. "Oh, I forgot you can't 'cuz you barely ever go to school. Can you even read?"

I was trying every attempt possible to hurt him like he was hurting me.

"Nope, but I can count. I been shootin' mama money for the past six months now. You been working a year and ain't gave her shit. She make me pay but don't even bother you. She sacrificed for you, even if it meant having me wear your stinkin' ass clothes, and you got the nerve to bitch about a lil' thousand. You fuckin' ungrateful and ain't nothing fair when it comes to po' lil Charlytte. I'm tired of you in my spotlight. Honestly, I'm glad to see you go."

Keyshawn's harsh words cut deep into my sensitive heart, like a machete threw a marsh mellow. Everybody was against me. Everybody.

"Oh, so this about them clothes? You blamin' me for that?"

"Charlytte, did you know that Evelyn's niece, that slut Kim, was in my third-grade class and she told everybody that I was wearing my sister's clothes. Huh, did you know that shit?"

Oh my. I thought. No I didn't know that. He never mentioned it before.

Even though I was beginning to feel sorry for him, I couldn't show it.

"That's not my fault! You should be mad at Auntie Jo for telling Evelyn all her business."

"It's not mama's fault either, but forget all that. The point is, I'm making money now, so don't be coming at me like you better than me because I'm doing what the fuck I gotta do to buy my own shit."

"That's no excuse. It's other ways to make money, jackass! It's called a J-O-B!" I yelled. "Why Auntie Jo ain't ask you to work for Mr. Otis? He already told her he needed someone to help keep the floors swept and stock up some-"

"I ain't no bitch," he quickly stopped me. "I ain't sweeping up no damn floors."

I was pretty sure he was going to say that, but it was worth the try. Bitch or not, he didn't need to be selling drugs at fourteen. He was a smart, handsome young boy and I cared too much about him to see him throw his life into the garbage can.

"One day you gone see that she don't give a fuck about us. Yo mama tells me to stay in school, hoping I make it through college and get a good job to help support her sorry ass. She's basically keeping you in the streets 'cause she knows you young, you black, and you got a better chance of making money hustling than graduating. Don't you think it's kinda triflin' that she lets her boyfriend teach you how to hustle, instead of teaching you how to be a real man, just cause she need yo lil' fifty dollars to help pay her bills."

Keyshawn just stood in silence. I could tell he was thinking hard about what I just said. I knew I had him second-guessing his mama's intentions, and that's all I wanted to do. Of course, he wasn't going to let me know that.

"Fifty dollars," he finally bounced back, and then reached down into the pockets of his gray sweatpants. "This look like fifty dollars to you?"

Keyshawn started fanning a small knot of money- that he had the nerve to put a rubberband around- up in my face. He really thought he was impressing me with his twenties and tens, but I wasn't one of his simple ass hoochies so I wasn't the least bit turned on by it. Besides, most of them were singles anyway. He just hid them between the larger bills. But even if they all were big bills, I knew he would eventually end up paying it all back to bond himself out of the juvenile.

Disgusted, I grabbed everything I needed and headed out of the room, pushing him out of my path.

"Get out my way boy," I told him. "And I hope you planning on buying yaself a good lawyer with that lil' change you call money 'cause you gone need it when you get jammed up."

"Whatever bitch," he said as he followed me out the door. He was five hundred degrees hot, but I didn't care.

As long as I had gotten my point across, he could have peed in his pants and it wouldn't have fazed me one bit.

I ignored Keyshawn and headed out towards the front door, moving as fast as I could. I tried to slam the door behind myself to slow him down, but he caught it and followed me outside.

"At least I got some place to say!" he yelled. "You ain't got no money. You ain't got shit, bitch."

As I walked away, I had to constantly tell myself to stay calm. I mean it took everything I had in me not to snap. Keyshawn was really trying to push me over the edge, and it was working.

"Oh, and they got cardboard boxes behind the liquor store too!" he continued. "Matter of fact, here go some money. Go buy yaself a house."

I watched as about five ones came flying in my direction. And as bad as I wanted to turn around and pick them up, my pride wouldn't let me do it. I didn't need Keyshawn or Auntie Jo for shit. The way I felt, I would have rather slept in the middle of the busiest street in Ordale than to go back to that house.

"Don't front like you don't need this money bitch!" Keyshawn still yelled. "I can help you if you wanna make a lil' change! I know a spot on the east where you can work. It's a lot of guys who would pay good money to get up in some young, tight pussy!"

I continued to walk away, trying my best to hide my shame from the neighbor, Mrs. Emily, who sat on porch and watched the whole thing go down. She was looking as if she so badly wanted to say something encouraging to me, but I knew that wasn't going to happen. Around our parks, people may have peeped out the window, but nobody dug their noses in anybody else's business.

I still couldn't believe my own brother would say those horrible things to me. But even though the argument was very hurtful, I was glad it happened. At least I knew where Keyshawn and I stood, and whether it was on a good or bad note, I didn't have to wonder anymore. Everything was becoming clear as everyone's true colors began to show. My family was never really my family; Auntie Jo didn't care shit about me, Keyshawn had more respect for a dog, Keisha abandoned me, and Korey reaching out to me was probably just a front. The more I thought about everything, the more I hated them all. I never wanted to go back there.

I headed back to Mr. Otis's store with nothing left of me but a backpack, a couple hundred dollars, and a small amount of faith. I knew I had to find some strength from somewhere because one was thing clear; from now on, I was definitely on my own.

PART TWO

1O: CONVERSATION RULES THE NATION

After I left Auntie Jo's I headed to Marco's, an all-day breakfast spot Mr. Otis turned me on to after I started working for him. Not only was the food there excellent, but the prices were reasonable too. It was owned by one of the coolest old white ladies I had ever met. She was very down to earth and had that cute, country girl accent. Sometimes Mr. Otis would make me walk there and grab him some breakfast. It was the only place in the hood I knew where you can get smothered shrimps, grits, and a drink for six dollars. That was my favorite meal.

I purposely took the long way because I needed time to organize the mountain-high thoughts that were piled up in my head. On my way, I passed the McApples's Shopping Plaza and spotted the clothing store that Keisha told me to NEVER shop at. It was owned by some foreigners and everything they sold inside was cheap and off-brand. Instead of Polo, they had Dolo. Nikes were Nikkis. And they even had an imitation U.S. Polo Association; it couldn't get any cheesier than that.

I had planned on buying clothes but never got around to it, and school was approaching in less than two weeks so I was in no condition to be picky. I had only grabbed one decent outfit from Auntie Jo’s house. It was a Polo fit that I had purchased a couple weeks before. I knew I needed more clothes, but I also knew I needed more money. It wasn’t easy, but I put my pride to the side and decided to see just what 'Fashion World' had to offer.

Upon walking into the store, I greeted the saleswoman. She was an old Chinese woman seated behind the checkout counter. I looked around at all the cheesy merchandise. I wasn’t a professional in judging fabric, but I knew those clothes were only made to be washed once. That’s if they could survive that.

By the time I was finished shopping, I ended up getting a weeks' worth of clothes, a couple pairs of earrings, two bracelets, and three belts. All for a little less than a hundred dollars. Truthfully, I was a little disappointed because I really wanted to start High School off with a bangin' car and some bangin' clothes to match, but somehow I managed to convince myself to just be thankful for what I was able to get.

I made it to Marco's around ten-thirty and ordered my usual. Then I seated myself at a table in the rear corner of restaurant and began to stare out the window at the passing cars. As I waiting quietly for my food, a tap on my shoulder interrupted me.

Surprisingly, I looked up to see this older, dark-skinned guy standing over me. The first thing I noticed was his slanted eyes. They were dark red. I knew immediately that he was under "Mary Jane's spell."

"I believe you left this on the counter," he said as he

handed me the small bag with my accessories in it.

"Oh, thanks." I grabbed it.

"It must have not been important. I can keep it if you like," he cracked.

"If you wear cheesy girl's earrings, then sure," I joked back.

We both laughed and then there was silence. Luckily, the waiter saved me from that awkwardness by calling out my ticket number. I started to get up, but the guy stopped me.

"Is that your number?" he asked.

"Yes," I answered, looking down at my receipt just to be certain.

"Sit tight, cutie. Let me grab that for you."

As he got up and headed for the food, I couldn't help but notice how sharp he was. He had on a pair of dark blue denims with an orange Polo shirt. His brown Rockport's brought out his classiness, and his gold chain and gold watch topped off his style. He wasn't the best looking guy, but his attire, along with his swagger, definitely brought out his potential sexiness.

He smoothly strolled back to the table with his order and mine. Then placed my food in front of me, put my straw in my cup, and laid my spork and knife out evenly on a napkin. I was impressed by his politeness, not to mention, the fact that he called me a *cutie*.

"I got some time to kill, miss lady. Do you mind if I sit with you?" he asked.

"No, I don't mind," I replied, but honestly, I wasn't at all okay with it.

I didn't like talking to strangers, especially men. I always felt nervous and uncomfortable. I would stutter, sweat, and sometimes hold my head down, embarrassed by my own scar. I really didn't feel like the discomfort, but I figured, why not have a quick conversation with him? It wasn't like I had anything else to do and it wasn't like I was ever going to see him again.

"So, what side of town you from?" he asked, while opening his box of food.

"I lived on the South. Right behind that youth center," I replied. "And you?"

"The west, near Balwin Avenue. You familiar?"

"Yeah, sort of," I lied.

"Can I ask you a personal question?" he asked.

"Sure, go ahead," I replied.

"Why are you sittin' here all alone?" he said as he took a huge bite out of his bacon, egg, and cheese sandwich, and then continued, "Where's your man, that's if you have one?"

"I don't have a man," I replied. "I had a boy, but that's why I left him. Guys are assholes."

"So, I take it you've been in love recently and got your heart broke," he said.

"How you figure?" I asked, amazed by how he was able to accurately guess that.

I dug my spork into my grits and took another swallow. The food was perfect. I wanted to eat it faster, but I didn't want to look like a pig in front of him.

"Because at first, most women do what they are naturally born to do- they welcome love with opens arms. That's until they get their hearts broke by one pussy poodle. Then they assume that all men are mutts, so they treat the rest they encounter like shit. Even if it means missing out on a *big dawg*."

I immediately realized that I was not talking to an ordinary guy. It was something special about this one. A mix of his demeanor, his style, and his intellect, captivated me and forced me to take interest.

"Generally speaking," I said, trying to sound just as experienced as he did, "what makes you feel like *you're* a good man?"

"I never said I was one," he joked. "I can't say that I'm a good man, but I can say that I know what it takes treat to a woman right."

After taking one more bite out of his sandwich, he closed his box of food, placed both of his hands together, and rested them on the tabletop. Judging by the serious look on his face, I knew that the conversation was going to get deeper. And I had a good feeling that whatever he said next was either going to be very important, or very interesting, if not both.

"It's like this," he said, "and I'mma keep it all the way real with you because that's the only way I know how to be...I can tell you're at a time in your life where you're just looking for someone to love you. They don't have to be rich or poor because currently you're not in need of much. You want quality time and intimacy, whether it be sex or cuddling, but nothing more or nothing less. Does that sound about right?"

I nodded.

"I'm twenty-four and I've learned throughout the years that as you get older, your demands began to increase and your standards begin to decrease. When you get that house, you gonna be looking for someone who can help you pay the rent, sometimes whether you like him or not. When you have those kids, you gonna be looking for somebody to take care of them, sometimes whether they're the father or not."

I listened to him closely. His delivery was so powerful that he could have said eeny-meeny-miney-moe-catch-a-tiger-by-the-toe and persuaded me to believe that it meant something great. He had all my attention and as long as he kept talking, I was going to keep listening.

He continued. "Every woman is different. Some want love. Some want shoes. Some just want a man who can come over and fuck her back loose. It all depends on her desires. It's a game. You just gotta know how to play it."

I didn't fully understand. All I heard was having babies, buying houses, and fucking backs out. I wasn't ready for any of that.

"Well, that's my problem," I said as I shied away from his creepy red eyes. "I don't believe that love is a game. I believe that people should act with their hearts and not with their strategies. Most men aren't interested in women's feelings. They only go for what they want. What you just said being an example."

"I can agree with that, to a certain extent," he nodded.

Yes! He agrees with me. I thought. *I'm doing fine.*

"But I just don't feel-"

Suddenly, his cell phone began to sound, with Eightball and MJG's *Space Age Pimpin'* being his choice of ringtone. The conversation came to a halt as he reached into his pocket and pulled out an all-black expensive-looking phone. He took a quick glimpse at the screen, then mumbled something to himself before sliding it back into his pocket. I watched his every move.

"So…now can I ask *you* a question?" I asked, attempting to pull his mind away from his phone and back to me.

He stared down at the pocket that contained his cell phone, obviously still thinking about the person who had just called. Then he slowly nodded his head, "Yeah, sorry about that. Be my guest."

I knew I was stepping way out of line with the next one, but what the hell. I was proud of myself for being able to indulge in a decent conversation with an older man, so proud, that I wanted to challenge him a little bit more.

"Do *I* interest you?" I asked boldly.

He chuckled to himself, like he was taken by surprise by my question.

"As a matter of fact, yes. I'm interested in getting to know more about you."

"Okay. So why is that you claim to be *soooo* interested in me, but you have yet to ask me my name?"

"Okay Miss-" he paused, and waited for me to fill him in.

"It's Charlytte."

"Okay Miss *Charlytte.* Now, let me ask you a question?"

"Sure. Go ahead."

"And by the way I'm Cederick. First off, you're probably about nineteen, right?"

Body wise, I could pass for twenty-one, but I still held the face of a twelve-year-old.

"No, I'm only sixteen," I exaggerated a bit.

Cederick's face lit up in amazement. He took a long look at me and sat speechless for about ten whole seconds. I was uneasy with him looking at me that way because it made his eyes look even spookier.

"You mean to tell me you're only sixteen!" he asked. "Wow...I never would have guessed. You speak with so much maturity."

"I guess so," I said bashfully.

"You work?" he asked.

"Yeah, I work over at Mr. Chills, what about you?"

"Yes I do, for myself that is."

"Oh, okay," I said, trying not to think too much about him telling me that he worked for himself. I didn't want to assume that he was in the drug business. There were a couple self-made entrepreneurs around our neighborhoods. Those guys sold anything from bootleg CDs to condoms, and they must have made decent money because they stayed in business.

Cederick didn't mind that I was only sixteen. In fact, it seemed as if that made him want to talk with me even more. He was amazed by how well I spoke and how I was able to keep up with him. We sat and chatted a bit longer, discussing everything from sports to his two kids. The both of us had gotten so lost in our conversation, that we didn't realize almost two hours had passed.

"Welp Miss Lady, or *Charlytte*, since I now know your name," he joked. "I hate to leave this way, but I gotta make a run. Do you mind taking my number so that we can pick up where we left off?"

I knew that was just his way of trying to get at me without feeling bad about my age.

"Yeah, write it down on this," I handed him a napkin.

Cederick wrote his number down and happily gave it back to me. His eyes weren't as red as they were before, allowing me to be able to look into them. There was still something very interesting about them- sort of sexy but malicious, all in one.

"Call me pretty lady," he said, before allowing me the pleasure of watching him walk away.

After he was gone, I gathered my bags, and my tray of food, then headed out behind him. Before leaving, I stopped at the trashcan that was located by the exit door. Surely I was interested in Cederick, but the last thing I was thinking about was getting involved, or becoming the least bit infatuated, with another man. I still had some hatred inside of me towards guys because of what Marcus had done to me. And on top of all that, I didn't even have a place to stay. I quickly came to the conclusion that I needed to rid myself from even the slightest idea of us getting together. So, I placed the napkin with Cederick's number on the tray, along with my grits, and watched it all fall into the garbage can.

Believe it or not, three o'clock was only around the corner so I wasted no time getting back to the store. I had accomplished everything that I needed to accomplish and still had about an hour to kill before my shift started.

When I got there, Mr. Otis was ringing up a customer. I watched him carefully to make sure he didn't show any signs of knowing that I had stayed the night, but he didn't seem to act any different. I greeted him, went straight to his office, and checked behind the cabinet for my backpack. Luckily it was still there, untouched and unnoticed.

"You're early," he said, after he finished trash talking to his one of his customers about a ball game.

He joined me in his office and sat down at his desk.

"I was out and about, just doing some school shopping," I held up my bag as a means to provide proof. "I got done early so I decided to come here, instead of going all the way home."

"You wanna go head and start?" he asked me before I got the chance to ask him first. "My back is killing me and Clarice been begging me to bring her some chicken noodle soup. I may have to make a run to the house."

“Okay, no prob. How is she?" I asked, hoping he would tell me something good.

Mrs. Clarice had been getting sicker and sicker. She was calling Mr. Otis for everything. One time she called him all the way home to fix her a glass of water because she said she was too weak to get out of bed. Mrs. Clarice was always an independent type of woman, so I knew she must have been really dying.

Mr. Otis held his head down for a second, and then looked back up at me.

"Not too good," he replied. "The doctor says there is nothing they can do at this point. Her cancer done spread too far."

"Aaw man, sorry to hear that," I sympathized with him. "But don't worry about what those doctors say. She'll be fine."

"I don't know this time. I told her ‘bout smokin’ all them damn cigarettes. That’s what happens when you abuse your body. She smoked them damn things for twenty-five years and now she wonder why she done caught that cancer."

"My grandma died of lung cancer and she never smoked a day in her life. It happens to the best of us. It's nobody's fault," I said, trying to take up for Mrs. Clarice.

I didn't like the way he was talking about her. It sounded like he felt that she had gotten what she deserved. His whole attitude about her sickness, to me, was very negative. If she called because she was in pain, he would call it nagging. I even noticed how he started hitting on some of the ladies that came into the store. Maybe that was just his way of trying to alleviate the pain of being so close to losing his wife. Shit, they had been married for almost thirty years.

"Yea, I guess," he sighed.

"I'mma put my bags in this closet," I said, drifting away from that depressing topic.

"You don't have to tell me that," he replied. "Go right ahead."

As I walked to the closet, I could feel Mr. Otis looking at my ass. He would watch it jiggle from left to right every time I made a move. It got so bad that it seemed as if his head would bounce to the rhythm of my butt cheeks. And to makes matters worse, he would let out little moans underneath his breath. I always had a feeling he would go home and jack himself off thinking about me. He just seemed like the type. It probably would have been less disgusting if he were younger and cuter. That short, stubby body along with that big, pop belly was nothing I wanted to even come close to imagining being sexual with. Yuck!

"Hey Charlytte!" he called out.

"Yes?" I answered, quickly wiping the look of disgust from off my face before I looked to him. He looked in the opposite direction, trying hard to act like he wasn't just lusting over me, but I knew better.

"Joe called today. He wanted to know what you're going to do about the car."

I was hoping Mr. Otis didn't ask me that. I didn't have time enough to come up with a good lie. And I still couldn't just come out and tell him that Auntie Jo stole my money.

"Oh…yeah…uhmm…," I quickly tried to think of something. "I…I think I'm going to save up some more money and get something better."

"And when did you decide on that?" he rose up in his chair. "You know that's a Honda. That's the best deal you gone get, Charlytte. It's real reliable and he just did all that work to it. Just yesterday you bounced up out of here ready to get it, now you changed your mind. Just don't make no kinda sense to me. You only sixteen, girl. What kind of car you tryna get?"

"I don't know yet," I said, getting a little frustrated, "a Camaro maybe." That was my dream car.

"That's what's wrong with y'all young folks," he fussed. "Y'all all about appearance instead of quality."

Mr. Otis couldn't tell me a damn thing about appearance. I lived with a permanent scar on my face. It meant everything, but nothing, to me. He had no idea how bad I wanted that car. It almost brought tears to my eyes just thinking about not being able to have it.

"Well I'm just gonna have to call and tell him to come back by and pick it up," he said. "But you need to make up your mind because it's gonna sell pretty quick."

A customer was coming up to the checkout counter just as we finished talking. Mr. Otis gave me 'the look' and I knew that was my cue to get to work. Then he grabbed his belongings and left out of the door.

11: TEACHER'S PET

Over the next two weeks, I kept the same routine. I would sneak back into the store after Mr. Otis closed it up and leave in the mornings, right before he arrived again. The nights he went home early were the sweetest because I didn't have to wait in the alley for him to leave. Come closing time, I would just lock myself inside the building, then call and tell him that I was gone. I felt really bad about lying to the man that was nice enough to give me a job, but I didn't have any other choice. And as the days went by, I didn't think I would ever get caught. I had become way too clever.

With school only one day ahead of me, I spent most of my night trying on my clothes. In the cooped-up dirty bathroom of the store, I slid my green and pink-striped Polo top over my head and pulled my dark blue denims up over my hips. I even put on the pink belt and the cheap pink earrings that I had purchased from Fashion World. I never got a chance to buy new shoes, so the plain white sneakers I already owned just had to do. But I wasn't trippin'- the outfit was so cute that the shoes didn't even matter.

Although I still had my microbraids in, I found the time to re-do the first couple of rows myself. One of the last things Keisha did before she left was teach me how to braid, and I perfected my skills by practicing on my dolls. Once I was finished, it looked as if my whole head was freshly done. It really amazed me how much better a cute outfit and a fresh hairdo made me look. I didn't even notice the scar on my face, and I hoped that the kids in high school would be mature enough to overlook it too.

When I finally got tired of looking at my reflection, I took my clothes off and laid them neatly out across Mr. Otis's desk. Then I grabbed my mama's picture, kissed it, and made myself comfortable on the couch. I was very anxious about going back to school, but I was also a little nervous. I couldn't help but think about what my first day would be like, especially since I was going to be *a freshman*. I wondered what the school would be like. I wondered what the kids would be like. I even wondered if they were anticipating my arrival. The Samantha Hutchinson incident should have died down, since it was over a year old. But of course, she was one of the most popular girls around school and in the city. And since I didn't have any heavy contact in either places, I didn't know what to expect. All I knew was that I wasn't taking any chances; I made my pencils extra pointy.

The next morning, the school bus picked me, and a couple other kids, up a few blocks away from Mr. Chill's. We arrived to the school a little after 7:30. Finding the courage to walk into the building wasn't as hard as I thought it would be; it was getting through the cluster of kids that were headed in every direction that was the real challenge. People were so busy looking down at their class schedules that they were bumping directly into each other. One girl knocked me so hard that my papers flew out of my hand. She didn't even say excuse me, or offer to pick them up. She just looked down at them and then up at me, smacked her teeth, and kept walking. I didn't worry about it though. It was my first day and I wasn't about to ruin it over some petty broad.

Principal Green sent me a letter in the mail with a list of all my classes, so there was no need for me to report to her office. When I made it to my homeroom, the door was already open. Small chitchat sounded from the inside, but it all seemed to have ceased when I entered the room. Clearly nervous, I found a seat in the very back of the class and began to observe everything and everyone around me.

The first person I noticed was my teacher, who was sitting quietly behind her desk scheming through some papers. I had plenty of time to check her out because she was very deep into what she was doing, only taking her eyes off her paper every time she ran her fingers threw her long, brown hair.

Her nails and feet were French-manicured. Her smooth, caramel skin was oiled up real good with baby oil. And I loved the cute black sundress, with the huge yellow flowers painted on it, that she was wearing. I was happy to see that she was young and black, and even happier to see that she was pretty. I couldn't wait until she started talking, so that I could see what her personality was like. Just seeing her sitting so peacefully, I couldn't tell if she was bougie or ghetto. She sort of struck me as the teacher-by-day-club-hopper-by-night type, but I didn't want to judge her- at least not just yet.

Once the examination of my teacher was complete, my eyeballs led me down each row of desks and I began to study every single kid in the class. I looked at everything from the way they dressed to their choice of book bag. I recognized a handful of them from Lee James Middle and a couple from my neighborhood. The rest I never saw a day in my life. Some people were already buddying up and getting to know each other, but I had no intentions on making friends. I figured the best way to make it through the school year drama-free was to stay to myself.

After the morning bell rung, our teacher strutted her perfectly shaped body towards the classroom door. Then she closed it softly and introduced herself to us.

"Good morning class, my name is Mrs. Johnson," she said. "I will be your homeroom teacher and your first period Social Studies instructor."

Ugh Social Studies. I thought.

"Let me tell you guys a little bit about myself," she started, "I am happily married with two kids, a six-year old and a four-month old. I was born in Charlotte, North Carolina and lived there my entire life. I only came to Ordale because my husband decided he wanted to join the military and he has been stationed here. Honestly, I can't say that I am pleased with living in this area, but I can say that I am very pleased to be your teacher."

"Trust me, I know how boring Social Studies can be, so I have come up with ways to make it fun and interesting for you. The kids from my previous classes enjoyed it and I am most certain that you will too. "

"Honestly, this class should be an easy 'A' for you all. The only way that you can fail is if you don't come or if you don't try. But whether you do or don't, class still goes on and Mrs. Johnson still gets paid."

Click clack, click clack went the sound of Mrs. Johnson's heels as she walked up to her desk and grabbed a stack of papers.

"I am passing out the syllabus for my class which lists all of the assignments and everything I expect from you. You can read over it yourselves because you're in High School now and I'm sure you're mature enough to comprehend on your own. I may quiz you on this syllabus so be prepared."

"Every week you will have a current events assignment to turn in. You must read the newspaper, find something that is currently going on the world, and write a one-page essay discussing what you have read. The guidelines to this essay, along with all the questions you will need to answer, are all in your syllabus. Again, you can read that on your own."

"Every week- particularly on Mondays- I will randomly call a different student to present their papers to the class. Does everyone understand this?"

"Yes ma'am," the class said collectively.

I was already getting overwhelmed with everything Mrs. Johnson was saying. I dreaded current events, let alone class presentations.

"Here are your class schedules," she said, holding up another stack of papers. "I want to get familiar with my students- especially those of you right here in my homeroom- so I have a little writing assignment that I need for you do. Take out a sheet of paper please."

The silence in the classroom immediately turned into ruckus, as the class began to scuffle around in their book bags for paper and pens. After the noise ceased and we were all ready, we gave Mrs. Johnson our undivided attention and waited patiently to hear what she had to say next.

"Okay, take about fifteen minutes to write about whether you feel the issue of racism has improved, or gotten worse, judging by what you already know about it." Mrs. Johnson began to write her words on the dry-erase board. "Your papers can be anywhere between one paragraph, to one page, as long as you cover the basis. This is your first assignment. I will be checking attendance with your work, so make sure you head them correctly. You may begin now."

Before I got started, I looked around at the rest of the class. Some of the kids were puzzled, and some were head first into their papers. I began to think long and hard about the topic. Then I gathered some thoughts, collectively organized them in my head, and began to let my pen flow onto my paper. Writing came easy to me. For as long as I could remember, it was the only way I could express myself.

Fifteen minutes flew by and I was already to the back of my sheet. When Mrs. Johnson called time, everyone put down their pens and pencils and looked her way.

"Ok class, I hope you did your best because when I call your name to give you your schedules, I want you to stand up in your seats and read what you have written," she said, surprising all of us. "If we are done before the bell rings you can use the remainder of the class to chat and get acquainted with one another."

I was already nervous from just having to sit in a class full of unfamiliar people, so when she said she wanted us to stand up and read, an unpleasant chill came trickling down my body. I wasn't expecting her to put us on blast like that, and I definitely didn't want to participate.

Mrs. Johnson grabbed her stack of schedules and picked one of them.

"Shaquita Lovett," she called her first name.

A very high-yellow girl sitting in the front row stood up slowly and grabbed her paper from off of her desk. It wasn't hard noticing her when I did my personal class rundown. I could tell she was straight out of the Garron Homes Project. All of the girls from Garron Homes went to the same hairdresser and all of their up-dos ended up looking exactly the same. The wrist full of cheap gold bracelets, the six gold teeth at the bottom of her mouth, and the ton of gold necklaces she sported around her neck was another dead giveaway.

Shaquita smacked her lips and placed her paper close to her face. I could tell she wasn't nervous. Not even a little bit.

"Well…I put that...I think that," she began to pat the top of her head and rock her body back and forth at the same time, "racism is progressin' because white people and black people can go to the same school and talk and be around each other without fighting. Rosa Parks had to sit on the back of the bus, but now we don't have to do that. We can sit anywhere we want. White people and black people can also go to the same stores, shop, and even white people get food stamps. Some people are still racists, but it is not as serious as it used to be back when my mother and grandma was going through it. Overall, I think progression has been good."

Shaquita cheerfully flopped down in her seat, as if she had said something great. I could tell by the phony smile on Mrs. Johnson's face that she knew she had a lot of teaching to do.

"Thank you Ms. Lovett, you made some great points," she said.

As Mrs. Johnson continued to call names, I listened to my classmates talk about everything from Martin Luther King and his dream, Malcom X and his vision, and Rodney King and his beatdown. Someone even reenacted a scene from the Kunta Kinte movie. After a while, every paper began to sound exactly the same.

"Charlytte Black," Mrs. Johnson finally called me, then looked around the classroom for a rising hand. "It's spelled with a y, that's different. I like that."

"Right here," I said softly, as I lifted my skinny arm and slowly rose from my seat.

I felt all eyes when everyone turned in my direction. I could tell some of the kids where staring at my scar. I even noticed Mrs. Johnson take a quick glimpse at it. My heart began to beat faster the closer I got to speaking, then I took a deep breath and released.

Here goes nothing. I said to myself.

"Back in time, slaves were used to do such labors as bricklaying, fieldwork, cotton picking, and housekeeping. They were the source of production in the North, but particularly here in the South. As technology advanced, the need for slaves began to decrease. So to me, slavery only started dying because they were no longer needed as much as they used to be. It became more convenient just to let our people "free," which we were not really free because most of us were let go with nothing, and many found wandering were hung and killed."

I looked up again and saw that I had everyone's attention. Mrs. Johnson had one hand on her chin and the other across her chest. She was all ears too. Their interest made me a little less nervous and a little more confident. I spoke much louder this time around.

"Racism is still a big factor, not just in the United States but around the world. Often, we as people just try to cover it up. Just because whites converse with blacks, doesn't necessarily mean that some or most of them actually want to. They still stereotype us. Some still disown their kids if they bring home a person from another race. And if you look closely, you can still see the hateful look in their eyes….Racism exists in the workplace, in the justice system, in the government, and in the streets we walk daily."

"But don't get me wrong, it also goes both ways. Blacks can be racists towards whites without even realizing it and even towards their own kind. The word 'cracker' is in the human vocabulary just as much as the word 'nigger'."

Surprisingly, I put my paper down and began to talk to the class.

"Think about the titles black and white y'all. On the color spectrum, black and white are two colors that are farthest from each other. One is over on one end, and the other is way on another. Technically, African Americans are not black and Caucasians are not white. So why the irony? Is it an innocent and convenient way to describe ourselves, or is it purposely a way to keep us distant and constantly remind us that we are different. Just something to think about."

When I finished my speech, I sat down quickly. The class looked both puzzled and enlightened at the same time. I glanced up at Mrs. Johnson and she didn't say anything for a couple of seconds. I didn't know if she liked my paper or not.

"Thank you, Mrs. Black. That was *very* interesting," she finally said.

Mrs. Johnson called the last couple of names and by the time everyone spoke there was about ten minutes left of class. Most of the kids chatted and shared their schedules with each other. I just sat there quietly and waited for the bell to ring.

When it sounded, the class quickly grabbed their things and headed out of the door. I was in no rush to enter that heavy hallway traffic so I took my slow time putting my notebook and paper back into my book bag. When I finally made my exit, Mrs. Johnson stopped me.

"Miss Black, didn't you forget something?" she said, while sitting with her legs crossed behind her desk.

Mrs. Johnson waved my schedule at me. I didn't realize she had not given it to me.

"Oh yes," I said as I walked up to the front of her desk and took it from her.

"Your paper was quite impressive," she said." In all my years of teaching and doing that exercise, I never heard anything like it. You even taught me a thing or two, and I know *everything* about my history."

"Thanks," I blushed.

"Honestly, did you think of that yourself, or did you read it somewhere?" she asked.

"Well, I got the facts from other history classes, but the opinions were all mine," I answered.

Mrs. Johnson took off her glasses and went scrambling on her desk for a piece of paper.

"How would you like to be my class reporter?" she asked. "It's a simple job that could even get you one extra point added to your final grade."

I didn't know what the reporter's job consisted of, but if it required any snitching, her and that extra point could kiss my ass. The offer did sound really good to my ears though.

"The job's instructions are on that paper I just gave you. Read over it when you get some time and tell me what you decide by the end of the week. Oh, and don't forget to read the syllabus. I may give a pop quiz tomorrow." Mrs. Johnson winked at me. I knew exactly what it meant; she was definitely giving that quiz.

First period went by smoothly. I was glad to know that I had already made a good impression on one of my teachers. Even better, my English and Science classes were just as sweet. In both classes the teachers' just talked about class rules, class expectations, and assignments that we would have to complete. I was beginning to feel really good about Franklin High.

After Science, the lunch bell rang and I raced to the cafeteria to sooth my grumbling tummy. When I got there, I watched everyone link up with their friends and it wasn't until then that I started to realize just how lonely I was. I always thought it was weird that I was never good at making friends, but I thought it was even weirder that I really didn't care to.

I noticed more kids that I recognized from Lee Ray Middle as more of them joined lunch. I even saw some of Samantha's friend staring at me while whispering to each other. Ironically, they were some of the same girls who sat there and did nothing when I did my homework on her face. The last thing I was worried about was them.

While everyone lingered around, I quickly eased my way through the small crowd of upper-class guys who were blocking the cafeteria entrance. The way lunch was set up, all grade levels ate together, which gave them a chance to scope out fresh meat- also known as young and dumb girls who were naive enough to give them some. I found my place in line and watched the cafeteria ladies as they worked hard to fill our trays up with fresh first-day food. I couldn't help but think about what Principal Green said about them in her office.

After I got my food, I led my tray of pizza, fries, and apple juice to a table ducked off by the back patio. And as I ate quietly, trying very hard not to look at anyone, I was interrupted by a loud squeaky voice.

"Someone sitting here?" the high-pitched ghetto sound irritated my eardrums. I looked up to see- not one, not two, *but three*- girls standing over me, and before I could even answer them, they sat themselves.

The girl who asked me for a seat sat directly across from me. She must have been the clique leader because her friends didn't move until she did. She was tall, skinny, and had caramel-brown skin with a very narrow, but beautiful, face to match. The word 'model' was definitely in her future.

On the side of me was this average pretty girl whose sew-in was fabulous and outfit was exceptionally cute. Judging by the coke figure shape she was blessed with, I knew she was the one who brought all of the attention to her crew.

As a matter of fact, all three of them were dressed down to a tee, but only two of them were pretty. The other one was big, black, and looked just like a gorilla. I could tell she was the bullying type and I was certain that they were just using her as their bodyguard. Of course, she sat right next to the leader.

I had no clue who they were, or why they decided to join me, but judging by the way they immediately started yapping and gossiping, I knew it wouldn't be long before I soon found out.

12: GO SHAWTY, IT's YA BIRTHDAY

Over the next four months, Mr. Otis still didn't have the slightest clue about me crashing in his store. Since school started, he had me working no later than eight in the afternoons. I dreaded that because I would freeze my butt off in the alley waiting for him to leave. On the weekends, I would be standing at the back door waiting for him to arrive. I knew I was making myself look suspicious, but it wasn't summer anymore. I couldn't go walk to the park or roam the streets. It had gotten way too cold for that. I needed to be inside, or as close to it as possible.

Although Mr. Otis was a little skeptical about me always showing up early, I managed to convince him that I needed to work extra hours to save money for some new car I was supposed to be buying. I think he bought it too, because every day he would fuss at me about how stupid I was for not getting Mr. Simmons's Honda. I continued to act as if I didn't want it and literally had to fight back my tears the day I watched his niece drive away in it.

As far as school went, other than the faded outfits I repeatedly wore each week, I was doing okay. It really wasn't hard for me to make good grades, especially since I spent most of my time in the store studying and doing schoolwork anyway. Because of my excellence, Mrs. Johnson favored me. She tried hard not to make it obvious, but I knew it, and the other kids did too.

Mrs. Johnson was also my favorite teacher, and because of her kindness, I happily took her up on her offer as the classroom helper. Thankfully, the job didn't involve any snitching. All I had to do was grade and pass out papers at the end of class. She was also trying to convince me to join the Advanced Social Studies Program, but I turned her down every time. I had so many other things to worry about; history just wasn't one of them

I found out that the girls sitting with me at the lunch table were long-time rivals of Samantha Hutchinson. The head chick was Patricia. The gorilla was Princess, Patricia's cousin. And Miss Coke Bottle was Brittany, Patricia's best friend since elementary school. There was no doubt that the three of them were flat-out drama queens. And they had almost been in three fights since school started, all of them being with either friends or relatives of Samantha.

So how did the beef between Samantha and Patricia's crew start, you ask? Well apparently, from what I gathered, Patricia lived across the street from Samantha. Her mom was on drugs really bad and Samantha's brother was her supplier. She told me that her and Samantha were very good friends, up until the day that Samantha- along with her older cousins- jumped her mom right in front of her because she owed a debt for some drugs that were fronted to her. The girls said that they had already known who I was because their whole school was talking about the fight at Lee James. She said everyone in Ordale knew about it.

Even though it gained me a lot of popularity, I wanted to leave that fight right where it started, in middle school. Unfortunately, that was impossible with the girls trying to talk about it every single day. They always wanted me to tell them details about what happened. I didn't entertain them though. Every time one of them would bring it up, I would just say that it was old news. In fact, barely even spoke at the table. I just listened to their drama and occasionally nodded my head or chuckled. I knew they were getting bored with me, and the only reason they kept me around was because of my reputation of beating Samantha.

• • • • • • •

Friday, November 17th, two days before my sixteenth birthday, I woke up not the least bit excited. I was never thrilled when that day came around. In fact, I was the complete opposite, because what was a celebration of another year of life for most people, was the devastation of another year of death for my mama.

I didn't look forward to cakes. I didn't look forward to parties. I didn't even look forward to gifts. Hell, the only person I planned on getting anything from was Mrs. Johnson. That was because every time one of her students had a birthday, she would bring in a huge cupcake and make the class sing to them. I always crossed my fingers and hoped she would somehow forget mine; I was way too shy for that kind of attention.

Unfortunately for me though, Mrs. Johnson didn't forget anyone. Not even a kid who celebrated a birthday during the summer break, or on a day that school was out. If someone's birthday fell on a Saturday, she would always do it the Friday before. If it fell on a Sunday, she would do it that Monday. That year, my day fell on a Sunday, so I assumed- like any other time- Mrs. Johnson would bring in my cupcake the day after. I was so serious about avoiding it, that I had planned on ditching school.

"Okay class, we're going to have to wrap this up early because we have another special birthday," Mrs. Johnson said to her students after we were finishing up on one of her essay assignments. I looked around to see just whose birthday was only a couple of days before mine.

"Charlytte," Mrs. Johnson shocked me by pointing the cupcake in my direction. "Could you come up here please?"

What? I said to myself. *It's not Monday.*

I rose from my seat slowly and walked to the front class, dragging my puzzled-looking face along with me. I could feel the sweat began to form beneath my armpits as I tried so desperately not to look nervous.

"But Mrs. Johnson, my birthday's not 'til Sunday," I said, hoping that she would hold off.

"I know, but I decided to bring yours today," she replied. "Besides, I was already in the store last night… Alright class, you know the drill. On three… *ONE…TWO…THREE…*"

I stood in the front of class blushing, while everyone dully sung the happy birthday song to me. Even though I was extremely embarrassed, I did feel a little special because although I had fifteen other birthdays, I never once remembered having it sung to me before. Korey, Keisha, and Keyshawn all had get-togethers, sleepovers, and cookouts for their birthdays. All I ever got was a card and an excuse.

"Thank you class and happy birthday Charlytte," Mrs. Johnson said after they had finished up. "I don't like to single students out, but your work has been so exceptional that I must tell you, in front of the whole class, that I am proud of you. Keep up the great work and I promise you'll go far. Y'all know I don't normally give cards with these, but this is for you."

I thanked Mrs. Johnson, and the class, then happily accepted my gift, before rushing back to my seat.

"You're welcome, Charlytte. And as I tell all my students… if you get caught in your next class eating that, you better not mention my name."

Our laughter was overtaken by the sound of the bell and Mrs. Johnson dismissed us. We all went our separate ways and the rest of my day was a breeze. I was feeling confident. It was Friday, and even better, it was payday. I saved my cupcake because I wasn't hungry, and didn't open the card because I wanted show it off to Mr. Otis.

When I made it to the store, I didn't see any cars parked or people standing around. That was very strange because between the hours of three and six, were when people crowded Mr. Chill's the most. I never felt too comfortable with the heavy traffic in and around the store, but Mr. Otis never seemed to mind. He said the hood was like his family and that he would rather see his people crowd around his store, than to see them out on the streets getting into all types of mischief. The police even warned Mr. Otis, plenty of times, about cleaning up the "trash" in front of his building, but Mr. Otis didn't pay them any mind. He even told the Sheriff one day, "People of all walks crowd around my store. Not just hookers and bums…but hustlers, working men *and* women, mothers, fathers, and some of your fellow co-workers. These people aren't just gambling and loitering, they're freeing themselves. They're laughing, joking, and taking their minds off of how hard life is, and how hard people like you are trying to make it for them. As long as that sign right there says Mr. Chill's, and as long as ain't nobody gettin' shot on my doorstep, then 'the trash' is here to stay."

The Sheriff's mouth was on froze. "You'll be hearing from me again," was all he could say.

Curious about how abandoned the store looked, I ran past the front door and headed towards the back. I got even more of a surprise when I saw that Mr. Otis's truck was gone. Walking closer to the door, I noticed a note taped to the handle. I snatched it off and quickly unfolded it. It read:

Charlytte,

Mr. Otis's store is closed until further notice. Mrs. Clarice passed this morning. Say a prayer for him and his family.

Love, Mr. Simmons

I dropped the note and fell to my knees. I only knew Mrs. Clarice for a short time, but when I met her she was healthy and happy. It was so sad to witness her die so quickly. Then I immediately thought about Mr. Otis, and wondered how he was taking it. After all, she was his wife. He used to complain about her being a pain in the ass, but every time she called, he went running. She was a big part of his heart, and without her, I couldn't imagine how he would go on.

I was so torn up that I forgot all about the cupcake and the card Mrs. Johnson had given to me. I wasn't in the mood to stay at the store either, so I decided to walk to a nearby shopping center and grab him a sympathy card. Afterwards, I stopped to a burger spot and got me some lunch with the couple of bucks I had left. My money from the bank was long gone, so I was expecting to get my check that day. But because of the tragedy, I didn't worry about it. I figured I would eventually get paid when Mr. Otis was feeling better. I knew that very soon, he would be back in business.

13: KEEP DANCING

Unfortunately, a couple days turned into a week, and a week turned into three. I hadn't heard a thing from Mr. Otis. How worried I was, I could have walked to his house to check on him, but I had no clue where he lived. I even tried calling his cell from the pay phone every day after school, but all I ever got was the voicemail.

Not only was I worried, I was also bored with not being able to work. I didn't realize how important my job was until I couldn't do it anymore. I complained about it being stressful, and surely it was, but at the same time, it relieved a lot of stress too. Plus, having a little extra money was always nice.

I didn't even have my homework to depend on. At school, both the teachers and students were slacking because the holidays were drawing near. The little bit of work I did have was caught up on. On top of that, Christmas break was around the corner. I was miserable. And slowly but surely, I was beginning to give up on myself, Mr. Otis, and Mr. Chill's.

There was one good thing I can say I enjoyed about him being gone though- freedom. I was able to walk around his store more openly in my little T-shirts and panties. I left things lying around, and I stopped cleaning up after myself. One day, I even accidentally left the back door unlocked. Surely, the longer he was gone, the more careless I became.

December 17th marked the one-month anniversary of Mr. Otis's disappearance. Yep, four whole weeks had passed since he had been gone, and there was still no sign of him. It was the last day of school before Christmas break, and while every kid was glad to see that it had arrived, I may have the only one who wasn't.

On the bus ride home, I sat listening to everyone talk about all the fun things they were going to do for the holidays, what they were expecting to get for Christmas, and how excited they were about spending time with their family and friends. One girl even had the nerve to complain about her family taking a trip to Florida. She said her mama's side of the family lived in Brooklyn and her daddy's side lived in South Beach. Her mom made her and her sisters vote on which two states they would rather spend the holidays in, and apparently she lost. She sat behind me the entire bus ride just crying about how unfair it was that she couldn't be in Times Square on New Year's Eve, and the more she opened her mouth, the more I wanted to turn around and slap the shit out of her in it. Not because her sobbing was aggravating me, but because I hated to hear people complain about things they should have been thankful for. Living with nothing made you appreciate everything. This chick was fortunate enough to be able to take trips, while the only trip I could take was a foot trip from Mr. Otis's store, on down to China Star, to get my starving belly something to eat.

Don't get me wrong, I wasn't a big fan of school, but it was my only source of motivation. That and work made the time go by faster and the days seem shorter. It took my mind off of all the painful things I was dealing with, and without them both, I was quickly stepping back into the darkness.

After I got off the bus, I took a slow stroll back to the store. When I made it there, the first thing I noticed was how messy the office was. I had snack wrappers everywhere, my clothes were scattered all over the couch and floor, and much of my schoolwork was mixed in with the papers on Mr. Otis's desk. The room was in desperate need of a good cleaning, and because I had nothing else to do, I decided to tidy up the entire store.

Using Mr. Otis's cheap boombox to play some music with, I found a good soul station on the radio and got to work. I straightened the counters, I dusted the shelves, and I scrubbed all the noticeable stains off the walls. After two hours had passed, the only thing I had left to do was sweep and wipe the fingerprints off the glass cooler doors.

Six o'clock hit quickly and sun seemed to have disappeared before I could blink my eyes. To add a little light to the store, I took the lamp from out Mr. Otis's office and plugged it up down on the floor by the check-out register. Then, cooler door after cool door I sprayed with Windex and wiped thoroughly, making sure I didn't miss a single spot.

Some of the beverages in the coolers were turned over, and clearly out of place, so I decided to arrange them too. I fixed the sodas, the water bottles, the juices- and when I got to the beers- I immediately smiled and reminisced back on Mr. Otis. He was very strict about me handling them. The only time I was allowed to sell alcohol was when he was gone, and even then I was only allowed to sell it to regulars. Mr. Otis said he could get in trouble because I was a minor, and the last thing he wanted to do was lose his business.

It wasn't until I spotted an Icehouse in the Budweiser section, that I started thinking about Auntie Jo. She drank them all the time. Don't get me wrong, she was mean and evil, but she was also funny, especially when she got drunk. One night I remembered her telling Evelyn that she was going to drink until she died because drinking took all her pain away.

Drinking takes the pain away, I thought to myself, as the fast circular motion of which I wiped the door began to slow down. I eyeballed all the alcoholic beverages- Mr. Otis had every kind you could name- and I suddenly felt an urge to try one. If what Auntie Jo said about drinking was right, at that very moment, I couldn't go wrong.

I stood there contemplating, like a five-year old left alone in front of the cookie jar after her mama said no more sweets for the night. A part of me said*, don't do it Charlytte*. But the other part said, *what you got to lose girl? Give it a try*. After all, what was the worst that could happen? I wasn't working, school was out, and the cleaning was almost done. I needed something new to explore and I needed it fast.

Unable to fight the temptation any longer, I grabbed a can of beer, popped the top, and took me a sip.

"Ugh!" I said as I watched all of it fly out of my mouth shortly after it went in. It tasted horrible. I couldn't believe people actually liked that stuff. I immediately concluded that beer wasn't my thing, but still not wanting to throw away the whole idea of me drinking, I schemed around for something else. Something that might have tasted a little better.

Wild Wine Rose, I said in my head, as I held the medium-sized glass bottle up to my face and read the label to myself. Then I put it to my mouth and took one big gulp. It wasn't that bad either. It had a strong tangy taste to it, but was also kind of sweet. Within three seconds, I had downed the whole thing.

At first I didn't notice any difference. But after just ten minutes, I started feeling my body changing. I was more excited and full of energy.

I knocked out the last window quickly and started sweeping. Koffee Brown's song, *After Party*, played on the radio and I was feeling the music like I never felt it before. I was so into it that I started dancing around the store with the broom, throwing my hands up in the air and singing like I was at a Mary J concert.

As I twist and turned my body, I pictured myself in a fancy club. And in that club, I was on the dance floor and the spotlight was on me. All the girls envied me and all the guys wanted me.

I imagined that the broom I was sweeping with was a sexy dark Tyson look-a-like, and I was winding and grinding on 'him' while looking passionately into his eyes. Everybody was at the club, even Keyshawn. He was mad as hell too, because Teon and all his homeboys couldn't keep their eyes of me. Yes indeed, it was my night.

After what seemed like an hour of prancing around daydreaming, I was starting to get tired. Plus, I reeked of chemical supplies and sweat. It was certainly time to give myself a good wipe-down. I got ready to head to the bathroom, but when Xscape's *Do you want to* came on, I was forced to keep at it. I slowly slid my red top over my head in a seductive manner, then let my dark blue denims roll down my thighs.

I walked to the doorway of Mr. Otis's office and threw my clothes on Raggedy Ann. As my arms went up, I noticed that the position of the lamp on the floor made the shadow of my silhouette appear on one of the walls in the office.

"Damn I'm sexy," I whispered, as I turned my body to its side and admired the arched shape of my backside. I may have been insecure about my scar and my face, but never about my body. My breasts were a perfect size, not too big but not too small. My nipples were almond-brown and the size of a nickel. And my ass was plump and juicy. Plus, I was the perfect height of five' two.

As I continued to let the rhythm of the Xscape song win me over, I swayed my hips from left to right, while touching all over my body at the same time.

"*Do you want toooo....like I want to make love to you....Saaaaay you dooooo,*" I sung as the fancy night spot I imagined, suddenly turned into a strip club. The boy shorts and cheap black bra faded away to allow room for the red string-up bra and thong set that appeared in my head.

Hopping on top of Mr. Otis's desk in my seven-inch string up boots, I danced some more and continued to admire my sexy shadow on the wall. And like the girls did in the videos, I closed my eyes and clinched my breast together. Then I turned to Mr. Otis's chair, looked down at it, and imagined that my Tyson look-a-like was sitting there with nothing but hundred-dollar bills in each of his hands. He was looking up at me with a slightly evil- but sexy- grin, while I held a seductive, serious face.

Giving him more of me, I turned around and allowed him to enjoy the view of my ass. Then I dropped my head and grabbed my ankles, letting him see all of me from the back. Everything felt so real. I knew dreaming was crazy, but since my life was boring, I was going to make the one I created very interesting. I even started talking to this invisible man in my sexy, soft voice.

"You like that daddy?" I whispered, while still bending down looking at him from upside-down.

I must have had a strong imagination because for a second there, I thought I heard him answer me. "Yes I do," he replied.

Ignoring it, I continued.

"Yeah, I know you do," I said, as I slowly lifted my head, rubbing my hands up my thighs as I came up. And when I did, I received the shock of my life.

"Oh shit! Mr. Otis!" I panicked.

And there he was, in reality, standing dead in the doorway with an indescribable look in his eyes and a shotgun by his side. I didn't hear or see him come in. I knew eventually I would get caught, but I had no idea it would be like this.

Mr. Otis just stood there with a smirk on his face. His eyes were a mix of red and yellow. They had no life in them. His beard and hair had grown out more than the usual length, and his clothes were wrinkled and dirty. He looked so bad that I could hardly recognize him. He had definitely let himself go.

"Uhmm...Mr. Otis! I can explain!" I cried, "Aunite Jo sto… sto… stole my money for the car…and…and…and we…we…started arguing and… and…and she kicked me out!"

My mouth was going full speed. I was rambling, stuttering, and trying to balance myself on top of the desk, all at the same. "I…I…didn't have no place to go! What...was I supposed to do? What am I supposed to do?"

Mr. Otis just continued to stand still. He had no emotion on his face, which made it even harder to tell what he was thinking. I just stood there waiting patiently- my heart seeming to be beating out of my chest- to hear his response. Finally, he cracked a creepy smile and said something I never expect to hear him say.

"Keep dancing."

14: SWEET FAITH

The very next day I woke up with a major headache. I was lying naked across Raggedy Ann prompted up on a new pillow and a fresh sheet covered my body. I immediately checked the time on my digital planner. It read 12:30.

My thoughts of where the fluffy pillow and crisp white sheet came from were shortly interrupted by male voices. I quickly figured out that it was Mr. Otis running his mouth with some of his partners out in the store area. I could hear his laughter getting louder as he walked towards the office, and when I saw the door handle turning, I quickly closed my eyes and pretended to still be asleep.

"Charlytte, wake up gurl," his raspy voice called out as he made his way over to me.

The minute I opened my eyes, I saw him standing over me with a cigarette resting on his bottom lip and his truck keys in his hand. Instantly, all the memories of the night before came rushing into my head.

"I'm about to go grab me some lunch in a second," he said. "I'mma need you to cover the register."

"*The register*?" I asked, wiping the crust from both my eyes.

"Yeah, the register," he answered. "We back in business. It's time to get back to work."

I heard Mr. Otis clearly, but I still was confused. I didn't know if I was more surprised that Mr. Chill's was finally open again, or that Mr. Otis was acting like nothing had happened the day after he just raped me.

"But what about last-" I began to say.

"Get to work," he quickly interrupted.

Without cracking a smile, he took one long glance at me and left the building.

Luckily business was slow in the store, probably because people were unaware that we had re-opened. I was glad to be standing behind the register working again, but I could barely concentrate with my head throbbing and my mind racing.

As my knees stood shaking behind the counter, all I could think about was me dancing on Mr. Otis's desk top. For two hours straight, I wiggled and twirled for him. Then, when my legs were too weak to stand, I pictured him laying his funky, drunken ass on top of me, pounding me with his short, wrinkled dick.

Every time I glanced over at that shotgun he kept under the counter, I kept remembering how he pointed it at me whenever I would scream. I remembered him telling me that if didn't do exactly what he said, he would simply tell the police he thought I was an intruder when he shot me. I remembered feeling the soft, loose skin from his arm on the left side of my face, and the hard steel from the shotgun on my right. Worst of all, I remembered being scared shitless that when he climaxed- if he could even do that- he might accidentally pull the trigger and blow my brains out.

Actually, the more I thought about it, the more I blamed myself for what he did to me. I kept feeling like I shouldn't have been in the store in the first place, and I sure as hell shouldn't have let him see me naked. Because I made myself vulnerable, just maybe, I got what I deserved.

Mr. Otis made his way back from lunch a whole two hours later. He continued to go about the rest of the day acting like nothing had happened. I, on the other hand, made it obvious that something went down.

When he would try talking to me, I would short talk him and try to avoid any eye contact. When he'd walked past me, I would move as far away as I could, sometimes knocking things over. I wasn't doing it intentionally, but the more I tried to act as normal as he did, the more I made myself look the opposite. I was sure he was aware of my discomfort, but he did a hell of a job ignoring it.

As the days went by, Mr. Otis still said nothing about our little surprise encounter. And the more he kept quiet, the more confused I became. In fact, he played it off so well that even I started having doubts about that night ever happening. Then again, I knew it had to, because he would have at least said something about me sleeping in his store now that he knew. Yet, he never did. He just left the keys on the counter every night before he went home, told me to make sure I locked up, and to call him if I had any problems.

After what Mr. Otis did to me, my peaceful nights at the store were no more. Instead of sleeping, I would lay lifeless on the couch, constantly having flashbacks about what went on between the two of us. And if I did doze off, I would always be awakened by nightmares or by the sound of a loud vehicle passing by. Hearing those engines made me think that it could have been him coming back for more.

After many restless nights, it wasn't long before my body grew weary. My eyes started to sag, I barely had any energy, and I slowly started to lose my will to do anything. Even my appearance meant nothing. All my clothes were dirty because I didn't have the strength to go wash them, and my hair looked even worse than it did before. I was in no mood to touch them up either, and the worse part about it, I didn't even care to.

Mr. Otis arrived to the store early on Christmas Eve. He showed up at six-thirty was even generous enough to let me sleep in while he took over some of my shift. He said that for what he had planned, I was going to need all the rest I could get. I was too tired to elaborate on his statement, and decided to just take advantage of the extra rest. I felt safe enough to sleep because as long as the store was open, I knew he wouldn't try anything.

And if I could've slept the whole day, I would have. But unfortunately the customer's high demand of last minute holiday items didn't allow that to be made possible. I personally didn't care about it being the day before Christmas. Well, at least that's what I convinced myself. My holiday spirit was lower than a caterpillar's pussy, and despite the extra rest I was given, my body was still exhausted. I was just ready for the break to be over so that I could have a reason to go back to school and get away from Mr. Otis. I was sick seeing him prance around the store like nothing seemed to bother him.

"What's with funky face? You scarin' all my customers away," Mr. Otis said about an hour after I punched in. It was now noon.

"Nothin." I mumbled, still upset that he had awaken me from my much-needed sleep, and even more pissed that he was making me wear those ridiculously-looking reindeer ears.

"Don't ya know it's Christmas, the season to be jolly!" he hummed a tune and continued to stock the cigarettes on the wall behind me.

"I don't care nothin' about Christmas," I sassed him, making it known that I was in no mood for him or his mind games.

Mr. Otis rose up from his squatted position, placed the pack of Kool's down on the counter, and walked over to me very slowly. I backed up, slightly afraid of him.

"Look, it's obvious you don't feel like working and I completely understand. Mrs. Simmons needs help baking some cookies for the church anyway, and I'mma be closing down shop little early, so why don't you-"

"I don't think so," I cut him off. "I'm fine here."

Even though I didn't want to work in the store, I most definitely didn't want to be sitting in some old woman's house listening to church music and baking sugar cookies. I refused to do that. Besides, the most Mrs. Simmons ever said to me was "smile sugah". I thought it was very unusual that she would be asking for my help.

"I really don't think you have much of a choice little lady," Mr. Otis said as he tilted his forehead forward and shot one eyebrow up. That was his serious face. I knew he meant business.

"And why is that?" I challenged him.

Mr. Otis took one long look at me, another long look at the office room, and an even longer look at the front door. Then he simply walked away. After quickly figuring out what he was implying, I grabbed my book bag and headed out the door.

Mr. and Mrs. Simmons lived only a couple of blocks away from the store in an average, middle-class home. You couldn't help but notice it, because it was painted an ugly, bright green color. I had been there plenty of times before delivering sweets back and forth for Mr. Otis. It was the only house with a porch full of flowers and a yard full of Gnomes.

Mrs. Simmons must have been expecting me, because when I arrived, she was standing up at the screen door just waiting to greet me. She still had on her oven mitts and from the way she was sweating I could tell she had been working hard in the kitchen.

"Come on in sugah," Mrs. Simmons said as she welcomed me into her antiquely decorated home.

Mrs. Simmons was a big-boned woman with smooth, dark skin and dark freckles above her cheekbones. She always wore her hair in the same style- fingerwaves. Her voice was a little deep for a woman, but every word she spoke was always sweet and pleasant. She was loved by everyone because of her graceful personality, but mainly because of her untouchable pies and cakes. She even sold sweets at her church after every Sunday service, with her pecan pies reigning the most popular around Ordale.

"How you doing Mrs. Simmons?" I asked politely, after I entered her home and closed the door behind me. I followed her into the kitchen where she already had two poundcakes and three pecan pies cooling on her wooden tabletop. Mrs. Simmons pulled out a chair from under her table and motioned for me to sit down. I did.

"I'm fine dear. That was so nice of you to volunteer your help. God bless your little heart."

"No problem. I really didn't mind," I lied.

"You can wash your hands in the sink," she said. "Would you like a slice a red velvet cake?"

"Yes please, but you can wrap it to go."

I gazed over at the white icing and shredded pecans covering the red velvet cake that was resting so beautifully on her marble kitchen counter. After we washed our hands, she cut me a slice, wrapped it in foil, and sat it on her countertop. Then she took her seat at the table and instructed me on what to do next.

"Alright. I already mixed the cookie dough. All I need for you to do is take a small piece like this," she demonstrated, "roll it into a ball, flatten it, and then place it on the pan, like that. You think you can handle it?"

"I think I can," I answered, then grabbed a chunk of the chocolate chip cookie dough and got started.

There was nothing but silence in the kitchen as we both worked. I watched Mrs. Simmons rotate the dough around in her palms with envy. Her arms were moving so fast. She was nothing less than a professional at baking and had already laid out five cookies to my one.

"You know Charlytte," she said, breaking the silence. "My husband was very upset when you turned down that car. He put a lot of hard work into to making sure it was perfect for you. I believe he really wanted you to have it."

I had prayed that the car situation was dead and buried deep under the ground, but I knew it would only be a matter of time before someone brought it up again. I was still recovering from the loss and hated thinking about it. I was tired of everyone criticizing me for something I really wanted, and it hurt even worse having to keep the truth a secret.

"I know," I told her, "but if I'm going to spend my money, I'd rather just get something that I want."

"You're young hun, what exactly do you want?" she asked.

"Uhmmm....I don't know, just something else."

"Well, that car was your best choice. I'm not going to get into it with you, because after all, it's your money and your decision. I'm sure one day you'll understand."

"Yes, ma'am." I replied, then quickly changed the subject by asking, "Mrs. Simmons, am I doing this right?"

Mrs. Simmons just looked at me with a broken smile that had 'poor little baby' written all over it. I could tell she didn't really believe that I understood her. And she knew I was just trying to blow her off.

"Yes honey, just add a little more dough," she answered.

We continued to work, chat, and get to know each other a little better. We talked about everything from our favorites T.V. shows to traveling the world. I was actually started to enjoy our little conversation. Well, up until she got all religious on me.

"So…what church do you attend, Miss Charlytte?" she asked me.

I sighed. "I don't go to church. I wasn't exactly raised that way."

"Well that's alright," she comforted me. "According to the Lord, it's never too late to start. You should come to our service this Sunday. Pastor Williams is very down to earth and he tells it like it is. Plus, between me and you, he doesn't keep you all day."

"I honestly don't know if I can make it," I told her, still rolling the cookie dough, hoping she would talk about something else. "I will just have to see."

"You don't have school on Sundays, right?"

"No ma'am."

"And if you're scheduled to work I'm sure Mr. Otis will understand. Correct?"

"Yes ma'am. I guess he would."

"Well then what's the problem? Do you have something else you have to do on that day?"

"No ma'am. I don't believe so."

"Well it must be something going on that's so important you can't make time for the Lord?"

Hold up. Slow your role old lady. I thought.

It wasn't that I couldn't make time for church; I just felt that I wasn't worthy enough to go. Truthfully, with all that was happening to me, I was starting to believe that God didn't even exist. And if he did, my only question to him would be "Lord, what have I done to you that you would repay me like this?"

Mrs. Simmons didn't know me at all, so of course, I felt like she was being a typical Christian, judging and assuming. Whatever the case, I just wasn't going to stand for it. Maybe it was because she brought up the car, or maybe it was because I really didn't want to be there. I really can't say why I snapped on her, but I did.

"How can I make time for someone that I don't even know is real?" I slightly blurted, pulling a little bit of overdue angry out of me.

Mrs. Simmons's face froze, her hands slowly went up in the air, and she started mumbling something underneath her breath. After she said what looked like a silent prayer, she paused, and stared at me once more before speaking to me again.

"Charlytte, may I ask you something?" she asked, and without giving me a chance to answer her, she went on. "Did He find the time to create you? ...Did He find the time to wake you up this morning? …Is He now finding the time to provide the oxygen that is currently allowing you to take your next breath?"

Mrs. Simmons was getting all worked up in her preaching mode. Her voice suddenly got louder, and even deeper, than it already was. Yet still, I was in no mood for any 'God talk.'

"Excuse me, I don't mean any disrespect," I said, hoping that I could stop her before she got started. "I just came to help with the baking."

Pushed to her limit, Mrs. Simmons slammed the cookie dough down in the pan. She made it very clear that she wasn't going to take much more of me, or my attitude.

"Let's get this straight young lady" she began. "Otis was the one who said *you* wanted to help *me* bake these cookies. I've been doing this for over forty years. No disrespect to you, but I don't need your help. Second, I don't need to physically see the Lord to know that he's real. My faith is strong enough to believe in Him. I am a faithful follower of His word and as long as I have breath in my body, I will praise Him. Anyone who has an issue with that is not welcome in my home."

I had never before saw Mrs. Simmons speak with so much attitude. I always wondered how she managed to tame a wild man like Mr. Simmons, but now I could clearly see that she had a different side to her. Knowing that type of anger could come out of a sweet old lady scared me something seriously. I had no choice but to apologize.

"I'm sorry, Mrs. Simmons. I really am. I'm just going through a lot right now. Sometimes I do feel like I really don't know if He exists."

"Baby," she sighed, "I'm not upset with you. You're just a kid. It's okay to feel like that. To be honest, you will never ever know if he truly exists. You just have to have faith and trust in His word."

"But what if I have trust issues?" I asked. "At this point, I don't know what's real and what's not."

"I find that hard to believe Charlytte. Like most people in this crazy world, you believe what you want to believe. You trust the people in the fast food restaurants with your food. You were going to buy that car and take your first ride in it, trusting that the brakes wouldn't give out on you. And don't you trust the people at the bank with your hard earned money?"

"I never understood it," she said, completely baffled. "Why is it that people can trust in things when it's convenient for them, but when it's time to put that same trust in the Lord, they start giving excuses?"

Although everything Mrs. Simmons had just said made perfect sense, all I could do was wonder why Mr. Otis told me that Mrs. Simmons needed my help, especially when he was the one who volunteered my services to her. She quickly interrupted my thoughts.

"I shouldn't have been so persistent like that in the first place. I'm sorry for that. All I am trying say is that, if He gives you seven days a week, if you're able, why can't you at least give Him a couple of hours."

"I understand Mrs. Simmons, really I do. But church ain't no place for a girl like me. You don't know how many times I have tried God. It just seems like the more I seek Him, the more I get lost."

Mrs. Simmons moved the baking pan and the bowl of cookie dough away from the both of us. Then placed my hands into hers and looked me straight into the eyes.

"Charlytte, I understand exactly how you feel. But you need to understand that you're still growing. It's much too soon for you to be talking like this. You're way too young to be giving up on your faith."

Mrs. Simmons looked down to the floor, shook her head from left to right, and then whispered another prayer. After she re-lifted her head, she continued.

"You remind me of a girl I used to know. She was young and lost, like yourself. She had nowhere to turn but to the streets, and to a man who believed that selling her to other men was showing her all the love that she deserved. She endured so much pain that it began to feel like pleasure, and any real blessings that came her way, she ran from because she perceived them to be curses."

"To her, the bruises were passion marks and the tears just washed away the old problems to make way for the new. Her life was surely headed for disaster until one day, her pimp and three of his *women* got into a terrible car accident, leaving only her and her pimp alive after the debris settled. The pimp was hurt badly, but the woman only suffered a mild concussion and a deep cut on her forearm from a huge piece of glass that dug into her skin. The doctor said it missed a major artery by less than an inch."

"After learning about the death of the other two girls, and how they too came very close to dying, the pimp and his hoe together vowed to change their lives. Although the surviving woman was the one he treated the worst, she was the one- the only one- who stayed by his side and helped him get better. And after a rocky road to redemption, not only did they find love in God and themselves, but also in each other. They settled down and even got married in the park, only a block away from where the accident happened."

Mrs. Simmons released my hands. Her eyes were a little teary and her hands were slightly shaking. Then she got up, grabbed herself a Kleenex, and dabbed her eyes with it.

"Sorry," she sobbed, "I don't mean to bore you with my old woman stories. Just know that God has plan for you. You just have to stand boldly in the fight. Understand that you must go through, in order to get to. Like Mrs. Wright used to say, "No pain, no gain."

"Mrs. Wright?" I asked. "Who is that?"

"You don't know who Mrs. Wright is?" She looked at me cock-eyed. "*The* Betty Wright? Mrs tell-it-like-it-is Betty Wright? Oh I forgot honey, that's way ahead of your time."

Mrs. Simmons rolled her eyes, disbelieving my ignorance to who Betty Wright was. She even sung some of her lyrics hoping that I would become familiar: the blank stare on my face clearly told her that I still didn't have a clue.

"Chile, you really do have a lot to learn," she shook her head. "See y'all kids so used to that Be-NON-say, Be-nonsense mess, that y'all don't know anything about that real soulful music."

"It's Beyonce." I corrected her, taking up for one of my favorite performers.

"Whatever, she ain't no Betty or no Gladys, and she sure can't hold a note like my girls," she laughed. "See, y'all generation is all about the looks and not about the talent. Back in my day, we could tell how good a woman could sing just by how ugly she was. If she was an attractive woman and she made it big, she may could hold a lil' tune. But, if she was butt ugly and she made it, you just knew she could blow!"

We both laughed, so hard that our stomachs tightened. Then the laughter slowly faded. There was another brief silence between us, but it wasn't awkward because we both were in our own little worlds. I snuck a glance at Mrs. Simmons and admired her bright smile.

"So… what were your friend's names?" I asked her, unexpectedly.

"Excuse me?"

"Your friends, the ones that died in that car accident you were in, what were their names?"

The way her eyes got big and her bottom lip started slowly sinking, I knew I had taken her by surprise. She sat silently for another couple seconds, just staring out her kitchen window.

"Gloria and Paulene," she finally answered. "But hold up- I never told you that the girl was *me*."

"You didn't have to. I never miss a thing," I told her. "I noticed that scar on your arm the first time I met you. And hanging up on your living room wall are weddings pictures of you and Mr. Simmons in Arsley Park."

Mrs. Simmons raised one eyebrow to me, very impressed by my attentiveness.

"They were all I had," she said. "We may have only been worth five or ten dollars to the world, but we meant the world to each other."

"No disrespect Mrs. Simmons," I said, "but I would have never guessed that you used to be a hooker, and I definitely can't believe that Mr. Simmons was big pimpin'."

She laughed. "I wouldn't say he was *BIG* pimpin', but he was doing his thang."

"I hear ya," I said, joining her in laughter. "You're alright with me, Mrs. Simmons. You're quite alright."

I must admit, maybe I was being a little judgmental myself. There I was thinking Mrs. Simmons was all bougie and highly sanctified, but really, she was just as human and down to earth as me or anyone else I knew. Our talk was helpful too. It opened my mind to the idea of having faith. I hadn't felt a sense of that in a very long time. She helped me realize that I didn't have to find God; all I needed to do was believe in Him.

I happily finished helping her bake the rest of the cookies and left as soon as the sun started to set. She offered me a ride home, but of course, I insisted that I walk. I even made arrangements to meet her at her house for church the next Sunday, and she packed me a goody bag filled with sweets as her way of thanking me for helping out.

15: MERRY CHRISTMAS

There was just enough sunlight out for me to make it back to the store, and when I did, I didn't see Mr. Otis or his truck. In fact, every car was gone from the lot and not a single soul was in sight. Relieved to see that he had already closed up and left, I unlocked the backdoor, rushed in, and let the warm heat sooth my body.

Surprisingly, as I walked towards the office, I began to hear soft music. It sounded like Boyz II Men. And the closer I got, the more I realized that it was that talented male group blessing the office with the sexy sounds of 'I'll Make Love to You.'

"Mr. Otis is going to kill me about leaving this damn radio on," I said as I slowly crept open the office door. And when it opened-

"Merry Christmas!" a drunken old man yelled out to me. Mr. Otis was lying on a twin-size bed, where Raggedy Ann *used* to be. Aside from his thick black socks, all he wore were some silky red boxers with a bunch little black Santa Clauses painted on them. His nappy afro was shaped up well too, with his hair neatly trimmed off of his face. And in both his hands, were two glasses filled with what looked like red wine.

In an attempt not to stare at him, and how disgusting his gut looked hanging over his boxers, I began to look around the room. It was even more surprising to see that he had taken all of his furniture out of the office and replaced them with a cheap bedroom set.

Where his desk used to be, was now a twin-sized bed. A wooden dresser replaced that big, ugly cabinet and my schoolbooks and supplies rested comfortably on top of it. He had also nailed two huge pictures of pink flowers up on the wall, one above the bed and one next to the window. I assumed that they were hot pink because they matched the hot pink bedspread. He even bought four pillows that exact same color, two of which he was prompted up on.

Stretched out across the bed, Mr. Otis's knees were bent and his legs were slightly opened. His eyes never left me.

"Do you like it, pretty girl?" he smiled. "I did all of this for you."

I just stood there, shocked and speechless, still looking around with my bottom lip nearly touching my collarbone. I didn't know what to think, let alone what to say. I didn't even know how to feel.

"So you just gone stand there or are you gonna say something?" he asked.

"Mer…Merry Christmas," I finally managed to let out. "Uhmmm…thank you, I guess."

"You're welcome sweetie. I'm just trying to make you as comfortable as possible. It's the least I could do."

Mr. Otis leaned up from the pillows, swung his knees around to let his feet hit the floor, and sat up on the squeaky bed. He moved very slowly, trying not to spill the two cups. Then he motioned for me to come to him.

"Charlytte, I just want you to know that you didn't have to hide anything from me. You could have said something about the situation with you and Joanne. I wouldn't have mind letting you stay here. Actually, I would have enjoyed you-I mean- your company."

"I know, Mr. Otis," I said as I slowly walked over in his direction and eased down on the bed beside him. He handed me a glass of wine and administered me a sip.

"But please understand, me and Auntie Jo just got into a little fight. It was nothing major. I just needed some time to get away from there. I'll be going back home very soon."

I knew that was a lie, but I needed to say something to make him think that I didn't have any intentions on staying with him for long. Plus, I wanted to remind him that I still had family and people to run to if I wanted to rat him out. Unfortunately, Mr. Otis was smarter than that. He was way ahead of me, and my games.

"Now Charlytte, you and I know that's very unlikely."

"How come?" I asked, testing his knowledge of the situation.

"Because, I ran into her not long ago and she didn't talk too fond of you."

"Really? You saw her! What did she say?" I panicked. "You didn't tell her where I was, did you?"

Mr. Otis tilted his glass to me, signaling for me to take a sip with him. He watched me very carefully as I took another hit of what I recognized to be that damn

Wild Wine Rose. It was very creepy how his eyes followed the flow of the wine, even after I drank it. It was like he could see it going down my esophagus.

"Now why would I do that?" he leaned in closer to me and began to slowly rub his rough right hand up my left thigh. The strong alcoholic scent coming from his breath confirmed to me that he was already drunk. I shivered in disgust.

"I don't know," I slightly eased my legs over, hoping I didn't make the fact that I was trying to pull away from him too noticeable. Unfortunately, he didn't care if I drew back or not. He had my pussy written all over his forehead, in hot pink letters. And he was sure to get it.

"I think you know why," he said, still rubbing me, only this time a little higher up. "You don't have to worry about that old hag. It was never *her* I liked anyway. If you don't want JoAnne, or anybody else in the world for that matter, knowing where you are, then you're safe here. I can keep your secrets, as long as you can keep mine. I can take care of you, as long as you can take care of me. You understand that?"

I understood actually what he was saying- as long we could fuck, I could stay. I wasn't sure if I was ready to make that commitment, although I knew I didn't have much of a choice.

"I really shouldn't be drinking this," I tried to steer the conversation into a different direction. "It made me feel really bad the last time."

"Oh don't give me that, Charlytte. You're a big girl. You don't have to be uptight with me. There are no rules around here. Anything goes. Absolutely anything."

His fingers continued to work their way up my legs and when he finally reached my spot, I knew it was that time again. I thought about begging him not to do it. I thought about taking my glass and dashing it into his eyes. I even thought about running as fast as I could out of the store and never looking back. But then I thought about where I would go afterwards, and decided against it all.

At that point, the only thing that could have helped me through what was about to go down was the drink in my cup. I murdered the rest of it and then asked him to fill me up again. I watched him as he intentionally poured the second glass up to the rim, and he watched me as I also took that one down like it was water.

"So, what do you want me to do for you this time?" I asked, after using my hands to wipe the access liquid from my mouth. I glanced down at Mr. Otis's boxers and stared at the one Santa Clause that rested on his genitals.

"Sit down right here," he motioned for me to swat down on the floor between his legs.

I did exactly what I was told and tried not to gag when he began to massage my shoulders. It was gross having him rub all over my upper body, but it felt just disgusting when he started talking dirty with it. I tried to create imaginary earplugs to block out of all the perverted nonsense he was saying in my ear, but that didn't work. All I could do was start praying, "*Lord please let this be over with quick.*"

"Turn around babygurl," he said after he was satisfied with his massage- either that or he realized that I just wasn't into it. Whatever the case, I was glad he finally took his filthy hands off of me.

Pressing both hands down on the floor in order to lift up, I turned my body around and found myself face to face with the slit in his boxers. A yucky-looking thing hung from out of it. I tried not to look at all the wrinkles and how small it was, but I couldn't help it. It looked absolutely *NOTHING* like Marcus's.

"You take care of me, and I will take care of you," he reminded me, then rubbed his hands through my nappy braids.

"But I'm not sure if I can do this," I said, referring to pleasing him with my mouth.

"I know you can't, but I will teach you. You want to live grown and on your own, you gots to do grown woman chores."

Chores? I thought to myself. *This ain't no damn job. This is supposed to be pleasure.*

After a long hesitation, I finally placed my mouth on his penis and began to slowly suck it up and down. The skin on it was very loose and it carried a slight odor. Mr. Otis immediately started moaning, and then started rubbing his hands through my hair again. I couldn't understand why he was so into the lame ass job I was doing. Giving head was more like a minor to me, not a major. Marcus and I tried it once, but that didn't work out. He stopped me after only a couple seconds and jokingly said that he would never let me put my mouth on him again.

"Get it wet," he demanded of me. "Put some spit on it."

I tried to accumulate some saliva, and when I built up a little bit, I slowly let it drip from my mouth, onto him. Apparently, that wasn't good enough for him.

"No," he stopped me again. "I want you spit on it. Spit on it like you're mad at me. Ya know, get nasty with it."

Poor choice of words, I thought. Because I was mad at him. And hell, I didn't have a problem biting it off, if that's what he wanted me to do. I even thought about hawk spittin', but realized that wouldn't have been such a bright idea, at least not for my sake. With no choice but to abide, I worked up even more saliva and let him have it.

"That's what I'm talking about!" he shouted, after a thick pile of warm mucus landed on him. "Do it just like that."

"Like that?" I asked him. "Is that how you want it?"

"Aaah yeah, you're doing good," he assured me. "You're doin' real good. Now use your hands and make some sexy noises for me. I want to hear that pretty voice."

I wrapped my fingers tightly around him. Even though I hated having to touch it, I was glad I didn't have to look at it any longer. All the sucking, him rubbing my head, and the sound of his nagging old voice, together just made me want to say fuck it, pack my bags, and sleep out on the streets. It was taking everything in my power to keep going.

"Oooh," I moaned, pretending with everything in me to be enjoying it. I knew that if I wanted it to be over, I had to turn him on.

"You like that, daddy?" I asked.

"Yeah I love it," he groaned. "Now squeeze it harder for me."

"I got you daddy, whatever you want."

I didn't know where the sudden confidence came from, but I spit on it one last time, grabbed it real tight, and started to suck on the head while moving my hands in an up and down motion. The faster I went, the louder he moaned.

"Just like that! Just like that!' he shouted. And just as I expected, within a minute, he was about to reach his peak.

Feeling himself about to climax, Mr. Otis grabbed me by my hair and yanked me off of him. "No! I'm not ready yet!" he shouted. "If I do this now, I might miss out on the rest!"

Ignoring him, I tried to dive head first back into his crotch to finish him off. I hoped by doing that, he would just cum and be done with it. Mr. Otis wouldn't let me though; he wanted the goods and nothing else, no matter how good it felt, was going to stop him from getting it.

"Lay down," he pointed to the bed. "Lay down right there for me."

I hopped up on the bed, and just so he wouldn't touch me, did the honors of taking off my own clothes. Then I laid down flat on my back and watched him as he stood up over me and pulled his boxers down to his toes. I looked away quickly, trying to avoid the sight of his awful looking body.

"Can we please turn the lights off?" I asked. "I'm more comfortable in the dark."

"Charlytte," he looked me up and down. "Don't be so insecure. You're beautiful, baby. How do you expect me to enjoy myself without being able to see *all* of you? Now take that bra off too."

"Alright," I sighed deeply, after realizing that Mr. Otis wasn't going to listen to anything that I asked of him.

The twin-size bed squeaked as he climbed onto it and the first thing, of all things, he did was try to kiss me. I turned away quickly. There was no way in hell I could let him do that to my lips. Luckily, he didn't pursue it; even he knew that was a bit much.

With me already in the position to be fucked, Mr. Otis grabbed himself, but just when he was about to put it in me, I stopped him.

"You got rubbers in the store," I reminded him. "Can you use one?"

"Don't you think it's a little too late to be asking that? If you got something from me, you got it last week. But if you worried, don't be. We didn't have all that floating 'round in my day like y'all do now. We stuck with one. Believe me, I'm clean.

"How do you know if I am?" I questioned.

"Really Charlytte, what an ole' man like me gots to lose?" he asked. "And you ain't got to worry 'bout having no babies 'cause my swimmers ain't never been no good."

Maybe that's why Mrs. Clarice never had any children. I wondered.

Whatever the case, clearly Mr. Otis wasn't going to let me call any shots, so I decided to just let him have his way. I shut my eyes really tight and bit down hard on my lips, trying not to scream in disgust. Then he entered me and began to poodle-stroke, fast and short. His loud passion roars and the squeaky sound of the flimsy mattress overtook the sound of the music.

Gripping the rusty metal rails of the headboard for support, Mr. Otis drilled me faster and faster. His head was buried deep into my neck, where his breath and saliva tickled me. I flinched and squinted with each one of his strokes, and felt the silent tears, as they began to slowly trickle down my face.

Looking around for anything to help me take my mind off it all, I spotted the aluminum foil with the red-velvet cake in it and immediately started thinking about Mrs. Simmons's and her words to me. They didn't seem to make sense now. Nothing did. Having faith wasn't so easy when you were sixteen with a sixty-year old man's dick inside of you. And hope sure as hell meant nothing. They only thing I could hope was that he'd hurry up and get the hell off me.

Five minutes seemed like five hours, but he finally finished. He pulled out of me as he came and I felt his warm semen hit my thigh. Then he leaned up and took a long, deep breath before collapsing back down again. He was exhausted.

Unable to stand the sight of him any longer, I pushed him off of me and ran full speed into the bathroom. After seeing the creamy residue on my leg, I stood over the sink and threw up quietly in it. Then I took some hand soap, put it on a rag, and scrubbed it away like it was poison. I used that same rag to wipe off my entire body, at least three times. I missed being able to soak in a hot tub or a take warm shower. Times like that, I had really needed to.

When I finally made it back to the room, Mr. Otis was knocked out cold. He was snoring very loudly and was stretched out so far on the bed that I couldn't have gotten in it with him even if I wanted to. I wasn't too big on sleeping next to him anyway though; I was only upset because he was hogging the pink comforter and all the pillows. I searched around the room for another bed sheet or something else I could use to cover me, but I didn't see anything. I did see that he had washed all my clothes and had them folded neatly in the drawers. *How thoughtful of him.*

I grabbed a Dark and Lovely T-shirt out of the bottom drawer and a fresh pair of underwear from out of the top, then put them both on. After hitting the lamp switch, I curled up like a baby on the cold tile floor, far far away from where he was. I knew I wasn't going to be comfortable sleeping like that, but I wasn't worried about it. Besides, sleeping was the last thing on my mind; I just needed time to think. But only after a couple minutes of me lying there, I found even that hard to do; Mr. Otis's loud snores were refusing to allow it.

"Ugh," I sighed as I got up angrily, grabbed two more T-shirts from out of the drawer, and raced to the bathroom. I cut the light on in there, stretched both shirts out on the floor, and then flopped my body down on top of them. I did feel a bit nasty curled up on the floor of a public bathroom, but it wasn't any worse than what I had just experienced. There were no windows in there either, so you could only imagine how dark it got when I turned off the lights. Unfortunately I had to, because they were just too bright to keep on. I wasn't afraid though. I wasn't afraid of anything anymore. I had been in far worse places. Besides, darkness was no stranger to me. In fact, we were becoming friends. If nothing else in my life was guaranteed, I knew pain and darkness would be right there when I needed it.

"Fuck faith," I said as I followed Mr. Otis's footsteps and let the effects of the alcohol guide me to sleep.

16: SWITCH-OUTS

As soon as the bell rang, I rushed out of Mr. Johnson's class. I could tell she wanted to stop and question me about what had just happened between the two of us, but I acted as if I didn't see her waving me down.

Christmas break was over and I was supposed to kick-off the first day back presenting my current events assignment. The problem was, I didn't have it ready. And not only did I not have it, I gave her much attitude when she asked me about it. No one in the class knew what was going on when they saw polite little Charlytte lashing out like that, and Mrs. Johnson was so disappointed in me that she could barely teach the remainder of the class. She just threw another one of her boring essays- that I didn't even attempt to do- at us before taking her seat behind her desk. Every now and then, I would peep my head up from the pillow that I created with my arms, and she would be staring at me as if she was trying to figure me out. It had to have been bugging her why her top student wasn't prepared. Especially after she had given me the heads up the day before Christmas break that I would be the one to kick off the new semester presenting mine.

Honestly, I had planned on completing it, but after being fucked by Mr. Otis on Christmas Eve and every single night after that, it wasn't that important to me anymore. In fact, nothing was important to me anymore. The only reason I even went to school was to get away from Mr. Otis. On top of that, I refused to be the one standing up in front of the class with my peasy braids and my last-year gear, while everyone else rocked their fresh hairstyles, nice outfits, and brand new shoes that they got for Christmas.

Mrs. Johnson wasn't a dummy by a long shot though. She could tell that something in my life was wrong. But I didn't care how she felt, as long as she didn't come trying to get all up in my business. To avoid that, I tried my hardest to dodge her, and all the other kids in school too.

The second half of the school year, I still managed to be on the same lunch as Patricia and her crew. I wasn't exactly excited about sitting with them again, but at least I could take my mind off of my problems by listening to some of theirs. Most importantly, I didn't have to sit alone. I would have much rather been a ratchet girl sitting with a group, then a ratchet girl sitting by herself.

Of course, I made it to the cafeteria before everyone else and grabbed my favorite meal, pizza and fries. I took a seat at our usual table and while I picked at my food, I watched more and more kids make their way inside. Everyone was so excited to be back, but even more excited to be showing off their new styles. Almost every guy had his hair freshly cut, his dreads neatly twisted, or his cornrows creatively designed. The girls all sported their new hairstyles that were so freshly done, the smell of gel and Spritz overtook the smell of the cafeteria food. Everybody- and I mean everybody- was clean.

After about five minutes of nibbling, I glance over to the lunch line and saw Patricia and Brittany sliding their trays down the counter. They were laughing and chatting it up with a couple more girls that stood in line behind them. I couldn't help but admire their beauty and both their styles. Patricia had on a navy blue and white Baby Phat sweat-suit and her weave was long and spiraled. Brittany wore a pretty white blouse and some dark blue skinny jeans. With just the slightest movement of her body, you could see her gold earrings and bracelets sparkling from across the room. I didn't see Precious, so I assumed she must have gotten switched to a different lunch.

After constant stops for hugs from many of their friends, the girls finally made their way out of line. Everyone that had eyes was checking them out. As they headed my way, I grabbed my bookbag from off the seat and moved over to allow room for them. I hurried up and swallowed my pepperoni, and just when I was about to fix my mouth to say hi, THOSE TWO-WIMING BITCHES WALKED RIGHT PASS ME!

They didn't even speak either. And I know they saw me too, because they looked my way and laughed. Embarrassed, I quickly looked down at my food tray to hide the I-just-got-my-face-broke face, only managing to pull off the, I'm-trying-really-hard-not-to-look-like-I-just-got-my-face-broke face.

I was confused. Just two weeks ago they were calling me their friends, now they weren't even acknowledging me. We even made plans to get matching T-Shirts for the pep rally. I was supposed to be there "I" in the word *GIANTS*. And tell me, how could they spell giants without the *I*?

I watched Patricia and Brittany from the corner of my eye as they took their seats only three tables behind me. Still a little in denial, I thought that maybe they didn't see me and that once they did, they would yell out something like "Hey girl, we were looking all over for you!" and then invite me over. But when I saw the two new girls who were in the lunch line behind them come and join their table, I knew that was a dead offer.

Trying not to act or looked bothered, I continued to eat my food. There were a couple of kids from the last semester looking like they were trying to figure out what was going on. It also didn't help that Patricia and Brittany's table was going ham, live in effect. Everybody stopped by to talk with them- the ugly boys, the cute boys, the ghetto girls, and the bougie ones too. Even a couple of teachers hung around for a little while. I tried hard to ignore what was going on over there, but they were so loud that I couldn't help but to think about them.

After all the kids had settled down, and I realized that I was the only one sitting alone, that was my cue to leave. Without even finishing my fries, I got up and threw my tray into the trash, then tried to slip out of the cafeteria unnoticed. And if I thought my first day back couldn't get any worse, I was wrong because as soon as I took two steps away from the garage can, I heard another loud outburst shoot from Patricia's table. This time I looked directly their way and was embarrassed to see Shaquita Lovett, and a boy named Dominic also from my homeroom class, pointing at my shoes while doing a tap dance. Their whole table was looking at me, all of them pointing and laughing too. That put all the other kids in the lunchroom's attention to them, which in turn, led them straight to me. My pride would let me run, but I walked out of there fast enough to win a speed walking competition.

17: LESS TALK, MORE WORK

At first my plans were to use school to escape from home, but where was I going to go to escape from school? There was no winning for me. I hated school. I hated work. I hated my life. I wanted to run far away but I had already learned that trying to avoid pain was actually more painful than the pain itself.

When I did go- to school that is- I did however much work I was in the mood for then I put my head down. That went for every one of my classes. And I sure as hell didn't involve myself in any group activities or discussions. My teachers, along with the rest of the kids at school, all thought I was weird and crazy so they never bothered me about anything.

Because of my lack of participation, of course, my A's turned to D's. And believe it or not, I had an F in Mrs. Johnson's class. She eventually got the drift that I didn't want to talk to her, so thankfully, she left me alone. She also picked someone else to be classroom helper. I was glad of that.

After one of the administrators caught me having lunch in the bathroom, which I had been doing for over a month, she disproved of it and found me an empty table out on the back patio. It was located directly on the side of a trashcan so nobody ever sat there. Even though it was in a smelly area, I liked it because I was secluded from everyone. Only a couple of tables got a good view of me sitting there, but most of those kids were nerds who were too busy trying to make volcanoes out of soda bottles to be worried about me. Occasionally, I would see someone from Patricia and Brittany's table come out and crack a joke on me, but after a while they eventually got bored with it. Plus, they had managed to get into some drama with some project chicks who sat on the other side of the cafeteria.

Not only was my attitude at school horrible, but at work it was even worse. There were many times Mr. Otis had to get on me for cursing out his customers. It didn't matter to me because I didn't care about him, or his business. Especially after I worked damn near three months with no pay, because he told me that he was charging me for rent, lights, and water. I thought that was what I was fucking him for.

Speaking of fucking him, at first we did it almost every day. Then every day turned into a couple days out the week. And then those couple of days turned into once a week. I don't think he got bored; I just think his old ass got tired. But even though he was slowing down, he showed no signs of completely stopping.

I eventually stopped resisting him because it was less painful that way. Mentally, I had to make myself believe that what he was doing to me wasn't all that bad, and it worked. I had gotten so twisted in the head, that I started asking him if he wanted it.

I learned a lot from Mr. Otis, like how to make an old man feel like a little bitch in bed. That man was not only a pervert, but a weird sex freak too. Sometimes he would bring home slutty animal outfits for me to put on and tell me to make strange noises while he fucked me. He even had me spank him with a paddle once. And I won't ever forget the night he came to the store pissy drunk, with a dog lease in his hand, and made me walk *him* around the room on his hands and knees with nothing but my heels on.

I hated him for that. I hated him for everything he made me do. I always told myself that if it wasn't for me needing to use his store, I would have killed him a long time ago. That's if his old ass didn't die first.

• • • • • •

One slow day at Mr. Chill's, I was sitting around picking at the flowers on my sundress. I was bored out of my mind just looking out the front door at everyone passing by. People were now spending more time outside because the warm spring weather was beginning to make its way into the city. Wishing I too was on the outside, my thoughts were interrupted by two guys entering the store. The one who I thought looked a little familiar to me, I focused on more. My eyes followed him as he walked to the back of the store and grabbed a bottle of Orange Juice from out of the cooler. It wasn't until he started walking towards the counter and stopped to pick up a bag of Doritos, that I finally recognized who he was.

"Cederick!" I accidentally said aloud. Luckily, no one heard me.

Oh shit! Oh shit! I then said to myself. *He cannot see me like this.*

Mr. Otis was back in his office, sitting on the bed counting the store money. I quickly made my escape and ran to him.

"Mr. Otis! I gotta shit real bad!" I stood over him, wiggling my hips slowly, but slightly sexually, so that he may be more persuaded to say yes. “Can you take those two customers?"

"Don't you see I’m in the middle of something,” Mr. Otis said as he looked out into the store area."It’s only two of them. Knock them out first, and then go."

"Pleeease?" I whined, like a two-year old who had drunk too much juice. "I really have to go now."

"You breakin' my concentration Charlytte. Take care of them first, then go," he repeated. "Now get outta here!"

Mr. Otis gave me the look- the one with his eyebrows- so I knew he wasn't about to do it. He never did anything I asked him to do. Disappointed, I slowly made my way back out to the register and hoped that Cederick wouldn't recognize me. Luckily, he had his back turned taking a phone call.

I grabbed the pack of Newport's that his friend-who looked like he was too young to even be smoking- asked me for and quickly rung him up. Without waiting for Cederick, he walked out of the store.

"Can I help you?" I said to Cederick really fast, so that I could get our little encounter over with.

"Oh, my bad shorty," he hung up his call and then placed the bottle of orange juice, along with the big bag of Doritos, on the counter.

"Oh. And lemme get two Swishers,” he said. He didn’t even acknowledge or seem to remember me.

"Regular?" I asked, trying not act to like I was offended by it.

"Yeah."

Although the Swishers were kept in a bowl right beside me, I went to the back wall, reached way up to the top row, and grabbed him a pack. I intentionally did it slowly so that he could admire my frame. After showing off a bit, I turned back around. I was almost one-hundred percent sure that by then he knew exactly who I was. Still, I got nothing out of him. He just exchanged his money for a receipt, and I watched him walk right out of the door.

My feelings were hurt when I saw him leave. I just didn't know what to think. Was it me? Had I become too ugly and down bad to be recognized? Or was it him? Maybe smoking hella weed made him forgetful? Worse, maybe he stopped to chat with teenage girls all the time.

"If you need me, I'll be in the bathroom!" embarrassed, I yelled out to Mr. Otis. And Although Mr. Otis heard me clear as day, he didn't respond. I didn't take it personal though. He always acted that way when he counted his money. Business sales had been falling, so every time he had to see those declining numbers, he got frustrated. Plus, half of the reason his sales were dropping was because of me and my nasty attitude, and it made him even more upset to see that I really didn't give a fuck.

Truthfully, I didn't have to go to the bathroom. I just needed some time alone to think. Why was it a big deal that some strange guy- whom of which I only met once- didn't recognize me? Plenty of guys tried to holla at me before, who I saw many times afterwards, and I didn't want them to notice me. It was different with Cederick though. I admired him for some reason and sometimes regretted throwing his number away. I often wondered if he was expecting my call, and in a way, I had just gotten my answer.

Maybe the kids at school were right. I locked myself in the bathroom and cried. *Maybe I am just a stupid nobody!*

After pitying myself I flushed the toilet, pretending like I had used it. Then I washed my hands, only because I had touched the filthy thing.

I made my way out the bathroom and my heart started to beat really fast when I saw the same guy, Cederick, standing up at the counter again. Ironically, in his hands, a bag of Doritos and a bottle of orange juice.

"Is there a problem?" I asked, wondering what was up with the unexpected return. Even Mr. Otis stuck his head up to see what was wrong.

"Uhm…yeah, a slight one," he answered.

"What is it?" I asked.

"Well," he began, "I came in here just a few seconds ago and I saw this beautiful girl that I ran into some time ago, and ya know what, she didn't even speak to me. I figured I must have been trippin', so I decided to come back and try it again."

Immediately I started blushing. Even though I thought his comeback was a little cheesy. Still, I couldn't help but be flattered by it.

"Cederick, right?' I asked, trying to act like I had just remembered him. I could never forget those eyes.

For a minute we both quietly gazed at each other, which was very uncomfortable because from the corner of my eye, I could see Mr. Otis staring too. Then, like the nosey old grouch he was, he made his way to doorway and acted as if he was looking through some of his paperwork. I knew better but I was so into Cederick that I didn't pay him any mind.

"How have you been? I asked.

"I'm good, maintaining. I most definitely can't complain," he said. "What about you? How's school?"

“School’s going very well," I lied. “Just ready for it to be over with.”

"I can dig it,” he replied, then changed the subject. “What ever happened to that phone call, miss lady?"

"I…I…I don't know," I stuttered, trying to think of some quick excuse to give him. But before I could open my mouth, Mr. Otis cut me off.

"You can go ahead and take your shit now," he said saving, but embarrassing, me at the same time. His face was really red. Clearly he was jealous. Cederick quickly caught on to Mr. Otis too, and not waiting to cause any problems, he backed off.

"Well shorty, I got my potna' out there waiting for me, so maybe I'll see you around," he said. "Oh, and if you don't mind, can you do me a favor and throw this away?"

Cederick peeped over at Mr. Otis to make sure he wasn't looking, then winked at me before handing me a folded piece of paper and a chewing gum wrapper. I threw them both into the small garbage can behind the counter, but made sure that I sat the paper on top because I knew it had Cederick's number written on it. He paid for his second purchase of juice and chips and I watched him walk out of the store one last time. Satisfied with his disappearance, Mr. Otis made his way back into his office and I made my way back to the bathroom.

Standing over the sink, I looked in the mirror at the huge smile on my face that I couldn’t get rid of, even if it was to save my life. It brought me great pleasure knowing Cederick went through that little bit of trouble just to talk to me. After all that, I knew I just couldn't have been some random chick to him.

Dead in the middle of my smile, unfortunately, I heard the sound of keys jingling at the door. It was Mr.

Otis barging into the bathroom. Startled, I jumped at the sight of him and quickly wiped away any signs of happiness from off of my face.

"Don't look like you shittin' to me," he said sarcastically, then immediately closed the door and proceeded to unbuckle his pants.

"I…I…I was just washing my hands first. Did you see how that jerk had the nerve to give me his nasty trash?" I fronted. "You can go ahead and use it first. I'll wait outside."

I headed for the door, but before I could get to it, he pinned me up between the sink and the toilet. With his index finger, he softly caressed the side of my face, and then planted one kiss on my lips just because he knew how much I hated that.

"You do know that the store is still open," I reminded him.

"I know that," he said.

"Then what are you doing?" I asked.

"I'm about to get my old-man wood sucked," he said, as if it was no big deal.

"Huh?' I questioned him.

"You heard me. Now... suck…my…dick."

Mr. Otis placed one hand on top of my head and started to push me downward. Normally when he gave me sexual demands I didn't resist, but this time, I had to.

"Mr. Otis, people are coming in and out of here. You sure you want to do this now?"

"I guess that means you better be quick."

Without asking any more questions, I got down on the hard tile floor and began to suck him as fast as I could.

He moaned softly, and within five minutes, he was cuming. When I felt the salty semen hit my tongue, I tried to move my head out of the way, but he grabbed my braids with both his hands and forced me to taste him while he let go into my mouth. After he was all drained out, he grabbed my chin with one hand and placed his other hand over my mouth.

"Swallow," he told me.

After hearing those words, I panicked. Immediately I tried to claw his hand from my lips, but his grip was too tight. While laughing at me, he so easily pushed my tiny fingers away, crushing my knuckles together as a warning for me not to try that again. With his right hand covering everything from my nose down, he showed no sympathy when he looked into my pleading eyes. I sat motionless for a couple of seconds, refusing to carry out his order. That was another thing I just could not do for him.

"Swallow," he said again.

As I began to feel the effects of the hard floor on my kneecaps, I continued to look up at him like a sad poodle. Mr. Otis was getting frustrated by my disobedience, but I wasn't giving in. He waited patiently for me to swallow his seeds, until thankfully, we heard someone come through the front door.

"This ain't over," he told me, then grabbed me by my hair, threw me down on the floor, and rushed out to politely greet his guest. I immediately ran over to the toilet to spit up the semen, and a little bit of food that I ate earlier. Then I waited for Mr. Otis to come back into the bathroom because I was smart enough to know not to go out behind him. When he re-entered, I was scrubbing my face and tongue with hand soap and didn't stop just because he was looking. I normally didn't do that in front of him because I felt like it was a form of disrespect. But this time, I wanted him to know how disgusted I was.

"I'm leaving for today. You can lock up at nine," he said as he watched me scrub away, not the least bit offended by it. "And remember Charlytte, less talking and more working."

18: ENOUGH!

A month had passed since Cederick dropped by the store, and because of it, Mr. Otis became more protective of me. He kept me busy working and I couldn't leave the building unless it was for school. Anytime I needed something, I had to tell him and he got it for me. I rarely asked to go places anyway because he wasn't giving me enough money to spend. He always tried to make it seem like he was in a financial setback, and even though that was true, I knew he was making enough to give me a decent check. Plus, he got a large amount of money from Mrs. Clarice's life insurance policy; Mr. Simmons came in one day and spilled the beans about that.

I was beginning to get smart about Mr. Otis. His plan was simple- to trap me. He needed me to stay vulnerable and keeping me broke was the best way to achieve that. He didn't want to worry about me saving up any get-away money and he didn't want me looking too good for any nigga on the outside who wanted to save me.

But not only was he becoming very protective, he was also becoming very grumpy. He was drinking twice as much, was never in a good mood, and was taking it all out on little ole' me. Most of it began when the foreigners started building a convenience store directly across the street from us, and it got worse the closer they got to finishing it. On top of that, his sales were still dropping.

The more depressed he became, the more shots of gin he took, and the more "visits" I received from him. When he first started having sex with me, ironically, he always made sure I was comfortable. But what was once gentle and patient, turned into roughness and aggression. He would dive straight in my shit and drill it as hard as he could, and even though he could only work it for one minute, the soreness of my pussy lasted for days. One night, he smacked my ass so hard that it formed a big red bruise on my buttcheek. I literally couldn't sit for a week. I always tried to tell him to stop it or be easy, but of course, he never listened. Besides, sometimes he was so drunk that it was pointless to say anything to him.

I despised that man. If I shot him in the head twenty times that still could not describe the hate I felt for him. I couldn't stand to hear him. I couldn't stand to see him. I even tried to stay at least two feet away from him so that I didn't have to breathe the same air as he did. My tolerance for Mr. Otis was fading and I knew it wouldn't be long before I found, or at least tried to find, a way out.

On the bright side, I thought about Cederick a lot. So much that every time the store bells jingled, I looked up to see if it was him. I knew I would never call him though, not only because of Mr. Otis, but because I didn't have the confidence to believe he would want a sad case like me. My hair was still a mess, I barely had any clothes, and I didn't have any money.

I skipped my way into Mr. Chill's afterschool one

Thursday evening in an unusual mood- a good one. Spring break had started a day early for me because even though we had school the next day, I had already planned on skipping. I wasn't happy about spending more time in the store, but I hated going to school much more.

Mr. Otis was getting ready to step out for a while, leaving me to do all the work once again. I didn't care though, I was in no mood to see his old, ugly face. He gathered his things, gave me the usual, *I'm-leaving-don't-try-nothing-stupid- look*, and left.

I worked until closing time, then locked up the store. Free from customers and homework, I grabbed the gallon of gin that Mr. Otis kept underneath the register, cut on some music, and poured me up a shot.

Tony Toni Tone's, *All I ask of you*, played on the radio and I immediately started thinking about Marcus. Even though he did me wrong, I still wished I was back in those days. I missed the feeling of being in love and being free from all my problems. With everything I had going on, I wanted that more anything else in the world.

After about two hours, I realized that I had taken about five shots. I knew it wouldn't be long before Mr. Otis came back for his night of having his way with me. He always arrived somewhere between eleven and twelve, and just as I predicted at 11:52, I heard his loud truck roaring down the street.

"Right on time," I said.

I clicked off the lamped in the office, and peeped out the window to see him staggering out of his truck. My plan was to get myself drunk, suck him dry, and have him snoring instantly afterwards. My vagina was still sore from letting him ram a dildo in me a couple of nights before, so there was no way I could take the pain of having him inside of me again. Just no way.

I got fully naked, like he trained me to do, and met him at the back door. He was drunk and dirty, which was no surprise to me. I had to practically carry him in because he was stumbling everywhere, and when we finally made it to the room, the first thing he did was go reaching for the lamp. He always wanted the lights on, but with him being extremely wasted, I had the opportunity to take advantage of him and do things my way. Before he could touch the switch, I quickly threw him against the bed and began to unbuckle his jean jumper.

When his clothes hit the floor, I pushed him down on the bed and got on my knees. Mr. Otis leaned back and moaned as I sucked him slow, then fast. I was no longer training myself to enjoy having sex with him. The more I hated Mr. Otis, the harder it became to stomach all that I was doing with him. It was taking more patience and more gin for me not to throw up all over his thighs, and in order to make it easier for me, I had to close my eyes and imagine him being someone else. Cederick was always that guy.

Mr. Otis's soft moans began to get louder as I used more to spit and sucked him faster. I moaned too because I knew how much it turned him on. Just as he was about to finish- and just as I was about to rejoice because he was finished- he grabbed my hair and stopped me.

"Wait…wait uh minute," he panted.

"What's wrong daddy?" I asked seductively, only trying to get him back into the mood.

"I don't want to finish yet," he said. "Turn over."

Mr. Otis tapped me on my ass and motioned for me to get on the bed. I knew he wanted me to bend over for him so that he could hit me from behind. That was his favorite position.

"Daddy, please let me finish. I wanna taste it." I said, still hovering over him. "I'll swallow this time."

"You can still swallow," this time he tapped the bed. "Now bend over."

Disobeying him, I flopped back down on my knees and went face first into his crouch. I got it halfway into my mouth before he pulled me back by my hair. By me being a little drunk and aggressive myself, I kept fighting to go down on him, and the harder I went in, the harder he pulled me back. One by one I could hear and feel my braids popping off from my roots, but I didn't care. I would have rather lost all my hair than to feel those burns every time he stroked me.

"Charlytte, stop!" he fussed. "Stop it right now!"

"No daddy, let me taste it," I pleaded. "I just wanna taste it!"

Tired of fighting, Mr. Otis picked me up by my waist and slammed me onto the bed. My head hit the railing and immediately it began to throb. While I lay on my stomach, with one hand on my aching skull, he quickly climbed over me, pulled me by both legs from behind, and tried to sit me up like a dog. Resisting him, I threw my body back down on the bed, only to have him slide me up again.

"Sit up Charlytte. I aint gon' tell ya again!" he yelled while he tried to push himself inside of me and force me into position at the same time. I clinched my pussy muscles together to block his entrance.

"Please daddy please, let me taste it! I just wanna taste it!" was all I kept repeating.

I didn’t want Mr. Otis to think that I didn't want him- just that I wanted to satisfy him. And as I expected, he didn't care to buy any of the bullshit I was trying to sell him. After a couple more minutes of tussling, he smacked me on one of my butt cheeks so hard that I had no choice but to contemplate on just giving in.

"With all this fighting, you must like it rough?" he smacked me again. "Answer me gal, is this how you want it?’

"Noooo, please nooo!" I cried, then tried to cover my ass with both my hands so that he wouldn't hit me there like that again. "Please Mr. Otis, can we do this another day. It still hurts from the last time, please!"

"You know daddy hates it when you whine like that, Charlytte. You're a big girl, I know you can handle ya old man by now."

I didn't try to deny him anymore because I knew I couldn't win. Besides, my ass was still stinging from the way he had just smacked it. All I could do was pray to God that it wouldn't hurt as bad as I already knew it would.

"Ok daddy," I surrendered. "Just be easy on me."

"*Easy*?" Mr. Otis repeated me, then chuckled to himself. "Okay babygirl, daddy will take it easy on ya."

I allowed him to slowly ease his way inside of me and although it was a little painful, I could manage at the steady pace he was going. He stroked in and out gently and I moaned softly for him just as he wanted me to.

Burying my face deep into the pink pillow, tears started flowing down my face. That was something that hadn’t happened in a while. I had become so numb from the pain that it was strange for me to be crying. And although they weren't tears of joy, I was glad to be feeling some kind of emotion again.

Escaping reality, I let my thoughts of Cederick help moisten my insides. I could tell Mr. Otis felt my flowing juices too because he began to moan louder. It must've felt real good to him too, because he forgot all about my little request to take it easy and suddenly started ramming himself in and out of me. The small amount of discomfort I was in was now replaced by a great deal of unbearable pain. I quickly tried to pull away, but he trapped me by grabbing my shoulders with both of his hands, and forced me to take in all of him.

"Please stop! Please stop!" I screeched. "You're hurting me!"

"Take it! You're a big girl!" he shouted. I could feel his warm breath hitting hard against my backside. "I know you can take it!"

My shit dried up soon as the pain started striking, which made the feeling even worse. Hurt awfully, I screamed so loud that the nearby neighbors probably heard me. Hell, I hoped someone would hear me and come to my rescue.

It seemed like the more I cried and tried to struggle, the more frustrated Mr. Otis got. I didn't care if he was close to getting his nut. It was hurting.

"Stop that hollering!" he yelled, while still drilling me from behind. "You fuckin' up my concentration."

"Somebody help me!" I ignored him and continued to scream out. "Somebody *please* help me!"

A little paranoid by my screaming, Mr. Otis pulled himself out of me, leaving me lying flat on my stomach, too weak and in too much pain to move. I prayed that his conscious had finally kicked him in the ass and forced him to ease up on me, but little did I know, he was only getting started.

"If you can't take it in this hole, then how about we try it in *this* hole!" he panted, then rammed his dick straight into my ass. I couldn't even scream, probably because there was no sound that could describe what I felt.

With his all of body weight thrusting on top of me, I couldn't have escaped from him if I tried. Besides, the more I did, the harder he forced it into me. Everything moved in slow motion- every strike of pain, every one of his deep breaths, every word to Chaka Khan's song *Sweet Thing.*

Push after push I cried, just wishing that he would do me a favor and shoot me in my head with his gun. I know it sounds crazy, but after all the times he raped me, that was the first time I felt abused. That was the first time I blamed someone other than myself. And that was the first time I realized that I needed to fight back.

I could feel his body getting weaker with every stroke. I knew he was about to cum because he started making those weird monkey noises. While I lay there taking the pain, I reached around the side of the bed for anything I could use to defend myself, and luckily, I rested my hand on his best friend and worse enemy, the bottle of gin. As soon as he started cuming, I lifted my body, pushed him off of me, and swung the bottle at his head so hard that it knocked him out cold. He let out one loud holler before he went down and I hit him once more, just to make sure he was down for good.

Quickly, I turned the lamp on to get a good look at him. His eyes were slightly open, but he was definitely out for the count. It almost looked as if he was dead, but I knew I didn't hit him that hard. Fearing that he would suddenly wake up like the people in the horror movies, I quickly grabbed a T-shirt and sweatpants from out of the drawer and got dressed. I also grabbed my backpack and started stuffing it with anything that I could fit inside, although it was nothing but a couple of shirts, two textbooks, and most importantly, my mama's picture. Then I took a big black trash bag from out of the cleaning closet and filled it with even more clothes. Anything I thought I needed, I tossed inside of it.

I took one long look back at Mr. Otis as I made my way to the back door. I was so furious with him that I just had to drop my things and attack him again. Grabbing the gin bottle, I hit him once more in the head, a couple times on his back, and then began to ram the top of the bottle up his ass. The same way he did me.

"You pervert! Is this how *you* like it?" I yelled, as I repeatly poked him in his anal. "Let's see how that feels in the morning you black nasty bastard!"

After I was pleased with tormenting him, I threw my backpack over my back with one hand, and grabbed the trash bag with the other. On my way out, I stop at the cash machine and took all of the money out of it. True, I was stealing a couple hundred dollars from him, but that was nothing compared to what he owed me.

As I exited out of the back door, not only did I leave it unlocked, I left it wide open just because I knew how much more upset he would be when he awoke and found it like that. And if he didn't wake back up until the morning and someone caught him passed out like that, he was going to have some serious explaining to do. Either way, he was screwed.

It was crazy. The same alley I hid in while I waited to sneak into Mr. Otis's store, was the same alley I was hiding in to make my escape from out of there. Walking quickly down it, my pussy was burning, there was a good chance my asshole was bleeding, and the spot where he spanked me had me wondering if I had sat on a flat iron. Also, it was dark and spooky, but I wasn't afraid. Like I said before, darkness was no stranger to me.

As I made my way further down the lonely strip, I stopped and placed the bag of clothes behind an old abandon house. I knew nobody would find it there. Heading for the street, I grabbed the digital clock from out my backpack to check the time. It read 12:32. I couldn't believe that my life had taken yet another major turn so quickly. I felt like I was one of those balls in that arcade game, where you push the button and it bounced from wall to wall until it eventually fell down into the a hole. Well, life was pushing my buttons and I was bouncing from one bad situation to another, only to find myself falling into the same dark hole that I had come out of.

Yep, I was definitely in that hole again- back at square one. But this time, I didn't have a plan. All I knew was that I only had enough money to last a couple nights in a hotel.

"Lord, it's gonna take a miracle to save me from this one," was all I could say to myself.

19: GHETTO SAVIOR

The red light from the Clean Stay hotel sign flickered, bringing a spark to the dark and deserted area on the Southside. The hotel was low budget and low class, but I was in no position to be picky. Although the walk from the store to the hotel was only about thirty minutes, it took me an hour to get there. The pain that struck my right butt cheek every time I switched wouldn't allow me to move any faster.

After a couple seconds of staring out at the rusty, beige two-story building, I pulled myself together, fixed up what was left of my braids, and entered. There wasn't a soul in sight, except for the foreigner who worked the front desk.

"May I help you?" asked the man, as soon as he saw me approaching. He looked like he was from India

"Yes, I would like to get a room for tonight. The cheapest thing you got, nothing fancy."

"Sure, just fill out his form," he told me. "I'm also going to need to see some ID. Are you 18 years or older?"

Shit! I thought.

"Yes I am sir," I lied. "But my purse was stolen. I don't have any type of identification on me. I promise I won't be a problem for you or your hotel. Just give me one night here and I will be out by the morning."

"I'm sorry miss," he shot me down, "but we cannot be of service to anyone without the proper form of ID. No exceptions."

It took everything in me not to burst into tears and beg him. If he only knew how badly I needed a place to stay. I just couldn't give up that easily.

"Sir, please, I gotta be honest," I said as I moved closer to him and began to whisper into his ear, "I'm only sixteen. I'm not a prostitute, or fugitive, or anything like that. I just need someplace to clear my head. You see, my mother is a full-time crackhead who likes being beaten by my alcoholic step-father, so you can only imagine how bad I need this favor. Please sir, I beg of you."

Although the story was a lie, the pain that showed on my face when I looked him dead into his eyes was for real. With both hands I tried to shield my tears, and when I uncovered them, I looked up to see the man staring back at me showing not even the slightest sign of sympathy.

"I'm sorry ma'am, rules are rules. But if you like, I will be glad to call the police for you and you can explain everything to them. I'm sure they can help you better than I can."

I could tell he didn't care about me, or my situation, and was only threatening to call the police so that I would leave. The last thing I wanted was the pigs involved so I quickly decided it was best I did just that.

"No sir, that's okay. But thank you anyway."

I felt many different emotions leaving that hotel- hurt, fear, and loneliness being the worst of them. I was hurting because I had just been raped brutality, I was scared because I didn't know what my next move was going to be, and I was lonely because I had no one to turn to.

I just felt like I was giving up on life. But suddenly, as the automatic doors swung open to see me out, a bright idea popped into my head.

"Excuse me!" I said as I ran back up to the desk. "I hate to bother you again, but can I at least use your phone."

"Phones are not for public use," he said.

"Sir, please," I flashed a five-dollar bill in his face. "It will just take a minute."

Just like I thought, the clerk quickly took the money and handed me the black cordless phone that rested behind the counter. I purposely snatched it out of his hand, then turned my back to him and began dialing. The phone rang and a male voice eventually answered.

"Yooo," it said.

"Hello, may I speak to Cederick?" I asked nervously.

"Dis me, who this?"

"It's Charlytte, the girl from Marco's and Mr. Chill's."

I hoped he'd remembered me.

"Oh, what's up babygirl?" he replied excitedly, but then his mood quickly changed. "It's kinda late, ain't it? You okay?"

"Yeah sort of. I'm at the Clean Stay in Richmond," I whispered while I peeped over at the hotel clerk. He was waiting impatiently for his phone. I knew I had to make it quick.

"If you're not too busy, can you meet me here?"

"Yeah, as a matter of fact, I'm about fifteen minutes away. I'll be there shortly."

Cederick hung up the phone before I could even say goodbye. I thanked the stingy old hotel clerk and left the building.

Just as he had said, fifteen minutes later, Cederick pulled up in the hotel parking lot driving a nice ass all black SS Monte Carlo. Without saying a word, he got out of the car, grabbed me by the hand, and escorted me to the back seat of it. Marijuana smoke brushed my face as soon as I entered, and although I didn't smoke, it was soothing to my nostrils.

"Charlytte, this is Ace. Ace, Charlytte." Cederick said, introducing me to a guy who sat in the passenger seat.

When I looked over at Ace, the first thing I noticed was how good he looked. That man was fine with a capital F. And not the regular fine, he was the fine that you pronounced with two syllables. He had smooth brown skin, his eyes were almond-shaped, and his lips were nicely shaped and firm.

"Whassup," we both said at the same time.

Everyone in the car was quiet as we cruised through Ordale vibing to a lil' Boosie mix. The base from the back speakers was so strong that it made my entire body vibrate. I watched as Cederick and Ace took turns hitting a well-stuffed blunt. Ace even tried to hand it to me once, and although I was tempted, I passed on it.

Cederick dropped Ace off in the projects, but they both got out of the car. Before closing the door, Cederick told me that he would be right back and gave me the okay to get in the passenger seat. Delighted, I climbed over to the front and began to check out all of his fancy gadgets.

Dayum. I said to myself as I rubbed my hands across the dashboard. *His whip is decked out! This CD player paints pictures...and look at this high tech ass navi system. I ain't never been in a ride this fly. Marcus's car is a hooptie compared to this shit.*

Outside of the car, the guys looked like they were having an interesting conversation. Only I wasn't interested in what they were saying, I was just fascinated by their styles. Cederick, who sat on the hood of the car, had on a red Polo top similar to the one he wore when I first saw him. And denims with dress shoes must have been his preferred choice of style. I still wasn't a big fan of his looks, but he certainly had some distinctive qualities that were strong enough to win any girl over. His swag being one of them.

But although I was fascinated by Cederick, it was Ace who I couldn't take my eyes off of. He, on the other hand, carried his conversation standing up. Every time he turned and faced the car, I caught a glimpse of his six-pack through his white tank top. Without question, he was a perfect ten and then some. I had to literally force myself to stop looking at him.

Cederick and Ace chopped it up about ten more minutes, dapped each other up, and went their separate ways. Making his way back to the car, Cederick peeped through the driver side window and pointed down to the switch on the door, which must have automatically locked on its own. Then he signaled for me to pop it for him. After I did, he hopped in the car and immediately turned the music all the way up to the max.

"Is this too loud for you, shorty?" he yelled, right before he pulled off.

I wish you would have asked me that when your speakers were caving in my chest back there. I said to myself.

"No, it's fine," I replied.

"If you say so."

Cederick put the car in reverse and made his way out of the projects. Now that we were finally alone, I knew that there were a lot of things that needed to be discussed. I wasn't going to be the one to break the ice though. I just quietly stared out of the window and waited for him to say something first.

"Can I ask you something?" he finally asked. What was left of the blunt that he and Ace smoked, he took out of the astray, re-lit, and took a puff.

Yeah, why not?" I sighed.

"Are you scared?" he questioned.

"A little," I answered, looking out the passenger window the entire time. As with everyone else, the less eye contact, the better.

"What's a little, shorty?" he turned down the radio a couple more notches. "Either you are or you ain't."

"I said a little, alright." I sassed him.

Cederick sensed my attitude and immediately let me know that he was not having it.

"Look lil' one, I ain't trying to be all up in ya business if that's why you trippin'. To be honest, I don't even know you well enough to care about what's going on in ya life, but I do know that when you called I came running, and usually, I don't do that." Cederick took another hit of his weed. His voice mumbled from trying to hold the smoke in. "You don't got to lie to me shorty, I came to help you. I'm not asking you to tell me your life story, but don't tell me nothing's wrong if that's not true. I hate being lied to."

He released the smoke and it came flying in my direction.

"Now again, is everything okay with you."

I paused and marinated on Cederick's last words before answering. "No. Everything's not okay."

"And would you like to talk about it?"

Nope."

"Fine."

Cederick turned the radio back up, and I continued to stare out of the window up until we made our way to Connor's Bluff. Although I was very curious about why we were going to the rich folk's neighborhood, I didn't ask him any questions. Besides, I was busy being hypnotized by all of the big, beautiful houses and nice cars that we passed.

Connor's Bluff, also known as The Bluff, was a small town on the outer skirts of Ordale. All the wealthy folks resided there. All the houses were divided into subdivisions, and all the subdivisions were gated and high secured: you didn't go unless you knew someone who lived there.

Cederick pulled up into the driveway of a beautiful two-story house. It was all white with black shutters. The drive-in garage door was left open so I was able to see the silver Benz, the '09 Camry, and the white sports car that occupied it. I knew it wasn't his spot because he didn't strike me as a guy who would be living that lavish. Plus, he had already told me he lived on the East.

"Where are we?" I finally asked him, but only after he parked his car and turned off the ignition.

"To a friend of mines," he replied. "You're staying here."

"What?" I questioned. "What do you mean?"

"Chill babygirl," he said, "and wipe that worried look off ya face. Just trust me, it's no big deal. He owes me a favor."

Although I wanted so badly to see what the inside of that house looked like, there was no way I was about to intrude on a complete stranger. I didn't care if he owed Cederick a million bucks.

"I'm not too big on sleeping in some stranger's place. I'd rather you just get me a room."

"You're gonna have to trust me. It's not like that," he said. "Now follow me."

As I was told, I followed Cederick out of the car and we made our way to the side of the house. I watched him as he used a strange-looking key to open up the tall, wooden fence that surrounded the huge backyard. My hopes of seeing nice interior decorations faded as we walked deeper into the backyard and headed towards an outhouse. It didn't bother me too much because the Jacuzzi and S-shaped pool were just as fascinating.

Even though it was dark, I could still see the fancy lounge chairs that were seated around the pool. I could also see a DJ booth and the built-in grill that was planted on the side of it. I got the feeling that whoever lived in that house must have thrown some crazy parties.

We walked deeper into the yard and as we got closer to the outhouse, I was able to see just how raggedy it really was. The white paint was chipping awfully, the screen door was filled with holes, and the three broke-down cars on the side of it made it look even more distasteful.

"I know damn well he's not about to throw me in no tool-" I began to think, but before I could finish my sentence, Cederick opened up the door and shut me up by revealing just how nice the inside of the shack really was.

When I walked in, I was surprised to be stepping on some clean, beige carpet and even more surprised when I looked up at the room where a queen-sized bed resided. The bed had a burgundy wood frame and one fresh white fitted sheet was spread neatly over its' thick, sturdy mattress. There was also a white wool blanket and a plaid comforter folded up on the edge of it.

To the right of the bed, was small space which held the kitchen. On the counter in there was a microwave, a toaster, and a black mini-fridge. It even had a stove. I just couldn't believe it.

Cederick glanced over at me, catching me almost drooling over the place.

"It's not a hotel, but it should do," he said, being sarcastic. He knew damn well that spot was much nicer than a cheap hotel room.

"It's fine," I said, still astonished. "Woooow. Is this like a guest house?"

"Yeah, and you're the guest for now," he replied.

I walked over to the bed and threw my backpack down on it, then turned to Cederick with the look of confusion all over my face. I didn't know why he brought me to that place, but I did know that I was lucky to have a comfy spot to rest my head. I hadn't stayed anywhere close to real home since I left Auntie Jo's house.

"Don't worry about anything else tonight," he said. "Just get yourself some rest and I will explain everything in the morning."

Cederick walked a little further into the house and pointed to another small room that I had overlooked. "There's towels, soap, medicines- just about everything you need in this bathroom right here."

"Ok thanks," I replied, then walked over to see it for myself.

"If you need anything else, just hit me up." This time he pointed to the nightstand that had only a telephone resting on top of it. "And there's the phone."

I glanced over at the phone, then asked, "You're not leaving me, are you?"

I wasn't too comfortable with being alone with him, but I would have been even more uncomfortable being left there by myself. Without saying a word, Cederick walked towards the door and grabbed the handle.

"I gotta make a couple of runs. But trust me, nobody is going to bother you here. I will be back first thing tomorrow morning," he finally answered. "And before I go, are you hungry?"

"No, I don't have much of an appetite."

"Well if you change your mind there are some snacks and TV dinners in the fridge. Lock the door behind me."

Before leaving, Cederick turned around and looked at me one last time. The sympathetic look he carried made me well aware that he could read the 'please don't leave' sign taped to my face. And I hoped that because of it, he'd pity me enough to stay.

"Both locks." He said, and then disappeared.

After securing the place, I immediately ran to the blinds and cracked them open. I watched Cederick walk to the back of the two-story house and knock on the door. Once again, I couldn't help but notice his demeanor. Even his walk was sexy, especially with those bowlegged and that slight limp.

Cederick waited a second and finally, a tall light-skinned man came out of the patio door and greeted him with a fancy handshake. That surprised me even more because I thought for sure that whoever owned that house was white. Most of the niggas I knew only dreamed of living in a house that big.

Cederick followed the man as he stepped a couple of feet away from the back porch. It seemed as if he was trying not to let anyone inside the house hear them. When they moved, it triggered a motion censored light to come on. That helped me really get a good look at this other guy.

Damn. He's cute too. I thought, as I squinted my eyes to get a better look at the very built dude who looked to be in his early forties. His moist, curly hair and pale skin made him look pretty-boyish. But his dirty red face, arm full of tattoos, and gold grill, made it very clear to me that he was no doctor.

The two of them didn't talk very long. Cederick handed him some cash. He counted it. They dapped again. Cederick split. And that was it.

When I saw the headlights from Cederick's car disappear down the quiet street, I did another run through of the house. This time I was in every cabinet, every drawer, and every closet. I wanted to see everything. I had never seen a shed decked out the way that one was.

In the kitchen, all the cupboards were nicely organized with snacks ranging from Vienna sausages to fruit roll ups. The fridge was very clean and neatly stacked with juice, fruits, and TV dinners. And in the bathroom, were traveler packs of toothbrushes, toothpaste, soaps, lotions- practically anything you could name. There were over-the-counter medicines of all kinds, alcohol and health supplies, and I almost choked when I opened the cabinet that contained the feminine products. I couldn't believe that there were about twenty boxes of Kotex tampons and twenty more packs of pads. They even had boxes of vaginal creams. I had to pick up the tube of Monistat and read it closely just to make sure my weary eyes weren't playing tricks on me.

After I ransacked the spot, I flopped down on the bed, letting the pain that kicked me in my right butt cheek remind me of the earlier events. The ones that had been suppressed by all of the excitement that Cederick had just presented me with. I was so thankful for that cute little bathroom because there was nothing I needed more than a long, hot soak in the tub. Some bath crystals, a box of Epsom salt, a dab of dish detergent, and a couple of drops of green rubbing alcohol were all the ingredients I needed to make the perfect wash.

After the water temperature was just right for me, I got naked and closed the bathroom door. Behind it, hung a full-size mirror that almost made me jump out of myself when it revealed to me my reflection. I immediately checked out how swollen my face was. I had a couple of red marks on the base of my cheek bones and my eyes were extremely puffy.

My hair looked a mess too. I counted six bald spots, and that was just in the front of my head. Then I turned around to see my back. It was awfully wept up, and just as I suspected, Mr. Otis's handprint was painted on my butt.

Still, with my back facing the mirror, I drop my head to the floor and split both my cheeks apart to see what my asshole and the inside of my vagina looked like. My clit was the size of my big toe and my ass was clearly broken in- the blood around it confirmed that. He had screwed it up so badly that it didn't even look like a vagina anymore. After seeing what he had done to me, I prayed that the bastard was dead.

Unable to put my eyes through any more discomfort, I got in the tub. The mixture of a warm sensation from the bath water and a cool sensation from the alcohol splashing up against my skin put my body at ease. After standing up in the bathroom of Mr. Otis' store, wiping down with rags for so long, I almost forgot what a good wash felt like. And I appreciated it more than I ever did before.

A half an hour went by before I found myself falling asleep in the tub. The last thing I wanted was to be found dead and naked in some strange man's hut so I quickly hopped out and dried myself off. I rubbed my body down with baby lotion, put icy hot on my scars, and carefully patted some Monistat cream on my vagina. I didn't know if it would help, but it was definitely worth the try.

Feeling much better and more relaxed after the wash up, I grabbed the remote from off the headboard and made my way to the bed. I happily dug my face into the fluffy white pillow, taking in the wonderfully pleasant feeling of being in a cozy bed again. Skimming through the channels, I rested the TV- a small flat screen that was mounted up on the wall- on the Golden Girls and laughed at Sophia until I drifted off to sleep.

20: DON'T SAVE HER

"Oh my Jesus!" followed by a burst of collective laughter was the first thing I heard as soon as I crept in thirty minutes late to Mrs. Johnson's Social Studies class. Dominic, the class clown, was losing his funny touch and joking on little old pathetic me was the surest way to crown him ringmaster of the circus again. That was the worst I had ever looked in school history; even Mrs. Johnson had to do a double-take.

I arrived late to school because Cederick had to practically force me to go. I knew he said he would be back the next morning. But I never guessed he would be standing over me as early as six o'clock, holding a T-shirt and grey sweatpants, pressuring me into going to school. I begged him not to make me, but he said if I did, I would never have to go back under those conditions again. I put up a huge fight, but eventually gave in and found myself sitting in the passenger seat of his car, headed back to the heart of Ordale.

"Settle down class," Mrs. Johnson said, trying to save me from any more humiliation. "One more outburst like that Mr. Williams and you will find yourself starting your break early."

I appreciated Mrs. Johnson for taking up for me, but really, I was unaffected by Dominic and the rest of the class. The physical and emotional pain that I already had to deal with made it impossible for me to endure anything else. I handed Mrs. Johnson my tardy slip, took my usual seat, and placed my head down on my desk until class was dismissed.

I tried to get through the rest of my day by not focusing on how bad I looked and felt, but that was hard to do when kids were constantly snickering, laughing, and pointing in my direction. Ashamed, I walked through the hallways with my head down and made eye contact with no one. I had even planned on skipping lunch, but my stomach and the fact that I hadn't eaten a decent meal in almost twenty-four hours, didn't agree with that decision.

Hiding myself outside on the patio, I devoured my food just as scavengers do road kill. The hamburger, curly fries, and fruit cocktail didn't stand a chance against me. The lunchroom was jumping as usual, but on that day it was extra live because people were so excited about Spring Break. I, on the other hand, didn't see what the big deal was. I wasn't going on any vacations, going to any major party events, or hanging out with any friends of my own, therefore I didn't care about it. I was just happy that I didn't have to step one foot in that stupid school for a whole week.

Once again, I was back to being the center of humiliation for the lunchroom. It seemed as if no one- nerds and geeks included- could stop talking about Charlytte Black. Of course, Patricia's and Brittany's table was flooded with people, and every once in a while one of them would make a crack on me.

Everyone enjoyed them tease me by yelling out everything from "take out that raggedy ass weave!" to "stop shopping at Goodwill bitch!" And they got the biggest laugh when they started passing around a brown box with the letters CC written on it, which stood for 'Charity for Charlytte.' Embarrassed, I kept my head down and continued to eat the rest of my food. I really tried to just let it all go, but I didn't know how much more of their jokes I could take. I had even planned on ditching school, but before I could get a chance to mentally scope out my exit route, my thoughts were interrupted by a familiar voice.

"Do you mind if I join you?" it asked.

I looked up to see Mrs. Johnson, who had a blue lunch bag in her hand, standing directly over me. The lunchroom had simmered down upon her entrance and the joking ceased a bit. Some of the nosey kids looked in our direction, trying to figure out what was going on.

She waited patiently for me to invite her to sit down, but I didn't say anything.

"I'll take that as a yes," she replied sarcastically, then cheerfully sat down across from me and began to empty out her lunch bag.

Looking at Mrs. Johnson up close allowed me to really see her true beauty. She was a natural. The innocence in her smile made her look way too young to be a teacher. Her eyes were hazel, her skin was smooth and blemish free, and she didn't have on any make-up because she didn't need it. Trying not to be manipulated by her striking presence, I buried my head down into my tray and began to eat very slowly. My food was almost gone and I didn't want any reason to look at her.

"I guess you're wondering why I'm here right?" she asked.

"No, not really," I said. "I think I know why."

"Good. I'm just going to cut to the chase Charlytte,"

she took a bite out of her sandwich and then covered her mouth so that I would not see her food. "I called your house yesterday."

Forgetting all about my plan not to look up, I lifted my head and stared straight into her eyes. I wanted to know what she knew, but most importantly, I wanted to know what Auntie Jo said. It would have given me some comfort knowing that she missed me even the slightest bit.

"I really can’t explain our conversation. It was kind of strange," she shot me down.

With Auntie Jo, 'strange' could only mean one thing; it didn't go well.

She continued.” Your mother-"

"She's not my mother," I cut her off.

"Guardian...grandma...Charlytte, I don't know these things, that's why I'm here trying to find out. Please, just tell me honestly, is everything okay at home?

"Yes, everything's fine Mrs. Johnson."

"Now Charlytte, we both know I have very strong reasons to believe that's not true. I can’t help you if you don’t say anything. Not many teachers will put this much effort into a student’s personal life, so you should appreciate that you have me. I'm not here to judge you. I'm here because I can feel that something’s wrong and I really want to help. Please, just let me do that."

"Mrs. Johnson," I sighed, “I'm good."

"Well I'll tell you what's not *good*,” she pulled a folded piece of paper out of her jean pocket and laid it on the table. "Your grades."

I grabbed the paper and began to open it. Sure enough, it was a history of my grades- a paper full of numbers declining from one hundreds, to eighties, to sixties- and sadly- to forties.

"I'm just not catching on to this new semester stuff," I finally said. "The American Revolution is not my strong point."

"I don't believe that Charlytte. You're an exceptionally bright young lady, one of the brightest I've seen in a long time. I've seen you pick up on new material in a day that takes other kids weeks to learn. You really need to stop making excuses and just tell me what's wrong. At the rate you're going, you won't pass my class and that would be very disappointing to me. Please Charlytte, just let me help you."

Mrs. Johnson looked me deep into my eyes and the passion in her face let me know that her concern for me was real. She paused, giving me a second to open up, but still, she got nothing out of me. After realizing I wasn't about to tell her anything, she finally gave up.

"Well at least I tried," she said to herself. "I guess you can't save someone who doesn't want to be saved."

Ignoring her comment, I continued to pick over my meal and for the remainder of lunch we both sat in silence, chewing on our own food and thinking our own thoughts. I could have opened up to Mrs. Johnson, but talking to her wasn't going to change anything. In fact, it probably would have just made things worse. At least that's what I believed.

I changed my mind about ditching school after lunch. After our talk, I had a slight feeling Mrs. Johnson was keeping a close watch on me. And thankfully I didn't skip because my third block teacher's phone rang in the middle of class. It was one of the administrators calling me up to the office. When I got there, Cederick was waiting in one of the chairs. I don't how he tricked Principal Green into believing that he was my older brother, but he managed to pull it off.

"How was school?" he asked, as he drove away from campus after kidnapping me.

"Fine," I replied.

"Then why the long face?"

"Look, I don't mean to be rude, but I really don't want to talk about it."

I was upset with him for making me go there and I wanted him to know that.

"Then I could take you back and tell them your doctor's appointment was cancelled." He took a sudden turn into the other lane. "That's exactly what I'll do."

“NO!" I yelled out, and then grabbed the steering wheel without even thinking.

"I mean...no," I repeated, this time in a much calmer tone. "Please, you don’t have to do that."

Cederick slightly grinned. He got a little kick out of seeing me panic like that. It wasn’t until he looked into my eyes and saw how scared and pathetic I looked, that he started to feel sorry for me.

"Had a rough day, huh?" he asked before quickly lighting up a paper joint. I still held on to the wheel.

After he was finished, I let go of it, purposely tried to inhale as much smoke as I could, then let out a deep sigh. "Yeah."

"Kids were hard on you?"

"Very. You didn't have to make me go through that. It wouldn't have killed me to miss one day."

"I see it didn't kill you to go either," he shot back. "You should be glad you did."

"Yeah right, and why is that?"

"Because, sometimes you have to go out really bad in order to make a real good comeback."

"Huh? Cederick, what are you talking about?"

"Didn't I tell you that if you went to school lookin' like that today, you wouldn't have to go back that way again?"

"Yeah, I remember you saying something like that."

"Well, just know that I'm a man of my word. When I say I'm going to do something, I do it. And when I do it, I do it big."

Cederick turned his radio up and didn't say another word, leaving me to wonder. He drove to a neighborhood on the eastside of town, and then pulled up to a place that was familiar to me, but strange at the same time. It was a place that, if you were a girl, you visited often. But since I wasn't a normal one, I had never been a day in my life. It was a hair salon.

21: MAKE ME OVER

The entire car ride I couldn't help but keep glancing at myself in the side mirror. You couldn't pay me to believe that I could have gone from a hot mess to a hot commodity in one day. It was just too much for me to take in at one time. Cederick knew I was full of myself, but he understood why. Hell, even he couldn't keep his eyes of me.

"I must admit Charlytte," he said as he pulled his car up to the gas station pump and came to a complete stop. "I'm lovin' this new look. Maybe a little too much."

"Thank you," I blushed. "I'm lovin' you right now for my new look. For real Cederick, I'm so speechless, I could almost cry."

"Well don't cry just yet," he told me. "The best is yet to come."

"What are you talking about *now*?" I asked.

Cederick looked over in my direction and removed a strand of my long, curly hair that was in my face, over to my ear. He had this look in his eyes as if he was still shocked by my attractiveness. I think he knew I had the potential to be beautiful, but he didn't know I was going to be that stunning. Mrs. Harriet, at House of Beauty, did wonders on my head. She took my braids out, sewed in some long black weave, and highlighted it with a couple honey-brown streaks. Then she added had some sex appeal by hooking me up with some loose, bouncy curls. Cederick even paid her extra to do my make-up and arch my eyebrows. It was a long five hours, but it was well worth me feeling and looking like a video vixen in the end.

"How many times do I gotta tell you, when I do something, I don't half step," he replied.

Without giving me a chance to respond, Cederick exited the car. It was a delight just to watch him walk away. His tanktop fitted him nicely and his pants hung just a little bit off his ass- but not too much. Seeing him looking all good like that quickly made me fantasize about having him sexually, but what I was mostly thinking about was what he had meant by his last words. If there was more to what he had already done, then I definitely would be crying by the end of the day. And at least this time, it would be tears of joy.

I sat pondering so long that I didn't see Cederick return until he tapped the side window and snatched me from my thoughts.

"Turn the car off," he pointed to the ignition switch. I obeyed, then watched him from the time he lifted the gas nozzle, up until he forced out the very last drop of oil into his car.

After gassing up, he drove us to a drive-thru for a bite to eat. Then we hopped on the highway. I didn't know where we were going, but I was reluctant to ask. I still liked surprises.

Resting comfortably in my seat, just listening to the music coming out of his speakers, I closed my eyes and enjoyed the ride. It would be an hour before I spoke again.

"We're a little too far out, ain't we?" I asked, after I noticed that we had been riding on I-95 for way too long. "Where are we going?"

Cederick cut down his music and turned to me. Unlike before, he was able to look me in the face without feeling uncomfortable. His eyes were bloodshot red from a Kush joint that he had just smoked, and even I was slightly buzzed from the contact.

"I guess I will just have to ruin the surprise," he replied. "We're going to Jacksonville."

"How is that a surprise?" I asked. "Don't you always go to Jacksonville?"

"Yeah but that's on business. This is pleasure."

I got a little nervous when he said the p word. I immediately thought that he wanted to have his pleasures sexing me. There was no way I could do anything with him. I didn't even know dude like that, and I hoped he didn't think because he put me up in a shack for a night and got my hair done, I owed him something. Besides, I was still sore and hurting after what Mr. Otis had done to me.

"Wha…what do you mean, *pleasure*?" I stuttered.

"The pleasure of treating you to a shopping spree, a mini one that is," he chuckled.

It took a minute for the words 'shopping spree' to sink into my head. Not only did he have my hair looking like my hairdresser was styling for celebrities, he was going to take me shopping in J-ville. I tried everything to tone down the huge smile I displayed on my face, but nothing worked.

Me? Shopping?" I asked, while still cheesing. "Cederick, are you kiddin' me? You don't have to do that. You really have already done enough."

"I know I don't have to," he sparked up another joint. "I want to."

Cederick inhaled the smoke, and then released it. Although I was happy he was treating me to all that stuff, I couldn't help but wonder what his real motive was. He didn't know me that well, and he didn't seem like the soft-hearted, cake-daddy type. It just had to be a catch. And if it was, I wanted to make sure my gloves were on when that curve ball came flying my way.

"So," I built up the courage to ask him, "you just pick up random women and treat them to shopping sprees, just because?"

Cederick was just about to take another puff, but he paused at the question. Then he turned and mugged me with those evil-looking eyes, and sat the blunt back down in the ash tray.

"You really believe that? You think I look at you as some random chick." He paused and waited for a response. Crept out by his eyes, I said anything so that he would hurry up and put his focus back on the road.

"I don't know. I mean, we talked a couple of times, but we really don't know each other that well. Honestly, I don't know what to think."

Cederick picked the blunt back up from out of the tray and inhaled it.

"Not trying to sound full of myself, little one, but I'm not your average nigga. And I'm definitely not one of those young bucks you're used to fucking with. I know you just met me and all, but I'mma need you to understand that, and fast....It don't take a year for me to figure a person out. I don't believe in that shit. I've been on my own since I was thirteen years old. So that means I done seen a lot of shit and met a lot of people in my lifetime. I can tell a lot about a person within in the first couple seconds of me meeting them."

He blew out some smoke, and again, took another long hit.

"And I'm not one of those thirsty ass niggas who lie and try to play hoes just to get some pussy. That shit is lame and elementary to me. I'm a grown ass man. If I want to fuck a bitch, she gone know it off the top. Plus, most of these hoes ain't worth the nut. There are only a couple of females out here that I trust, and that's my sister and my mama, and even they questionable at times. It's not every day that I meet a young woman who catches my attention, but when I do, I'm interested in learning more about her. And if I see that she's in need, I definitely don't mind helping her out. Point blank."

I was hypnotized by his words. How he looked when he said them. How he sounded when he said them. The way his lips formed when he made S sounds. I was captivated by it all, and luckily, he continued on.

"Look shawty, what I'm trying to say is…I'm a young nigga gettin' to some paper. Hoes practically throw they pussy at me, I don't have to bribe some teenage chick. Besides, I'm about to be twenty-five and you're just sixteen. I wouldn't ruin your life like that. I done fucked sisters, mamas and daughters, best friends- that shit is old to me. Now I'm all about getting to this money, so you don't ever have to think that I have some secret agenda."

"I sat at the table in that restaurant with you and was completely amazed by the way you held an intelligent conversation with me. I would have never guessed that you were only sixteen, that shit just did something to me. So, when I saw you last night I knew that a strong-headed young lady, like yourself, must have been going through some crazy shit for you to be asking for my help."

Cederick rubbed my left cheek softly with his index finger. I almost melted at his touch.

"You a queen little mama, and you deserve the best. You too special to look the way you did earlier today. Plus, the fact that you were willing to go to school looking tore up like that, showed me just how strong you really are. A nigga understand that, and that's why I'm doing this. That's the only reason."

Cederick words encouraged and made me feel good again. They were exactly what I needed to hear. Honestly, I believed him when he said he wasn't trying to fuck me, and that made me want him even more.

After hearing everything he had said to me, all I could do was just sit back and listen to the remainder of his Tupac's *Greatest Hits* CD.

When we made it to Jacksonville, I stared out my window, amazed by all the beautiful attractions. It was my first time being out of state, so even the traffic lights were a site for me. The Town Center mall was lovely too. It housed some of the most expensive name brand department stores. A rush of excitement hit me as we passed each one.

After two hours of shopping, Cederick had already spent about seven-hundred dollars on my stuff alone. With a little help from him, I picked out a nice Jean all-in-one Guess short-set, a couple of casuals fits from the Gap, a cute linen Ralph Lauren dress, a pair of Polo shoes, a pair of Jordan's, and two pairs of Gucci heels. I felt like I hit the jackpot because I had never worn anything that came from the Ordale City Mall, unless it was one of Keisha's hand-me-downs.

The last place we went was to Juicy Couture. Cederick said he wanted me to pick out something nice because he was taking me to a fancy Seafood restaurant. Juicy Couture was just a small boutique, but their clothes, their purses, and their shoe collection was amazing.

Going for something classy, I skimmed through the rack of dresses. Of course Cederick was trailing right behind me, also searching. He knew that I didn't have a very good fashion sense, and if I was stepping out with him, I was going to have to be on point.

"How about this?" Cederick asked, holding up a black silk mini-dress with the back out. I loved the dress, but I knew the bruises on my upper body wouldn't go very well with it.

"I like it," I replied, picking up something that was a little less revealing. "But let me just keep looking."

"Aaaw c'mon Charlytte, I really think you'd look good in this one," he said.

Attempting to persuade me furthermore, he called out to the petite white saleswoman. "Hey Miss! Wouldn't this dress look fly on her?"

Stepping out from behind the counter, the woman answered, "Yes, of course."

Then she led herself over in our direction to get a better look. "I've had my eye on that dress since it first arrived here. Honey, I think you're the perfect fit for it."

Of course you're gonna say that. You work off commission. I said to myself.

I looked up at Cederick, then over to the woman. They were looking at me as if I was about to reveal their fortunes, just waiting for me to give them my answer.

"Uhm...I don't know about that one. It's a little too short," I disappointed them both. "Cederick, can I please just look some more?"

Unfortunately, Cederick wasn't taking no for an answer. He saw me in that dress and he wasn't going to leave me alone until that vision became a reality. He thanked the lady for her advice, grabbed me by the hand, and pulled me over to a full-sized mirror in the corner of the store.

"Look at you," he said as he pushed my fragile body up in front of it. "Can't you see that you're beautiful?"

I just stood there, shamefully looking at my reflection. My long, wavy locks and my cute made up face almost made me look unrecognizable to my own self. But even though I was standing before a new and approved me, I wasn't completely happy about it.

True enough, the person I saw was very beautiful. You couldn't tell just by looking, that I was going through so much. Still, I didn't see the Charlytte that I was used to seeing. The smoky gray mascara did a good job of covering up the pain that manifested in my eyes and the ruby red lipstick coated with the cherry favored lip gloss, made it very easy to believe that nothing but sweet stories could exit my lips. Don't get me wrong, it was cool and all, but it just wasn't me. And strangely, that bothered me.

"I know Cederick, I feel beautiful." I said, pulling my eyes from my reflection and placing them back on him.

"Then quit being so afraid to embrace it," he told me. "What's the point of having something nice and not being able to show it off?"

Cederick stood behind me and also looked in the mirror. I couldn't help but notice that we looked really cute together. I knew we weren't a couple, but if we were to hook up, it wouldn't have been a bad look. He wrapped his arms around my waist, put the dress in my hand, then said, "Now I let you pick out whatever you wanted today, just do me this one favor and try this on. Is that too much to ask?"

I sighed briefly and finally surrendered, "No, I guess not."

Although I wasn't happy about it, I took the dress from Cederick and stared down at it. I mean, it was perfect, if I was twenty-one. But I wasn't, and I wasn't comfortable putting it on. I really wanted to tell him that, but the look in his eyes and that power he carried in his deep voice just made me want to do whatever it was he asked of me. Without saying another word, I grabbed the dress and headed for the fitting room.

Cederick stood at full attention, watching me as I did a three-sixty-spin-around while modeling for him the silky black dress that hugged my body oh so tightly. My pecan brown thighs were smooth as a baby's back and nicely structured like a Michael Angelo sculpture. My stomach was flat and well-portioned with my waist, and the lumps from my small breasts were slightly revealed in my cleavage. I must admit, I looked damn good.

"I like, I like," Cederick smiled, looking very proud of the job he'd done on me. I looked to see if he noticed the marks on my back, but he seemed to be too caught up on my ass to recognize it.

"Hold up, wait right here for a second!" he said, then ran off and came back with a pair of black heels. They were open-toed and they strapped around the ankles. Basic and simple, but still cute. I wasn't the heel wearing type of chick and Cederick knew that, but that's what he wanted, so that's what he got.

I tried the shoes on with the dress and they both went hand and hand. He also picked out some gold accessories for me and a small clutch bag, and even told the saleswoman to throw away my old clothes. In the end, we both were pleased with the way I looked.

It took a couple of hours for me to get used to walking in those heels and even then I still was staggering a bit. Cederick kept me on his side all the way up until we took our seats at the Crabshack Cafe. He played that father figure role really well, but deep down, I knew he liked the idea of me looking like his woman.

Politely, the waiter greeted us and then took our orders. While we waited for the food, I couldn't help but think about how different I felt walking out of that last department store. It was crazy how much more friendly people were when I actually looked like something. Normally when I walked the streets, they would just stare in disgust or try to avoid me by looking in the opposite direction. Now they were speaking and couldn't keep their eyes off me. I had the pleasure watching people- guys and girls- lust over my beauty, and I must say that I really enjoyed it.

I also enjoyed the fried shrimps, fried oysters, and crabcake platter that Cederick and I both ordered. We found out that we both shared similar taste in food, music, and had a deep interest in arts and literature. We talked about all sorts of things, picking up where we left off at Marco's. I felt like Cinderella in a make-believe world. The perfect clothes, perfect restaurant, and what seemed to be the perfect man, was all something I only dreamt about. There was no denying that Spring break for me kicked off with a blast, and even if it got worse, it would have still been the best. Cederick and I devoured our food, leaving no trace of anything behind. He paid for the meal and tipped the waiter twenty dollars for her very friendly service.

After we ate, we headed straight to the Howard Johnson hotel. Cederick didn't plan on staying the night in J-ville, but after his boss, Hi-C, called and asked for a favor that required him to stay a little while longer, he had no other choice. Besides, we were worn out from all the shopping and site-seeing we did, so it wasn't a problem for either one of us.

Cederick checked us into a king-size room and made sure I got in safely.

"Can I come with you, pleease?" I begged, hoping that he would feel sorry for me and let me ride. I knew that sympathetic crap didn't work with him, but I tried anyway. When Cederick meant something, he meant it. If I didn't know anything else about him, I knew that.

"No babygirl," he rejected me. "This is business. You know I don't get down like that," then he kissed me on my forehead. "I'll be back in about two hours. There are a couple things I need to talk to you about anyway, so try and stay up if you can."

"Is something wrong?" I worried.

"Naw, everything's fine shorty. It's nothing major," he assured me. "I'll be back, so stay put. Don't leave this room for anything. Not even for a drink at the soda machine. I don't want anything to happen to you on my watch."

"Now you know you don't have to tell me that," I said, sarcastically.

"Oh c'mon now Charlytte, don't act like you don't walk the streets," he joked. "I gotta keep my eyes on you. Ya know, guide you a bit."

"Yeah whatever, just hurry back," I rushed him.

"I will."

When Cederick closed the door, I locked it behind him. Then I took one last look in the mirror before undressing for the night. Once I had gotten over myself, I took an unusually long shower, wrapped my body up in a towel, and waited up for Cederick until I couldn't wait anymore.

Cederick and I made it back to Ordale around noon the next day. He woke me up very early that morning and before leaving, we caught a breakfast buffet, browsed around the flea market, then headed out. I didn't know what time he made it back to the hotel, but I do know that when I woke up, he was curled up in a blanket on the floor. My time in J-ville was fun, and although I didn't have a home there, I was glad to be headed back to Ordale.

Cederick needed to talk to me about some party that was being thrown at the place where I was staying. Hi-C's, the guy owned that big ass house, younger brother Richard, was a part of some entertainment group and every year he hosted a Spring Break Pool Bash in his backyard. By the way Cederick described the party, it must have been very well-known and exclusive. And after he mentioned it, I did remember Keisha and Shannon bragging one year about getting into some guy named Rich's Annual Pool Bash. I assumed it was the same guy that Cederick was referring to.

Cederick's problem with me was simple; he didn't want me there. He told me he just wanted me to study and prepare for school, which would be approaching right after the weekend was up. I wasn't too upset at the fact that I couldn't attend, and at first, it was no big deal to me, but when Saturday came around and all those beautiful people crowded up in Hi-C's backyard, staying in the shed was harder than I thought it would be.

The evening was bright and shiny, perfect weather for a nice swim. The D.J. was playing all the latest feel good jams, the bar stand was flooded with every kind of alcohol, and the smell of barbecue maneuvered its way through the crevices of the shed door. I knew I was supposed to be studying, but I spent most of my time peeping out the window, looking at everybody in their swimwear with envy. It seemed like every girl was beautiful. That was a requirement. The promo flyer Cederick showed me clearly said, "If you aint cute, expect to get the boot."

People were mangling with one another, some were taking a swim, but most of them were lounging around just grooving to the music. Every now and then I would hear the crowd cheer loudly as someone got dunked into the pool. Cederick explained to me the famous tradition where, in order for a girl to get into the water, a boy had to dunk her in it. That signified that he liked her and if she felt the same about him, then by the end of the night, the pool wasn't going to be the only thing getting her wet.

They got one girl so good. She was standing up in a circle talking with her friends when a real sexy chocolate guy scooped her up from behind and threw her straight into the pool. The crowd cheered and laughed as she hopped up from under the water, laughing right along with them. After wiping the water from her face, I couldn't believe who I recognized the girl to be. It just couldn't be. I pressed my eyes against the window to get a better look, and sure enough, that sexy dark man was choosing on my cousin Keisha.

"Keisha!" I shouted as I ignored Cederick's wishes for me to stay in the shed and ran full speed to get my shoes. I already had on clothes, a bad Guess outfit at that. I made sure I was cute just in case Cederick changed his mind about letting me come out to join them.

Scrambling around the room, I gave up on finding my sandals and just grabbed the pink bedroom slippers that Cederick had also bought for me. I ran straight out the door towards Keisha, not caring at all if Cederick saw me. I hadn't seen my cousin in years and nothing was going to stop me.

Keisha had made her way out of the pool by the time I made it out of the door. She was so busy laughing with her friends, and cursing out the guys, that she didn't even see me walk up on her.

"Brandon, you play too damn much!" she shouted at him and his homeboys, while they all just laughed about it.

"Keisha?" I said as I approached her, then asked just to be sure, “Is that you?"

Keisha turned around to me slowly with a, *who-is-this-bitch* look on her face and I just stood there looking pitiful, hoping that she recognized me. It was undeniably an awkward moment for everybody. She was wondering. I was wondering. Her friends were wondering too. With her face still tooted, she looked me up and down and it wasn't until she focused in on the scar, that she finally recognized who I was.

"Oh my Gosh! This my little sister Charlytte y'all!" she yelled out to her friends, and then ran to me. "Come here girl and give me a hug!"

I embraced Keisha whole-heartedly and almost cried just knowing that I had reunited with her again. We screamed a couple more times and hugged some more too. People were looking and wondering what all the hype was about but we weren't thinking about them.

"Goodness Charlytte, you have gotten so big girl! I see you stylin' too!" she said as she checked out my denim Guess jeans and my yellow Guess shirt. "It's good to see that you have been keeping up with yourself."

"Thank you," I blushed, but inside I was secretly saying, *if you only knew the half.*

"And look at that ass!" she spun me around to get a full look. "Yep, this is definitely my little sis. What you doing here girl?

"Oh nothing, hanging out," I said, trying to leave out the details. "I'm a just friend of Cederick."

"Oooooh Ced, that's what's up sis, doing big things I see. How about I take you to grab a drink and you can come kick it with us for a little while? We got some catching up to do."

Keisha grabbed me by the hand, then turned to her girls. "I'll be right back y'all."

I followed her like I was seven years old again, but instead of going to an ice-cream truck, we were going to a bar stand. As she walked a little ahead of me, I noticed how well she maintained her beauty. With her hair cut in a bob, she still looked seventeen; only now she had a firey red highlight in the front to spice it up.

Nope, Keisha hadn't changed a bit, and if she did pick up weight, luckily it was only in her hips and breasts. She had not one stretch mark or discoloration on her body and her stomach was just as flat as mine. I saw that she finally got that rose tattoo she always wanted on her lower back too. She even sported a small nose ring. *Cool*. I thought.

When we made it to the bar, Keisha got herself an apple martini and a shot of Parrot Bay. Just as she was about to order my drink, a male hand firmly gripped my wrist and pulled me in the opposite direction.

"She'll pass on the drinking," Cederick rudely said to Keisha and began walking me back towards the shed.

"Wait a minute," I whispered to him, trying not to make a scene. Then I looked to Keisha who had a confused look on her face. "That's my sister. Please let me talk to her."

Cederick ignored my plea and continued to pull me away. He had no expression on his face and said not one word as he flew me through the crowds of people. Completely embarrassed, I looked to see if anyone was watching. Luckily, they were too busy having their own fun.

Once we made it inside the shed, Cederick broke out of his silence and immediately began to give me a piece of his mind.

"I thought I specifically told you not to come out of here!" he shouted as he slammed the shed door. I jumped at the sound of it. Cederick was normally a laid back type of dude, so to see him lash out like that was a scary surprise.

"That was my cousin!" I yelled. "I haven't seen her in forever!"

"I don't care if it was Jesus Christ himself! I told you not to go out there. You should have listened to me!"

"You mean to tell me I can't even holla at my cousin without goin' through you first. I just knew it was a catch to this shit."

Cederick walked up on me slowly. I back up on the bed, afraid of his approaching presence.

"I told you, you gone have to smarten up if you want to stick around. You think this shit is about control?"

"That's what it seems like to me," I said, giving him much attitude, but still moving backwards at the same time. "What's the point of me not being able to go out there anyway? It's just a party. That's stupid. I don't care if you got girlfriends. I wasn't going to be all up in your face, if that's what you were worried about."

"You know you really startin' to get on my nerves with all this assuming and shit." By now he was all up in my face. "This shit ain't about me being in control or you gettin' up wit' ya cousin."

"Then what is it about?" I asked. "You say you always keep it real, but yet you always acting so secretive about shit."

"It's a difference between being real and being real stupid. Remember that."

"No," I disagreed. "What's real stupid, was you snatching me up like that. You really didn't have to embarrass me that way."

Cederick was so close to me that I could feel the air that was seeping out of his nostrils repeatedly tapping my forehead.

"You think I give a fuck about you being embarrassed? No!" he answered his own question. "I got bigger problems...The folks have been on this man's ass lately, just waiting for him to slip up so that they can throw him in jail. This party's been going on at this same spot for damn near twelve years, and that's exactly how long they've been trying to shut it down. You don't think they will be glad to know that an under-aged girl is at a party where alcohol is being served. It's small petty shit like that that could fuck up our whole operation."

Cederick walked back towards the door and grabbed the handle. "I think that's well worth you getting your little fucking feelings hurt."

Cederick slammed the door behind him, leaving me all alone and feeling like shit. After hearing the real reason he wanted me to stay inside, I started to feel guilty, and hoped that he wasn't too upset to forgive me. Worse, I didn't even get a chance to tell Keisha goodbye. There was no telling when, or if, I would ever get to see her again. I tried to forget about everything that had just happened and started doing something I should have been doing all along, studying.

"Charlytte, Charlytte," someone called. "Get up, babygirl."

It was a couple hours later. Cederick was sitting up on the edge of the bed, nudging at my thighs. I opened my eyes and looked around. It took a minute, but I finally realized that I had fallen asleep with my face in my Social Studies book. Quickly, I sat up and wiped the drool from around my mouth, hoping he didn't see it.

"Wha...what time is it?" I whispered, "And why are you sweating?"

Cederick touched his forehead with the tip of his index finger, and then looked down at the moisture.

"It's 2:12. We just shut everything down. I had to put all those chairs back up by myself. That's the last time I'm doin' that shit. Niggas love to party, but get ghost when it's time to clean up," he said, then swiped the sweat from his finger onto his jeans. "I'm good though, just tired."

"Oh, I bet. Was there any food left?" I asked, after a hunger pain suddenly struck my stomach.

"Yeah, I put you a plate up in the microwave," he said. "If you were hungry you should have called me."

I watched Cederick carefully as he rose slowly from the bed. He stretched his arms way up in the air, yawned, and then walked over to the closet to grab himself a blanket.

"I know, but you seemed to be really mad at me. I didn't want to bother you any more than I already have."

"I was mad at you. But that doesn't mean I was going to let you starve," he frowned.

For better cushioning, Cederick folded the maroon comforter in half, before laying it out on the floor. He had been spending the night with me the last couple of days, but never once did he sleep- or even try to sleep- in the bed with me.

"That's why I woke you…to tell you that I apologize for embarrassing you like that. I understand that you're probably feeling alone out here, so seeing your cousin must have really made your day. I get that."

After his cot was laid out perfect enough for him, he made his way back over to the bed and sat down on the edge of it. "I just got a little upset because shit has been really crazy lately. Niggas snitching, the folks lurking, and I just keep having these crazy ass dreams about me being trapped a brown box. I'm protective like that because it's some heavy shit going on around here. And I would hate to see Herb, or any one of us, go down for some bullshit. Especially not for some I caused."

"I understand," I simply said.

"For real, Charlytte. I just need you to trust me. Trust my judgment and understand that if I tell you something, you need to respect it and abide, no matter what the situation is. Got that?"

"Yeah, I got it." I answered softly, like a four-year-old getting chastised by her father. I swear that boy had that kind of power over me.

"Good," he said. Then he planted one wet kiss on my forehead. I loved when he did that. It made me feel like a woman and a little girl at the same time. "And cheer up, why you still look so sad."

I dropped my head down and felt a little cool air hit my forehead, where Cederick had just kiss me. "I'm okay. I just wish I could have at least got her number."

"Who Keisha?" he perked up. "That's not a problem. I can give you her number right now."

Cederick reached for his touch screen phone and began gliding through his contacts.

"You know my cousin Keisha?" I asked excitedly, but curious at the same time.

"Man, who don't know Keisha?" he replied. He got up and tore a piece of paper out of the phonebook. Then took a pen from out of his back pocket and wrote her number down on it.

When he finished, I snatched the paper right out of his hand. I didn't know what he could have possibly meant by that *'everybody knows Keisha'* comment, but I was too excited about having her number to dwell on it. With the help of Cederick, once again, I felt much better. He knew exactly how to cheer a girl up. I definitely felt a sense of security with him. And even though he wasn't sleeping in bed with me, I was sure as hell glad that he was there.

22: SOMETHING TO DO

Tupac's *All Eyez On Me* was all I could sing in my head when I walked into Mrs. Johnson's class, because every jaw dropped and every eye was centered on ya' girl. Nobody could believe that lil' rachet ass Charlytte Black was walking into the class with some bad ass weave, a fly Guess jean dress, some black Nine West sandals, sixty-five dollars' worth of gold accessories, and a nice ass black Juicy Couture bag.

Cederick dropped me off to school bright and early, but I purposely walked into class a couple minutes late so that I could make my grand entrance. All of the kids were stunned by how beautiful I was. Even Mrs. Johnson, although she tried to hide it, was completely in shock too.

I walked to my seat slowly, so that everybody could get a fair opportunity to check me out. I even dropped my pencil when I passed Dominic, just so I could bend over and show him my pretty, plumped ass. His captivating stare, along with the dropping of his bottom lip, let me know that he was lovin' it.

The entire first period, Mrs. Johnson tried so hard to stay focused on teaching us, but it only made her stutter and choke up every time she took a single glance over in my direction. Although I still didn't participate in any of the class discussions, I paid way more attention to my lessons than I did before. I was feeling a lot better about myself; therefore I was more interested in learning.

Thanks to all the attention my classmates were giving me, first period went by pretty quickly. If being a celebrity was anything close to what I experienced when I walked the halls after Mrs. Johnson dismissed us, then I must have been a superstar. The guys were staring, the girls were glaring, and I knew within minutes, that I was the talk of the school.

I also knew that Patricia and Brittany had already gotten the 'Charlytte Black Makeover' memo, because when I got out of the lunch line, both of them were posted up near my table. They were too thirsty to see if the rumors were true. Of course I strutted passed them, and made sure I looked them dead in their eyes when I took my seat. They both tooted their noses up at me and displayed a disgusted look on their faces. I just knew they were saying to themselves, '*this bitch looks so good til it makes me fucking mad.*' And I knew I must have been killing 'em, because they even felt the need to walk by my table just so Brittany could say, "bitch you still a bum" underneath her breath. I wanted so badly to respond by saying, "that beats being a jealous hoe," but I didn't give them the satisfaction.

I wasn't worried the least bit about those hoochies. I was too busy enjoying my day, which started off good, but ended even better when Cederick pulled up illegally on the bus ramp, and almost every kid in the school got the pleasure of seeing me get escorted into his fly ass ride.

Over the next couples months, at school I managed to bring all my D's and F's up to C's and even got a chance to re-do my current events presentation. Just to be fair, Mrs. Johnson promised all her students- who did the assignment when asked- one extra toward point towards their final grade. Of course me, and the other two kids who failed to have theirs on time, didn't get the extra point. But we weren't complaining about it.

Cederick continued to take me shopping and would even drop by the shed to bring me clothes and shoes every time he went for himself. The kids at school were waiting for my downfall, thinking that my flow of new fits would soon run short. But I proved them wrong and kept them guessing each day I arrived wearing something different. Disappointing for them, down to the very last day, I never wore the same thing twice.

Speaking of the last day, as usual, Cederick came to scoop me up from the bus ramp. The teachers were complaining, constantly telling me that he wasn't allowed to do that. But he didn't care. Cederick was his own boss. He did what the fuck he wanted to do, when he wanted to do it.

As we drove off, I turned around and looked back at Franklin High, and at Mrs. Parsley, who was shaking her head at his disrespect. Although I had fun showing off that last semester, I was ready for the summer. I needed a break.

"So, where we headed today?" I asked, after I put on my seatbelt.

Cederick was looking very good, if I must say. He was wearing a white tanktop with some dark blue Sean John jeans. Friday's were causal days for him, so I knew he would also be sporting one of his fitted hats with the letters O-R-D custom-stitched on it. And as it usually did, the car smelled like straight weed smoke.

"*You're* going back to the spot, *I'm* going to make a couple of runs."

"Aaaw man," I whined like a little girl. "Why can't I go with you this time?"

Cederick made his way off of the school premises and then lit his joint. "Because, we been over this a million times… *my* business is *no* business for you."

"I understand that, I promise I do. But Ced, you don't think I get tired of being cooped up in that shed all day? It's been like two months now, and with school being out, I really don't have nothing to do."

Don't get me wrong, I loved the fact that he was feeding and clothing me. And I didn't want to seem like I was complaining- even though that's exactly what I was doing- but I really was growing tired of being shut in all the time. Cederick would leave for days, then come back for days. Leave for hours, then come back for hours. Some nights he'd stayed, and some he didn't. It was just too confusing for me. Like him, I wanted to get out and do more things; and getting a summer job, so that I could make my own chips, was definitely one of them.

"It's plenty to do out here, Charlytte," Cederick said as he took a puff of his joint. "You just gotta put yaself out there. It's not like I'm holding you hostage."

"I know that Ced," I sighed. "I know."

"And what about Keisha?" he asked excitedly, as if a great idea just popped into his head. "She just been around Herb's crib the other day. You were in school though. She didn't exactly come for you, but she did ask me why she hadn't heard from you yet. You should call her and see what's up."

After stopping at a nearby gas station, Cederick found Keisha's number in his phone and handed it to me before hopping out of the car. I had been wanting to call Keisha, but I was too nervous. We just seemed so different. She was glamorous, popular, and had a lot of friends: I, on the other hand, didn't know who or what I was. At the party, I thought she was more fascinated with how well I looked and dressed, that once she got to know me and found out that I was a homeless desperate chick, she would just abandon me like she did ten years ago.

Courageously, I pressed the talk button, placed the phone to my ear, and jammed to Keisha ringback- Kelis's Bossy- until she answered the phone.

"What it do boo!" someone answered.

I knew it was Keisha, but I asked for her anyway.

"Hello, may I speak to Keisha." I said, bashfully.

"Speaking," she answered. "This must be Charlytte?"

"Yeah, it's me," I confirmed.

"Bout time, bitch!" she shouted, sounding very excited to be receiving a call from me. Although I wasn't too fond of her calling me a bitch, I knew she didn't mean any harm by it.

"I swear I was just talking about you," she said. "What's going on hun?"

"Oh nothing. Just glad school is out, trying to find something to get into."

"Look at you, trynna talk grown. Ain't like you can get in the club," she laughed. "Hol…hold on for a minute, sis."

Keisha placed me on hold and began talking to someone else." This Charlytte on the phone right now, bitch! Talk to her."

There was a quick pause, which gave me time to wonder. I didn't know who could have possibly wanted to speak with me. Could it be Korey? Keyshawn? Or even worse, Auntie Jo? My thoughts were suddenly interrupted by another female voice."

"I know this ain't lil' bad ass Chartlytte!" the mystery girl said.

"Yeah this me," I chuckled. "Who this?"

"This Shannon gurl."

"Shannon?" I perked up. "Oh my gosh! What's going on!"

Just as I could never forget Keisha, I could never forget Shannon either. They were like two peas in a pod. Shannon was the one who took up for me and saved me from getting beat by Keisha, so many times. I was glad to hear from the both of them.

"I didn't know y'all still rolled together," I said.

"Yeah, you know we the ghetto Thelma and Louise," she joked.

"True homies," I agreed. "I heard you got kids too. How are they?"

"Yes gurl, I got four of them little monsters and I ain't having no' mo. They 'bout to run me crazy."

"Damn, four! I bet!" I laughed. "I see y'all ain't changed a bit."

"Girl nope. Same people, just different situations, ya know?"

"Trust me, I know."

Shannon got really quiet, as if she went into deep thought, or maybe was just reflecting back on her life. After a few seconds, she snapped back into the conversation.

"But speaking of changes, Keisha tells me you're all grown-up and fresh to death!"

"You know how Keisha is, always overdoing something," I said trying to be modest, but on the contrary, I touched my soft, dark weave just to remind myself that I was definitely hot. It still looked just as good as it did the first day. I had that expensive hair: it could last six months if I wanted it to.

"Well when I'mma be able to see you and judge it for myself?" Shannon asked me.

"Shit, what are y'all doing now?" I asked, hoping that they could squeeze some time in for me.

"Hold up, Keisha's the one driving. Let me let you talk to her."

Shannon and I said our farewells and then she gave the phone to Keisha, who was now ordering some food at a drive-thru window. She was arguing with someone about not getting her drinks right. I had to wait a good little minute before she came back to the phone.

"These muthafuckas act so fucking slow! First one person take your order, then somebody else start taking ya order, and then they wonder why they keep fucking people shit up!.. Hello," Keisha finally said to me. "I'm sorry Charlytte, what's up."

I laughed on the inside after hearing how upset she was about her food.

"I just wanted to know what y'all were about to do. Maybe we could get up," I said.

"Hell yeah, that's cool sis. We just left the mall and now we're grabbin' a bite to eat. After that, we're gonna head over to the nail salon. I see yours wasn't done," she added. "Just meet us down at New Millennium and let me treat you to a lil' mannie and peddie."

"Okay cool. I will see if Cederick will drop me off. He’s pumpin’ gas right now, so I’ll just have to call you back."

"Okay boo. If I see you, I see you. If I don't, then I understand," she said, clearly referring to the pool party incident.

"Oh no, don't worry. I will be there."

23: YEAH I'M DOWN

Cederick agreed to drop me off at the nail salon, and Keisha agreed to take me back to Hi'C's when we were done. When we got there, he gave me a hundred dollars for spending money, kissed me on my forehead, and sent me on my way. The forehead kiss wasn't as cute as it used to be anymore, probably because I was starting to want more. My body was all healed up, and the scary thoughts of Mr. Otis weren't haunting me like they used to. I wanted Cederick in every kind of way. Although sex should have been the last thing on my mind, I had gotten used to having it- whether it was with someone I wanted to have it with or not.

I really liked Cederick though. He just didn't seem to show any type of serious interest in me. I wanted to tell him so badly how I felt, but I didn't want to push him away, or possibly get rejected.

"Call me when you're on your way back, so I could open up for you," he said.

"Okay, I will."

As I walked away, I could feel him watching my ass as it moved from left to right in my Dereon jeans. I was satisfied with that, because I knew somewhere deep down inside of him, he wanted me.

When I walked into New Millennium Nails, Keisha and Shannon were in the waiting area. They were so busy talking that they didn't even noticed me approaching them. They were having a heated conversation about who was the better rapper out of Young Jeezy and T.I.

Surprising them, I blurted, "Told y'all I would be here!" and as soon as they saw me, they both stopped bickering and rushed over to greet me.

"Girl, you really have gotten big!" Shannon said as she checked me out.

And so have you, I said to myself when I saw that she had put on a few extra pounds herself. But even though she was a little on the pudgy side, she still had that same pretty face and didn't look too bad considering the fact that she pushed out four kids. I had definitely seen worse.

We all sat down, and I joined them in their Jeezy verses T.I. dispute until it was Keisha and Shannon’s turn to be pampered by the two Chinese women. It wasn’t until that moment that I started to wonder what I was doing in a nail salon. The hair, the clothes, and all the cute little accessories were one thing, but getting my nails done, I knew for sure just wasn't me.

We were only in the salon for a little over an hour before we all were finished. Then afterwards, we hopped into Keisha’s all Black 2005 Impala and I just couldn't help but keep playing with my nails in the back seat. I really didn't like way they felt on me, but it was no denying that they made my fingers look much prettier. Thanks to Keisha, I had a French manicure on both my hands and feet and I even got my eyebrows waxed. I could only wonder what Cederick was going to think.

"It's Friday bitches!" Keisha shouted as she pulled out of the Ordale City Shopping Plaza. "What y'all wanna do?"

"I don't care, as long as I'm home by ten-thirty. You know Monde works that eleven-to-seven shift this week," Shannon reminded Keisha.

"Oh yeah, I almost forgot about that. I don't want that nigga callin' and cussin' me out like he did the last time for bringing you home too late."

"Shut up bitch, leave my man alone," Shannon said, defending her boo. "You know that boy is fool the fuck up."

"Yeah I know, he's a good dude though," Keisha said. "Besides, we got Charlytte anyway. Ain't like we can go out for no drinks. I just let Lexis hold the fake I.D to go to Miami."

"Damn shol' did," Shannon remembered. "That's cool, we can just grab a bottle and go to yo'spot. I ain't trying to be out like that anyway."

"Yeah, me neither." Keisha agreed. "I ain't wit that shit today. These mutherfuckas losing they minds out here in these streets. Safest place to be is in the house."

Keisha quickly glanced at me, then turned back to the road. "Is that cool with you Charlytte?"

I didn't care what we did, as long as I was out of that shed.

"Yeah, that's cool."

Shannon turned her whole neck around to face me. I was sitting directly behind her. "Charlytte, you drinking and all now?" she asked.

"Yeah, every now and then," I replied.

"Oh shit nye! What you be sipping on?"

"Wild Wine Rose," I said, with confidence.

Shannon and Keisha looked to each other at the same time and bursted out into laughter. I didn't know what was so funny, but I wanted to.

"What?" I asked, puzzled.

"Girl, that's that old people, cheap shit. Keep drinkin' that and you gone be fool the fuck up too," Keisha joked.

"Don't worry lil' sis, we gone put you up on some real shit. What you know 'bout that Grey Goose?" Shannon asked, still chuckling.

"I heard of it, "I said," but I ain't never had none."

"Well that's all we drink," Keisha replied. "That expensive shit, and all we smoke is that loud."

"Speak for yourself Keisha," Shannon said to her. "I'm smoking whatever's being put up in the air. You smoke too, Charlytte?" she asked.

"Nope, but I do get tempted at times."

"Well sis, you ain't gotta be scared *nor tempted* around us. All we do is get high. It's just weed, ain't nothing wrong with that," Keisha said. "You down to hit it?"

I wasn't really sure what I was down to do, but I did know that I always wanted to smoke weed every time I would smell it, or see that face Cederick made when he took that first puff. Hell, I was already stepping out of my character, so why not give something else a try. I flicked my long, luxurious hair with my newly pressed fingernail, then threw my Juicy purse over my lap and answered them with class.

"Yeah, I'm down."

24: ADAM'S APPLE

Classic hits from a Best of Mary J. Blidge CD blasted from Keisha's car speakers, and I almost caught a cramp in my stomach from laughing so hard at her and Shannon sing every word to 'Not gon cry.' Watching them really made me think of true friendship and how important it was to have that. I knew that over the years they probably had their differences- especially dealing with Keisha's crazy ass- but at the end of the day, they were still holding on strong and I was proud to see that. I only hoped that me and Keisha could have eventually had that same type of bond. That would have made life a whole lot better for me.

We made a stop to the liquor store for the Grey Goose, hit the convenient store for the two-for-three blunt special, and then headed to Keisha's spot. She lived in a gorgeous townhouse on the Southside of Ordale. It was a two bedroom, up and downstairs, with a nice front yard and upstairs balcony. I didn't know what Keisha did for a living, but I was hoping she told me, so that I could know what I needed to do to have a place as nice as hers.

It was around seven o'clock when we finally made it her house. We only had a couple of hours to chill before Shannon had to go home to her kids, and I had to be back to Cederick. Keisha led me threw her fabulously

decorated hallway, to her even more fabulous den, where I had the pleasure of taking a seat on her lovely leather loveseat. Then she immediately livened up the atmosphere by turning on her mp3 player and letting some mellow sounds pour out of her nice Rocket speakers that were planted up on the wall. A combination of the sounds, the sweet mango smell of the house, and the calm, relaxing colors of the furniture, put me at ease and made me feel like I never wanted to leave there.

Shannon didn't follow us. Instead, she went to the kitchen to unpack the brown bag. I got a good view of her from where I was sitting and watched her as she began filling Keisha's blender up with ice from the ice machine. Then she took a pack of daiquiri mix and some fresh strawberries from out of Keisha's frig, and began whipping us up some drinks.

I could tell the room that I was sitting in was the smoking area because on Keisha's all black coffee table was a weed grinder, a bong, an ashtray full of roaches, and a blunt cutter. With all her supplies prepped and ready in front of her, Keisha began to do surgery on the blunt.

"Come over here Charlytte, let me show you something." Keisha stopped what she was doing and waved her freshly-painted candy pink nails in my direction.

I walked over to her slowly and sat down beside her on another comfy leather couch. I didn't know why I felt nervous, but I did.

"Yes?" I asked, shaking a bit.

"I wanna teach you a lil' something," she said, then handed me a cigar. "How 'bout I show you how to roll a blunt."

"Uhm...okay," I replied.

Although I tried to hide it, I was excited about her teaching me how to do that. I wanted so badly to learn ever since the day Cederick had to pull over on the side of the highway just so he could do it himself. As he stuffed his blunt with weed, he made a comment to me saying, "damn, this would be much easier if you knew how to do it," and ever since, I wanted to learn. For some silly reason, I thought that me being able to roll Cederick's blunts for him would make him like me more.

"Hey Shannon!" Keisha yelled in the direction of the kitchen.

"What's up," Shannon answered.

"Is it okay if I let her practice on ya bogus ass weed?" Keisha yelled.

"Hell no!" Shannon yelled back. "And I'm 'bout tired of you disrespectin' my shit."

Keisha insulted Shannon even more when she broke out into a serious laughter. Then she ignored her and continued to talk to me.

"Anyway, ya see Charlytte," she said, purposely speaking loudly so that Shannon could hear her over the sound of the roaring blender. Then she picked up the two sacks of weed from off of her coffee table and showed me both of them.

"Smell this one," she said, putting the sac that she held in her left hand up to my nostrils. "This is what you call Kush. See how the weed in this sac is like a bright green color? And you see how the leaves are kinda flufflylike?"

I nodded my head, pretending to know what she was talking about.

"And you see those little orange hairs in there?" she continued.

"Yeah," I answered. I actually did see those.

"What about stems or seeds, do you see any?"

"No."

"Good. This is how weed is supposed to look," she said, then snatched the sac away and put another one in my face.

Shannon turned the blender off and peeped out from the kitchen to hear exactly what Keisha was saying. When Keisha saw her looking, she began to talk even louder.

"Now smell this sack," she said, putting her left hand down and her right hand up. "You see the difference between the two?"

"Yeah," I said, noticing that the smell of the weed in that sac was much weaker than the other one. I also noticed how brown the weed was and all the stems and seeds it had in it.

"Enough said," Keisha laughed. "This sack is what you call boo-boo. Don't let nobody give you this shit. And I prefer you don't smoke it either."

Shannon was so offended that she stormed into the den and tried to snatch her sac, but Keisha was too quick, only allowing her to grab thin air.

"Charlytte, weed is weed." Shannon said to me as she panted a bit from the brief little tussle with Keisha. "If you can't afford to get Kush, get mid. Hell, get Reggie for all I care. It's cheaper, and best of all, you don't have to sleep with a man just to smoke it."

Shannon must have struck a nerve because Keisha went off. She dumped the guts from the blunt into a plastic bag and sat it down on the table, just so she could say what she had to say.

"No bitch, the runs I go on pay for my weed, so technically I work for mines. Maybe if you stop being so scary, quit that lil' bump ass cashiering job, and come make some real money, you wouldn't have to come round here with that bullshit ass weed."

Catching Keisha completely off guard, Shannon ceased the opportunity to grab her sac from out of her hand. This time she was successful.

"No, I got kids. A little downgrade of weed is worth the sacrifice," Shannon said, waving the sac in her hand while sporting a childish smirk on her face as if she was saying to Keisha, nanny-nanny boo-boo bitch. With her head sitting high, she confidently dismissed herself from the room and headed back the kitchen.

After I broke down Keisha's weed and twisted it up into a blunt, surprisingly, I was pleased with what I had done. Keisha too was impressed with my first attempt and decided to let me keep my little project as a reward. And she must have been in a giving mood because she gave Shannon a sack of Kush too. Although she did keep Shannon's "boo-boo" because she said she was going to give it to some smoker to wash her car later.

Just as we were finishing up with the blunts, Shannon was finishing up with the daiquiris. She poured each of our tall crystal glasses up to the rim with it, and we all met up on the outside balcony. When I saw the view of the small, beautiful lake with the two little ducks swimming in it, I knew for sure that I didn't ever want to go home.

We each took a seat in one of the four white lounge chairs that looked like they were just waiting for us, and

Keisha grabbed both me and her drinks from between Shannon's fingers.

"Aaaaah, this....is....the....life," Keisha sighed, after she first took a sip of her drink and then handed me mine. "Doing little work, but making lots of money."

“Speak for yourself," Shannon disagreed. "They working my ass like a slave down at the job."

"Shannon, I told you," Keisha sat her cup down on the table beside her and sparked up the blunt with her Bob Marley lighter. “That’s your own fault. You need to stop playing and come make some real money. You know it's always a spot for you in the business."

Shannon took a sip of her drink and made a frown. "I think I may have put a lil’ too much in here, y'all better sip slow." Then she turned to Keisha. "Now Keish, you know if I ain't had my babies I would be all the way down for it, but I aint tryin' to do nothing now, that can end up causing me to lose my kids later."

"Damn Shannon,” Keisha threw her hands up. “Why you always gotta think so negative? Your kids should be more of the reason for you to go out and get this money. You don't want lil' CiCi having to grow up and be begging no nigga fa' shit. With the money you could be making, all yo’ kids could be straight."

Keisha looked to me. "Charlytte, this bitch used to roll with me hard, but ever since she had them kids she done up and got all soft on me. This the same bitch that did a couple runs with me back in the day. The same bitch that used to be playin' these weak ass niggas right along with me. And the same bitch who used to be Coach bag to Coach bag with me up in Club Paradise almost every damn weekend. Now she wanna act all holy and shit. I miss my homie, fa real."

"I'm still yo' homie,” Shannon said. “I'm just a lil' mo'

mature. Kids do that to you, ya know, and you don't have any so therefore you can't speak on it. You damn right, I needs the dough, but my kids are more important. And me making a couple extra bucks, just to have a flatscreen and some fancy furniture, ain't worth me going to jail ten years for."

"Who said *anything* about jail?" Keisha asked as she hit the joint. "I fa sho ain't going to jail for no damn nobody."

"Well what you think gone happen to you if the state patrol pull yo' ass over and find all that shit in yo' trunk? You think they gonna give you a pat on the back 'cause you cute?"

Keisha began to laugh, as if what Shannon said was a straight up joke to her.

"You think I'mma go to jail?" she asked. "Hell no, I already got this shit figured out."

"Then whatcha gone do?" Shannon asked, eager to hear Keisha's reply. I was tuned in too.

"I'm snitching." Keisha said boldly.

"*Snitching*?" Shannon threw her hands up, completely taken by surprise. "So you think it's that simple, huh? You know what niggas who that deep in the game do to snitches. You think they gone spare you because you a bitch?"

Keisha freed some smoke from her mouth. "Let me explain something to you…the police don't care nothing about locking no female trafficker up. You and I know that they would be willing to cut me a sweet deal if I gave up the source. I know that's fucked up, but that's just how it is. I'm not gone be sitting in jail while them niggas run free. Shit no. And by the time they make their arrest, I will be *looooong* gone."

I just sat there quietly, listening to Shannon and Keisha talk. I knew by how serious their conversation was that Keisha had to have been involved in some serious shit.

"So you don't think Herb got niggas on the outside that will handle that, even if he does go down?" Shannon asked.

"Trust me, I *know* he got plenty niggas that will handle that. That's why I said I will be loooong gone, I'm talking o-u-t, out, of Ordale."

"And where you gon' go?" Shannon continued to drill her.

"Bitch, didn't I tell you I got everything planned out!" Keisha shouted, then handed her the joint. "I'm going to stay with Poncha in L.A."

"*Poncha*?" Shannon asked. "Just like you would snitch on Herb, how you know Poncha won't snitch on you. She works for him too, ya know."

"*Beee-cause*, my girl Poncha is a down ass bitch. I know she wouldn't rat me out. Besides, me and her talk about this shit all the time. She said she would snitch too. And if she ever needed me, I would do the same for her."

"If you say so Keish," Shannon gave up. "All I can do is pray for you. But on the real, I still feel like you shouldn't jump in that car if you ain't willing to take that ride."

"I got this," Keisha boasted.

I just continued to sip my drink and tried to stay out of it. I understood both of their sides, but I did feel that Shannon made a better point. I didn't want to see anything bad happen to Keisha. I, too, just didn't believe it would be worth it.

After the bickering died down, we all just sat quiet for a minute and stared out at the lake. I took a couple more sips of my Daiquiri. It was so good that if it wasn't for the possibility of a brain freeze, I would have sucked the whole thing down in one slurp. After the silence became awkward, I tried to start up a conversation of my own.

"So," I turned to Keisha, "is Herb the guy who owns that big ass house?"

Keisha took another sip of her drink, threw her index finger up as if she was ready to give me the 4-1-1, and then placed her cup back on the ground after she had swallowed.

"Yeah, that's Herb," she answered.

"Oh, okay. I kinda figured that. How do you know him?"

"Chile, to make a long story short, I used to fuck wit' him. Now we just do business together. I really don't mess with him on a personal level anymore."

"Yeah right bitch," Shannon butted in. "You always say that, then you right back fuckin' his ass."

Keisha rolled her eyes at Shannon, and then focused her attention back to me.

"Anyway, see cousin, his real name is Herbert Issac Cooper, but people call him Hi-C for short. I hate that name so I just call him Herb- even though he don't like nobody calling him by his government. 'Hi-C' was probably started by some lame kid in elementary school and it just stuck with him. Hell, I don't know, but anyway," Keisha paused, grabbed the blunt from Shannon, then passed it to me. "He used to small hustle, just nickel and dime. That was back before he got busted and did a couple years in jail on minor drug charges. As far as all the money he's making now… I don't know how true the story is…but I heard that he saved some wimpy ass Mexican kid from getting pounded by one of those jail bully types, and evidently, the punk ass kid was the son of a well-known drug dealer in one of them foreign countries. So, in return for Herbert saving his life, he turned him on to his father, the father fronted him some dope, and he's been the man ever since."

"Damn, I know he's glad he helped *that* kid," I said, completely entertained by Keisha's story.

"Hell yeah, that lil' bitch turned out to be a sweet ass lick," she replied.

"Don't forget to mention that he's married," Shannon glared at Keisha.

"Yeah and so what?" Keisha got all defensive, like she was ready to take Shannon's head off. "That's not my fault. I ain't got no rings on my finger. Plus, I heard she fuckin' around with her ex on the side anyway."

Keisha took another hit out of her cup, but this time it was a big gulp.

"If I was her I'd be creeping around too. That nigga can't do shit with that little ass dick of his."

"Oh my god, Keisha, T-M-I!" I laughed. "And I can't believe you messing around with a man who's married."

"I tried to tell her triflin' ass the same damn thing," Shannon agreed with me. "She ain't no damn good."

"Oh, shut the fuck up Shannon," Keisha finally snapped. "You know you just mad cause you ain't fuckin' him. You talk all that shit, but I don't see you complainin' when we in the mall and I'm buying the *both* of us shit with the money he's giving me."

Shannon was about to say something else, but she quickly got quiet and went back to her drink.

"Yeah bitch, that's what I thought. I'm 'bout tired of you judging me. I know I keep fuckin' his weak ass, but this apartment, that sweet Kush, and that Grey Goose y'all sipping on, is compliments of this sweet pussy and that lil' pencil he calls a dick."

Just as Keisha's last words came out, I inhaled the weed and choked. The smoke burned the hell out my throat, causing me to cough drastically.

"See Charlytte," Shannon said, looking over at me coughing "That's what you get for hitting Keisha's grimy ass weed."

“Oh hush trick!” Keisha shoved her.

We all laughed, but deep down inside I knew that it was bitches like Keisha that made it hard for decent girls like me and Shannon. As we continued to sip our drinks, I decided to wee myself away from the bickering and just enjoy the breeze and my high. It felt good having people I could kick it with, but it was even better that those people were Shannon and Keisha. We were all reunited again, and this time, I was grown enough to join in on their conversations, and their 'festivities’.

"So, what about you *miss thang*," Keisha changed the subject. "What's up with you and yo boo Ceddy?" she said in her best 'Lovita from the Steve Harvey Show' voice.

"What do you mean?" I sighed, knowing she was about start up a whole new complicated issue. I had to take another hit of the blunt just to stop myself from blushing.

"The way he scooped you up from that party, I knew something must have been going on between the two of you."

"No. There's nothing going on," I assured her. "What we have is kind of weird. I can't really describe it."

"Well can you describe that dick of his? I heard he has a third leg, if ya know what I mean." Keisha reached out and grabbed the blunt from me, then turned all the way around in her seat just to hear my response. "Is it true bitch?"

I looked up to see Shannon and Keisha staring me dead into my eyes. They were so hungry for the scoop that I could almost see the drool pouring from out of their mouths. It was kind of cute in a pathetic sort of way.

“I really wouldn't know,” I disappointed them both. "To be honest, we never did it."

Shannon and Keisha both gasped in disbelief.

"You mean to tell us that you sitting over here in some two-hundred dollar weave- that he paid for, a Coach purse- that he paid for, and an Enyce outfit straight off the manikin- cause I saw it there the other day- and you gone tell us that y'all ain't fuckin’. Shannon, can you believe that shit?"

"Uhmmm, I don't know Keish. That's a hard one," she replied. “But not all girls have to be fuckin’ a man to get shit from him.”

"Exactly," I agreed.

"Look bitch, don't be no fool," Keisha threw her hands up at Shannon as if she was dismissing her from the conversation. "If a nigga buying you shit, he either fucking you or trying to fuck you. No exceptions. That's why you stuck with four kids and no money. You gotta smarten up, hun."

I could see the rage as it began to appear in Shannon's eyes and I couldn't help but notice how harsh Keisha could be to her at times. It seemed as if she downed her for every little thing. But I decided not to look too much into it. I figured that was just the way they did things. Besides, Shannon knew how to hold her own and didn't have a problem telling Keisha about her ass.

"I love every last one of my kids," Shannon fired back. "And if it wasn't for all them abortions you done got, you would've had a daycare by now. Just because I was woman enough to take care of mines, don't make you no better than me."

"Yeah whatever," Keisha hissed. She tried to act like she wasn't bothered by Shannon's last comment, but we knew differently.

The two of them seemed to be arguing a little too much, and I didn't want our good girls' time to be ruined. Besides, I was supposed to be the topic of their conversation so I quickly put the focus back on me.

"Shannon's right Keisha. There have been plenty of times when we were alone that he could have, but he never went for it."

"Well, do you *want* to fuck him?" Keisha asked, while motioning for Shannon to talk-to-the-hand.

"Yeah," I answered. "Sometimes I think about it."

"Evidently not bad enough, because if so, you would have had been hittin' that by now. The power is all in the pussy," Keisha said. "A real woman knows that."

"Oh brother, here she goes with that power of the pussy shit again." Shannon flung Keisha's hand down, then made sure she made direct eye contact with me. "Charlytte look at me. Please don't let her poison you with that bullshit."

"C'mon now Charlytte," Keisha defended herself, "as much as I looked after you, you know I wouldn't tell you anything wrong. So trust me when I say that men ain't shit. None of them. They all have an agenda, so if you want to protect your little heart, you need to make sure you have one too."

Keisha was about to hit the blunt again, but realized it was Shannon's turn and passed it over to her. "The rules are simple: show no weakness. Get what you can get out of them dirty bastards and move the fuck on."

"Is it really that easy?" I asked.

"Simple as one, two, three," Keisha replied. "If you want the dick, take it. Guys need that extra push. They love a woman who takes control. Don’t be afraid to use your powers. God gave them to you."

Shannon sighed. "Oh lord, now the bitch wanna bring God into this."

"Hell yeah, I take Him with me everywhere I go-even on them runs. This shit real. It dates back to biblical times. Why you think we living in all this sin now?"

Keisha looked around and waited for a response from one of us. Shannon just looked as if she was done with trying to get through to her, and I was just too afraid to talk about God in that manner. When neither of us replied, Keisha answered her own question.

"Because of the power of the pussy!” she shouted. “Get up on y'all shit bitches!"

Shannon sighed once more, but this time it was a much deeper one. "Explain please. I gotta hear this."

Keisha began to whisper as if what she was saying was some top-secret CIA shit. "See, it was the pussy that made Adam betray God. The bible speaks of it. You just gotta read between the lines. You really think we going through all this hell because Adam bit a piece of fuckin' fruit?!"

Keisha waited again for a response, but I was still staying out of it. And so was Shannon.

"Hell fucking naw!" Keisha shouted once more. "Adam ain't ate no damn apple… he ate Eve's pussy!"

Shannon and I both leaned up in our seats, shocked by what Keisha had just suggested, and couldn't help but break out into laughter.

"Y'all hoes laughing but y'all need to open ya eyes to some real shit. See, God ain't gonna put *that* in the bible because kids read it. So what they did was say 'apple' instead of 'pussy.' Think about it; an apple is sweet but bitter, just like some pussy."

"Girl, just when I thought you couldn't get any crazier, you hit me with this shit," Shannon giggled.

"I'm not crazy y'all. Just picture this…one day many years ago, Eve fell asleep all naked in the woods while Adam was out hunting tigers and shit. Then, along came this wandering snake- that's how he got into the picture- slithering up her bare little legs, sticking out that tiny little tongue of his…" Keisha looked back and forth at the both of us and mimicked a snake's vibrating tongue motion, "…well see, the snake moved up her thighs and accidentally brushed his little tongue up against her pussy. Eve woke up just as it happened and realized that she liked the little sensation it gave her. Y'all follow?"

Shannon and I nodded.

"Ok, so then, Eve threw the snake off of her and ran to Adam. First, she told him what it had done, and then she told him that she wanted him to try it. Now mind, God had already told Adam that he could screw Eve, but that he could only do her missionary. You do know what missionary is right, lil' sis?

"Yea, only on top," I slurred, starting to feel an even greater buzz from the weed and alcohol.

"Yeah, I think that's somewhere in the bible too. But anyway…at first he told her no. Then she told him that if he didn't eat her pussy, he couldn't fuck her. She wanted it so badly that she started using her body to tempt him, walking 'round the forest brushing up against leaves and shit. She teased the fuck outta po' Adam for a whole week until eventually he gave in and did it."

"Oh really," Shannon chuckled. "And how did God find out?"

"Shit, He's God, and plus," Keisha took a little bit of the daiquiri, dabbed it around her lips, then pointed to it, "the evidence was all over his face!"

Shannon, Keisha, and I laughed so hard that our stomach started tightening up.

"I'mma blame it on the weed, but you still going to hell first class," Shannon told Keisha. "We need to move from around you. I don't want to be nowhere near this bitch when the good Lord strike this motherfuckah down."

Shannon and I laughed some more. I just couldn't believe Keisha had come up with that crazy ass theory. But that was one of the reasons why I loved her. Keisha was still the same old Keisha. She may have been a little worse than when we were kids but some of the stuff she said really got to me, especially the part about me taking control of my situation. I mean, I was feeling Cederick a lot and not only did I want him to have me, I felt that he deserved to have me. He treated me very good and he made me feel like a woman. Maybe it was time for me to stop being so afraid of rejection. After all, no guy in his right mind would turn down some pussy. And what better night then a night that I was feeling so right to make my move.

Keisha dropped me off first since it was more convenient for her. I called Cederick off of her cell phone, just like he instructed me, and let him know that I would soon be arriving. Thankfully he was already there waiting up for me. It was a little after ten-thirty and I was still feeling pretty damn good. The Grey Goose mixed with that sweet Kush we smoked was definitely a feeling I could get used to. I went back to that shed with one thing on my mind, and that was giving Cederick the pussy. I didn't know how I was going to pull it off, but I knew I wasn't going to bed unless he was putting me to sleep.

When I entered, Cederick was lying across the bed prompted up on a pillow watching the Sports Center. All he had on was a pair of black sweat pants and black socks. It was unusual to see him dress so loosely, but I remembered him saying earlier that he was taking all his clothes to the cleaners.

With sex being the only thing on my mind, I came into the house immediately trying to draw attention to myself. Not knowing exactly what to do, I threw my purse down on the bed beside him and loudly fumbled through it, pretending to be looking for something. Paying me no mind, Cederick continued to watch the game. He didn't even ask me what we did or where I had been, like I was expecting him to.

After I gave up on the phony purse act, I decided to heat things up by taking a bath. But instead of undressing in the bathroom like I normally did, I sat on the edge of the bed and began to unbutton my white Dereon collar shirt right in front of him.

Slowly, I slid my sleeve down one arm, revealing my sexy black bra with the lace trimming. Then I peeped out the corner of my eye to see if he was watching, but he still didn't seem to be paying me any attention. When that wasn't good enough, I stood up from off the bed and slowly rolled my jeans down my legs- the matching black boy shorts with the red laced trim should have definitely been enough to win him over.

I seductively bent over to pick up my clothes, purposely letting my precious ass face him, and when I looked up- expecting for sure to see him drooling over me- I was disappointed to see that his eyes were still glued to the television set. Unable to stand him ignoring me any longer, I stormed into the bathroom, taking only a couple of steps to get there, and slammed the door.

In the bathroom, I immediately looked in the big mirror and studied my body to figure out what he didn't see that I did. My scars and pussy had healed, my breasts were a little small but still big enough to cuff, and my ass was nice and voluptuous. Any man would have loved to have me bent over and pressed against the headboard, but Cederick didn't seem to be one of them.

Feeling a bit emotional from the weed, and bold from the alcohol, was a bad combination because that had to have been the only reason why I snatched my bra and panties off and storm back out the bathroom to confront Cederick.

"What the fuck is wrong with you?" I rudely asked, as I stood in front of him butt ass naked.

He glanced at my small round breast, and then at my naturally shaved-looking pussy, before looking up at me.

"Excuse me?" he asked, with a bewildered look on his face.

"Are you scared of pussy or something?" I made myself clearer.

Cederick thought for a minute about what I had just said, and then he laughed in my face. I think he thought my little attitude was cute more than anything, and I got even more upset just knowing that he wasn't taking me serious.

"What the hell Keisha do with my little Charlytte?" he said while he pretended to be looking around the room for somebody. He still couldn't stop laughing.

"Keisha didn't do anything to me," I replied, ignoring the fact that she was the one who boosted me up in the first place. "I just wanna know one thing… why won't you fuck me? Is there something wrong with me? Is it the scar?" I pointed to my face.

Cederick sat up on the bed and tried really hard to stop himself from laughing. "Don't you think your jumping the gun a little bit, little mama?"

"Or maybe it's because I'm sixteen?" I continued on. "Because I may be young, but I'm still a woman."

Cederick chuckled again, almost about to really make me boil over.

"You don't know the first thing about being a woman, Charlytte," he said to me.

"Why don't I? I know how to work hard *and* I know how to survive out here on these streets on my own. I saw more in my sixteen years than most grown women see in their lifetime. So I believe that makes me a woman."

"You got it all wrong. It's not about how hard you work, or your life experiences. And believe me, Charlytte, it's not about your age either. No offense, but I know thirty-year olds who are more immature than you. Stop taking everything so personal and understand that there is a time and a place for everything. I just don't think you're ready or even sure of yourself yet, that's all."

Cederick fell back on the bed and continued to watch the TV. "Now go wash up. And please, act like a lady and keep your clothes on around me."

After seeing that Cederick really meant business, I let out a gut-wrenching sigh and then stormed back into the bathroom. As I quickly walked away, I heard him chuckle one last time and it took everything in me not to tell him to shut the fuck up. I still couldn't figure out why he dismissed me the way he did, especially after I had given him the green light.

Being rejected in that way really hurt me like hell. I knew there was a time and a place for everything, but judging by the clock on my pussy, the time for me to be fucked by Cederick was then. On top of that, I was even more confused. I didn't know exactly what he meant when he said I wasn't ready. If I could have took Marcus's huge dick, and put up with Mr. Otis's old ass, I knew I was ready for Cederick. And with the combination of the things I learnt from the both of them, I knew I was no amateur. I just wished he could have given me the chance to show him that.

I hopped in the tub and soaked my body while thinking about what had just happened. Still in denial and not wanting to give up so easy, I started thinking to myself that maybe-just maybe- he really did want me. I thought that after I got out the shower he would be laying naked on the bed, just waiting to give me some of what he had to offer. The night wasn't over just yet.

After I gave myself a good bath, I dried off thoroughly, and rubbed my body down with some green apple scented lotion. Then I powdered up my pussy, cleaned all the wax out my ears, and sprayed the matching green apple fragrance on my neck and backside. Finally, I made my way back to the room and hoped to see Cederick up waiting for me, or maybe waiting to creep up behind me, once he thought I was fast asleep. But instead, all he gave me the pleasure of seeing was him spread out over the bed, with his eyes closed and his mouth wide open, snoring hard as hell.

I was so pissed that I stormed over to the closet, pulled out the comforter, and made my bed on the floor where he normally slept. Then I put on a t-shirt and turned off anything that gave off light so that the entire room could be just the way I liked it, dark and familiar.

25: BONNIE AND CYLDE

I was having the best summer ever hanging out with Keisha. She picked me up almost every day, and we got into something new each time. We went shopping together, we got our nails and toes done, we went to the spa for massages, and once she got her fake ID from that Lexis chick, she had me up in all the exclusive parties. Shannon hung out with us whenever she didn't have to work, or if she could get free from the kids, but mostly it was me, Keisha, and one of Keisha's other homegirls, Alicia. In a very short time, I went from being bored out of my mind, to having a blast. No doubt, I was living the fast life and doing shit that was way ahead of my time. And I gotta admit, it was fun.

Cederick was still looking out for me financially and even paid for our outings a couple of times. He didn't mind me spending so much time with the girls either, probably because I was out of his hair. As long as I was with them, he didn't have to hear me complaining about how lonely I was in the shed, and he definitely didn't have to worry about me begging to tag along with him every time he made a move.

After facing that horrible rejection, I let go of the idea of being with him in any kind way. I decided that if he wanted me, he was going to have to be the one to make the move. But even though I was done with it, I was still a young woman who was growing more confident, much happier, and a lot hornier by the day. There were many times, when I was out partying with Keisha, that I almost had to sew my pussy up to keep myself from fucking one of her sexy ass homeboys. They were always hitting on me. I could've had my boots knocked up many times, but my loyalty to Cederick wouldn't allow me to do it. Yet still, the boy was going to have to make a move on me pretty quickly. I was a ticking time-bomb ready to blast off on somebody's dick, and Keisha's friend Andre was looking like a good target.

• • • • • •

It was on a beautiful day in the middle of June when Cederick called Keisha's phone looking for me. We were doing happy hour at Chili's. He told me to get my stuff together because he was on the way to pick me up. He never interrupted my girls' time, so I safely assumed that something was up.

I slurped down my half of glass of Mango Margarita, grabbed my Michael Kors purse, and headed for the bathroom to gloss my lips. When I made it back to the table, I quietly explained to Keisha what Cederick had told me and she completely understood. Besides, Shannon and Alicia were there too, so she wouldn't miss me too much. On my way out, I hugged Shannon, and from the way she hugged me back, I knew that she was truly sad to see me go.

Alicia, on the other hand, shot me the deuces. She didn't care one bit about me, and was probably glad that I was leaving. She made it very clear from the moment she met me that she didn't like me very much. Alicia was Keisha's homegirl that she met through Hi-C. They did runs together and ended up clicking tight. She was a petite, mixed girl with a short blonde texturizer that fit her Halle Berry-shaped head perfectly. She always looked at me funny with her Asian eyes and rolled her long slender neck anytime she saw me coming. And she couldn't get enough of pouting those anorexic lips up at me whenever I spoke to her or entered in her presence. I didn't like the stuck-up bitch either, and I couldn't figure out, for the life of me, why Keisha even hung out with her ass. They surely didn't have anything in common.

Keisha was way cooler. Even though she was pretty, she didn't act like she was. She laughed, joked, and practically got along with everybody. While Alicia, better known as Mrs. Diva, acted like she was a thousand-dollars grand. Every movement she made was vital, and every time she spoke the entire room was supposed to be quiet and bow down to her. I didn't pay her ass any attention though. Instead of shooting her the deuces back, I walked over and hugged her too, just because I knew how much it pissed her off.

After leaving the girls, I waited by the entrance door until my Cederick arrived. Smiling brightly when I saw him pull up, I entered his car and gracefully consumed the fresh air smell that immediately hit my face. For the first time, his ride didn't smell like weed, and it looked as if he had just got some detail cleaning work done on it. I was impressed.

"Sup Miss Lady," he said, admiring me in my mini-skirt and pink halter-top that revealed my stomach, and my newly pierced belly button ring.

"Nothing. What's up?" I replied, checking him out as well.

Cederick was also looking and smelling very good. He wore a dark brown Polo shirt and some khaki Ralph Lauren jeans. He even had on a fitted hat, and some Gucci sunglasses, which he didn't normally wear.

"So what's going on?" I asked curiously. "Why you pick me up?"

Cederick pulled a freshly rolled blunt from out of his ash tray. I knew it would only be a matter time before his car would smell like weed again.

"Because," he sparked it up. "I've been on the move a lot lately and I realize that we haven't really kicked it in a while. I had a little bit of free time today so I just wanted to hang out with you, before I have to get back to business."

Cederick was right. He had been on the move a lot lately. Not to mention, he had also been very aggravated about some of the things that were going on in the hood. He never personally gave me any details. But, I did overhear him telling Ace that some dude name Squirrel got arrested. They must have done business with him, and were worried that he was going to snitch or have one of them set up. After learning of the news, I purposely stayed of his way because when Cederick wasn't making the type of money that he was used to making, his attitude could be really fucked up.

“Okay,” I said, impressed by his efforts. "So what did you have in mind?

“You wanna hit up Jacksonville?" he asked.

"You know it!" I replied. I knew exactly what that meant.

Cederick and I took the two hour drive to J-Ville and the first thing we did was exactly what I predicted we'd do- go shopping. He bought me two causal outfits, and a short red mini-dress with some gold six-inch stilettos to go with it. I got dolled up in the red dress right in the department store, and because it was so good, we headed straight to the same seafood restaurant that we had been to before.

The sun was slowly dimming down when we made it there, which created the perfect atmosphere for a nice romantic evening. Cederick was a complete gentlemen. He proudly walked into the restaurant with me close by his side, pulled my chair from under me when we got to the table, and ordered my food. He even requested to have my tartar sauce poured on my shrimp, instead of on the side, just the way I liked it. Cederick was even lucky enough to land us a table by the window, so this time we had a great view of the beautiful outdoor lake. After we placed our orders, I immediately got lost looking out at the view, appreciating its beauty and thinking about how lucky I was to be able to see it.

"What's wrong?" Cederick asked as he followed my eyes and looked out the window to see what I was staring so deeply at.

"Nothing, just thinking."

"About...."

"I don't know....about where I would have been if I never met you."

"Who knows? You may have been better off, you may have been worse. You can't waste time thinking about the what-if's. What's important is that you *did* meet me. I know everything ain't exactly how you want it, but in time, it will be."

I was a bit shocked, but please, with how caring Cederick was being towards me. He rarely showed that affectionate side of him, but I knew it was there. He proved that just by taking me under his wing. I loved every single thing he had done for me. The only thing I wanted more was for him to love and be with me. But even if he didn't, he had still done enough.

"But everything is exactly how I want it to be," I assured him. "I wouldn't change a thing."

"You sure about that?" he questioned.

"Yes, positive." I said.

"So there's absolutely nothing that bothers you about this situation?" he asked. “I know you appreciate everything, but can you *honestly* say that there isn't one thing you would change?" he asked.

Cederick paused, and waited patiently for an answer. Even though I was dying to tell him how much I wanted to be with him, all I managed to say was, "No, everything's fine."

Unfortunately, Cederick wasn’t buying it.

"So, you mean to tell me that you’re out partying on the regular, getting drunk and shit, and you never once wanted to be fucked or laid up with someone?"

His bluntness came as no surprise to me; I was used to getting that honesty from him. But what I wasn't used to was him putting me in an uncomfortable position. I knew he was too smart to be lied to, but still, I just didn't have the courage to tell him the truth.

"No, never." I lied again.

Cederick drew himself closer to me, forcing me to look him into his dreadful eyes.

"Ok," he said calmly, as if he was giving up on the conversation. But unexpectedly, he flipped the script.

"What about Andre, you never thought about bangin' him?"

I looked down into my lap, trying to shy myself away from his powerful glare." I don't know what you're talking about?"

In reality, I didn't have anything to hide from Cederick when it came to Andre. He was only a guy I met a couple of times when Keisha and I went out, and the most we ever did was share a drink and a conversation. Although I must admit, I did dream about caressing his big, firm muscles and rubbing my hands all over his smooth, brown skin.

"Aaw c'mon Charlytte. The streets talk, ya know. You mean to tell me that you don't know who Andre is, goes by the name 'Slick'?" he asked. "Can you look me in my eyes and tell me that you don't like him, or even think about him just a little bit. Don't lie to me. You know how I feel about being lied to."

Cederick continued to trap me in his pupils. He knew just what to say and do to get the truth out of me. Unable to cover it up any longer, I let it all out.

"Honestly, yeah," I sighed. "I have thought about him. But that doesn't mean anything. I don't care about that guy. I'm just using him."

"Using him?" Cederick raised one eyebrow at me.

"Yes, using him to take my mind of the only person I really care about, which is you."

I couldn't believe I let those words slip out of my mouth, but I did, and there was nothing I could do to take them back. Cederick leaned back into his seat and stared at me even harder. His face suddenly grew emotionless, which made it very difficult for me to figure out what he was thinking.

"What?" I asked, breaking the silence to see just where his head was. "Did I say something wrong?"

"No," he said, then quickly pulled himself together. "Not at all. It's natural for you to feel like that. You can tell me anything and I won't trip. I know that you dig me and I'm cool with that, but I do feel that you should stay away from that dude Dre."

"Why?" I blushed, because he seemed to be a little threatened by him. And if he was the least bit jealous, then he must have felt a little something for me.

"Because, the dude's a square. Why you think they call him Slick? And how you think I found out about you and him?"

Just when I was about to answer him, the waitress interrupted us with two steamy plates of seafood. Cederick made room for them. Then ordered two shots of patron for us, and tipped her really good so that she wouldn't ID me. Luckily, it worked.

After thanking the waitress, we dove into our food and right back into our conversation.

"Because," Cederick picked up where he left off without even giving me a chance to respond to his question. "He told me. The nigga bought an ounce the other day and was generous enough to smoke one with me and Hi-C. He was cool until his water-faucet ass mouth started running. He started talking about a bunch of different hoes in the city, including Keisha. Then he had the nerve to say that he smashed her lil' young ass cousin after the club one night. He couldn't remember yo' name, but I knew from the description he gave that he was definitely talking about you. I already knew the nigga was lyin' because anytime he lies, his eyes start twitchin'. And plus, he always lyin' about something. I can't stand the nigga. The only reason I fuck with him is 'cause he shop good and bring me high paying customers."

"*Dayum*," I said, shocked by what Cederick had just told me. I didn't know grown ass men told lies on their dicks. If Cederick was right about Andre, I was completely turned off by him.

"Why would he do that?" I asked. "I mean, how could he just lie like that?"

"Cause he's a lame." Cederick said. "That's what lame people do. They're miserable. Every step they take is pre-planned. Their personalities change with their environment. I don't want you getting caught up with him because you can fall in love with a lame nigga, but a lame nigga can't fall in love with you."

Cederick peeled the tail off his shrimp and tossed it into his mouth. Then he swallowed it down along with a spoonful of his baked potato.

"And you know why?" he asked.

"Why?"

"Easy. Because he never mastered the art of loving himself, so how couldn't he possibly love anyone else?"

My mood changed from happy to bittersweet when Cederick told me what Andre said. I was hurt and mad at the same time because if Andre told Cederick and Hi-C that he'd slept with me, I could only imagine who else he told and what else was said. Plus, I was starting to like him more than what I told Cederick, and soon planned on giving it up to him. I even knew when and where.

The waitress came back to our table shortly with our shots. We each grabbed one and when Cederick sensed the sudden change in my mood, he tried to cheer me up.

"Let's just drink to that one," he joked. "Don't take it personal, lil' mama. It's nothing you did wrong. It's not even his fault. Lameness is just a terrible disease that's spreading and affecting our people, just like AIDS and the rest of that shit."

"I see," I agreed with him.

"And don't think that I'm just hatin' or trying to control you, or anything like that. I just care about your heart and I'm trying to look out for your best interest. I would hope that you would do the same when it came to me."

"Yeah right, Cederick." I shot him down. "I doubt there will ever come a time where you need me to think for you. You pretty much know the answer to everything."

"That's not true." Cederick laughed. I could tell he was a little flattered by my compliment. "I've just been around, that's all. I still make mistakes too. You never know, I may need you one day, just like you needed me."

"We'll see," I said, still not convinced.

"But if I did, would you be willing to ride for me like I have been ridin' for you?"

"If you Clyde, then I'm Bonnie," I joked, then we both took our shots and enjoyed the rest of our meal.

26: HAPPY BIRTHDAY!

By the time Cederick and I left the restaurant, we both had taken down three shots of patron each. Buzzed and feeling real good, we laughed and joked all the way to his ride. Cederick even held the car door open for me and made sure I got in comfortably. There was something very different about his attitude. The always very serious guy was now joking, playing, and catering to my every need. He told me he had booked us a nice suite at the Hilton's. I didn't want to jump ahead of myself again, but I couldn't help but think that he wanted to do more than just spend some lost time with me.

Before we headed out to the room, Cederick had to make a quick stop to handle some business. When he pulled up to a red brick house in a middle class neighborhood, he kissed me on my forehead and told me he would be right back. I was feeling pretty tipsy from the drinks, so the kiss alone got me wet. I watched Cederick up until entered the house, then I closed my eyes and leaned back in my seat. Cederick was jamming

T.I.'s *I'm serious* album. I changed the song to "Hotel" and immediately started singing the words, while thinking about all the things I wanted to do to him when we got to the room.

After jamming the song three times in a row, I brought myself back to reality and quickly began to worry. Cederick had not come out of the house and he never had me waiting in an unfamiliar place longer than two minutes top. I sat up and turned the music all the way down, but shortly after I did, thankfully, I saw him coming out.

Walking swiftly to the passenger side door, he stopped at the window. Judging by the way he banged on it, I knew something was wrong.

"Get out for a minute!" Cederick panted, while at the same time opening the door. He had a very serious look on his face.

"Is everything okay?" I asked, beginning to get a little worked up myself.

"I honestly don't know. I'll tell you everything when we get inside."

Cederick grabbed me by the hand and led me to the house, as if I couldn't see the trail of cement that led up to the glass screen door with my own two eyes. We barged our way inside and entered a small den area, where about four young guys- one of them being white- were all sitting down on a couch smoking weed and playing Madden on the XBOX. The darkness in the room mixed with the thick fog from the smoke made it very hard for me to see any of their faces, but I knew they must have been stoned because they all were quiet, very still, and had their eyes were super-glued to the television set.

Without saying a word, Cederick and I eased by them and entered a long, dark hallway. Every room door we passed was closed and I could only hope that no one was trying to sleep, because the sound of my heels tapping on the hard tiled floor, along with my wrist bracelets

knocking against one another, were loud enough to wake the entire house up.

Cederick escorted me to the very last room at the end of the pathway. When we were in, he closed the door behind us. Then he flicked on the light to reveal the one lonely mattress, with the crisp white fitted sheet, lying smack in the middle of the floor. Once we were locked up on the inside, Cederick let out a huge sigh and the emptiness of the room made a big echo out of it. Then he began pacing back and forth, mumbling something to himself. I didn't know what was going on, but I wanted to.

"What's wrong Ced," I trembled. "Is everything okay?"

Still pacing, Cederick finally decided to talk.

"I don't know man. Herb's cousin- the guy who lives here- told me that he just got a call from a homie back home saying that Herb's entire street was blocked off with cops. Man fuck!" he yelled, then punch the door. "I knew I shouldn't have left Ordale!"

"Oh my Gosh!" I gasped, not expecting to get that news, but relieved that it wasn't as bad as someone dying.

"But did they say they were at Herb's house?" I asked.

"Naw, he said he couldn't tell because they got the whole street blocked off. But why else would they have the shit sewed up like that? Plus I keep calling the man and he ain't fucking answering!"

With one last failed attempt to reach Hi-C, Cederick took his flip phone and slammed it down onto the mattress. The phone hit so hard that it bounced off of the bed and landed on the floor, separating from the battery.

"Don't get upset. Try to look on the bright side," I said, trying to calm him down and piece together his phone at the same time. "Anything could have happened on that street. White people get into shit too, ya know. Just don't get worked up until you know for sure."

"I don't know man, I just got this feeling.... and them dreams..." Cederick dazed off for a second and when he brought himself back to reality, he began to pace even faster across the room. His breathing picked up and he even managed to work up a sweat.

"And if that nigga Squirrel snitched, I swear before God I'mma kill his ass!"

Unable to stand him panicking and popping off like that, I ran over to him and wrapped my arms around his waist. Then I rested my head on his chest. The warmth of his skin and rhythm of his heartbeat made me want him just the way he was.

"Calm down boo," I said in a seductive tone. "I think you're overreacting. It could be a house fire, a robbery, a dispute. Just don't jump ahead of yourself."

I rubbed Cederick's back slowly with both my hands and I could literally feel the tension in his body beginning to lessen.

"You really think everything's cool?" he asked.

"Yes, honestly I do." I told him. "You just need to relax."

Cederick wrapped his arms around my waist firmly and began to rub my lower back. I moaned softly at his very touch. It was the first time in a while that I had been that close to a man I actually wanted to be that close to, and the fact that it was Cederick, made the feeling even better.

"Ok, I'mma trust you," he surrendered." And I apologize for that. I just got a little nervous. You ready to get out of here?"

"Yeah, let's go."

Pleased with the way I was able to get Cederick under control, I smiled to myself and began walking to the door. And as soon as I opened it, surprisingly he crept up behind me and closed it back, then turned off the light. At first I was confused, but when he grabbed my face and began to kiss me slowly, it all made sense.

Without thinking twice about it, I kissed him back and began to caress his arms, starting by rubbing his wrist then making my way on up to his shoulder bone. Cederick and I only shared tongues for a minute, but it felt like a lifetime. His lips were soft and moist, just the way I imagined they would be.

Still smooching and wrapped in each other's arms, Cederick slowly walked me over to the mattress and threw me down on it. I hadn't noticed the glow-in-the-dark stars that were stuck on the ceiling until the room was dark. Who would've thought that of all the times he had put me up in a nice hotel, we would be experiencing our first time on a mattress of some strange man's house, but at that point, none of that mattered. I wasn't going to let anything get in our way, not even a quick trip to an expensive hotel. I even purposely forgot to turn on his phone after I put it back together. I, myself, wasn't quite sure if it was Hi-C's spot that was raided, but that was the last thing I was thinking about. I knew I was being selfish, but all I was concerned with was me, Cederick, and the passionate love that we were about to make. My mind was clear of everything else. I even managed to tune out the sound of the video game been played in the other room.

Blinded by the darkness, Cederick used his hands to search my body for my panties and when he found them, he slid them down my legs and made them disappear. When he pulled my red dress over my head and I lay before him with nothing but a black-laced thong on, I knew it was definitely about to go down. He got on top of me and began to kiss and suck on my neck in a slow and circular motion. With each touch I moaned, letting him know that he was definitely doing the right thing.

Cederick's tongue guided him on down to my breast. He cuffed and sucked each of them fairly, causing my nipples to harden instantly. He knew just how to handle my A-cups and somehow maintained an equal balance between being firm and being gentle with them.

He also did a magnificent job of making sure he didn't leave out one part of my body. After he spent enough time on my breasts, he then rolled his tongue on down my stomach and did circles around my navel. The little tickling sensation made the foreplay even more exciting. He continued to move down to my legs and kissed my inner thighs, teasing me in the worst way. I had never had anyone take their time with me the way that Cederick did, and there was no greater feeling than when he planted kisses from my right thigh to my left, letting nothing but the air from his warm breath brush over my goods as he pass over it. He continued to do this until I literally started begging him to fuck me.

"Ohhh...Cederick," I cried. "I want you *sooo* bad."

He just smiled at my begging and after he had gotten enough of teasing me, he dug his face between my legs and began to French kiss it like he had just said 'I do.' I moaned uncontrollably as he ate it slow, fast, in, and out. He made circles and squares with his tongue, sucked my both lips, and literally did a drumroll on my clit until I busted a nut all over his face. Then he finished the job by pinning me down and sucking every bit of it up like it was some type of crackjuice. It felt so good that I literally almost cried.

"You okay?" Cederick whispered, after he made his way back up to me. He kissed me once again on my lips, forcing me to taste my own juices.

"Yeah," I moaned, trying to regain control of myself after my entire body had went into a paralyzed state. The way my muscles locked up and the series of shivers passed through my legs, I got to experience firsthand the difference between a nut and an orgasm. "I'm cool."

Pleased, Cederick rolled over on the side of me and we both just looked up at the glowing stars. I didn't know about him, but I was still buzzed of the Patron.

"Can I tell you something funny," I asked him.

"Yeah, go head," he permitted.

"For second there, I thought I was really in space."

Cederick and I both laughed.

Then he said, "I told you when I do something, I don't half step. But look," he rolled back over and made his way on top of me again. "You think you ready for the rest of this?"

"Cederick, I know I'm young but I'm not that little girl you think I am. I can take a dick."

"I'm not even talking about like that. I mean, are you ready, not just sexually, but mentally too. I'm a nigga who stays on the move and the last thing I need is another young-minded chick stalking me and trippin' because she fell hard after I fucked her too good. We can do this, but you gotta promise me that you can maintain our friendship. Now I'm not puttin' no gun to your head. It's your decision, and if there is even the slightest bit of doubt that you won't fall in love with me after this, then you shouldn't do it."

I thought hard about what Cederick said and I understood him well. Honestly, I wasn't sure that I wouldn't fall head over heels for him, but I was sure that if I did, I could do an excellent job of covering it up. His question tainted my perception of being with him a bit, but there was nothing that was going to completely turn me away. Absolutely nothing.

"Yeah, I can handle it." I told him. "I'm ready."

"Alright," he shrugged. "Let's do it."

Cederick stood up over the mattress and pulled a condom from out of his pocket. He put it on carefully and made his way back on top of me. Boldly, I laid there with my legs wide open just waiting for him. I wasn't scared. I wasn't nervous. And I wasn't backing down.

I was already soaked from all the foreplay, kissing, and climaxing I had done. That made it much easier for Cederick to slide his nine plus inches into me. He knew that he was way too much for me, which is why he moved very slow and was extra careful not to be too rough.

Damn, the nigga really does have a third leg. I thought to myself as my vagina stretched apart to accommodate his thickness. Once he managed to get pass the minor struggle of entering me, he began to pick up the pace.

Cederick moved in and out, out and in, and the more he did, the more I adjusted to him. For a second, I doubted if I would be able to take it, but tapping out was not an option for me. He did have me feeling like a virgin all over again and by the first two minutes, I understood why the pep talk was needed.

"Oooh Cederick. Give it to me," I tried to play big girl. And just as I requested, Cederick began to move faster. He, too, was groaning with pleasure. The way my tight, wet insides gripped around him, I knew he had to have been in ecstasy.

"Damn Charlytte," he moaned. "You just don't know how good this feels."

And he was right. The better it got, the better it felt. Everything began to sink in; I was finally fuckin' somebody I wanted to fuck and that feeling alone was satisfying. I missed having that mutual connection and I suddenly felt the urge to just let loose.

"Turn around," I told him, taking control. Just like Keisha had schooled me.

Without question, Cederick turned over on his back and watched me sit up on top of him. I slowly slid my body down on it and began to ride him slowly. He exhaled deeply, rubbed his hands all over my breast, and he completely loved it when I grabbed his index and finger began to suck on it. Afterwards, I placed my hands down on his bare chest for support and began to ride him like I was in a rodeo. The more comfortable I became on top of him, the faster I moved.

Cederick began to breathe harder and groan louder. "Shit girl," he tried to keep up. "You sho' you only sixteen?"

“I’m sure,” I cried confidently, knowing that I had him right where I wanted him.

I wanted him to regret treating me like a little girl and making me wait so long. Each time I thought about how he rejected me, the faster and harder I worked my body on top of him. I was bouncing, twirling, and shaking my ass like was I never going to see a dick again in my life. Cederick had to hold on to both ends of the mattress in order to keep up.

The mattress springs squeaking, our bodies smacking against each other, and our heavy moaning, made it impossible for us not to be heard throughout the house. Normally I would have been embarrassed, but I didn't know those people out there and probably would have never saw them again in my life. Unable to hold back any longer, I gripped the thin, fitted sheet and let out a loud moan as I hit my peak for the second time. Cederick squeezed me tightly and made me sit still while I pumped my juices out onto him.

When I was all drained out, I collapsed down on top of him. And without giving me time to rest, he slid from under me and fixed my body up in doggy-style position. Once my back was arched perfectly for him, he pushed himself all the way inside of me and held it, causing me to climax, yet once again. With three nuts down, I was now even wetter than before.

"Aaaw Cederick!" I screamed. "I fuckin' love you!"

“I know you do,” he replied.

Cederick began to drill me from the back and the feeling was one that I could not describe. I felt every bit of his nine inches and took it all in like a champion.

"Faster, baby!" I screamed, placing one of his hands on my stomach so that he could feel just how deep he was inside of me. He like the idea of feeling his grown man poking at my navel and he began to play around in it, moving from right and left, even going in circles. I dug my face into the sheets and squealed in pleasure. Then I began to throw it back, allowing him to see the ripple effect of my butt-cheeks every time my ass bounced against his chest.

"Yeah, throw that shit back!" he yelled. "Shit yeah, lil mama, you definitely ready."

"I told you I was," I moaned as I drilled my body up against his chest. I was doing everything to prove to him that I was a woman.

In return, Cederick smacked my ass and gripped my cheeks firmly.

"You like that?" he asked.

"I love it!" I replied. "I love you Ced! Please don't ever leave me! Please don't ever hurt me!"

"I am hurting you now?" he asked as he sped up and pushed it in as deeply as he could. Then he held it there. It felt so good that I couldn't even get a sound out.

"Answer me!" he yelled. "I am hurting you now!"

"Noooooo baby!" I cried. "It feels so good! Please don't ever leave me!"

I don't know why I was begging Cederick not to leave me. Maybe it was because my dependency on him was now greater than it ever was before. He provided me with shelter, he provided with clothing, and not only did he provide me with food, but he was feeding me some good quality dick too. I didn't want to lose that.

Cederick continued to work me until we both came together. I fell flat on my stomach and then he collapsed on top of me. We both were tired and sweating, but satisfied. Despite everything he warned me about, immediately, I was in love with him and was already beginning to feel all those feelings I knew he wouldn't have wanted me to feel.

After Cederick took a much needed breather, he rolled from off my back and curled up next to me. I welcomed him with open arms, but before I had the chance to experience the best part of sex- intimacy- he suddenly went into a weird flip mode.

"Shit! I'm trippin!" he said as he quickly sat up and began patting on the mattress in search of something.

"What's wrong?" I asked. "Whatcha lookin' for?"

"My phone," he panicked.

I reached around the side of me and grabbed his phone from between the wall and the mattress where I had pushed it to avoid him spotting it. "It's over here."

Cederick snatched it and mumbled to himself. "Fuck man! My nigga could be jammed up and I'm sitting here fucking around with a *bitch*."

That was the first time he had ever referred to me as that, but I decided not to take it personal. It was really hard to get mad at someone who had just given you the best sex of your life. Plus, I knew he was worried and frustrated with everything he thought was happening with Hi-C.

"Fuck!" he yelled again, once he realized that his phone was dead. "And the shit been off! What if he tried to call me?"

When he turned the phone back on, the light from it added dimness to room. I was now able to see his face a little bit. He wore that same worried look he had before we fucked, except now it was a little bit worse. And when the phone finally finished loading up, he really flipped out.

"Man fuck! Aint this some shit! Eight new voice messages!" he said as he got up, hit the light switch, and began pacing again.

Cederick placed his phone on speaker and listened to his voicemail while he rushed to put his pants back on. I followed his lead and began to do the same.

"*You have 8 new voicemails. Two saved messages,*" the computerized voice from the answering service said. *"To check your messages, press one."*

With his pants still halfway down, Cederick used his free hand to press the number on his phone.

BEEP. "FIRST NEW MESSAGE:"

"Ced this Peaches. I'm just letting you know that ya boy ain't showed up so don't expect to your cu...."

Cederick quickly skipped to the next message when he heard the loud ghetto voice of some girl who said her name was Peaches. The way he shut her up so quickly, almost seemed as if he had something to hide. But like everything else, I overlooked that too.

The next couple of messages where blanks. And by the time Cederick got to message number seven, he was just about to press the END button on his phone until he heard and a woman speak.

"NEXT MESSAGE:"

"Hey Cederick, it's Isis. I need to get in touch with you, asap. I got some good news and some bad news, so I'mma go ahead and give you the bad news first...

The bad news is- and I don't know if you heard yet- but the folks got my boo. I can't really talk much over the phone, but they ran up in the spot around eleven tonight, searching and shit.

The good news is that, of course, they ain't find shit. They only took him down for obstruction, which I feel was some bullshit because he ain't did nothing more than just curse they asses out for waking him up out of his sleep. But you know how the folks can play it…I just left the jail and his bond is thirty-five hundred. He told me when they were puttin' him in the cuffs, not to give them nothing more than what we had to and he specifically said to let him sit until Monday. I know you wanna get him out, but Ced, just do as he says. Plus, I think he wanna peep some shit out while he's in their too. Trust me, I know my husband…My phone and everything is back at the house. They wouldn't let me take shit from out of there. I'm staying to my sister's. This is her cell phone if you need to talk to me, but I pretty much just summed up everything for you. I will let you know if I hear anything new. Oh, and by the way, if you planning on staying out back tonight, you shouldn't. I think you should just lay low for a while and take your company elsewhere. Hi-C ain't taking no chances trusting anybody unfamiliar at this point. This is just until the weather gets cooler, if you know what I mean. In the meantime, holla at me and be safe brother. Peace."

I slowly put on my dress and pretended not to be listening, but really, I heard every word Isis said. I felt bad for manipulating Cederick, not to mention, I felt that he was probably going to blame me for my misjudgment. Luckily, the circumstances weren't as bad as Cederick thought they would be, but that didn't change the fact that his main homie, and his number source of income, was jammed up.

Cederick checked the rest of his messages to make sure nobody else called- possibly with more news- and once he was fully dressed, he grabbed his phone and headed for the door. I followed him, but he stopped me.

"Look, I'm about to step outside and call Icey real quick," he said. "I'll be right back."

Icey was Isis's nickname. She earned it honestly from being spoiled by Hi-C. I didn't see her much, but when I did, she was always shining and never rocked cheesy accessories, no matter how expensive or cute they were. Everything she wore was real gold, real diamond, or real silver.

She was the most beautiful chocolate woman I had ever laid eyes on, and she wore the face of a strong and powerful woman. Her skin was extra dark, but smooth and flawless. Her eyes were naturally hazel. And her hair was long, black, and silky. Keisha told me that Isis had a promising future to be an international model, but as she put it, "the dumb bitch gave it up just to be with Hi-C." Based solemnly off of Isis's beauty and slender physique, I found it highly believable. And if it were true, I only wished she would have pursued it because I knew she would have been sharing the throne with Naomi Campbell.

Isis was Hi-C's queen. And she knew it too. She even had the name plate with the words 'Icey the Wifey' printed on the front of her 2012, smoky-black Toyota Camry, to let hoes like Keisha know that they may have had him once, but she had his every dime.

"Okay, you want me to wait in the car?" I asked.

"No," he said. "There's a bar right across the street. I'mma run in there real quick, grab me a drink, and head straight back. You wait here in this room. I just need a little time to myself, you know, just to figure out what's going on."

Badly, I wanted to beg Cederick not to leave me again. We had just made passionate love and all I wanted to do was lie next to him. Isis said herself that there was nothing to worry about, and even I knew that an obstruction charge was just a misdemeanor. On top of that, I didn't know whose house I was in.

"But Cederick," I pleaded, "I don't even know these people like that."

"I know," he answered. "And you didn't know them when you were butt ass naked in their bedroom, screaming my name to the top of your lungs either, now did you?"

Cederick had a point, but still, when I was screaming his name, he was right there with me. I decided not to argue back with him because he had already made it clear that I couldn't go. It wasn't my first time waiting around for him, and it probably wouldn't be my last.

"No, I guess I didn't," I sighed.

"Look, there's nothing to worry about. I wouldn't leave you here if I thought for a second that you wouldn't be safe. I'm going to have one drink, talk to Icey, then I'm coming right back."

Cederick planted a wet-one on the top of my head. I couldn't believe that after everything we had just done, we were back to the forehead kiss. Then he glanced at me one last time, told me to lock the door, and disappeared down the hallway.

After Cederick left, I didn't bother turning the lights back on. There was nothing in the room worth seeing anyway. It was just me, the mattress, and the smell of Cederick and I marinating in the sheets. That made me instantly flash back to everything that had just went down. All the oohing and aahing, the sweating, and the sexing flooded my mind, causing me to smile. The way we made love was too intimate to be just another hook-up. I was confused. *If Cederick didn't want to be with me, then why would he fuck me like he loved me*? It wasn't fair. He was making it impossible for my feelings for him not to become stronger. I sure as hell didn't regret making love to him, but I did regret making that promise.

Two whole hours had passed when I found myself waking up to a single flick of the light.

"Charlytte. Babe, wake up," I heard Cederick's voice say.

As my pupils tried desperately to adjust to the light, I could make out Cederick standing over me with a Styrofoam cup in one hand and burning blunt in the other.

"Wha...what time is it?" I stuttered.

"It's two a.m.," he answered. "Sorry I took so long. The boys went with me and we ended up having more than just one drink."

Cederick was laughing as he spoke to me, even though nothing he said was funny.

"Aaaw man," he chuckled once more. "What a night?"

"What's so funny?" I asked him, then waited to be clued in.

He laughed again. "I just let them jerks talk me into betting some arrogant ass lil' nigga on a pool game, and guess what happened?"

"What?"

By now, I could tell that Cederick was buzzed. He was acting really weird and I could smell the vodka on his breathe.

"I underestimated that lil nigga and I'm damn near broke, that's what happened." Cederick laughed again.

"And that's funny?" I asked, not the least bit amused. I didn't think there was anything funny about him leaving me in an unfamiliar spot, just so he could go lose money on a pool game.

"Yeah," he answered. "Sometimes you gotta laugh to keep from crying."

I sat up and started putting on my shoes. The room was beginning to feel like a prison cell and there was nothing I wanted more to do than to just leave. Besides, I saw him blow two thousand alone on clothes in less than three hours, so what he told me about losing a couple hundred on a pool game was no big deal to me. And it definitely didn't prepare me for what he said next.

"Oh, and I talked to Hi-C too," he said.

"Oh good," I replied, anxious to hear what they discussed. "What did he say?"

"He's good, just a lil' shook and 'noid. He shuttin' down shop for a little while."

"What shop?" I asked, green to the street vocabulary.

"The business Mrs. Nosey, you sho' you ain't the damn police?" he laughed. I sucked my teeth and then roll me eyes at him.

"Naw, it's cool though," he continued. "It's happened before. Normally we don't move for like three months, but now he's talking six to a year."

"That's a long time," I said.

"Yeah I know it is, and it affects all of us, *even you*."

"What do you mean, even me?" I questioned. "I don't hustle."

"Welp babygirl," he sighed, then sat down on the edge of mattress and motioned for me to come and sit next to him. I obeyed. I didn't have the slightest clue what Cederick was talking about, but I was definitely all ears.

"Unfortunately, if you're involved with a hustler, you may as well be one too. That's just the way it goes. With that being said, I got some good news and some bad news for you."

"Aaaw hell," I said, trying to mentally prepare myself. "Hit me with the bad."

"Well, it's like this," he said, clearly trying to get his words together. "Hi-C told me that he doesn't want any more traffic at his home, not even in the shed. That means, we can't go back there."

"Shit," I blew out a deep sigh. "That is bad."

But not bad enough to have me worried. I had gotten so comfortable with trusting Cederick, that I just knew he wouldn't have helped me out that much, just to leave me out in the cold again.

"And what's the good news?" I asked, already believing that he had everything under control.

"The good news is that I got a quick gig for you, a possible way for you to make some fast money, you know, for yourself."

"What type of gig?" I asked excitingly. I had already been talking to Cederick about me getting a job for the summer, but he kept telling me to just focus on school. One thing about me, I knew how to work and I didn't mind taking on a job. "How soon is the job and how long would it take?" I asked.

"Honestly, you can make some money as soon as now, and how long it takes- three minutes to three hours- all depends on you."

"Three minutes to make some change? I'm down with that. Just tell me what I need to do."

"Well....," Cederick began to look around, then he held his head down and spoke in softer tone, as if he thought someone could have possibly been listening, "you know those guys we passed when we came in…"

"Yeah, I saw them" I said, trying to match my tone of voice with his. My smile slowly began to fade away. "Who are they?"

"A couple of nobodies really. Just some young cousins of Hi-C, making way more money than they should be. Their willing to pay two hundred and fifty dollars each, just to be with you."

"What do you mean, *be with me*?" I asked. My eyes lit up, my body straightened, and my smile hadn't just faded, it had turned into a complete frown.

"Aaw c'mon Charlytte, you young but you ain't dumb. You know exactly what I mean. Do I really have to break it down for you?"

"If you're saying what I think you're saying, then yes, I need you to break it down for me. I gotta make sure I'm hearing this right."

“Okay then, listen closely," he began. "It’s two lil’ niggas in there who are willing to pay two-fifty each just to fuck you. Individually or at the same time, whichever you prefer."

I didn't want to believe it. Maybe, just maybe, I was dreaming. It wasn't the two guys that wanted to sleep with me that got to me. It wasn't even that they offered me money to do it. It was the fact that Cederick was willing to allow it that got me heated. I thought he respected me more than that. And even though he didn't show it, I really believed in my heart that he loved me.

"Cederick, you gotta be kidding right? Please tell me that this is some type of joke. How could you insult me like that?"

"Now I'm insulting you?" Cederick rose up from the mattress and stood over me. "I'm not insulting you. I'm trying to fuckin' help you."

"Help me?" I looked up at him. "You're tryin' to help me by asking me to fuck, not one, but two guys that I never met before for some money!"

"Look," he said, managing to shout and keep quiet at the same. "I'm trying to help you by putting some money in ya damn pockets. This ain't about them two lil' niggas. I don't know if you were listening, but I just told you that Hi-C is shutting down shop. This shit is about to hurt *all* of us. I'm already struggling now with it slowing down, but with a complete shutdown, shit really 'bout to get ugly. I got two kids to take care of and with money not coming in like it used to, I just can't care for you the way I did before."

"I will find a job," I whispered. "Just give me a little time."

"We don't have a little time."

"Why not? I just watched you blow over two stacks in less than a day. You mean to tell me you can't put me up in a hotel for a couple of nights."

"Don't try to count my money, Charlytte. That's the best way to get put on my shitlist. I can't stand a muthafucka all in my pockets," he warned. "But since you wanna know, I only got a couple thousand dollars left to my name and at this point, I need every dollar."

"No, I can't." I whispered. "There's no way I can do this."

"Fine, have it your way. Just let me know where you want me to take you when we get back."

"What do you mean Cederick? You know I don't have anywhere to go."

"Cut the bullshit Charlytte," his voice began to rise. "You can go home, you just don't want to. You're just another stubborn little girl who can't follow rules. Well the charade is over. It's time for you to go back to your family."

Cederick was judging me, and I didn't like it one bit. He didn't know my situation. He didn't know about Auntie Jo and all the shit I had to put up with. I wasn't going home, no matter what.

"I'd rather die before I go back there. You haven't lived in my shoes, so you can't tell me a damn thing about the path I walk. I don't care what you think. I have *nowhere* to go."

"Exactly," he said. "Then what better reason for you to get this money."

I chuckled, trying to hide my hurt. "Cederick, you really have some nerve disrespecting me like this."

"I have some nerve?" he snapped, not caring anymore about who was listening. "No. *YOU* have some nerve! Was I disrespecting you when I turned ya penny pinching ass into a dime? Was I disrespecting you when I told Hi-C to keep that money he owed me and let you stay at his spot? Was I disrespecting you when I made sure you got back and forth to school? Or what about when I used come around you horny as fuck, and had to see yo' pretty lil' ass walking round in them tight booty shorts, but never once touched you? You're the one who has some nerve. I did everything and more for you, but the minute shit gets ugly and I ask you to do something, not even for me, but for yourself, you try to make me out to be the bad guy. What happened to 'if you ride for me, I'll ride for you? If you Clyde, then I'm Bonnie'...What happened to all that shit...huh?"

"No, it's not even like-" I started to defend myself, but Cederick cut me off.

"What's the problem, Charlytte? You afraid of what people gone say? You think I'mma look at you different? You think you gone feel like less of a woman?" he asked. "You think you grown because you had a lil' job and you 'supposedly' out on ya own? My nine-year old nephew got a job sweeping up at the barbershop, but that don't make him a man. You not grown Charlytte and you're not on ya own. You just getting by depending on people. But what if everybody was gone? What if I walked out of this house right now, never looked back, and that two-fifty was on that kitchen table waiting on you? What would you do then?"

Cederick moved closer to me and got up in my face. I sat there quiet, showing no emotion.

"You think being grown is about whether or not you got a job? No! It's about knowing how to survive. I been out on my own since I was thirteen, and unlike you, I didn't run into people that I could mooch off of. Nobody took me in and helped me get on my feet. I had to do what I had to do to see the next day, and that meant I had to learn the streets. When I needed money, if I had to small hustle on the block to get it, then that's what I did. I had to eat, so if that meant I had to rob a nigga, then that's what I did. I had to live, so if I had to shoot first, then that's what the *fuck* I did."

Staring up at the flimsy light bulb in the ceiling, I could feel a teardrop roll down my cheekbone. I tried to turn to the right side of my face so Cederick wouldn't see it, but I was never really good at keeping anything from him.

"There's no need to cry, babygurl," he consoled me. "Listen, if I made my decisions based on what people thought, I'd be dead by now. You can't be worried about what the world says is right or wrong. Those same people you're worried about are gonna judge you either way. Those peers, those Christians, those guys in there," he pointed, "they all got places stay and half of them never had to want for nothing a day in their happy little lives. They got family and support, you don't. God's not like them. He's not judgmental and he'll still love you the same. I don't care what 'man' tells you, life ain't about making good or bad choices, it's about what you do, verses why you do it. Nobody's situation is the same so you can't make decisions based on anybody 's circumstances but your own."

I don't know why I just couldn't tell myself that Cederick was running game on me, and how did he have the power to make something so bad seem so good? Worst of all, why did I always believe that he was right?

"I don't know if I could do this Cederick. I really don't know."

"Okay, it's your choice babygirl, I won't put no gun to ya head and I don't wanna keep pressuring you," he said. "How 'bout this?...I'mma go out front and send one of 'em back here in ten minutes. I want you to lock the door behind me and when he knocks, if you don't want to do it, don't open it. If you do, then you know what to do."

Cederick handed me his cup and the blunt- that because he abandoned it when he was preaching to me- had burned out.

"It's goose and cranberry. Drink all of this and hit that a couple of times. I promise you won't even think about it. And if it makes you feel any better, just imagine he's me."

Cederick kneeled down on the cold, bare floor and lifted up my dress. He kissed my thighs and twirled his tongue around my clit softly. Just when I was getting into it, he drew back. Then he walked to the door, flicked the light off, and right before he closed it all the way, peeped his head back into the room, "Just think of it as your birthday, the day you did what the fuck you had to do to survive: the day you became of woman."

I watched Cederick as he closed the door, leaving me in the dark to make my decision. I didn't need ten minutes to decide what I was going to do because I already knew the answer. In attempt to drown out everything I had just heard, I took a sip of the goose, lit the blunt and took one long pull, then blew out my troubles. In fact, I spent the entire ten minutes sipping, puffing, and thinking. I thought about my life. I thought about how when everything seemed to go so good, it always turned out bad. I thought about my mama. I thought about Auntie Jo. I even thought about my grandparents. Who in my family could have done something so terrible that I was suffering the consequences of it? I didn't have all the answers, but either way, I always found myself getting the short end of the stick- or in this case- the short end of the dick.

My pitied thoughts were shortly interrupted by a tap on the door. My ten minutes were up. I still hadn't brought myself to believe it. I thought perhaps it could have been Cederick telling me that I had been punked, but when I saw the shadow of a taller dude with medium-length dreadlocks entering the door, I knew it was the real deal.

I couldn't get a good glimpse of the guy and I wasn't trying to. All I know was that he was standing there waiting for me to "okay" his presence, and I laid stretched out with my legs busted wide open on the mattress, giving him my answer.

"Happy birthday Charlytte," I whispered to myself, as I watched the guy pull down his pants and bring himself closer to me. "Happy fuckin' Birthday."

PART THREE

27: FIERCE

"See, that's why she's my top bitch!" Cederick said to Peaches, who sat jealously in the back seat as he sped out of the gas station parking lot.

I had just pulled up my shirt and showed some stockbroker-looking white dude my pretty brown nipples. I was pumping gas in my short black mini-skirt and he was filling up at pump right behind us, staring at me so hard that he almost waste gas on the ground and on himself. The fact that he was checking me out wasn't the problem- when you're wearing a skirt with your ass cheeks hanging out it's hard not to be watched. But what I didn't like was that his wife was sitting in the passenger seat of their BMW giving me dirty looks. I tried to ignore the both of them, but that last little roll of her eyes from up underneath those thick, bulky glasses made me wanna leave her with something that would put a permanent stain on them. So, before getting back in the car, I lifted my shirt and gave them both something to talk about on their way home to the suburbs.

I didn't care nothing about disrespecting an elder, and probably happily married, couple. And I didn't mind that other people were at the gas station and saw the whole thing. Showing strangers your tits was no big deal when you slept with random men for a living.

"And that's what he gets for staring so damn hard, trying to act like they don't like dark meat," I laughed, while pulling down my red halter top blouse. "Did y'all see the look on his wife's face?"

I turned to Cederick, who was quite amused by what I had just done. I guess transforming me from the girl I used to be, to the girl I was now, was one of his proud accomplishments.

"Yeah, I saw her. That bitch was picking up the phone to dial 911, trying to get my tag number and all," he laughed right along with me. "I had to peel out. I don't need that heat, especially not on this highway."

"Yeah, you right," Peaches butted in. "We got impo'tant business to 'tend to, and way too much weed in here for me to be sticking up my pussay, and she wanna be out here doing hawt shit. But this yo' top bitch though, you sure know how to pick 'em Cederick."

"Oh shut up Peaches, with yo' hatin' ass," I teased her. "You just mad you ain't had the courage to do it."

Peaches was sitting in the backseat with a lollipop in her mouth and two more in her hands. She kept a stash of any type of hard candy because she had become so used to sucking dick, that when she wasn't sucking on something, she started freaking out.

She was nineteen years old and a long time employee of Cederick. Like me, she had been out on the streets since she was fifteen, but Cederick didn't have trouble trying to turn her out. She had already been tricking before they met, and had even taught him a little bit about the game.

See peaches used to be what Cederick called his 'top bitch', that was until she started sniffing powder and popping pills heavily. Cederick didn't mind if his girls did drugs, but if it started to affect their minds- and most importantly- their bodies, then it became a huge problem for him.

"The courage?" she looked at me sideways. "Ced, I know she only been knowin' me for a year, but you better tell her…"

"Yeah, Charlytte, you gone have to put in a lot of work to come anywhere near as close as my girl Peaches here." Cederick defended Peaches, then peeped in his rearview mirror and smiled. He was truly proud of her for putting a price tag on her body and making lots of money for him.

"That's right!" Peaches threw her hands up, twirled them around in the air, and moved her hips seductively. "You may be the 'Top Bitch' but I'm the 'Queen Bitch'. Remember that," she bragged. "Cederick knows it, he just doesn't know how to be loyal."

"*Loyal*?" Cederick asked as he passed me and Peaches both a White Owl blunt and a sack of weed to roll up. We were going to smoke while we were on the road. "Peaches, what are you talking 'bout now?"

Peaches took the bluntcutter off her keychain and slid the blunt through its' hole, exposing the guts. I didn't own one, and I wasn't about to ask for hers, so I broke mine down manually.

"I mean damn, Ceddy Boo, I worked for you all these years, took in plenty dick, and brought you in a good bit of money. I manage them stupid ass little whores in that hot ass freakhouse, do your job and mine, then soon as the stress from all that starts to take a toll on me and I need a lil' powdery boost to keep me focused, you just kick me to the curb for some for some young ass, inexperienced broad. That's fucked up."

Cederick smacked his lips. "No, what's fucked up is how skinny you gettin' and niggas starting to notice that. Like you just said, you the Queen Bitch and nobody gone take that title from you. But you know like I know that the Top Bitch is always the one bringin' in the top amount of dollars, and that bitch just so happens to be Charlytte."

Peaches rolled her eyes at the sound of my name. She acted like she couldn't stand me but I knew deep down she loved me, probably even more than I wanted to imagine. Peaches might have been a dumb broad who was only good for sucking and fucking, but she was smart when it came to money. And she knew that when me and her did shit together, we got paid.

As a matter of fact, we were on the way to Jacksonville to visit our number one paying customer, G. He was getting married and his homies were throwing a bachelor party for him at the house where I turned trick. I ended up having sex with three guys that night- four if you included Cederick. And it must have been good too, because the first two went back and told another guy named G about me, and Cederick convinced him to pay up too. We made seven hundred dollars in less than two hours, drove back to Ordale in the middle of the night, and with the money I had just made, Cederick put me up in a hotel. At first I was hoping that it was just a one-time thing, but after Hi-C never got out of jail, Cederick started going broke, and the hotel-stay days were running out, I was begging him to turn me on to another gig.

"Face it Peaches," I said laughing in her face. "You fallin' off!"

Peaches slapped me in the back of my head and we all laughed. We hated each other, but loved each other just the same. I couldn't be mad at her. Especially since she was the one who taught me the most about tricking, and I hadn't started seeing the real dollars until niggas started paying to see us eat each other's pussy.

Truthfully, the first day I met Peaches she went down on me. Shit was crazy because G, the guy who we were going to put on the bachelor show for- and who after that first night had been paying me at least once a month to hit it- told Cederick he wanted to try something new. Then, six months into me tricking, Cederick comes to the hotel, throws six one-hundred dollar bills the table, and tells me that it all could be mine if was willing to sleep with G and his fiancé.

As usual, Cederick convinced me that it was no biggie. He said that they just wanted to do something wild before they got married, and out of all the things they could afford to do- jet skiing, sky diving, or even bungee jumping- a threesome was what they decided on. As much as I had fucked G, I would have never guessed that he had a girlfriend, let alone one who he'd soon be making his wife. And I sure as hell wouldn't have thought that she'd be willing to participate too.

I wasn't big on the idea of sleeping with another woman. As a matter of fact, I was completely against it. And besides, Cederick had opened up and told me about a girl name Peaches who handled all the same-sex affairs. He also told me about the small whorehouse that he was running, which I had no clue about when we first met. He said he didn't tell me because as long as the money he was making from hustling was good, he let the girls do their thing and run the business on their own. But after Hi-C got jammed and the money got low, he tightened up and became boss again, having all types of jobs lined up for the girls and taking unfair percentages.

The whorehouse was the house where the ugly, the crackhead, and the ratchet girls fucked for a couple of dollars. It was pretty much walk-ins, no appointments. The badder girls like me, Peaches, and another girl named Monique- who was on a standstill because she had just had a baby- had the appointments and got to the bigger bucks.

Fortunately, threesomes were Peaches specialty, but G requested me personally. I was scared, and Cederick knew it, so he felt that it would be a good idea for Peaches to come in and 'break me out of my shell.' Cederick called up Peaches right there at the hotel and offered her a hundred dollars, out of my cut, just to perform oral sex on me and help me get comfortable with being with a girl.

It was around three o'clock that afternoon when Peaches stormed into my hotel room with her let's-get-this-over-with attitude. I immediately noticed how beautiful she was with her caramel brown complexion, her nicely shaped fish lips, and her long blonde weave. It wasn't until later, when I saw some of her older pictures, that I realized just how badly she had fallen off.

Peaches was the bold and bossy type. Without caring how nervous I was, she laid me out on the hotel bed and ate my pussy better than Cederick did. Then after I climaxed, she opened her legs and told me to try. I spent the next fifteen minutes doing to her what she had done to me. Cederick just sat there watching the whole thing, not even turned on the slightest bit. Everything was strictly business with him.

After I returned the favor and made Peaches cum, she told Cederick that I would do just fine, took the hundred dollars and left. I never saw or heard anything from her again until Cederick was calling us back to do business together.

In the car, Peaches was already sparking up her blunt, while I was just starting to roll mine and I was upset because I didn't beat her to it. Secretly, we felt the same way about our man and although we didn't say it, we both wanted to be with him. It got so bad that we'd often compete for his attention. So of course, instead of obviously hitting it first because she rolled it, Peaches puffed it once- just to get it burning nicely- then boastfully passed it up to Cederick.

Knowing exactly what she was doing, I turned around in my seat and gave her a dirty look. She shot one back at me and then decided to keep the act going by really trying to make me jealous.

"Hey Cederick!" Peaches called from the back seat.

"What's up babygirl," he answered, as he examined her perfectly rolled blunt of Kush.

"What's that lil' nickname you gave me when we used to roll together a couple years back?" she asked.

Oh shut...up! I said to myself.

"Oh, yeah I remember...it was uhm...uhm..." Cederick thought long and hard. Then he took long pull from the blunt and released the smoke from his lungs, as if it was supposed to help jog his memory. Apparently, it worked.

"Pecka!" It finally came to him. "That's what it was...Pecka."

"*Becka*?" I burst out in laughter." What type of name is Becka."

"No, not Becka," Cederick corrected me. "Pecka."

"Ooookay, let me rephrase that." I said, starcastically. "What type of name is *Pecka*?"

'"I named her Pecka back then because the way she sucked a dick, she had to have been born half-man and half woodpecker," he laughed.

It took a second for me to mentally visualize a woodpecker and actually get the joke, and even when I did, I still didn't think it was funny. I had seen Peaches give head a couple times before, and I must admit, she invented the shit, but I didn't think it was appropriate for her to be bragging about it- especially considering the fact that my head game wasn't nearly as strong as hers was. Peaches was really trying to piss me off and was doing a good job at it. I just couldn't let her win like that.

"That's not fair Cederick," I cried, patching the last little piece of my blunt together and waving it in his face to let him see that I too was finished. "How come you never gave me a nickname?"

"I did," he replied. "I just haven't told you it yet."

"Well," I said, hitting the blunt I just lit and allowing the smoke to enter my lungs. We always kept at least two in rotation. "What is it?""

"It's Fierce," he told me.

"*Fierce*?" Peaches and I both said at the same time.

I liked it. I just didn't see how it fit me.

"Why Fierce?" I asked.

"Because, of the way you were when I first met you- how you were so timid and shy, and submissive. But I knew deep down that you had a raspy side. You just needed to right level of confidence to bring it out. Plus, the way you rode the dick really shocked me. You were just sixteen but *dayum*, you was mean wit' it."

Peaches laughed in jealousy, then mocked me. "Oh, I thought it was because of that *fierce* looking cut on her face."

Even at the maturing age of seventeen, I was still sensitive about my scar. I never really knew how Cederick felt about it because he never spoke of it or asked me any questions. I always took it as he was just being nice.

"Fuck you Peaches, wit' yo fish lips," I said, trying to get even. "Ced, I know you'll keep it real wit' me. Honestly, what do you think about my scar? Does it make me look ugly?"

"What? Are you fuckin' crazy?" he asked. "That's what makes you sexy."

"Sexy?" I asked, in disbelief. "Now I know you just talking."

"Mmm...hmm," Peaches agreed. "Don't believe the hype. He just doesn't want to hurt your feelings."

"Peaches chill," Cederick said, getting very serious with her. "All jokes aside, don't try to think for me."

Once again, he looked into his rearview mirror at Peaches, but this time he wasn't smiling. He made direct eye contact with her and she immediately knew that she had better get quiet. He always made sure he looked us in the eye when he was getting on us about something. Cederick was willing to laugh and joked, but he always demanded respect when it was time for it. There was two things he didn't play around with- his word and his money.

When Cederick felt that Peaches had completely understood him, he took the floor again and continued on. "What I'm trying to say is that your scar is what defines you. You wouldn't be who you are without it. It shows your pain, but also your desire for pleasure. It's what makes you look fierce."

Cederick grabbed the side of my face with his right hand and rubbed his fingers across my wound. "Mix your personality and your sexual aggression with that scar, and you've got yaself got one helluva combination."

I turned around to Peaches, who had her lips pouted and her head facing out the window. She clearly didn't want to be a part of the conversation any longer. I stared at her, just waiting for her to look my way so that I could give her the same clever smirk that she had given me.

"One fierce combination huh," I said, while still looking at Peaches.

"Exactly," he answered.

Peaches remained silent and never looked my way. As a matter of fact, nothing was said from any of us for a while afterwards.

Weed smoke fogged the air and we were buzzing like a motherfucker, all of us quietly thinking about our own little problems. We silently listened to the sounds of Lil' Boosie and a half hour later, as we got closer to our destination, Peaches started pouring up the liquor in the back seat.

"Alright nye Charlytte, we're almost there," she said, clearly over the earlier incident. When Peaches knew she was about to make some money, nothing could keep her discouraged. "You know the rules right?"

"Yep," I answered, digging in my purse for my make-up kit. "Don't give them no more than what they pay for. Start off with a lil' bit and work my way up. Basically, the more they pay, the more I give."

"You got it!" Peaches said as she handed me my cup of pineapple juice and grey goose.

This was my first party and it was dear to me because that month made a full year since I started tricking. I was a little nervous, but I knew a little Vodka and Ecstasy would rid me of that. Plus, Peaches had taught me everything I needed to know about the game. She told me all the do's and dont's of putting on a show. Cederick even said if we played our cards right we could end up bringing home five stacks. I wasn't a big fan of bachelor parties, but twenty-five hundred dollars was just what I needed to put down a security deposit and pay the first months' rent for that apartment I was looking into. I was planning on putting the rest up with some other money that I had stashed, so that I would finally have enough to get that 98' T-top Camaro I always wanted too.

We pulled up to the house at exactly eleven o'clock and were stunned by all the cars that filled up the street. At the sight of them, I downed the rest of my drink and held my cup out for Peaches to pour me up another round.

"Slow down girl," Cederick said. "Don't get too fucked up before the night even starts."

"Cederick, you must not see all these cars," I said. "I thought this was a private party, not a block party."

"Shit, the more cars, the more money," Peaches said. "And these ain't just cars, dey nice cars. You better pay attention and observe."

Cederick agreed with Peaches, then they both snorted their lines. Sad to say, that was another thing she was proud she could share with him that I couldn't. I willing let her have that one because there was no way I was going to let what powder was doing to Peaches, do to me. Plus, even though Cederick started doing it very heavily after Hi-C got locked up, he still didn't recommended it for me, or anyone else who hadn't already gotten hooked on it.

I wanted so badly to go ahead and get the show on the road, because I knew once we started, the knot in my stomach would disappear. I didn't know which was worse, my nervousness because I was about to perform, or my anxiousness to see how much money we would make by the end of the night. Not only was I depending on that change, but I had begun to believe that I needed to trick in order to survive and stay fly. Besides, I never made it to high school my sophomore year, and I knew it was too late to go back.

Once Peaches and Cederick were done geeking themselves up, and I had swallowed my half of pill down with a shot of vodka, we dashed across the street, cut through the front lawn, and headed towards the front of the house. Peaches and I had on our long, black trench coats with our matching lace thong and bra set underneath, except hers was red and mines was black.

A couple guys were standing on the porch already drunk as hell, a few were passed out in the grass, and the rest were crowded around a dice game. When they saw us, all heads turned our way and all bodies- even the passed out ones- immediately started following us like we were Jesus. They were yelling out all types of perverted stuff, but at least we managed to get passed them without being physically harassed. Cederick made sure of it. He was our protector, sort of like a bodyguard. He made sure nobody touched us without paying and I knew he was going to be in the party watching every guy, making sure that no one got over on us.

When we entered the house, all the men, or should I say ghetto disciples, praised Cederick for bringing in the two young hotties. They had two poles already set up in the middle of the front room floor just waiting to be put to use. G was sitting in a chair directly in between both of them. He was already filthy drunk and ready for his show, and although Peaches was the pro at stripping, I wasn't the least bit intimidated because anytime I popped ecstasy, I felt like I could do anything.

The lights suddenly flicked off. I saw Cederick take his place in a corner. G signal for the camera man to begin rolling the footage. Peaches and I both took our places at our poles. Then the D.J. bumped the record, and yelled out to the audience, "ALRIGHT EVERYBODY, LET'S GET THIS SHOW ON THE ROAD!!!"

28: CLUB KARMA

Peaches and I did our business together, but we never personally hung out. Sometimes I would see her around town and wouldn't even acknowledge her. I didn't have anything against the girl; she was just too 'open' for me. She didn't care about what people said or thought about her. She was the type to tell the Pastor what she did for a living, then ask him if he needed a blessing, if you know what I mean. I would sometimes see in her the mall wearing practically nothing, trying to catch plays all out in the open and I wasn't with that. Shit, I was tricking too, but I wasn't boastful about it. I tried to be as low as possible and I didn't think too many people knew or even cared about what I was doing. Besides, most of the guys I was sleeping with were much older than me, or out of town.

I stayed so low key that even Keisha hadn't found out- until one month after I moved- that I had my own apartment. We really didn't hang out as much since Hi-C had gotten arrested. Like Cederick, Keisha was also affected by the bust and wasn't able to go on runs, therefore she wasn't bringing in the chips that she was used to. In attempt to make up for her lost, she was spending most of her time trying to find niggas with money, to keep up with her expensive spending habits.

Although Keisha and I didn't see each other as often, we still kept in touch by phone. I always called to check up on her, but mostly when I needed to talk to her about something Cederick did. She, in turn, mainly called me when she had something juicy to gossip about. And as far as us going out together, it was either on a holiday or if a famous celebrity was coming into town.

In fact, we had been planning for months to go to the R.I.P Bash that went down every summer. A very talented local rapper in our city was shot down in front of his label's studio with his kid in his arms. His name was Army Boy and everyone in the hood respected him. Nobody could paint pictures, give you the real, and reach out to the hearts of the streets like the boy Army. If he wouldn't have been killed, he definitely would have been a rap superstar. Club Paradise threw a party each year dedicated to him, and anyone else who had fallen victim to the cold streets of Ordale.

I was sitting at home one lonely Saturday, and the only thing stopping me from dying of boredom was that the Bash would be going down in less than three hours. I called Keisha to make sure we were still on, and to find out who else was going with us. She answered her phone on the first ring.

"Hey, what's up cousin?" Keisha asked.

"Nothing much girl," I yawned. "Just a little tired. I was up since eight trying to get my fit before everybody else crowded the mall."

"That was smart. You know they gone be deep up in that shit today," she replied. "Did you find something?"

"A green top with some camouflage Capri's from Macy's," I told her.

Green wasn't my thing and camouflage definitely wasn't my pattern, but everyone wore it to pay tribute to Army boy's name. Not to mention, it got you in the club much cheaper.

"You wearing camouflage too, right?" I asked her.

Keisha paused for a minute, and then sighed deeply.

"Uhmm…I don't know Charlytte. I don't even think I'm going."

"What!" I shouted. "Aww…c'mon Keish! You know I never been to one before. I really want to go."

"I know, I know, I'm sorry. But me and Michael got into a really bad argument earlier. I have a major headache and I'm just not feeling it tonight."

Michael was a gastrointestinal doctor that Keisha met while shopping downtown. He was the high-class type who would not have been talking to Keisha had he known who she really was, and what she really was all about. Keisha was smart though. She knew how to turn her ghettoness on and off, and she knew how to fit in with the uppity folks. She had him thinking that she was the treasurer at a church, and that she had gotten her bachelor's degree in Accounting. The conniving bitch even had a fake ass graduation certificate planted up on her living room wall.

"But that's why you need to go out, to release some of that stress," I tried to convince her. "I'm on my way there now. Which one of your spots are you at?"

"The projects," she said.

Just like the hustler Keisha was, she had applied for housing, got a two bedroom apartment in the projects, and rented it out to one of her homegirls, all in the same month. I thought it was highly unusual for her to have gotten a place that fast, especially since she didn't have any kids. But leave it up to Keisha, she knew how to work the system.

Conveniently, the housing project was in the downtown area, and was just a skip and a hop from the club. As a matter of fact, we normally parked there and walked to avoid the heavy traffic of flashy, flexin' ass niggas.

"What happened now?" I asked her, knowing that the only time she went to that spot was when she was trying to dodge someone, or when she wanted to get back to her roots by creeping around on Michael with some good ole hood dick. Her homegirl, Shameka, who rented out the place, worked overnight at a gas station. She was rarely ever there, but she didn't mind that Keisha came by quite often. Actually, she felt better knowing that someone was there with her six, nine, and thirteen-year old while she worked.

"I ain't gone lie," she said, "I stole some stash from one of these lame ass niggas yesterday and he's been comin' round my place like he's crazy. He popped up last night when I was there with Michael, and if it wasn't for that cableman uniform he had on, I would have been busted."

"Oh shit," I gasped. "Girl, you gotta be careful."

"I know man," she agreed. "Last night was one helluva night. Speaking of last night, what did you do missy? I tried to call you."

I instantly had a flashback of the old white man who paid me three hundred dollars just for a thirty-minute striptease and a blow job. Then I looked over on my dining room table and saw all of the ones scattered over it.

"Nothing much. Just chilled," I told her.

I don't know why I couldn't tell Keisha that I was tricking. Even after she admitted to me plenty of times that she fucked niggas just to get money from them, I still couldn't come clean. For some reason, I just wanted to pretend like I had everything together.

"I know you really wanted to go, but I can't lie sis, I'm just not up to it. Alicia and Shannon are still going and I think their meetin' up over here around ten. How 'bout you go with them."

Ugh, Alicia. I thought. I wasn't comfortable stepping out with anybody other than Keisha, and I definitely didn't want to go out with Mrs. Hollywood. But still, I hadn't enjoyed myself in a long time and I really wanted to be at that party. Besides, I had just got some new weave *and* had a couple extra dollars of my own to spend. I thought long and hard, and since Shannon was going to be there, I decided that, yes, I would join them.

"I really wish you would change your mind, but okay, I guess I'll go."

"Good. Alicia has to go by and pick up Shannon, so I'll tell her swing by and grab you too. I know you just got your car but you don't need to be riding until you get that insurance on it, miss hottie."

"Yeah, I know," I replied, even though I wasn't so happy about not being able to show my car off to Alicia. I had finally gotten that Camaro I always wanted, and maybe seeing me in my own place and driving my own car, she would have respected me for the woman I thought I was.

"Cool. See ya when you get here," Keisha said.

“Later," I sighed.

"Hey Charlytte wait!" Keisha yelled, just as I was about to hang up the phone up."

"I'm still here. What's up.”

"Is Ced there?" she asked.

"No. I don't know where that fool is."

“Did you talk to him today?"

"Earlier, why?"

"Nothing major, I just needed to talk to him. I don’t like to talk over the phone, but you know I gotta answer to him since he's in charge now."

"Yeah, I know. How fun." I said, sarcastically.

Herb had finally given Ced the connect, and the okay to pick the business back up. Although they hadn't started making any major moves yet, Keisha was making sure she still had her job and that the routes were still the same. I knew that was exactly why she wanted to speak with him.

“Extremely fun,” Keisha chuckled, slightly though. "When you see him, just tell him I’m trying to reach him."

"Okay, if he calls me I will definitely let him know."

"Thanks, sis."

"No prob. See you later."

We both said our goodbyes and I headed straight for the shower. I was dressed and dolled up in less than an hour, and was looking damn good too. My camouflaged pants stopped a little passed my knees and wrapped around my calves tightly. The way they fitted me and had my ass sitting high, I knew I was going to have all of the local soldiers at my attention.

Even my top was cute. It exposed the line in the middle of my breast and I had purposely failed to mention to Keisha that I got one of Army Boy's famous rap lines, *Y'all Don't Want Da Drama,* airbrushed on the back of it. I just wanted to see the look on her face when she saw it for herself. I finished the outfit off with some gold accessories and some gold heels.

My hair was pretty too. Mrs. Harriet had it looking stunning, as usual, with some long, wavy curls and honey blonde highlights. This time she also spiced me up with some red streaks in the front. It sounds a little ghetto, but it was far from that.

Alicia picked me up a little after ten and we headed straight to Keisha's spot. I had hoped that when Keisha saw everybody dressed up and looking cute, she would have changed her mind and decided to come along. But once I saw her hair sticking up all over head and that weary look in her eyes, I knew that wasn't going to happen. We sat with Keisha long enough to take one shot of Goose and smoke one blunt, then we were all on our way. Luckily, we didn't have to wait in line, or pay a thing because Alicia knew the club owner and she used to fuck with the doorman. Selfish of me to say, but that was the only reason I was glad she was there.

Club Paradise wasn't a fancy club, but the dance floor was huge. It had floors up and downstairs and the bar stand was long enough to sit about fifty people. On top of that, one drink was guaranteed to get you fucked up.

Just as I thought, the inside of the club was already packed and everyone was paying tribute to Army Boy by sporting their camouflaged gear and R.I.P t-shirts in their own unique way. The D.J. was bumping some good warm-up songs, but anytime the girls and I went clubbin' we never hit the dance floor.

As usual, we headed straight for the bar. Alicia bought herself an Absolut and pineapple drink, and Shannon and I grabbed us a blue motherfucker. After two hours passed of sipping, mangling, and enjoying ourselves watching everybody dancing and having a good time, I looked across the bar and surprisingly saw someone that I hadn't seen in a long time taking a seat.

Oh shit. Marcus! I said to myself.

That familiar-looking guy was very much Marcus, my high school sweetheart and first love. I watched him as he ordered himself a Corona and a shot of something brown. As I sat staring at him all alone under that bar light, a ton of memories flooded my brains. It had been years since we last spoke, and although I never thought more of him after my heart had finally mended, I still felt the need to go say hello and show him exactly what he said goodbye to.

"I'll be right back," I told Shannon and Alicia who were both chatting with a mutual guy friend of theirs, while still keeping Marcus in my eyesight.

They both nodded their heads and continued on with their conversation. After getting the okay from them, I maneuvered my way through the crowds of people, managing to dodge two older cats who were trying to get my attention. Marcus was too busy staring up at the flat screen T.V. monitor, to see me when I snuck up on him.

"Nice to see you again," I said, catching him completely off guard. Then I sat down on the bar stool beside him and crossed one leg over the other seductively.

Marcus turned and looked at me strangely, and the first thing I thought to myself when I got a closer look at him was '*damn homie, in high school you was the man homie.*' I couldn't help but notice how dry and small his face was. He didn't at all look like the same Marcus I knew a couple of years ago, but at least I recognized him. Marcus just looked at me like he never saw me a day in his life. Then, after long hard stare, it all seemed to come back to him.

"Miss Feisty?" he finally asked, breath smelling like a whole case of beer. He had that drunken gloss in his eyes; I just knew he was tipsy.

"Yeah, it's me." I said as I flipped my hair from out of my face, showing it off a bit. "How you been?"

"I've been good, maintaining," he said, then reached out for me to hug him.

"That's what's up," I embraced him, then released my arms from around his shoulders and slowly brushed my fingers across his neck as my hands slid down. I did that on purpose.

"How's college?" I asked.

"I wouldn't know. I never made it there," he replied.

"What?" I said, completely shocked. "Why not, if you don't mind me asking."

"Naw, it's cool," he said with a sad, blank look on his face. "Just made the wrong decisions and got myself into a little bit of trouble."

"Oh, sorry to hear that," I sympathized, but in reality, I wasn't sorry at all. "Are you going to go eventually?"

"Naw, I don't think so," he said. "That school shit ain't for me. What about you? You should be getting close to senior status, ain't it?"

"Nope. I dropped out. Apparently it ain't for me either," I co-signed. "Besides, people don't necessarily have to go to school to get money."

"Yeah, true dat," he replied. "I think that college shit is just a scam anyway."

"A big one," I agreed.

Marcus and I both shared a laugh that we hadn't shared in a long time. For the next ten minutes we chatted and I learned a lot about him. He explain to me why he didn't make it college, how the felony charge he caught was making it impossible for him to find a job, and the possible baby he had on the way. You would think that after hearing how fucked up his life seemed, I would have felt sorry for the boy, but deep down inside, I was glad that he was doing bad. And the entire time he talked with me, all I kept thinking was, *at least I got a drink out of this pathetic bastard.*

I listened to Marcus a little longer and continued to act interested, but really I could care less about his problems. I was working on my second blue motherfucker, getting hornier by the second, and would have loved to fuck him for free that night. I would have enjoyed showing Marcus how much my sex and head game had grown.

There was just one problem; nothing about him turned me on. I tried everything- looking into his eyes, reminiscing back on the past, imagining that he was someone else- but all I ended up feeling like doing was getting the hell away from him.

"I hate to cut you off there bae," I said, interrupting his story about his mama's cancer coming back, "but my homegirls over there should be expecting me back any minute now."

Marcus got quiet and a devilish smirk appeared on his face, as if he just knew I was lying to him. Then I watched his eyes as they went from my lips on down to my breast, where he boldly glued them and clearly began lusting over me.

"What's wrong?" I moved my face closer to his, trying to snap him out of his daze.

"Nothing, just thinking."

"About?"

Marcus paused for what seemed like forever. "Us," he finally said.

"What about us, Marcus?" I asked.

"Nothing serious, just about what we used to have and how much I've I missed you."

I knew Marcus was full of shit and was just saying anything to make his move on me. The way he was drooling, and how unstable his life seemed, I knew that the last thing on his mind was trying to rebuild a relationship.

"Did you miss me?" he brushed his index finger across my cheekbone.

I snatched his hands away from my face before answering. "A little, Marcus."

It seemed like the whole club went crazy when the D.J. played Army Boy's number one hit 'Cut Buddies.' "I can't hear you," he leaned in closer to me. "What did you say?"

"I... SAID," I yelled a little louder, while slowing my words down for him, "A LIT-TLE."

"What exactly did you miss?" he hollered back.

I hesitated. "Uhm…everything, I guess."

Marcus paused and waited for me to finished talking, but after he realized that I wasn't going to give up anything else, he continued.

"I missed you too. You wanna know what I missed the most?"

"What?" I answered, not at all curious.

"I missed your lips," he said to me, "...the way you said 'hello' with them, the way you smiled with them, how soft they felt when I kissed you..."

Marcus chuckled a bit, probably laughing at how cheesy he sounded. Then he took another sip of his Corona and flagged the bartender to pick up his tab before he continued on. "And I miss the way you-"

"I get it." I said, cutting him off quickly. The more intimate his thoughts got, the more disgusted I became just knowing that I used to fuck with his sorry ass.

A little thrown off by my snappy attitude, he said, "What? I'm just letting you know how I feel about you. Is that a crime?"

It wasn't a crime for him to tell me that he missed me, but it was a crime for him to tell me that he missed me just so he could get in my pants. Marcus wasn't fooling me one bit. I knew exactly what he was trying to do-slide his way back inside of me by bringing up old times. I could tell he still thought I was that same gullible chick I used to be, and if he did, I had bad news for him.

"Naw, not at all," I said. "But it is a fee."

Marcus laughed, stared down at me silently, then laughed again.

"Come again?" he said, putting his ear up to my mouth.

"Just cut to the chase, Marcus," I told him. "It may have been a while since we kicked it, but I still know you like the back my hand. I know your eyes get low when you get horny and I know how your left legs starts rocking back and forth," I pointed down to his knee caps.

"I can't deny that Charlytte, so yes, I'll admit, I do want to fuck you," he confessed. "You're sexy, I mean sexier, than I have ever saw you before and just looking at you is making my dick hard. Is that what you wanna hear?"

Marcus took a deep breath, relieving himself, then swallowed down another sip of his beer. "Besides, I kind of miss yo lil' ass, for real."

I always wondered if he ever thought about me in any type of way, and him telling me that at that very moment, whether it was true or not, satisfied me. That was all I really wanted, to know that I could be longed for by somebody.

"Things have changed since we've been together," I said. "Actually, alot has changed. I'm not the same little naive girl you used to know. All I'm saying is that we can hook up again, but this time you gotta pay a price."

Marcus still held a look of confusion on his face, like he didn't know whether to take me serious or laugh at me. And since he didn't seem to be understanding, I decided to get straight to the point.

"Look, if you want a little quickie out in your car, you can give me a hundred. But if you're trying to do the hotel thing we can talk about all of that on the outside."

He snickered again.

"If this is some type of freaky sex game you trying to play, then I'm down with it. But if it's not, then I hate to upset you, Miss Cinnamon, but I don't pay for pussy-especially for some I done had for free before."

Marcus impressed me with the whole 'Miss Cinnamon' thing, and even put an idea or two in my head about the name. But I wasn't trying to hear nothing else from him if he wasn't paying me for my time. I sipped the last little bit of my drink and said whatever I had to say to get away from his cheap ass.

"Like I said Marcus, I gotta go. I need to get back to my girls. It was good talking to you and very nice to see you again."

I grabbed my purse from the table and threw a ten-dollar-bill down on it, right next to my empty plastic cup. Peaches taught me that. She said "if a guy turns you down, you pay for the drink to let him know that you didn't need him as much he thought you did, when you were asking him to bang you for a couple of dollars." She said it made me look more professional and independent, and "when a man senses that you don't need him, then he suddenly tends to feel like he needs you." According to her, it was all just a mind game, and sure enough, it worked.

"Wait!" Marcus allowed me to take about three steps away from him, then grabbed my arm forcefully.

"My car is parked underneath the bridge. Meet me there in ten minutes."

Got 'em! I thought. *I knew his down bad ass wasn't getting no pussy to be turning any down, free or not.*

I thought about going back over to Shannon and Alicia to make them aware of my brief departure, but they were too busy vibing to the music and laughing it up with their friends that they didn't seem the least bit worried about me. Fifteen minutes of me being missing wouldn't have matter too much to them.

I dismissed myself from Marcus and pushed my way through the heavy crowds of drunken people to get to the bathroom. When I got there, I had to push even harder to get to a toilet. A couple of girls were running their mouths by the sink. Judging by what they were saying, some shit must have went down or was about to go down. I listened to them carry on while I swatted over the toilet seat, took a long piss, and wiped myself thoroughly with my *handy-dandy* baby wipes.

After I was finished, I waited for the crowd of girls to dismiss themselves and when the coast was clear, I flushed the toilet and opened the bathroom door to make my exit. Unexpectedly, someone blocked me in.

"Where you think you goin' bitch?" a heavyset dike-looking chic caught the door as soon as I was opening it. The first thing I noticed was how much she looked like a man with her Red Polo shirt and her 5-0-1 shorts on. Then I started to notice how much her face looked a little familiar to me.

"Excuse me?" I asked puzzled. She pushed herself closer into the door, then repeated herself.

"I SAID.... where the *FUCK* you think you going? Can you hear me now?"

“I'm going to wash my hands if you don't mind, gosh, ease up off the liquor. Apparently you got me mistaken for somebody else- your girlfriend perhaps."

I tried to ease my way through the freckled-face dike bitch but she wouldn’t budge. As my body rubbed against hers, she smiled and consumed my every touch.

"Damn," she said seductively, as she caught my waist with her arms. "You done changed a lot since middle school."

Hearing those words, I finally recognized the stranger, and she too could tell by the surprised look on my face that I now knew exactly who she was.

"That's right bitch! *Samantha Mu-tha-fuck-in' Hutchinson*! Can't you tell?" she pointed to her face.

Damn. I said to myself when I realized that those spots weren't freckles. I had really fucked her up. As much as I hated Samantha, seeing the healed puncture wounds all over her face didn't make me proud of what I did to her.

"What's wrong? Cats got yo' tongue, or you ain't tough without your number two pencil?"

"Excuse me?" I said, trying my best to get myself out of the awkward situation. Money was calling me and I had no time for the bullshit. "I have to go now. My girls are waiting for me."

"She thinks she's going somewhere," Samantha said looking to her left, and then to her right, to address her crew. I didn't know how many girls were in the bathroom because I couldn't see from inside the stall, but judging by the size of their laughter, I knew it had to been a whole cheerleading squad.

"Naw, you aint getting off that easy," she said as she pushed her way inside the stall and let the door close us in.

I backed into a corner, finding myself stuck between the wall and the toilet seat. Samantha moved her large, stalky body towards me and got so close that her titties were touching my shoulders. I could even feel the wind from her breath hitting up against my forehead.

"What? You surprised to see me like this?" she asked. "You don't have to be afraid. Come closer, I wanna tell you a little secret."

Samantha leaned in, put her lips up to mine, and pressed her bodyweight up on me. "Niggas hate a bitch with an ugly face, but for some reason, the hoes love it."

I shot her down immediately. "Too bad I'm not one of them."

"Yeah, you're right," Samantha agreed. "That's just too bad. But either way, none of that's important now ‘cause it’s not about what you want, it’s about what you owe. Now you took something *precious* from me a couple years ago, so I think it's only right that you give me something precious in return. A face for some *face*."

Samantha flapped her tongue up and down like Tony Montana's friend did on the movie Scarface, and although I wanted to slap her like that white bitch slapped him, I let her slide.

Not stopping there, she boldly cuffed my pussy and went in for a kiss. Without thinking twice about it, I pushed her off of me and watched her stumble back and hit the door. Samantha picked herself up like it was nothing, jumped forward, and caught me with a right hook to the face. I took the hard hit like a champ, and then swung back. Sad for me though, my blows didn't seem to affect her. She hit me again with another right, and then a left, knocking me to the floor.

Samantha continued to swing down at me, hitting me in my head, shoulders, and arms. Realizing that I was no match to the she-man, I curled up like I did in elementary school during a tornado drill to protect my face and my stomach. Even though it felt like lightening was striking my back, my only concern was to not get kicked in my face or let my head go anywhere near the base, or the inside, of that toilet.

"Bitch...didn't...I...tell...you...that..I…was...going....to. ...whip....yo... ass!" she yelled, swinging and stomping between each word. With my eyes closed tightly, I didn't know what was going on around me, or better yet, how long it was going to last. All I could hear was a bunch of footsteps and people screaming out things like, “beat her ass!” and “fight!”

Samantha continued to punch, kick, and stomp me, while I remained curled up like a fetus. I heard a little more screaming and yelling, before I heard Samantha yell to someone, "Get the fuck off me." After that, I felt no more hits. That's because, thankfully, someone had made their way into the stall and thrown Samantha off of me. Then they picked me up and tossed me over right shoulder. When I finally opened my eyes, I realized that it was one of the club bouncers carrying me out of the bathroom. The big, thick baldheaded dude who held me, was fighting hard to get through the crowd of girls who were still trying to get licks off me as I defenselessly dangled over his shoulders. Some of them were even grabbing my money out of the purse that hung with me. It got so bad that more security members had to rush into the bathroom to contain them.

"Back up! Everybody back the fuck up right now before I gas this bitch!" one bouncer threatened, as he tried to clear a path to get both me and the officer out. Hearing that, the crowd obeyed, and a couple seconds later, we were moving forward.

We made our way out the bathroom, on to the main part of the club. I couldn't see a thing, but I knew we were near the dance floor because I could now hear the music blasting from out the speakers. People were yelling things like, "oh shit, she fucked up" and "aye man, record that shit." A couple of the sick bastards even had the nerve to smack my ass as we passed them.

When the music began to dissolve and all the voices I heard slowly faded away, I knew I was finally away from the crowd. The bouncer led me down a lonely hallway to a small office in the back of the club. Once we were in safely, he sat me down in a wooden chair. My head was spinning, my body was aching, and I was still trying to bring myself to at least begin to piece together everything that had just happened to me.

"Don't move," the man, who I now saw to be a very built dark-skinned dude with a cute baby face, said to me as he ran out the door to help the other guy.

I heard him clearly when he told me to stay put, but waiting on him to come back with the police was definitely not an option for me. The last place I was about to find myself on a Saturday night was in jail, especially after I was the one who got my ass beat.

It took some heavy concentrating, but the minute I was up on my feet, I made a run for it. Luckily, there was an emergency exit door right outside of the office. I ran out of it, sounding off the alarm, and it put me out on the side of the building. Within seconds of the loud beeping, I could hear thunderous stomps trailing in my direction. I didn't know whether it was the bouncers, or some people who were panicking and trying to exit the club, but I wasn't trying to stick around to find out.

Running away from the building, I didn't care about Marcus, who was probably in his car with a hard-on, or about Shannon and Alicia not being able to find me-especially since I couldn't find them when I was getting my body caved in. It felt very painful to run, especially in my heels, but I wasn't going to stop, not even to take the sons-of-bitches off. I dashed through the parking lot, crossed paths with the traffic, and headed to Keisha's.

Ironically, the closer I got to the projects, the safer I felt. I knew what had just happened at the club had to have been karma, because I hadn't run like that since I ran home after fighting Samantha back in middle school. I must admit, the shit had caught up with my ass. But I wasn't sweating it, because at least I had paid my debt. My wounds would heal in time and I could finally close that chapter of my life. Best of all, the worse part of my night was over. Or so I thought.

When I made it Keisha's front porch, I took a quick rest and a couple of gasps of breathe before banging on her door.

Shameka's six-year-old daughter opened it.

"Yo mama didn't teach you to ask *'who is it?'* before you open the door for somebody!" I snapped on the little innocent girl. "Where's Keisha?"

"She's in there," she said frightfully, allowing the beads in her hair to dangle as she swung it in the direction of one of the bedrooms.

Without even thanking her, I rushed into the room that she pointed to and found two sleeping bodies all covered up in a queen-sized bed. The smell of fresh ass in the room let me know that Keisha was definitely having a little *session* with one of her many niggas. Examining the big hump in the sheets from her wide ass, I could tell which side she was on and immediately ran over to wake her.

"Keisha! Keisha! Wake up right now!" I shouted.

Keisha slowly opened her eyes and frantically jumped at the very sight of me. It was like she had seen a ghost. I hadn't taken a glimpse of myself since the fight, and I knew my nose was bleeding a little, but the way she looked at me made me feel like I must have needed plastic surgery.

"Shit Charlytte! Wha..what you doing here?" She said as she looked into my face, down at herself, then over at the guy who laid next to her.

"Don't you mean, what the fucked happened to me?" I asked, tapping the blood on my nose with my index finger to show her that I had some serious explaining to do.

"Yeah, I...I...I was getting there," she stuttered. "Wha..what happened?"

"Samantha and her girls jumped me in the bathroom at the club, that's what happened!"

Keisha already knew who Samantha was because she used to fuck with one of the Hutchinson brothers. I told her about the pencil jabbing incident back when we first started kicking it again. She said she was impressed with my courage, but she also told me to watch my back. She knew firsthand how that family got down.

"Huh?...for real?' she asked with a stoned look and a still demeanor. There was something very different about her actions. Normally, in an instance, she would be ready to jump up, grease her face and go find the bitches, but this particular night she wasn't acting at all like that. She was just way too jittery and paranoid. You would have thought she was the one who had just gotten her ass whipped. I tried to overlook her weirdness, especially since she had just woken up from what looked like some hot and wild sex.

"Yes! For real! Just now at the Bash! I ran all the way here!"

"Where's Shannon and Alicia?" she asked, but then she cut me off before I could get my words out. "Wait...let's talk in the other room."

Keisha quickly, but quietly, hopped out the bed and ran to grab her bra and panties. Unfortunately, the squeaking sound from the loose mattress springs awoke her guy friend. He pulled the cover from over his head and sat up.

I couldn't believe my eyes.

29: ULTIMATE BETRAYAL

I had to make sure the blows I suffered weren't causing me to see things, and after about a minute of deep staring, I had realize that what I was witnessing was no illusion, it was actually real. You would have thought that after everything I felt for Cederick, and how much respect I had for Keisha, I would have been hurt to see that it was them in bed together: but no, nothing.

I guess after all the physical pain I had just suffered, I had no room to endure anything more. Even though Cederick and I weren't a couple, and probably would have never been one, Keisha knew how I felt about him. It was her who sat on the phone and listened to me talk about him for hours at time. It was her who kept telling me that no matter how bad things got between us, to never give up on trying to make him mine. She knew how much I loved him. She was family, and yet, she still betrayed me.

"How could you, Keish?" I finally broke the silence.

"It's not what it looks like sis, just trust me on this one," she said as she hysterically began to search around for her clothes.

"Trust you?" I asked. "How could I possibly trust you after this?"

"Because Charlytte, it's not personal, it's just business. You know how that goes."

"No, I don’t know how *that* goes, Keisha."

"C'mon Charlytte, quit acting like you green to shit and stop trying to play Miss Goody-Goody all the damn time! I knew the minute you said you were with Cederick that you was either trickin’ or about to be. Don't play stupid. You know how to fuck a nigga, get his money, and walk away without having any connections. That's all this is, so don't let it come between us."

I couldn’t believe my ears. "If it wasn't such a big deal, then why didn't you tell me?"

"I was going too."

"I seriously doubt that Keisha. Here I was all along thinking you changed, but really, you haven't changed since we were younger. Always thinking about yourself. You see Cederick taking over the operation and you're all over him, just like you did with Hi-C!"

"Oh, so you judging me now, bitch!" Keisha threw her baby blue Hollister t-shirt over her head. "I'm not the one hoping and praying that one day the ghetto Cinderella is somehow going to make the broke down Prince fall in love with her!"

Keisha continued to talk shit as if Cederick wasn't even in the room.

"You damn right, I'mma eat off of these pussy ass niggas. They don't give a fuck about us. All they care about is money, and that's all you should be worried about too. We're like sisters, and if you let this come between us, then you were never my family in the first place."

"Bitch, how-" I said, right before Cederick cut me off.

"Enough!" he shouted. "I can't take much more of this soap opera shit!"

Cederick then rose from out of the bed and let his big, hard dick dingle in our direction.

"It's real simple; Keisha, you a hoe, and Charlytte, you a trick. This whole fantasy about me and you being together, GET RID OF IT! I will never be with you. You fuck random niggas for money. You can turn a housewife into a hoe, but you can't turn a hoe back into a housewife. Once it's done, it's done. I don't care about either one of y'all slut bitches, so both of you need to just stop it."

"Oh please Cederick, shut the fuck up!" I cursed him for the first time ever.

I never disrespected him before, but seeing what I just saw, and hearing those words leave his lips after all I had done for him had me five-hundred degrees hot.

"You try to act like you so real! Nigga you ain't shit! You fake and phony as a fuck. You just a wannabe pimp and Hi-C's yes man, you fuckin' powderhead junkie!"

"You dumb trick!" Cederick ran towards me with his right arm up in slap-a-hoe position. "I'mma fuck you up worse than ol' girl did!"

Keisha jumped on Cederick's back to try and stop him from getting to me, and I made a run for it. When I got a couple steps away from the bedroom, I turned and looked back to see Cederick standing over Keisha slapping her up as she tried to fight back from on the floor. Even though I didn't like seeing him handle her in that way, I couldn't help but feel like the bitch was getting what she deserved.

I headed for the front door and saw Cederick's keys on the dining room coffee table. Out of spite, I picked them up and took them out the door with me. I told the kids, who were watching everything, to call the police. Without his keys, I knew that when they arrived, he wouldn't be too far.

I left Keisha's with no plan, other than to stay out of sight for a couple days. I didn't have my car with me, so I decided to catch the bus back to my apartment. I could've called Peaches for a ride, but I wasn't sure if she would have dropped the dime on Cederick.

Fortunately, I got a big break on the way to the bus stop when I spotted Cederick's car ducked off in a cut. I had no intentions of stealing it when I took his keys but I didn't have much energy left to do anymore walking. I thought long and hard about taking it- especially after I knew how much he didn't play about his shit- but I needed to get home, and I needed to get there fast.

"Fuck it," I said as I popped the lock, hopped in the car, and quickly sped off.

I raced all the way home, dippin' and dogdin' threw traffic, but still being careful enough not to get pulled over by the police. When I made it inside my apartment, I immediately made sure all my doors were locked because I knew it wouldn't be long before Cederick made his way to my place. After they were secure, I quickly stuffed my backpack. There was no way I was staying in that house. Shit was just way too hot.

Once my bag was packed, I headed straight for the front door. But as soon as I grabbed the handle, I stopped myself. There was just one more thing I needed to do before leaving.

"I'll show that nigga a dumb trick," I said as I ran to my bedroom closet.

I took all his dope from off of the top shelf and began flushing it down the bathroom toilet. Zip lock bag after zip lock bag, I dumped and flushed, flushed and dumped. I didn't even think about selling it for myself. I was too young to really understand how much money I was throwing away, but at the time, I really didn't care. The only thing that was on my mind was getting revenge.

I believe I was so hurt because even though I was tricking, I was doing just fine. I wasn't depending on anyone but myself and my men, and I finally had time to sit down, put my life in prospective, and think about what I really wanted for myself. I had friends and people who I thought cared for me, and for the first time ever, I was getting out and enjoying my life.

But, none of that mattered when I let those drugs hit that toilet water. I knew, in that moment, I had thrown away my apartment, my money, and probably my life.

"I wish I would have never went out to that club," I said as I continued to dump, also wishing that Keisha wasn't my family and that I never ran to her for help. And I sure as hell wasn't happy about catching her and Cederick in bed together. If I could have chosen between knowing and not knowing, I would have rather it been going on under my nose and not even have the slightest clue about it. The blindness of their lies would have been less painful than knowing the truth.

Once again, in the blink of an eye, my life was falling apart. At that very moment, nothing was important. Not getting those couple of dollars from Marcus, who was probably still out in his car waiting for me. Not Samantha and the beatdown she had just handed me. Not even the obvious fact that Cederick was going to kill me when he found out that I just flushed his dope down the drain. I didn't care about any of it. I had bigger problems to face and I didn't even know how to begin to deal with them. So, I answered them just like I did with any other tough situation I faced; I ran.

I wasn't about to have Cederick or one of his goons spot me riding around in my car. So, after I had gotten all my things together, I hopped back into his and drove it out to the Mall, where I parked it right in the middle of the Belk's lot. I knew he would be pissed, but eventually he would find it there.

There was a bus stop near the J.C. Penny's store. I ran to it and waited for the next one to come. The night was still early, just a little before twelve to be exact. Bus 731 arrived only after fifteen minutes of me waiting for it. I got on board, and even though it was empty, I took a seat to the very back.

"Where are you headed?" the old, crispy black bus driver said, trying to spark up a conversation with me. He smiled as if he was happy to see a woman, no matter how tore down she looked.

"Wherever the wheels take me," I replied.

• • • • • •

A huge sign with $19.99 printed on it was exactly what I spotted beside the Budget Inn Motel after riding the bus for about twenty minutes. I wasn't too happy about a cheap motel stay, but the price sounded real good. Not to mention, the three hundred ones I went to the club with,

was down to only fifty-six after the girls in the bathroom got their share.

I had already made my decision to stay there the minute I saw the motel, and luckily, the bus stopped directly across the street from it. The building resided in a dark, deserted area on the Westside of Ordale. I knew I was in for rocky stay when I walked closer to the building and saw just how run down it really was. I didn't even think I was going to be able to get a room there because of my age, especially after I remembered how the last jerk refused me. Yet, I didn't have any other choice but to take a chance, and that's exactly what I did.

I stumbled my way inside the motel, finding myself in a small lobby. A ghetto ass blue hair, green contacts wearing chick was working the front desk all by herself. She was watching the Fresh Prince of Belfair on a very small T.V, while at the same time, talking loudly on the company's telephone.

Cynthia, or at least that's what her name badge read, was so busy running her mouth that she didn't even see me approaching. And when I finally did catch her eye, her whole facial expression changed at the very sight of me. With an obviously disgusted look on her face, her eyes scanned me up and down, looking at everything from my wild hair to the dried up blood on my nose. Thirsty to get the 4-1-1, immediately, she told whoever she was blabbing on the phone with that she would call them back, "pronto."

Cynthia unprofessionally greeted me, and without letting her know anything more than what she had to, I got straight to the point. I asked her what was the possibility of a seventeen-year old getting a room at her motel. At first, she quickly refused and said that nothing was worth her losing her job, but when I offered her an extra twenty dollars to keep her mouth shut, ironically, she decided otherwise.

Once I exchanged the cash for a room number and a key, I walked back outside, took a right turn, and counted six doors down just as I was instructed to. The painted numbers on the doors had chipped off and in order to find my room, Cynthia said that I had to start at the top of the building and count six doors down. She even offered to walk me down herself, but I told her not to bother.

One, two, three, four, five doors I counted in my head and when I got to door number six, shaking a bit, I quickly put the key in and opened it.

The room looked as bad as I thought it would, but I didn't care about any of that because for the first time that night, I felt safe. I dashed straight into the piss-smelling bathroom to get a good look at myself and almost cried when I saw how beaten up I was. To get a better look, I stripped down to my underwear, stood on the tub, and when I saw that my back looked like a tie-dyed shirt, the way the black, red, and purple bruises were painted all over my upper body, tears began to swell up in my eyes.

It didn't look at myself too long because I couldn't handle the awful sight of me, plus my wounds were beginning to remind me of that dreadful night with Mr. Otis. I walked back to the bed and slowly eased my way down on it to avoid any further pain. Then I tried my best to relax my body. I was a little more comfortable, but sadly, my nerves were still in a frenzy. I could tell by the way my arms and legs were still shaking.

For a while, I laid still in the dark, before remembering the blunt that I had stuffed in my bra earlier. I normally took one to spark up in the club when the high from the one we smoked before we got there started to wear off. I dug around in my black-laced Wonderbra and found it tucked up under my left breast.

It was a little wet from all the sweating I did, but a little titty juice wasn't about to stop me from hitting it.

I sparked it up and took one long pull, making sure I took in every bit of smoke. Then I held it in my lungs for a second and slowly exhaled while beginning to put the events of my night into perspective. It was the first time I had ever smoked an entire joint by myself. Without a doubt, I was planning on getter higher than I had ever gotten before.

"Aaah," I exhaled, thinking that smoking weed would help me to forget about my situation; ironically, it only made me dwell on it.

I couldn't see a thing in the dark room, other than the little bit of light that peeked through the blinds and hit the carpet. Strangely, I started to feel a little paranoid and my heart began to pound even faster than it already was. Then, after many pulls and puffs, I began to hear voices in my head. I wasn't sure if it was just me tripping off of the weed, but this is what they said:

"Look at you Charyltte. Look what you have become. Nothing. You're family hates you. Korey doesn't care. Keyshawn would shoot you if he could get away with it. And you can't even bring a man around Keisha without her fucking him. You have nothing and you are nothing. Why are you sitting here holding on to your miserable life because some old slut told you to have faith? Have faith in what? God. Tuh, God doesn't even love you. He hated you since the day you were born. Why else would he take your mother away? Can't you see. You're almost grown now and nothing good has ever happened to you. While your friends, and everybody else in the good old world, are out having a good time, here you are

all alone crying, with no one to call on. Just face it. You're stupid. You're broke. And once again, you're homeless. Without Cederick, you know you can't make any money, so you might as well just kill yourself. He's going kill you anyway once he finds out what you did with his drugs. There's no way you will ever be happy again. Your life is through, just like your pussy. Now take that jar of aspirins from out of your bookbag and kill yourself. It's the only way you will be at peace."

The voices continued to whisper sweet sounds of death in my ear and I honestly tried to fight them off. The more I convinced myself to take my own life, the more I tried to find something in it to hold on to. I had never before in my life considered suicide, and even used to wonder what could make a person want to kill themselves. But the way I felt that cold summer night, I didn't have to wonder anymore.

I was used to feeling hurt, but I wasn't used to feeling empty. I couldn't feel pain, and this time, I wanted to. I couldn't even cry. That at least, would have let me know that something in my life was still real. Finding myself giving in to my demons, I started scrambling around the bed for my backpack. When I got it, I shook it to locate the pills, then took them out and opened the bottle. But, before I could turn the cap on it, I paused and heard another voice say:

"Hold on Charlytte, you are stronger than this. You think God brought you this far just to let you do this to yourself? Everything happens for a reason, just be patient and soon you'll see. Don't listen to that devil. He hates you and will say anything to make you

hate yourself. Do not to give up and that easily. Do not give him that power. This is just a storm, it shall soon pass. Just hang in there."

I laid across the bed with the aspirin bottle in my right hand and a hand full of pills in my left. I was listening to one part of myself battle the other, while I stood helplessly in the middle. I felt like I was the rope in one of those tug-of-war battles, and if one side of me didn't win, I was eventually going to snap. The confusion alone was too much to withstand.

"Aaaaaaaaaaaaaaahhhhhhh! I can't take this anymore!" I cried, releasing a long overdue scream. With all my strength, I slung my backpack down on to the ground, causing the objects inside to fly out.

"Lord please!" I began to sob. "I'm on the edge of giving up now! Give me a reason to stay here! Show me a sign or something!"

Trying to show God that I meant business, I held up a bald fist to the sky, then waited a couple seconds to see something. Unfortunately, silence was the only thing that came to me and then I was convinced; God wasn't going to show up. He hadn't been there for me once in my life, so what would make my little naive ass think anything was going to change on that day? I had made up my mind, there was no use for me to live on and be another burden to someone else. I put the pills up to my mouth and softly whispered, "Mama, see you on the other side."

"For whoever wishes to save his life will lose it, but whoever loses his life for my sake will save it." -Luke 9:24

30: GUARDIAN ANGEL

"I wish I could have done something to stop her. I swear I tried, but maybe I should have just pushed a little more. She probably would have opened up to me," one lady said to another.

"I know Mel," the other lady responded. "But it's not your fault. One of the leading causes of death for teenagers is suicide. Sad to say, but she probably would have done this whether you tried or not."

"But how do you know that? I could have saved her. I just didn't try hard enough. I can't help but feel like this is all my fault," the lady cried. "Oh my God, what have I done?!"

"Please, quit blaming yourself. You're only making things worse," the other lady comforted her. "Did you ever get in touch with anybody in her family to notify them of this terrible situation?"

"I left over twenty messages on her Aunt's answering machine and even stopped by this morning. Someone peeped out of the blinds, but no one came to the door. I even tried yelling from outside, but still, nothing. I gotta tell you Nurse Kathy," she began to whisper, "I really don't think her family even cares about her."

"Well, there goes your motive," the nurse said.

I slowly began to open my eyes and once the big blur in my vision started to clear up, I saw my old homeroom teacher, Mrs. Johnson, and someone who looked like a nurse, standing over me. I tried to sit my body up a bit but the drastic aching I felt in my stomach only allowed me to moan out softly in pain.

"Oh my God, she's up!" Mrs. Johnson shouted to the nurse after she heard my cry. Immediately they both ran over to take a look at me.

The nurse, who was a chubby, white woman with bright red hair, examined my body, flashed her light into my pupils, and then took a quick look at the computer monitor.

"I'll go get the doctor," she said, then took off.

Mrs. Johnson stood over me and began thanking Jesus. She touched my face, and then my hands, and smiled down at me as if I was her new born baby. I still hadn't come to figure out what had happened and where I was.

"Girl, you almost scared me half to death. You have no idea how much I have been worrying about you," Mrs. Johnson finally said to me.

"Whe...where am I?" I whispered, the pain also striking in my throat with the release of every syllable.

"Try not to talk too much," she said to me. "You threw up quite a lot and Nurse Kathy said your throat will be sore for a couple of days. You're in the hospital Charlytte. You tried to kill yourself."

When Mrs. Johnson informed me of my suicide attempt, I started to remember the motel room and me swallowing the pills, but what I couldn't figure out was why I was still alive?

"Do you remember anything?" she asked. "Don't talk. Just nod your head."

I did exactly what Mrs. Johnson said and gave her one slight head bob, but there were some questions I needed answers to and a little pain in my throat wasn't going to stop me from asking them.

"But why am I here, and why are you here?" I whispered.

"You're here because the good Lord was on your side, and I'm here because you called me. My God Charlytte, don't you remember?"

Even though I didn't remember anything after I swallowed the pills, I knew it was impossible for me to have called Mrs. Johnson. I didn't even have her number. Sure enough, I was completely confused and began to believe that I could have been having an after death dream or something.

"There's no way I could have called you, Mrs. Johnson. I don't understand."

"But Charlytte, you did call me. It was almost one somethin' in the morning when my phone started ringing. You were rambling on somethin' awful. You just kept saying, *'I don't want to die'* and you were begging for my help. I asked you where you were and the word 'budget' was the last thing I heard you say before we lost connection. The number was on my caller ID so I immediately called back and it connected me to the front desk of the Budget Inn Motel. I had a feeling that you were in trouble, so without asking the clerk any questions, I hung up the phone and just rushed over to find you."

Mrs. Johnson pulled her chair closer to my bed and chuckled a bit to herself. "Charlytte, you just don't know what kind of trouble I was about to get into behind you. I was almost about to catch a charge because I was about to put my hands on that lady at the front desk- and you know I'm not the violent type."

"The one with the blue hair?" I giggled.

"Yes, her," she said. "She had the worse attitude ever and was denying your stay. It wasn't until I had to show her the number in my cell phone, and threaten to call the police, that she finally admitted to me that you were there. Then we both went down to your room to find you stretched out on the floor, passed out in your own vomit. Charlytte, just thinking about the sight of you laying there was, and probably will be, the hardest thing I ever had to witness in my life. I honestly thought you were dead."

"Oh my," I whispered, then felt a tear drop fall from my eye.

"Your fist was bald up so tight that it took the both of us to pry your hand open, and when we did, we found that it was full of white pills. I don't know how long you were lying there like that, but judging by the way they had begun to dissolve in your palm, I knew it had to have been a while."

Mrs. Johnson handed me a cream-colored envelope, and when I took a closer look at it, I realized that it was the card she had given me for my birthday back in her classroom. I remembered that I forgot to open it when I found out that Mrs. Clarice had passed. It must have fallen out when I slung my bookbag onto the motel room

I slowly pulled the card from out of the envelope and read it to myself.

Keep up the good work, Charlytte. Never give up and I promise you will go far. If you ever need me, my number is 912-082-2208. Much love, Mrs. Johnson.

Another tear dropped because I knew Mrs. Johnson must have been my guardian angel. I know she told me not to move much, but I just felt the need to reach out and hug her. She saw my weak arms extending out into her direction, and as soon as she tilted her body my way, we were suddenly interrupted by a tap at the door.

"I hear someone woke up," a doctor poked his long, bold head into the room and smiled at us.

"Yes, she did Dr. Connor," Mrs. Johnson informed him.

"Wonderful," he replied.

Dr. Connor entered the room and greeted me with a handshake. He was an elder white man with a wide face and thin, curly hair. I tried not to laugh at how much he resembled Shaggy from Scooby Doo.

"So...how do you feel?" he asked me.

"I feel okay," I whispered.

"You scared us quite a bit there, young lady," he began to examine my body with his eyes. "But I must say that you're a strong one. You took in quite a high dosage to still be alive."

"I know," I said softly. "I'm sorry."

"What's going to happen from here, doctor?" Mrs. Johnson interrupted, as if she was unable to stand hearing him talk about me almost being dead. "When do you think she will be able to go home?"

"Welp, the good news is...it looks like she will pull through just fine. Her heart rates good and her blood pressure is stable. We're only going to keep her here for about two more days, just so we can monitor her a little more. Then we will run some kidney and liver test to make sure there were no sever internal damages. After that, she can leave," he said. "But, the bad news is that when she leaves here, she won't exactly be going home."

"What do you mean *she won't exactly be going home*?" Mrs. Johnson asked.

"Well...," the doctor took a long pause, and then a deep breath. "Unfortunately, because she did try to harm herself, it's mandatory that she goes straight to a psychiatric facility so that they can make sure she's mentally stable."

"Oh God no!" Mrs. Johnson cried out, holding the palm of her hand up to her heart. Her startle frightened me, almost causing me to panic, and she must have sensed that, because she quickly pulled herself together. "I mean, is that really necessary?"

"I don't know if it's necessary or not, but I do know that it's the law," he answered her. "We don't want to release her without making sure that she's completely okay. We just can't risk the chance of her going home and harming herself again, or worse, someone else. It's just procedure."

Mrs. Johnson couldn't argue with that. But that didn't stop her from trying.

"But say, hypothetically of course," she tested him, "that she does have to go there, how long will she have to stay?"

"Anywhere from three weeks to three months. That depends on Mrs. Black here," he tapped my right leg.

"But doc, is there any possible way that she can come home with me and just forget that step? She's not crazy or anything. She's actually very bright and I know that there's a reasonable explanation for this."

"She tried to kill herself," the doctor reminded Mrs. Johnson. "There's always and never a reasonable explanation."

Not giving up, Mrs. Johnson asked, "Doctor, may I speak with you outside please?"

I admired her for the way she challenged him. In any situation, she knew how to hold her on. She may have been just a teacher, but she was just as bright as any doctor and was smart enough to make a successful negotiation with him.

Doctor Connor followed Mrs. Johnson, who was already walking to the door before she even got a response from him. From the way he lifted one of his thick eyebrows and smiled at her, I knew he was also intrigued by her assertiveness.

"Sure, right this way," he said, sarcastically of course.

While I waited for them to return- and with a T.V. but no sign of a remote- I entertained myself by scoping out my surroundings. I examined the IV in my hand first, then let my eyes follow the tubes all the way up to the machine it was connected to. Finally, I stared up at the jug of fluid that was circulating into my body and everything now felt real. I couldn't believe that I had actually tried to kill myself.

Then I started to remember why. Keisha and Cederick in bed together would forever haunt me and seriously fuck up my trust for anyone else. I touched my face and remembered that Samantha had put a nice beat down on me. And I remembered that mirror image of how she left me looking. I remembered that I didn't have any money or any place to go. I remembered that I had flushed Cederick's weed and figured that him and his crew were probably already out looking for me, or the drugs. Honestly, after recalling it all, I wasn't quite sure if I was happy to still be alive.

Evidently they didn't take too long negotiating because Mrs. Johnson walked back into the room shortly after they stepped out. The doctor didn't come back with her, and from the stressful look on her face, I knew that they must have had a pretty intense conversation.

I wiped the weary look off my face because I didn't want her to be any more worried than she already was, then asked, "Where did the doc go?"

"He went to get some paperwork ready and check on another patient," Mrs. Johnson said, then pulled her chair up to the side of my bed and took a seat. "Charlytte, I really need to talk to you."

"Sup?" I replied, not trying to be hip, but because my throat was really starting to bother me.

"I have convinced the doctor to release you under my care. Maybe it's because I'm a damn good flirt, or maybe it's because he found out that he spent some time in the service with my husband a while back. Whatever the case, he agreed to skip the whole psych care process under the condition that you change your story about what happen that night."

"What do you mean?" I scratched my forehead.

"He's gonna send in a mental health doctor shortly. I just need you to tell them that you got drunk. Tell them that you had a slight headache, but you must have ended up taking too much medication. Assure them that you love your life and you would never ever imagine harming yourself. Got that?"

"Yeah, I got it," I answered. That wasn't going to be a problem. I was pretty good at lying.

"A friend of mine works at that ward and I can assure you, it's no place you want to end up. That medication they're gonna give you will have you messed up for real."

"Ok Mrs. Johnson," I said, frightened. "I will tell them."

"Good. Charlytte, the doctor and myself are going out on a very shaky limb with this one, and jobs are at stake. We really need to know that you won't ever try that again," she said as scooted her chair even closer to the bed and grabbed my left hand. "Please, look me in my eyes and tell me that you want to live."

"Yes," I answered, trying to look directly into Mrs. Johnson's eyes, while at the same time, trying not to think about all the bad stuff that was going on in my life.

"Good dear, because if not, I can let them take you there and I will just put it in the Lord's hand. I've always believed that you can't save someone that doesn't want to be saved. I just don't think it would be fair for you to take myself and Doctor Connor down with you."

"I understand," I sighed.

"And besides," she added, "it's not just you that you have to live for now."

"What you do mean, it's not just me I have to live for. Nobody else cares about me."

"Believe it or not, somebody does care about you and is depending on your safe recovery?"

"Who?" I asked.

"Your baby," she replied, now throwing me completely for a loop. "Charlytte, did you know that you were pregnant?"

Pregnant? I thought. There was no way that could be possible. The words Charlytte and pregnant didn't even belong in the same sentence. I just didn't seem right.

"No, that can't be possible," I denied.

"How so? You're telling me you haven't been sexually active," she questioned.

"Yes, but I have been careful."

"How careful?"

I shrugged. "Condom careful."

"Charlytte, those things break. They're not one hundred percent dependable. I'm sure you know that."

"I know, but I'm a hundred percent sure I have been-"

I stopped in the middle of my sentence and went off into a blank stare as I began to think back to the time Cederick came home drunk and high off coke. It was one night in May. I remembered it so well because it was after his big birthday celebration at the club. He fucked me hardcore the whole night and when the rubber broke, he busted one big nut off into me. And when he was finished, he snagged the condom from off his penis, looked at the semen dripping from it and said, "Oh well, I got money to pay for an abortion." I didn't think any more about it after that, especially since my period came on a couple of weeks later.

"How far along am I?" I asked. It was now the end of June and if I was pregnant by Cederick, then I knew I would have had to been about eight weeks.

"Eight and a half weeks, according to the doctor."

Shit. I thought. It was Cederick's.

Of course I had slept with many different guys, but I always checked the rubbers afterward, just as Peaches had taught me to. I had been tricking for a year and never once did I slip until that night with him. I knew it would be hard getting Cederick to believe that I was carrying his child, especially since we only fucked a few times, but I didn't care. In my heart, I knew it was his.

“Two months?” I sighed.

"Yep,” Mrs. Johnson said, then sandwiched one of my hands between both of hers. “Charlytte, you really need to let me help you. You need to open up to me and tell me everything that's going on with you, even if you have to go back to the day you were born. Let me get you back on the right path. You are too beautiful, too smart, and too young to be even thinking about doing this kind of stuff to yourself. I know I can help you, I can feel it. You just have to be willing to trust me. Do you think you can do that?"

I hesitated for a second. Her mentioning the day I was born made me think about my mother. *What would she have wanted me to do*? I definitely did not believe that she would have wanted me to be lying up in some hospital because I tried to take my life. I had a dream once that she had showed up at my college graduation, was at the bottom of the steps when I walked off the stage, and hugged me before whispering, "this is the happiest moment of my life" into my ears. Deep down, I knew that she wanted to see me successful and happy. I could have been dead, but I was alive and given a second chance, and I didn't believe that it was by coincidence. Besides, I now had a child of my own growing inside of me; it wasn't just about me anymore.

"Yes I can," I answered.

Mrs. Johnson leaned over and got the hug that I had been waiting to give her, then we cried in each other's arms.

31: DECISIONS, DECISIONS

I stayed in the hospital two more days until the doctor said it was okay for me to leave. Mrs. Johnson was there by my side everyday feeding me good food and good words of encouragement. She even read a couple of scriptures out of the bible for me- once in the morning and once before she left in the evenings.

I began to open up to her, just as she asked me to, telling her every single detail of my life. She literally had to fight back the tears when I got to the part about Mr. Otis. I also told her the whole situation about Cederick and what I did with his drugs. She felt it was best that I didn't go back to my apartment to retrieve anything, not even my car. And she also told me that I was welcome to stay at her place.

At first I was a little hesitant at the offer. I didn't want to have to depend on anyone else. But after she wouldn't take no for an answer, I eventually gave in and agreed to it.

Mrs. Johnson lived about thirty-five minutes outside of Ordale in a small two-story house. It rested beautifully in a gated community right outside of an army base, and was home to many other military families. I was blown away when I saw how well-decorated the inside of it was, and the guest room she fixed up for me had me speechless.

For the first time in my life, I got to sleep on a queen-sized bed. I also had my own half bathroom and although I didn't have any clothes, I had a huge walk-in closet. She even fixed up a studying section in one corner of the room for me, with a computer and desk filled with learning books and school supplies. I guess it was necessary since she was making me get my GED.

After seeing my room, I hugged Mrs. Johnson to show her my appreciation. She embraced me too, but told me not to thank her just yet, because she hadn't even showed me the best part. Then she grabbed me by the hand and led me to the backyard, where I got to see the beautiful lake that her and her neighbors all got to share. From many conversations Mrs. Johnson and I had back in her classroom, she knew just how much I loved water. I had a feeling that I was going to be just fine staying at her place.

• • • • • •

Over the next couple of weeks, Mrs. Johnson kept me busy by having me run all over town with her. There was not a day that I got to sleep past eight in the morning. Not even on Sundays. Those were church days. And even then, we had to be there extra early because she was the Sunday school teacher, and helped assist with the praise team every now and then.

When Mrs. Johnson told me that I had to attend church, I quenched at the idea of it, but I knew if I was staying at her place, I had to follow her rules. And although I would've never believed it, I really enjoyed myself each time I went. Mrs. Johnson even tried to get me to become a member. Of course I refused, but I did go as far as helping her assist her Sunday school classes whenever she got backed up on her work.

Mrs. Johnson was a work-a-holic. I never knew a person could stay so busy. She told me that part of the reason she had to keep herself occupied was because she didn't teach in the summer. And with no job, no husband, and the kids spending every break with their grandparents back in North Carolina, she sometimes got bored.

Fortunately, the kids being gone really gave us a chance to get to know each other better. One day, when we were out and about, Mrs. Johnson took me to the hair salon. She said she couldn't go another day seeing me wear a scarf on my head. At first I cried when the hairdresser told me that cutting my hair was my only option- after she saw how Samantha had ripped out most of it from the root- but after I saw how cute the small layers of curls and the little spikes at the top of my head were, I couldn't do anything but thank her. Besides how much it made me look like Keisha, I loved my new look. That change was exactly what I needed.

I was very grateful for Mrs. Johnson. She helped me out in more ways than I could have ever imagined. She even bought me a couple new outfits, of course they weren't top notch, but I didn't mind. She also picked me up some Chicken Soup books, a GED guide book, a Bible, and my own personal electronic tablet. I couldn't figure out if it was just pity or if she genuinely saw something special in me, but I told myself that I was going to worry less about her reasons, and just be thankful for what she was doing.

Besides, I honestly didn't think that she was plotting on turning me into a trick. Because unlike Cederick, Mrs. Johnson wasn't just buying me stuff, she was teaching me things too. Whether it was having me in the kitchen with her when she cooked her turkey wings, or reading scriptures from the bible, I was learning something positive every day. She even gave me advice on what it took to be a woman and a good mother.

I still hadn't figured out what I was going to do about the pregnancy situation. I just coped with it by simply trying not to think about it. I was just learning how to care for my own self, so how could I possibly know what it took to care for a child? I had no money, no job, no type of education, and I really wasn't a hundred percent sure who the father was. I just wasn't ready.

Thankfully Mrs. Johnson didn't bring the issue up too much, allowing me the freedom to think for myself. Even though she didn't believe in abortions, she didn't pressure me with any of her opinions about it either. She just told me that children were blessings and that I could handle it if I put my mind to it. But no matter what I choose to do, she would still be behind me one hundred percent.

One Saturday night, Mrs. Johnson and I decided to stay in because it was storming pretty bad outside. We had just finished watching a good chick flick over pizza and wings, when Mrs. Johnson decided to pull out her photo book and show me some pictures of her and her family. A little emotional, she cried with the turn of each page over the absence of her husband and kids.

"Those were the good ole days," Mrs. Johnson pointed to the picture of herself in her teenage years at her old house in North Carolina. "If only they would bring those hairstyles back."

"Oh gosh, no way!" I begged to differ, frowning my face up at the ugly pinned-up do Mrs. Johnson was rocking.

Mrs. Johnson and I looked at a few more photos and laughed a little while longer. Then she closed her book and got up to put her bed slippers on. I followed her up from off the couch, only to look for the remote though. She was going to bed, but I wasn't quite ready to take it in yet. I wanted to stay up a little while longer and maybe watch another movie.

"Goodnight Charlytte, I'm taking it on in now." Mrs. Johnson dragged her tired body over to her pink, fluffy bed slippers, then slipped into them. "You know the rules about the television. Make sure you turn it off before you go to sleep."

"Oh, and before I forget," she recalled, "I wanted to talk to you about something."

Oh boy. I thought.

We both met each other back at the couch. I gave Mrs. Johnson my full attention and was very curious to know what she had to say to me.

"Lay it on me," I said.

"Well, you already know the kids will be back tomorrow and school will be starting Monday, so that means nobody will be here with you during the day. Truthfully, the reason I have been keeping you busy is so you wouldn't have time to think about all the negative things that you had- and probably still have- going on in your life."

I cut her off quickly because I felt I already knew where she was going.

"Mrs. Johnson, I'm fine. I haven't been thinking about

Cederick, Keisha, Mr. Otis, my Aunt Jo, or any of that other mess. With your help, I'm getting over it all. You don't have to worry about that."

"I know, but except for when you’re sleeping, I've been constantly around you. Lonely minds wander, ya know. And you just never know where yours will take you when you're all alone. All I ask is that you keep yourself busy while we're gone. I have already found you a therapist. Would you be willing to go?

"Yes ma'am," I said, although I wasn't big on the idea of talking to a complete stranger about my problems. But even though I was feeling a lot better, I couldn't deny that I still needed some type of help. I figured that maybe going to see a professional wouldn't be so bad after all.

"Good. I also brought you those GED practice books for a reason. You should discipline yourself to study for about three hours a day. You need to be ready when you take the test," she sounded like my teacher again. "And if I have any house chores, I will leave them on a sticky note on the refrigerator for you. There may even be some Sunday school cut-outs that I will need your help with, but for now everything looks taken care of. I'm pretty much caught up with church activities, but by the time school starts I know I will backed up again."

"Yes ma'am," I repeated. I wasn't happy hearing about all the work she was throwing at me, but I didn't mind feeling like I was her child. In fact, I appreciated her for it.

"Most importantly Charlytte- and no ifs, ands, or buts about it- absolutely no company! Do not let anyone in my house for any reason at all. If you wake up and someone is cutting my grass, don't be alarmed, it's just Jeremiah, the neighbor’s kid."

"You don't have to worry about that, Mrs. Johnson. I don't have anyone to invite over here even if I wanted to."

"I ain't worried honey," she said. "I'm just letting you know."

"And one more thing," Mrs. Johnson said before she rose up from the couch. "I don't mean to put any pressure on you, but have you decided anything about this pregnancy. You're a little over three months and you don't have much time left."

Oh Gosh. Not tonight. I thought.

"Mrs. Johnson, I really don't know and honestly I'm trying not to think about it. It still doesn't seem real to me."

"Did it seem real when you were throwing up all morning?" she reminded me.

True, if it weren't for me being slightly nauseated, and for the couples of times I vomited up egg-yolk looking stuff, I probably would have never believed it. But either way, I was still indecisive about what I was going to do. Sad to say, I could see myself being a crackhead before I could see myself being a mother. That's just how much it scared me.

"Yeah," I thought back to me throwing up that morning. "It seemed pretty real then."

"That's because it is real, hun. That baby's little heart is beating inside of you as we speak. You really need to sit down and think about this. If you're going to terminate the pregnancy, you need to do it before it's too late. And if you do decide to keep it, you need to go and see a doctor. This is the most critical time for your baby right now."

"Okay Mrs. Johnson. I will think about it," I lied. "I promise."

Mrs. Johnson walked towards her beige carpeted stairs and took two steps up them before stopping again.

"And just for the record, there is one other thing you can consider."

"What's that?" I turned my body around on the couch just so I could see her face.

"Adoption," she replied.

"Oh, no way!" I stopped her right in her tracks. "There's no way I'm giving my baby up for adoption."

"So you mean to tell me you would think about killing your child before you'd think about passing her on to a great family, or a woman who may want kids, but just isn't as blessed as me or you to have one?" Mrs. Johnson continued to walk up the stairs slowly.

"I just couldn't live with myself knowing I had a baby out in the world somewhere, that's all."

"But you can live with yourself knowing that you killed her, right? I'm not quite following you."

"I don't know." I said, feeling myself getting overwhelmed by it all. "I just don't know right now."

"Look, I'm not trying to come down on you, but truth is truth. Most people choose abortion over adoption because they just can't live with the fact that they have a baby out in the world that they aren't caring for. For some people, abortions are just a quick way to put the past behind you, and sad to say, but for some, it's also a form of birth control. I'm not very particular about abortions or adoptions, but my best friend can't even have a baby and it really hurts me to see people just kill their children as if they weren't real lives."

"It's just a fetus now, Mrs. Johnson. It's not even a life yet."

"Your baby isn't just a fetus. Fetus sounds just like feces, and it's simple mind tricks like that, that make it easy for you to dispose of them. Life doesn't start after three months like they tell you; it starts the minute that egg and that tiny little winning sperm cell connect. That's when your life started, that's when my life started, and that's when those evil ass doctors who tell you this stuff, life started too…My mother had me when I was sixteen and if she felt like she wasn't ready to be a mother, I wouldn't have been here today. And being that it was me who God sent to save your life, you probably wouldn't have been here either. So think about that."

Although what Mrs. Johnson was saying made sense, I didn't want to hear it. I know it wasn't right, but I would have rather aborted the child than put it up for adoption. I couldn't just have a baby and give it away, and I couldn't help that I felt that way.

"I understand Mrs. Johnson. I will think it over. See ya in the morning, I can't wait to meet the kids," I said, trying to fool her by changing the subject. Luckily, she fell for it.

"Yeah, I miss them little jokers. I can't wait to see them too. Of course Kay-Kay is too young to understand, but I haven't told Michael Jr. about you staying here just yet. He's been a little on the edge since his dad has been gone, so if he doesn't open up to you like that, don't take it personal."

"Trust me, I understand."

When Mrs. Johnson disappeared, I let out a deep sigh and flopped down on the couch. That adoption thing made things even more complicated for me. I really didn't know what to do. I couldn't live with myself giving my baby away, I couldn't live with myself killing my baby, and I couldn't live with myself having her either.

I heard Mrs. Johnson's room door close, and not feeling like watching a movie anymore, I made my way up to mine. I had been praying quite a lot since I moved into her home. She taught me that prayer had the power to change any situation.

I shut my room door, walked over to the side of my bed, got on my knees, and began to pray, "Dear God, it's me again."

32: THERAPY

Life was going good and Mrs. Johnson turned out to be the best thing that happened to me. I was finally getting on track, getting closer to God, and getting some real business about myself. Yep, the former trick, Charlytte Black, had a baptism scheduled in a couple of Sundays and was even dedicating my services to the Youth Usher board. And, I still found time to help Mrs. Johnson out with her Sunday school programs.

I enjoyed being a member of Giving Glory Ministries, but sometimes I would get a little aggravated when some of the good ole 'Christian' folks would toot their noses up at me and my big round belly. I wasn't saved just yet, so a part of me wanted to curse them out. Honestly, if it wasn't for the respect I had for Mrs. Johnson, and for the Pastor giving me a job with the church's Day Care Center, I probably would have.

Being on the church's payroll, or anybody's payroll for that matter, was the best part of it all because I was finally making some money again. Of course, it wasn't as good as the tricking money, but at least I was getting it honest. Plus, I only had three months left until the baby was born and I needed some type of cash of my own. I still wasn't completely sure if I wanted to keep the child, but I decided not abort it. I made a deal with Mrs. Johnson that if by the time I had him, I still wasn't sure what I wanted to do, then I would give him to her best friend and let her care for him. I was happy with the arrangement, but the more I felt him moving and kicking inside of me, and the more we grew together, the more I fell in love with him.

When my eighteenth birthday came around, Mrs. Johnson and the kids took me out to a fancy Japanese restaurant. Just when I thought that being able to see my meal being prepared right in front of me was special enough, she gave me a cupcake and a card to go along with it. When I opened my card there was a car key taped to it and the fine print said:

Congratulations on everything that you have achieved. We are proud to have you as a part of the Johnson family and it is a pleasure to see how much you have grown. Here is a token of our appreciation. Love Melissa, Little Mike, and Kay-Kay.

I had told Mrs. Johnson about the two-thousand dollars Honda incident, but I would have never guessed that she would go out and buy me one just like it. It was the same color and everything. When we got back to the house, as cold as it was outside that November evening, Jeremiah was rinsing it off and drying it down with a towel. I was so excited that I ran and hugged Mrs. Johnson, little Michael, Kay-kay, and Jeremiah- whom I had a secret crush on- and squeezed him a little tighter than I did everybody else.

Everyone, including Jeremiah, hopped in and I took my first spin around the block. After we got back, Jeremiah asked Mrs. Johnson if he could take me for a quick ride, just the two of us. I still didn't have my license and he knew that Mrs. Johnson wouldn't have let me gone any further than around the corner by myself.

At first she was hesitant, because although I tried my best to tame the butterflies I got in my stomach every time I saw him, Mrs. Johnson was a woman who was no fool. She never questioned me about it, but I knew she could sense that I liked the kid. And just maybe, she could even see that he had a little thing for me too.

The first time I saw Jeremiah was about two weeks after Mrs. Johnson went back to teaching. It was about seven o'clock in the morning. The baby had been tossing and turning all night in my stomach so I had hardly gotten any rest. On top of that, Mrs. Johnson and the kids usually got up at five in the morning, and Kay-Kay almost always had to come into my room to make her early morning presence known. I never minded it though. She was just too cute, that getting mad with her was impossible.

They all left about six-thirty and my time for a much needed rest had finally come. Unfortunately, I wasn't even asleep for a good hour before I was awakened by the sound of a loud lawnmower roaring up against my window. I put a pillow over my head, then tossed and turned a few minutes, before I finally got angry enough to let my blinds up and shoot a dirty glare at who I thought would be an old drunk named Jeremiah, cutting Mrs. Johnson grass. But, as soon as I began to frown my face the way I wanted to, the calm morning sun shined its light on one of the most adorable guys I had ever saw in my life. All I could do was stare at Jeremiah, who didn't see me because he was deeply concentrated on what he was doing. The only time he would lose focus was when he would stop to rub his hands through his curly afro. I could only wish that he was as dedicated to his women, as he was dedicated to cutting that grass.

As Jeremiah continued to be distracted by his duties, I studied his entire body frame, noticing everything from the way his firm muscles formed under his long John tank top, to the way the sweat rolled down his golden brown skin. He was so red that he looked mixed, but still, he didn't have that light-skinned prettyboy type of look. It was sorta cute, but dirty, and that turned me on even more.

Finally taking his eyes from off the grass, he must have felt me looking at him because he turned directly to my window, catching me in my daze. Embarrassed, I quickly snapped out of it, closed the blinds, and ran back over to my bed.

Please don't come over here. Please don't come over here. I kept praying to myself, only to be disappointed when I heard him tapping on my window. *Shit!*

I quickly adjusted the scarf on my head and tried to wipe the mucus out of my eyes. I let out one big yawn to release some of the morning breath from out of my mouth, then went back to the window.

"Yes?" I said as rolled the window up only a couple of inches.

"Hey," said the cute guy who stood outside my window. "You must be-"

"Charlytte." I finished his sentence, trying to rush him on.

"Yes, that's right. Mrs. Johnson told me she had a guest staying over, but I didn't know if anyone would be home today. If I'm bothering you, I don't mind coming back a little later."

Jeremiah was so polite when he spoke to me. I wasn't used to it, but I liked it.

"Oh no. It's fine. I was just getting up anyway," I lied. "Go right ahead. If you need a drink of water or something, just give me a tap."

"Ok, thanks," he said, then walked away.

"*Oh my gosh, even his teeth are perfect*," I said after I closed the window and made sure it was secure. I cheesed all the way back to my bed and couldn't go back to sleep if I wanted to because all I could think about was the boy outside cutting Mrs. Johnson's grass.

Jeremiah never came and asked for that glass of water like I had been hoping he would, especially since I went and put on my best outfit for him. And the only time I saw him after that was when he would pass by his in loud Ford pick-up truck. We would wave to each other, and maybe smile, but it never went any further than that.

I didn't start to really get to know him until late September, when I started my counseling sessions. That's when Mrs. Johnson told me that Jeremiah would be taking me to them. I tried to act like it was no big deal, but deep down I was thrilled. Adding on to the front, I even told Mrs. Johnson that I didn't think I would feel comfortable riding with a guy I barely knew. Mrs. Johnson assured me that I would be nothing less than safe, and even filled me in with a little bit of info about him.

She told me that Jeremiah was only sixteen when his mom died fighting in Iraq. That was when he started getting into trouble. She said one day he had gotten upset because his dad had asked him to take out the trash, and slung his baseball into her yard, breaking her expensive glass screen door. Jeremiah's father was very close to throwing him in juvenile, but Mrs. Johnson convinced him not to.

She said the first thing she did was make him pay for her window by cutting her grass and doing chores around her house. And she said that ever since she had been letting him spend a little time with her, his attitude had been improving. She told me he was good people, and I had my own secret reason to believe that she was telling the truth.

The sessions were on Mondays, Wednesdays, and Fridays at ten o'clock in the mornings. Jeremiah was always on time to pick me up. The first week we rode silently with each other, barely saying two words. But by the second week- after we got into a huge argument about what was better- a Butterfinger or a Snickers- we began to open up a little more. And hell, after a month had passed, I was skipping my sessions and hiding out at the park, just to spend time with him. I knew Mrs. Johnson would kill me if she knew I was doing that, but I couldn't help myself. Jeremiah was all the therapy I needed.

What could I say, he made me feel comfortable. I didn't have a problem telling him about my life and everything I had been through. Never once did he judge me and always simply respected me for just being honest. He was such a sweetheart that being in his company was always a joy for me. But even though I had strong feelings for him, I knew not to overthink them. I had just been through a traumatic situation that I was still trying to bounce back from and falling in love with someone else would not have been the wisest choice for me. So I decided to just take everything very slow with him, and I always managed to value our friendships over anything else.

Mrs. Johnson agreed to let Jeremiah take me for that spin. Surprisingly, we only swerved around the block, parked at his friend's house, and snuck back to his crib. When I saw the beautiful candlelight dinner set up in the living room, I immediately knew the real reason he wanted me to ride with him.

Jeremiah's dad was working the evening shift at his factory job and wouldn't be home until twelve in the morning, so we didn't have to worry about getting busted. I had been inside Jeremiah's home a couple of times before, but never had I seen it so beautiful. The mood was set with the lights dimmed, and the soft tunes of R. Kelly played out of his dad's expensive surround-sound speakers. The table was beautifully decorated with white roses and vanilla-scented candles. Best of all, he made my favorite, chicken alfredo. Of course it was straight out of the box, but it was the thought that counted. And even though I had just eaten a big meal, I still decided to try some. Besides, I knew he took his precious time making the perfect dish for me so I refused to let him down.

As we both talked and ate, I couldn't stop myself from smiling.

"This is really good," I said as I forced myself to swallow the spoonful of creamy white noodles and the fat piece of chicken breast.

"Thanks," he said. "I told you I could do a lil' something in the kitchen."

"You did *aite*," I said, stroking his ego a bit.

"Judging by the way you're licking that sauce off your lips, I can't tell."

"I think the baby's enjoying it more than I am," I said, rubbing the six-month-old in my belly.

"Don't you mean *our* baby?" Jeremiah corrected me.

"Oh lord, here you go with that again. Not today Jeremiah. Please, don't start this today."

"I don't care what you say," Jeremiah flung his arms up. "That's my baby."

"How is this *your* baby if we never even *did it* yet?" I flirted.

"If it worked for Mary and Joseph, it could work for us too," he said.

After we both got finished laughing, Jeremiah took his napkin and used it to wipe away some of the sauce from off the side of my mouth. He was so sensitive the way he touched me. Loving the way it felt, I closed my eyes and dreamt that we could go further.

"Why are you so afraid?" Jeremiah asked, as he brought his chair closer to mine and ripped me from my thoughts.

Completely caught off guard by the question, I answered, “Afraid of what?”

"Letting your guard down,” he replied. “I told you, I'm not like those losers who hurt you before. Just give me a chance to show you that I really do like you Charlytte."

"I never denied that you *really like me*, Jeremiah. It's just that it's only been a couple months. I got a really good feeling about this and I want to do everything right this time around. Besides, what do I have to offer you and what do you see in me? I'm a pregnant hooker. Are you sure you’re not blind or a bit crazy?"

"No Charlytte, you're the one who’s blind and crazy for seeing yourself as anything less than a queen. You're not all those bad things. You were just a little misguided, that's all. All you ever needed was a little bit of love and someone to show you the right path. Mrs. Johnson did that for you. She did that for us."

He continued. "Now look at the both of us. We may not have our mothers, but we have each other. And that's all we need."

"I know, but so much could go wrong, just trust me." I assured him. "I told you, you are my friend above anything else. I don't want to mess that up. It's very easy for friends to turn into lovers, but it's hard for lovers to turn back into friends."

"Who said that I wanted to turn back?" he asked. "I only want to go forward. You know just as well as I do, that little boy of yours is going to need a father in his life. You got someone right here who is willing to be with you and willing to be the person he can look up to. Don't let him miss out on that because of your fears."

"*My child* is not *your child*. You are not obligated to him. You have every right to walk away from the both of us at any given moment. I'm trying to protect him, not deprive him."

"Stop making excuses, Charlytte. You mean to tell me that you don't feel anything when we're out and people mistake me as your baby's father? Or when I take you to your doctor appointments, and the nurses- even the doctors- think I'm that child's father. I know I'm not his *real* dad, but who cares about some stupid DNA. Just trust me on this one, I promise I will always be here for the both of you."

That feeling of being able to rely on him felt so much like the right thing to do, but I just couldn't set my heart up for another possible failure.

"I believe you Jeremiah, but let's just let time reveal everything. If I decide to keep him, I won't keep you from being a part of his life, but I won't be looking forward to it either."

"That's fair enough," he replied.

I leaned over the table and gave him one smooch on the cheek. In return, he grabbed my face and we shared our first intimate kiss.

33: POWER

"Power Isaiah Black! Get your bad butt over here and put these pants on right this minute!"

Power waddled his little bowlegs over to my direction. He had just recently learned how to walk and it was becoming extremely hard for me to keep up with him. I was in a rush to get him dressed because Jeremiah was on the way to pick him up. He had finally got to work a half-day and wanted to take my little man out to Chuck-e- Cheese. I wanted to go with them, but I had a little studying to do for a final exam that was coming up in my Anatomy class. It was my first semester in school and I took my lessons very seriously.

I finished putting on Power's clothes just in time for the doorbell to ring.

"*Coooming*," I sung, full of joy, as I skipped all the way to the front door and then opened it.

"Hey, what's up babes," Jeremiah walked in and planted one big kiss on my lips. He always greeted me that way, and it never got old.

"Looking mighty nice for a guy who just worked six hours," I complimented him.

"I know. And it wasn't easy," he replied. "You know that lazy ass nigga Mark might have unloaded two boxes today. One more day of this and I'm going to the boss."

"So my baby's a snitch now?" I sucker punched him in the shoulder.

"Man, call me what you want. We both get paid the same amount of money, therefore we should be doing the same amount of work. Shit, I be wore out. But it's all good though," he ran towards Power, "my lil' man gonna cheer me up."

Jeremiah scooped my son up like a football and began to tickle his stomach. Power giggled at every silly noise that Jeremiah made and I just stood there silently, admiring them both.

Power loved Jeremiah. He always let out a loud scream and smiled from ear to ear every time he saw him. I was proud of that guy. He had kept his word by treating my baby like he was his own son, and he stood by my side up until the very day I had him. He even waited outside the hospital the entire eleven hours that I was in labor.

My whole life changed the second I laid my eyes on my baby boy. He was so cute when he came busting out of me, even with all of the blood and slime covering him. And when the nurse cleaned him up, he was even more precious. His skin was as white as the blanket that covered him and I knew the second I looked into those manipulative and slanted eyes, exactly who his father was.

In fact, it gave me the chills, what his eyes did to me. They had that same look of control as Cederick's. And just like I was with his father, I wanted to give my all to him. I wanted to dedicate my life to him. I had no choice but to name him Power.

"I wish you could come too," Jeremiah hinted at me. "Take a break for a change and come spend some time with your two favorite men."

I looked at Jeremiah and Power, who both were looking at me with sad eyes, just hoping that I would change my mind. I wanted to join them, but I couldn't. My final was in two days.

"As much as I want to, I can't. This test is really important. Radiology ain't easy, ya know."

"I know, I know...but between me working and you working, your school and your studying, and little man, we barely get to spend time together."

"I'm already ahead of you. We'll spend time together real soon, I promise. After this semester is over, we're going to all take a trip. I already started saving for it."

"I'll believe it when the day comes," he sighed.

Jeremiah carried Power to the door and kissed me one last time. I watched them walk all the way to his truck, and I laughed as Jeremiah struggled to put him in his carseat.

"And don't be blasting all that loud rap music in my baby's ear. He's too young for that!" I yelled out to him.

"Young my ass! This boy's fifteen months going on fifteen years!" He shouted back.

"Whateva, just be careful what you play around him. He's picking up on words now and if he comes back cursing, then us not spending time together ain't gon' be the only problem we're gonna have!"

We both laughed and I waved goodbye one last time before closing myself inside my apartment. Finally, the moment that I had been waiting for had arrived: peace and quiet time. Sure, I was a little upset that I couldn't go play with my boys, but I was physically and mentally drained from school, work, and Power. A couple of hours to myself was just what I needed. Plus, being alone was the only time I had to sit down and smile about how much I had accomplishment over the last couple of years.

My life had changed drastically since Power was born. I was a working mother, a student, and a best friend. It wasn't easy trying to be all three at once, but the benefits were well worth it. The minute I realized what my purpose was in life was the minute I felt like I was born again. And the most interesting part of it all, was that it was only the beginning.

I took a seat in my work area that I had created for myself, and before I opened my book, I stopped for a second and began to reflect a bit. The manifestations brought a huge smile to my face because never before had my heart been filled with so much joy. My life was almost close to perfect. I had a man who loved me, prayed with me, and treated me like the queen I was. I had the most handsome baby boy who motivated me to stay on my shit. And best of all, I had a place of my own that I was legally maintaining.

After Mrs. Johnson told me about the local Housing Program, I jumped right on it and got approved for one of those low-income based apartment homes, better known as, the projects. Luckily it came through for me just a couple of months after Power was born. It wasn't much, but it was a start. I wasn't happy about going back to the hood, but what choice did I have? Besides, Mrs. Johnson said that there was nothing wrong with living in the projects, as long as I didn't get too comfortable. I had been there for over a year and had boxes that I still hadn't unpacked- the last thing I was trying to do was get comfortable.

Jeremiah, on the other hand, still lived with his dad, but was working a full-time job at a warehouse making more money, in a week, than I did in a month. He was definitely my man now and as much as I wanted him to move in with us, I was sticking to my "take everything slow" motto because I wanted to make sure things we're perfect for when we finally did start to make bigger commitments.

I loved Jeremiah because he was a real man and he respected every decision that I made. As much as he also wanted us to live together, he never pressured me into doing anything that I didn't want to do. In fact, Jeremiah and I didn't even have sex until Power was about five months old, which by the way, was incredible. He wasn't the biggest in size, but he sure did know how to work with what he had.

I can truly say that life was a lot less stressful. I didn't have to hide, fearing an encounter with Cederick. It didn't long for my absent family members, because I now had a family of my own. And with Jeremiah's encouraging words, I didn't feel that I had to belittle myself because of the things I had done in the past. Ordale and everything that happened there was history to me. The city, the drama, the lifestyle- it would always be in my rearview and I had no plans of ever moving back. I absolutely loved my new life and new family; but as usual, me and good things didn't last long.

I had been studying for about an hour when my cell phone started to ring. I knew it wasn't Jeremiah because we had talked literally two minutes prior, and his cell phone number never came up as private when he called me. At first I didn't answer it because I didn't have the slightest clue who it was, but after I got that same estranged phone call five times in a row, I figured I had better see what was up.

I grabbed the phone from out of my lap, flipped it open very slowly, then placed it to my ear.

"Hel-lo," I said, hesitantly.

No one said anything.

"Hello," I repeated.

"Hi, is this Charlytte?" The cracking voice on the other end asked.

Damn. I knew dis shit was too good to be true. Please don't let this be some chick talking bout she got a baby from Jeremiah. Lord please, don't do this to me again.

"Yes, this is she. Who is this?" *Go ahead. Drop the bomb on me.*

I waited for her to hit me with the bad news about my man.

"Charlytte, this is Keisha."

Keisha? I thought.

I heard her clearly, but it still didn't register in my brain. Plus, something about the phone call just didn't feel right. She didn't sound like herself at all.

"Keisha who?" I asked, just to be certain.

"Your big sis," she mumbled.

Immediately I snapped. "Look, I don't know how you got my number, but I honestly don't want to hear no sob stories about how sorry you are! My life is perfectly fine and I'm over that. Goodbye."

"Wait!" she cried, tears included. "I'm not calling to apologize. Something terrible has just happened."

I never heard her sound so distraught before. She was always the strong one. Keisha cried for nothing and no one. She didn't even shed one tear the time she found out that one of her old sex partners had H.I.V; neither did she rejoice when the nurse revealed to her that her test came back negative. All she did was get up a say, "C'mon sis, I got a taste for a Big Mac."

When I heard Keisha breaking down the way she was, family instincts immediately kicked in. I didn't care about how she betrayed me in the past. I just wanted to make sure that she was okay.

"Keisha, what's wrong?" I began to panic. "What happened?"

"It's about Keyshawn!" She started to cry even louder.

"What about Keyshawn?!" I asked. "Keisha, calm down. What happened to Keyshawn?"

"He's…he's...he's dead!"

My cell phone hit the carpet as I let out a heartfelt scream. Following my phone, I collapsed down to the floor and all I could do was lie there motionless, stare into space, and try to piece together the words that I had just heard. Keyshawn could not be dead. God wouldn't take my mother *and* my little brother away from me. He just wouldn't do me like that.

Even though the phone was a couple inches away from where I was laying, I could still hear Keisha crying. And each sob was letting me know that what she told me about Keyshawn was really true. After a little bit of weeping myself, I finally found the strength to pick the phone back up and get some more info about it.

"Charlytte, you there?" I heard Keisha ask right before I answered her.

"Yeah, I'm here. Just trynna get my thoughts together." I answered. "You okay?"

"Yeah, I'm just in a state of shock right now," she replied. "I still can't believe it."

"Me neither," I sobbed. "Do you know what happened?"

"A little," she sniffed. "You know I barely watch the news, but something just told me to watch it today. A story came on about a drive–by shooting turnin' fatal. As usual, I thought it was some ol' stupid motherfuckers out the hood, until the news anchorman said the two victims were twenty-three year old Teon Albright and sixteen-year old Keyshawn Black. I was hoping and praying that it could have somehow been another kid who goes by that name, but after they showed a clip of Teon's orange chevy, I already knew."

The more Keisha spoke, the more the tears rolled down my eyes. But still, I tried to be strong for myself and for her. Although I knew Keisha wouldn't lie about her little brother being killed, I knew that the only way for me to accept the fact that Keyshawn was dead was for me to see him for myself.

"Is Teon dead too?" I asked.

"No, they say he's in the hospital with minor injuries. I think he got hit twice in the arm or something. The police are questioning him down at the hospital and from what I hear, he ain't talking. His cousin Sharice say they got him handcuffed to the bed and all. Apparently they had guns in the car, and you know he a felon so he going straight to jail, probably five to ten."

"Damn," was all I could say.

"What about Auntie? Does she know?" I asked.

"She's out of town with Lewis. I'm not telling her until she comes back. I don't want to ruin her vacation. Keyshawn wouldn't have wanted that. And she don't have a cell phone so hopefully the word won't get back to her, but Korey is on his way down here as we speak. The whole neighborhood is meeting up at mommy's house tonight. You should come."

"To be honest Keisha, I can't go back there. I'm just not ready for that. It's too many memories. The last time I saw Keyshawn we-"

Unable to fight back any longer, I really started to let it out because I remembered the last conversation Keyshawn and I had. I remembered those harsh words that we said to each other, and the part that hurt me the most was that I couldn't go back and change any of it. If I knew then, what I had just learned, I would have hugged Keyshawn and told him I loved him, even after he said all those mean things to me.

"Nevermind that story," I said, then tried to pull myself together. "I'mma just have to pass on that. I'm in no condition to drive anyway."

"Okay, but if you change your mind, we'll be there."

"Okay thanks sis."

I got myself ready to hang up the call, but had a terrible thought in my head.

"Hey Keish," I called to her quickly, trying to catch her before she hung up on me, "can I ask you a personal question?"

"What's up?"

"I know I may just be being a little paranoid, but honestly, do you think that this has anything to do with Cederick retaliating for that little debt I created?"

"I heard about that. You a fool for that one, but naw, I'm positive Cederick didn't have anything to do with this."

"How can you be so certain?"

"Because he's in jail, and has been for the past year."

"Oh," I said, slightly relieved. Not only because Cederick was in jail, but because the last thing I wanted to do was find out that I had something to do with my brother's death. I couldn't possibly live with that.

"It's not your fault Charlytte," she said. "Keyshawn made mistakes and he paid for them with his life. We'll talk more in person."

"Okay sis," I dismissed her. "Stay strong."

"I'll try," she replied.

We both said our goodbyes and I immediately called for Jeremiah's support. When I last spoke to him, he told me that Power wasn't ready to leave Chuck-e-cheese and that they were going to stop and get a bite to eat before they came home. But after I had told him about the phone call I had just received, he dropped everything and came straight to me.

Power was worn out when they arrived home, so Jeremiah washed him up and put him to bed for me. Then he consoled me until I finally managed to get some rest.

34: 'HIPPO'CRITES

"Look at my baby brother," I whispered to myself while I just stared at Keyshawn's lifeless body, shaking my head from left to right in sorrow. It still seemed unreal and I still had not begun to accept the horrible truth that he was really gone. I just couldn't.

The funeral was held at a huge church in our hood that was known for holding homegoing services for people who didn't have an established church home. I arrived almost an hour early to beat traffic. Jeremiah, Power, and I took a seat on the side of the church where the friends sat, because I didn't care to walk in with the family. Even though the tragedy should have helped me overlook it, I still couldn't help but feel like I didn't have any ties to my blood relatives. Besides, I wasn't ready to face Auntie Jo again and was trying my best not to be seen by her.

Not even thirty minutes after we arrived, did the church begin to fill up with all types of folks. Not counting Mrs. Johnson- because she had already told me she was going to be a little late- but along with its members, there sat a couple of Auntie Jo's friends, a sprinkle of our distance relatives, and damn near everybody who lived in Ordale. I wasn't aware that Keyshawn- who was looking like he was sleeping so peacefully in his casket- was so popular. He looked nothing like the Keyshawn I knew, but he did look sharp in that white Armani suit. Not to mention, the gold watch and chain he wore on his wrist was dazzling.

Even though we were only sitting a few feet away from where his casket was, I was able to look at him without shedding a tear. Besides, I did most of my crying the day before at his wake service where I, all by myself, met Keisha and we saw each other for the first time in over two years.

I gotta admit, the encounter with her was awkward, but we managed to put aside our differences and focus on what was more important- the loss of our brother. We even cried a little bit in each other's arms before taking turns saying our final words to him. It wasn't until Keisha walked me to her car that she told me the whole story about what really happened.

"Take a seat," Keisha said as she moved a couple papers off of her passenger seat to allow room for me to sit down. Keisha was no longer driving the Impala. She was in a new Toyota Camry that was much nicer, and obviously much more expensive. I didn't know what lawyer she was screwing just to have it, but truthfully, I didn't care.

"Gotta make this quick 'cause I gotta meet mama back at the house," she told me. "I don't like to leave her alone. She's taking this pretty bad."

"I bet she is," I said, then rolled my eyes. *Keyshawn was her favorite.*

Keisha pulled her short jean skirt down, just so she could face me without showing off her panties. She always made sure she looked a person dead into the eyes when she was about to spill some juicy gossip, so I knew that whatever she was getting ready to tell me was going to be interesting. I wasn't comfortable staring her in her face like that because she still carried the look of a traitor, and honestly, it made me even more upset that despite her ugly acts, she was still beautiful. The only difference was that her hair- that was once in a bob- had grown out just a little past her shoulders. She still kept that ruby red piece in the front though.

"I still can't believe this shit," she said. "But let me give you the 4-1-1."

"I'm listening," I calmly replied.

"See, I don't know if you heard or not, but Keyshawn was making some major moves in the city. That lil' nigga was a beast- young, dumb, and really didn't give a fuck."

Keisha took a pause and glared out of her mirror at some people walking into the funeral home. We were parked right across the street from it.

"He was the one who niggas called when they wanted to get a job done. They say lil' bra was heartless and wasn't scared to do shit. Hell, he even earned himself a little nickname 'Savage.'

"Fa real?" I asked, already shocked by the little bit of info she had just given me. "And you didn't try to talk to him, tell him to chill?"

"No," she answered. "C'mon Charlytte, you know I barely went around there. I mean, I knew he was getting into trouble, but I just thought it was some misdemeanor shit. As far as him thuggin' hard, hitting major licks, and being wanted by the Feds for his involvement in some shootings, I ain't knew nothing."

"Wait a minute...slow down," I told her. "Involvement in what?"

"Some shootings…but I'll get to that, just let me finish," she said. "See, a little after Cederick got jammed- which was only a couple months after you disappeared- I ran into Teon. We started talking and you know me- old or young, I don't discriminate- I started fucking with him."

"The lil' nigga was lame as fuck, but shit, he used smoke hella-good weed with me and the dick was A1. He was just a lil' boytoy, nothing I took seriously though. Anyway, the young nigga eventually catches feelings and starts pillow talking, telling me how he gets his money and shit, so of course, I wanted in. That's when I started going on runs for him and his-"

"Hold up. Wait another minute Keisha," I cut her off. "If you finna tell me that you had something to do with this, then I honestly don't want to hear it. I don't care what happened."

I hated to have jumped to any conclusions, but Keisha was grimy, and it wouldn't have surprised me if her selfish ways contributed to some, if not all, of it.

I grabbed my purse and cell phone to leave, but Keisha snatched my arm in attempt to stop me.

"Charlytte, hell no! Just listen to me dammit!" she shouted. "If anything, blame Lewis and mama, but I ain't had shit to do with it."

"Auntie Jo?" I asked. "Keisha, what the fuck have y'all done!"

"Y'all ain't done shit. Keyshawn got his first major front of dope through *Lewis. Lewis* was giving him weed to hustle. *Lewis* was using him to set niggas up and rob them. *And mama*, of course, knew about everything and was just sitting back enjoying the profits."

"See, I knew that was going to-"

"But on the flip side," Keisha cut me off, "Keyshawn was doin' business with Teon too. And one day, I met up with him- him meaning Keyshawn- for a drop. Before I hit the road, we smoked one in the car and he started telling me about this sweet lick Lewis had lined up for him. He said that some Mexicans who lived in a trailer park a couple of miles away, in one of them country ass towns, were stashin' about ten pounds of weed and almost twenty-thousand dollars in cash. Lewis gave Keyshawn and his homeboys the address, told them what time to run up in their spot, and just like the hungry and dumb ass niggas they were, they strapped up and made their move on 'em."

"But apparently, shit didn't go as plan. They did get away with some cash and a couple pounds of weed, but one of the niggas in Keyshawn's crew was shot- and you know they just left his ass behind. Later on, a video gets back to the hood showing the Mexicans making a deal with the kid, saying that if he gave up the names of his partners, he wouldn't kill him for trying to rob them. But, as soon as the word "Keyshawn" came flying out of the boy's bloody mouth, they put one in his head anyway, for snitching."

"*Dang*. Some real live gangsta shit," I groaned.

"I know right. And get this, a couple days later, Keyshawn ends up dead, and all witnesses see is a car driving away with the county named Springfield on the tag. That's the same county the dudes they robbed lived in. You do the math."

I sat in silence, trying to take in everything Keisha had just told me. I didn't know who I blamed more- Auntie Jo, Lewis, Keisha, or myself- even though I was the only one in the family who tried to tell him better. I was even considering blaming Korey. He was so wrapped up in Patricia's arms that he never took the time out to help his little brother become the man that he had become. I just didn't know. All I knew was that there was no reason for Keyshawn to have been dead. No reason at all.

There was nothing further that I needed to hear from Keisha. We said our goodbyes and I went back to my car and cried a little bit before I pulled off. I was saddened, angry, hurting, and still in a little bit of shock. The half hour drive back home was one the hardest and longest rides I'd ever taken. I even cried some more when I made it home that night.

Back at the church, at exactly eleven a.m., the pianist and the six-member choir started the service off with a soulful version of Amazing Grace. Everybody in the building stood as the family made their entrance.

It took three people to hold up Auntie Jo as she cried all the way up to the front pew. She was dressed to a tee, wearing a long black dress and one of those huge, extra ass hats that old ladies usually wore. And I couldn't help but notice that beautiful gold necklace she sported around her neck.

"She hasn't changed a bit," I whispered to Jeremiah after I was finished studying her. She was still big. Still loud. And still made me wanna throw up every time I looked at her.

Keisha, Korey, Patricia and the kids followed behind her, picking up things that were falling out of her purse from her bouncing around all over the place. My two uncles, who I hadn't seen in forever, came in behind them and I didn't know anyone else who trailed after, even though they were crying just as hard as the people in our family. I figured they must have been some of

Keyshawn's homeboys because they all wore black RIP t-shirts- all twenty of them. There were even some too-grown-for-their-own-good little girls mixed in the crowd too. One of them was crying uncontrollably. I assumed she was his main chick because she too had on a RIP t-shirt, with a picture of the two of them all cuddled up at a teen night club.

After the family settled in the pews, everyone else took their seats. Well, everyone except for Auntie Jo, who was still hovering over Keyshawn's casket, crying her guilty heart out. Judging by her professionally styled hairdo and her freshly did nails, I could tell she had her hands on a little bit of 'dirty' money.

Finally, after taking about three ministers and two ushers to calm her, she found her seat. And the more she played that innocent 'oh Lord why me role', the more disgusted I became with her, because after what Keisha had told me, there was no doubt in my mind that she was responsible for Keyshawn's death. Yes, of course he made his own decisions, but she was his mother; she was supposed to tell him better. Not have her boyfriend help destroy his life by giving him poison to sell on the streets. He was way too young to know as much as he did about hustling. She could have convinced him to get a job, or stay in school, but instead, she convinced him to make fast money. Because of it, Keyshawn was dead, and it really burnt me up to see her putting on the way she was.

Thank Gosh. I said to myself after she took her seat. She howled a couple more times before she finally put her mouth on mute, the church proceeded with its services, and I watched happily as family members, friends, and teachers spoke about their experiences with Keyshawn. I almost even cried when his little league football coach told the story of how, when he was eight, he poured a whole jar of salt into the team's water cooler as a prank. I remembered that so well because Auntie Jo tore his ass up, not because he put salt in their drinking water, but because he used her new container that she had just bought. I could never forget that.

After the reflections and one solo, the six-member choir sang another selection, then the pastor, John Williams, rendered a thirty-minute sermon. I sat there quietly listening as the short, stubby pastor preached solely about the resurrection drawing near, and how people needed to get saved before it was too late. Now that I was a faithful church member, I was able to keep up with him and even nodded my head from time to time whenever he said something really deep. Pastor William's sermon was so powerful, that after he was finished speaking, the entire congregation- young and old- stood up and gave him a standing ovation.

Next, the funeral providers opened the casket once more, but because the church was so packed, only the family members could view the body. Once again, Auntie Jo was the last person still standing over Keyshawn, screaming and carrying on. I still couldn't believe my eyes.

"Oh God!" she threw herself over the black steel casket with the silver trimming. "Why did you have to take my baby? Lord why!"

Keisha and Korey tried to comfort her as she continued hollering, while the people of the church sympathized with her. Some of them crying themselves. Not me though, I felt awful about Keyshawn dying, but I didn't feel one bit bad for Auntie Jo. And if the Pastor the rest of them knew what I knew, they probably wouldn't have felt bad for her either.

In fact, the more I listened to her crying, the more I could feel myself shaking in anger. Not only that, just seeing her for the first time in a long time, brought back many horrible memories. Everything from her putting me out, to me moving in with the child molester, to me tricking up in them hotel rooms, to Keisha sleeping with Cederick behind my back- even my suicide attempt- was making it really hard for me to continue watching her keep up with her little charade. On top of that, one of the choir members started singing an acapella to one of my favorite gospel songs, *Open My Heart* by Yolanda Adams.

Fallen deep into words, while trying to drown out my inner evil thoughts, I rocked back and forth and began to sing the song in my head. Jeremiah and I were like soul mates and he always felt whatever I was feeling. Whether it was joy or pain, he could sense it. And he must have sensed that I was getting upset, because out of nowhere, he leaned over and whispered into my ears, "You okay bae? If you need to cry, just let it out."

"Yeah, I'm fine," I said, not wanting to tell him what was really bothering me. "Just trying to be strong for little Power."

"Okay, but you sure you don't want to go up there one last time," he pointed to the casket. "I'll walk with you if you need me to."

"No, this is already too much. Power doesn't need to see him like that. He's probably already scared as it is with *that woman* carrying on the way she is."

I looked down at Power, who was sitting next to me playing with the flowers on my colorful sundress. Clearly he was not fazed by what was going on in the church. True enough, I was worried about keeping him safe, but I was more worried about encountering Auntie Jo, who had been so worked up that she hadn't yet realized I was there. I just didn't know what to expect if, or when, we laid eyes on one another. But the way I was feeling, if she did or said anything out of the way, I was going off. I was just that pissed.

"I just need to go to the bathroom, dab some water on my face or something. Maybe that will help me calm down."

I held my hands up to Jeremiah to show him just how badly they were shaking.

"You need me to go with you?" he asked, convinced that I needed to do something about my uncontrollable nerves.

"No, I'll be fine," I assured him.

Before I got up, I glanced back up at Auntie Jo, Keisha, and Korey, who were all still standing up over Keyshawn's body. Keisha was holding Keyshawn's cold hand crying. Auntie Jo was damn near inside the casket. And Korey was patting their backs with each of his hands, trying to be strong for the both of them. I assumed that the church must have decided to just let them vent because nobody interfered.

Unable to stand the site of them any longer, I skimmed the emotion-filled room, looking behind and around me at everybody. Some people were singing the words to the song, some were watching Auntie Jo displaying looks that said they could feel her pain, and some were crying themselves. I even spotted Mrs. Johnson who was sitting alone at the very back of the church. I was glad to see that she had made it. She gave me a smile and I gave her one back, before turning my attention back to my family.

"Lord no! Not my baby! Not my baby!" Auntie Jo continued to cry out. “Lord no!”

While her back was turned to the casket, I ceased the opportunity to make a silent getaway and shot for the bathroom. But, as soon as I was up on my two feet real good, her never-miss-nothing, big, popped eyes turned in my direction, catching me dead in my trail and leaving me lost for words.

Shit. I thought as I stood there motionless, not wanting to look at her, but unable to take my eyes off of her either. Her tears and her make-up played with one another, leaving one helluva dark painting on her plump face. That made it even harder. Suddenly, her cries slowly faded, and her interest in Keyshawn seemed to be no more. Even Korey and Keisha had to stop consoling her just to see what had so quickly stolen their mama's attention.

With the song now over and everyone in the church- including the Pastor- looking at the both of us as if they had all personally known of our quarrel, a nervous feeling came over me. I could feel myself beginning to shake all over, and it seemed as if my whole body went numb.

Even though I was certain I wasn't going to be the one to break the ice, a part of me thought that Auntie Jo would have shown me even the slightest bit of love when she finally saw me. I thought that just knowing I was alive and well would have given her joy. But to my very surprise, she just turned to both of her children, who were standing side by side each other, held their faces in the palm of her big hands, and said in her best I'm-trying-to-impress-people voice, "We must be strong children. We're all we got, just the three of us." Then she grabbed their hands, purposely looked at me with an evil glare, and began to lead them back to their seats.

I was crushed. I don't know why, but I was. I had done so well getting over my past, but as soon as that happened, all the depressing emotions came rushing back to me, as if I never even started the process of recovering from them. I guess after all those years of being on my own, I still had a little faith that Auntie Jo had some good in her, that she still cared somewhat about my well-being. But after that little stunt she had just pulled, I knew I was wrong.

I looked at Jeremiah, who then looked at me. There no way he could have sensed what I was feeling that time because I didn't even know what I was feeling. Even Mrs. Johnson had peeped what she had done, and the sympathetic look on her face showed me that she felt really bad for me too, especially when she saw the tears starting to crawl down my face.

Like a quiet statue, I just stood still, watching as Auntie Jo, Keisha, and Korey took their seats. I got the feeling that people were looking at me and wondering why I hadn't sat down yet, but I didn't care about what they thought. As a matter of fact, at that moment, I didn't care what anyone thought.

From the corner of my eye, I could see Mrs. Johnson running up to me, but before she could get close enough to try and comfort me- which was exactly what she was coming to do- I pushed her away.

"I'm okay," I told her, then turned towards Auntie Jo, who was looking straight ahead as if she did nothing wrong. Unable to hold back any longer, and from the top of my lungs, I yelled out to her...

"YOU HYPOCRITE!"

35: CONFESSIONS

Whatever little noise being made in the building came to a halt, and immediately Jeremiah and Mrs. Johnson, both shocked by my outburst, tried to pull me back to my seat. Of course, I wasn't trying to hear it.

Everyone else in the church- downstairs and up in the balcony- quickly looked my way.

"Charlytte," Jeremiah called out to me. "Please calm down. This is not the time, nor the place, for this."

Mrs. Johnson nodded her head, siding with him.

"Why is it not?" I said loud enough so that everyone could hear me." This is a church, a place to lay down your sins right? I think this is the perfect place for this."

Silence, confusion, and fear filled the air. No music played. No choir sang. No pastor preached. There was nothing but heavy tension between two very angry women, and a good chance that all hell was about to break loose.

"I'm talking to you, *Joanne*," I said to her as I excused myself and made my way up to the front of the church. I had held my tongue long enough for that evil old lady. It was time for everyone to see who she really was.

"I see you taking this real hard," I continued. "It must really hurt having that guilt eatin' at ya cold little heart, doesn't it?"

Auntie Jo rose up, taking me up on my challenge, but Keisha tried to pull her back. As much as she liked drama, even she wasn't ready for it.

"No!" she screamed at Keisha, and then snatched her heavy arm away from her. The fat from it jiggled a bit as she drew back. "She wants to start something, I'll finish it. I'm about sick of this brat anyway."

Auntie Jo slowly walked towards me and Pastor Williams met us in the middle. We were now in the front of the church. I was to the left of him and she was to the right. The looks in both of our eyes let him know that if it was going to be battle in the church, it wasn't going to be a spiritual one.

"I was a good mother," she fixed her mouth to say. "How dare you challenge that? You still the same old Charlytte, ungrateful and nothin' but trouble."

"A good mother?" I shouted. "It's your fault Keyshawn is dead!"

Collective gasps all over the church overthrew the silence.

"You knew what he was doing in those streets! A good mother would have told him better, not have him out there hustling just so you can buy beer!"

More gasps sounded from the crowd. This time I turned to them. Everyone looked like Zombies the way their eyes were glued to us. They were thirsty for a good show, and I knew it wasn't right, but I was going to give them just that. I wanted to expose Auntie Jo to her friends, to her family, but most importantly, to herself.

"The bible says spare the rod, spoil the child!" she balled her fist up at me. "And my God if we weren't in the church, I would go upside your head for disrespecting me like that!"

"Go ahead!" I screamed, the tears still falling. "It wouldn't be the first time you hurt me, but I can promise you this...it will be the last. Besides, I just want you to admit that you caused this! That you never put your family first! That all you ever cared about was men and money!"

"You ungrateful bi-," she was about to say, but stopped herself. "Is this about you leaving my house? Because if it is....you left because you wanted to leave! You wanted to be grown and on your own! You knew you could have come back, but *YOU* chose not to!"

"You threw me out!" I reminded her. "And didn't even come looking for me the next day, but you did find the time to take my clothes to Jeans for Green. How do you live with putting me out on the streets, and not even caring about whether or not I had clothes on my back?"

"I paid for those clothes," she reminded me. "And if I could pay for them, I could take them back. I did the same to Korey and Keisha when they left, so what makes you think that I would treat you any different."

"I don't ever remember you throwing their stuff out! Ever!"

"You disrespected me in my house, so you had to go. Period. And as far as me chasing behind you Charlytte, Joanne Black don't chase behind nobody. You know you really kill me, always trying to play the victim. You know you just wanted to be like the rest of those little fast girls and chase them big head boys. I heard ya had baby too," she pointed at Power, "evidently you ain't been doin' all that bad."

"Don't bring my son into this...and definitely do not judge me," I got up in her face. We were in arms reach of each other now and I could see it in his eyes that Pastor Williams was becoming more and more afraid that someone was eventually going to get violent.

"You have no idea what I have been through out here on these streets!" I yelled. "No idea!"

"And *miss thang*, you have no idea what *I've* been through at home," she shot back. "Charlytte, I hate to break it to you, but the world don't revolve around just you. We all got problems."

Some of the older women nodded their heads in agreement. That only got me more heated. I had to strike back.

"I hear you been doing wonderful at home, with the help Keyshawn hustlin' and robbin' people for you and your no-good boyfriend. Ooh looky," I pointed to the necklace she was wearing, the one that was sparkling so beautifully that I couldn't take my eyes off of it. "You always did say that when you got your hands on some money you would get a necklace like that. Well, let me ask you this... having something that valuable, was it really worth your son's life?"

Without thinking twice about it, Auntie Jo pulled her arms back and slapped fire to my face. The entire church screamed out in unison and the Pastor, along with the some of the ministers, immediately jumped between us.

Keisha, Korey, and Patricia ran up and grabbed Auntie Jo. Mrs. Johnson and Jeremiah rushed to my aid. Little Power was falling asleep on Jeremiah's shoulder-thank goodness. And both my uncles turned their heads away in embarrassment. I can't say I didn't blame them though. They all had seen enough.

"I'm fine," I told Mrs. Johnson as I held my face where it stung. I wasn't worried about getting slapped. She might have hurt me on the outside, but I was hurting her on the inside. That's all that mattered to me.

"Are you done now?" I asked her, after the stinging started to wear off.

"How dare you!" she yelled. She was really upset now. Her breathing heightened and she began sweating even more than she already was.

"Charlytte, you listen to me and you listen to me good! I never want to see you again! You are NOT any family of mine. You're the devil. Out to ruin my life... JUST LIKE YOUR MOTHER DID!"

Before I could even get a chance to think about what she had just said about my mama, Auntie Jo dropped to her knees, and for the first time in my life, I saw her break down. She began to cry so hysterically that she could barely stand on her own two feet. Everyone in the church stood looking, and my uncles, who before didn't want to take part in the confusion, now ran to help her.

For a short period of time, but what seemed like forever, she wailed and wept- the way you were *supposed to* when you'd just lost a child. It was so intense that even I could now feel her pain. No one knew what to say or what to do. We all just stared at her.

Auntie Jo didn't cry for long before she slowly eased her way back up on her feet, holding Uncle Johnny by the shoulders to keep her balance. And when she was finally rose completely, she had a different look in her eye- that look a crackhead gets when he just took a hit, that look a drunk gets when he's had too much malt liquor, that look that had no soul behind it. It scared me.

With her body loosely moving all about, her eyes pierced mine as if a bomb would have exploded if she took them off of me.

"Yooou are yooour mother," her words slurred. "Just alike. The same eyes. The same nose. The same stuck up attitude. The same joy stealer."

"That's enough!" Uncle Johnny stepped in, trying to stop her from saying anything further.

"NO!" she yelled back to him. "She needs to hear this."

I didn't know what I needed to hear. I didn't even know what to think. All I knew was that there were questions that I needed answers to. Like, how did my mother ruin her life? What was the real reason behind her sudden break down? Just really, what did it all mean?

"*Poor little Charlytte*," she sung the words so beautifully. "*And poor little Jonell*, always somebody's victim. No regards for anyone else. You act so much like her, but you look so much like him. I can't stand it."

"I said that's enough!" Uncle Johnny said again, knowing deep down that his sister wasn't about to listen to him.

I was definitely confused now. We all were- the pastor, the church, and it seemed as if Auntie Jo herself- was a little confused.

"My little sister Jonell, I should have never taken her into my home," she cried.

Uncle Joey who was silently standing by watching it all, now butted in, "Joanne, when are you going to stop this. You know that wasn't her fault. You were twenty-five, she was only sixteen. She was just a kid."

Auntie Jo slowly turned to Uncle Joey, her finger pointed at his brim hat that sat so low on his head, it almost covered his big, beady eyes.

"You can believe that all you want," she said to him. "She knew exactly what she was doing. Prancin' around in those tight pants and things. Showin' her skinny ass all over my damn house. Mama knew how she was. She didn't even want her."

"No, Joanne," Uncle Johnny said. "Jonell moved in with you 'cause mama got too sick to care for her. You know that."

"I should have went with my first mind," Auntie Jo ignored him, her face soaked from the tears. "I should have never let her stay!"

"Joanne, admit it," Johnny said. "You hated her ever since the day she was born. You wanted to be the only girl, and when she came along, you didn't like that she was getting all the attention. At least admit that you were *a little* jealous of her.

"Jealous?" she laughed out loud. "I wasn't jealous. I was angry. It was always *Jonell* this, and *Jonell* that. Jonell was smart. Jonell was pretty. Jonell was skinny."

"So that's what this is all about," Uncle Joey said, his full-length beard moving along with his lips. "You were fat and she was skinny?"

"It's deeper than that, my brotha," she sassed him. "You were Mr. Athletic, you wouldn't understand. You never had to go through what I went through. You never had to worry about people smacking you with honeybuns, or being called 'fatso' all the time."

She began to cry again, obviously reminiscing back on her hurtful past.

“All my life I wanted to be a majorette, but the team told me that all my fat ass was good for was holding the damn flag."

Uncle Joey tried to use his towel to wipe her tears. "Jonell couldn't help how she looked, but you couldn’t have helped the way you treated her."

"Are you trying to say that I treated her bad?" she snatched away from him, then looked to both her brothers as if she needed confirmation of their feelings. "I didn’t see y’all offer to take her in when mama got sick, and neither did you take Charlytte after she died."

"You knew I was in military. I wasn’t in no position to take in a child. And what was Joey gone do with her, he was barely in a position to take care of himself."

"It doesn’t matter! Why are y’all siding with her? She ruined my life! And the only person who loved me, she took away!"

Uncle Johnny tilted his head down in disappointment.

"Joanne, I love you, but I can no longer accept you as my sister if you continue to go on living this lie. You know deep down Jonell did nothing wrong. For once, you need to face reality and own up to what happened. If not, you will forever be bitter."

"What was I supposed to do!" she screamed. "I was wrapped up into the arms of the only man who ever truly loved me! A man who didn’t care how big I was. A man who didn’t care how many times I went to the buffet table when we went out to eat. A man who didn’t care how I looked underneath my clothes. He simply loved me for me."

"You thought he loved you for you, but you were wrong," Uncle Johnny corrected her. "Jose Pablo was a no-good cheater. He preyed on low-self-esteem-having women like yourself. I never got good vibes from that cat, and even warned you about him over a million times. You were just too blinded and too wrapped up in compliments to see the truth for what it really was. Too in love to realize that you were the only one in love."

"How dare you!" Auntie Jo smacked Uncle Johnny in the face, just as she had done to me. More gasps sounded from the crowd. "Jose loved me, ya hear me! He loved me!"

Uncle Johnny didn't get mad. He didn't yell. He didn't even raise his voice. He knew like I knew that the only way to get back at Auntie Jo was to hit her with something that she couldn't handle, something that she tried all her life to get away from- the truth.

He slowly walked up to her with no expression. His tall height had all our heads bent upward in the direction of him. Then he grabbed Auntie Jo's face, firmly put her cheeks between both his hands, and carefully pierced her with his eyeballs.

"If he loved you," he held her tightly. "Then why *for four years,* was he molesting our baby sister."

Auntie Jo's eyes widened and before we could even grasp what he had just said, she pushed him away from her and covered her ears with both of her hands. "I'M NOT LISTENING! I'M NOT LISTENING! I'M NOT LISTENING," she hollered out like a mad woman. "THE DEVIL IS LIAR! THE DEVIL IS LIAR! THE DEVIL IS A LIAR!"

Her screams became background noises as I slipped into my own zone and began to let the words that Uncle Johnny had just said marinate in my head. I knew firsthand how it felt to be raped, and I wouldn't have wished that on Samantha Hutchinson. To even think that it was possible for my mama to have gone through that was harder than swallowing my prenatal pills.

"Face it Joanne," both Uncle Johnny and Uncle Joey tried to get through to her. "It's time for you to face the truth."

"THE DEVIL IS LIAR! THIS DEVIL IS A LIAR!" she continued to sing out. She was rocking back and forth in a psychotic manner. Her eyes still refusing to display any sign of a soul within her. Her mind still not accepting the truth.

"How could you ignore her?" the never-show-no-emotion Uncle Johnny surprised all those who knew him and also began to breakdown. I had never seen him like that. My uncle was always tough and assertive- a sergeant in the military and a boss on the streets. I never even remembered seeing him smile, so to see him cry started to bring tears to my own eyes.

"How could you just ignore her after she told you what he was doing to her! What kind of person are you?" he continued to question her integrity. "It was going to take some time, but I would have forgiven you. All I ever wanted was to hear you say that you were sorry. And it's been almost twenty years and you still haven't. That night Jonell died, not only did we lose her, we lost you too. No longer can I live with this on my heart. I'm leaving now."

Uncle Joey followed Uncle Johnny, and they both slowly walked down the center aisle towards the outside of the church. I wasn't far behind them either. I had heard enough. Knowing what I now knew, as much as I loved Keyshawn, there was no way I could stay at his funeral and look at Auntie Jo any longer. I signaled for Jeremiah and Mrs. Johnson to gather our things, but they were already three steps ahead of me. Even Keisha and Korey had to take a seat and let everything sink in, leaving Auntie Jo up at the altar all alone.

"So you just gone leave me like that!" she yelled out to her brothers. "Y'all are all I got left and you just gone turn ya back on me! ...Because of her!"

Uncle Johnny and Uncle Joey continued to make their exit, only giving her the privilege of looking at the back of their black suits as they silently walked away. They were through with Auntie Jo and her bullshit. And she knew they meant business.

"Well gon' then! I don't need you!" she yelled with all she had left. She didn't mean it though. And although they knew it, they continued to walk out on her.

As they got closer to the wooden double doors- and it seems as if it was just seconds before they reached it- she cracked.

"ALLLLRIGHT," from the top of her lungs, she yelled so loudly that I had to look over at Keyshawn and make sure she didn't wake *him* up. "YOU'RE ALL RIGHT!...CHARLYTTE'S RIGHT! JOEY'S RIGHT! JOHNNY'S RIGHT! AND ANYBODY IN HERE WHO HAS EVER SAID ANYTHING HORRIBLE ABOUT ME IS PROBABLY RIGHT TOO! I'M A WRECK AND I HAVE BEEN THAT WAY FOR A LONG TIME NOW! MY SISTA'S DEAD! MY SON'S DEAD! AND I HAVE NO ONE TO BLAME BUT MYSELF! SO HERE, I'LL ADMIT-IT'S...IT'S...IT'S...IT'S ALL MY FAULT!"

Everyone moving completely stopped in their tracks and turned to Auntie Jo. Everyone except for Uncle Johnny, who restrained himself from pushing the door open, but still wasn't convinced enough to turn around and give her his full attention. I, on the other hand, did. If Auntie Jo was about to apologize and admit that she did something wrong, I wanted to look her right in her eyes when she did it. That's the only way I would have believed it.

The Pastor looked as if he was about to try and stop her from saying anything else.

“I’m not ashamed,” Auntie Jo snatched away from him, then turned and faced the congregation. “Everyone in here needs to hear this.”

She waited for silence, cleared her throat, and spoke.

36: FORGIVE ME

"Since I was a child, my mama treated me special 'cause I was a little 'chunkier' than the other kids my age. She told me that God made me biggah 'cause he favored me and wanted me to take up more space than everybody else...I remember it like it was yesterday. Kids can be something awful I tell ya. They have no regards for anyone's feeling but their own."

"Anyway, one day I ran home crying to mama 'cause the kids where teasing me....Mama got all upset too. Not with the kids. But with me, for letting them get to me. Then she took some make-up, smeared it all over my face, showed me how ridiculous I looked in the mirror, and told me that I never needed to wear that stuff just to feel beautiful. She said that the only reason children picked on me, was not because I was fat, but because I was weak. After that, I made a promise to her that I would never be weak again."

"And I'll be darn if the very next day, Beverly Jackson threw a honey bun at me in the cafeteria. Seemed like the whole lunchroom was laughing. Nobody cared about my feelings, so I didn't care about Beverly's face when I took my food tray and beat her upside her head wit' it."

Auntie Jo paused for a minute, clearly thinking back on the incident.

“Mama was right ‘bout me being weak, 'cause after that day, no one messed with me again. They were all scared of Big Joanne, and sho nuff, that made me feel proud. So proud that I ran home to tell mama the good news, but instead of her listenin’ to my story, she screamed at me for wakin’ Jonell up. Then she told me that she was tired, and that she just didn’t feel like dealin’ with it at the moment. I was already upset that mama got pregnunt again. ‘Specially after she promised that I would always be her one and only queen, so her brushin’ me off like that, really made me click. And shortly afterwards, I was a different person."

Auntie Jo sighed deeply. “I spent my whole fifth grade gettin’ into trouble by doin’ silly things to get mama’s attention. I was wearin’ her out, mentally and physically, because I wanted to get revenge on her for neglectin’ me. But little did I know, mama wasn't just tired because of baby Jonell, she was tired because she was dying of that cancer. Worse, my little sister was growing up to be much prettier, and much skinnier, than I ever was, and I hated that. Any little attention she got from mama, and ‘specially daddy, would just make me go out and do some more damage to somethin’ or someone.

“And when I turnt twelve, things only got worse, ‘cause that’s when I met a man," she paused for a minute, before continuing. "I was skipping school one day and went to Stillwood Park- where I did most of my thinkin’- when a guy in a beige, beat-up old van pulled up beside me and asked me to come to him. He was a Mexican. Mama told me to never talk to them kind, and that’s exactly why I did it."

"I walked over to this guy all shy, trying to squeeze my stomach in and lock my jaws up to make my face look skinny. And when I got to him, he asked me my name. I told him. Then he asked me where my folks were. I told him. Finally he asked me why I wasn't in school. And truthfully, I told him."

Auntie Jo cracked a smile for the first time. For some reason, I couldn't help but feel that she still loved this mysterious Mexican man.

She continued. "He just laughed with his cricket yellow teeth and his wicked smile, and told me that if the police caught me wandering around like that, they would take me to jail. Then he told me that if I went with him he could protect me, and I wouldn't have to worry about them. So, like the little naïve child I was, and against everything my mama had ever taught me, I hopped into this man's car and rode with him to some abandoned house. And it was in that house, where he told me I was beautiful over and over and over again, and before I knew it, he was touching me in places I knew my mother would not have approved. That's the day I found out what it meant to be a woman- a big, beautiful woman that is."

Auntie Jo's eyes began to water. But I couldn't tell if they were tears of joy, or tears of sorrow.

"A year after that, I was laying up in a hospital bed havin' Korey. And believe it or not, shortly after, I was pregnunt again with Keisha. Mama was really tired now, with me slapping two kids on her and all. I sure as hell wasn't mature enough to take care of them on my own. And for all she knew, I didn't even know who their daddy was. Jose told me he was an illegal immigrant and that if the people found out, he would be deported back to his country. I didn't want that 'cause I loved him. So just as he had asked, I told no one. I was too young to realize he was just telling me that to cover up the fact that he was molestin' me."

Auntie Jo looked to Uncle Joey as if nobody was in the room but the two of them. Uncle Johnny still had his back turned. "The day I left mama's house to move in that trailer with Jose, when I was eighteen, I could see the pain all through mama's eyes. She knew I wasn't gonna do right by those kids, but she was too weak and too sick keep them with her. She begged me not to take 'em, but with daddy workin' those long hours and creepin' around with that chick on Staley Avenue, Johnny in the service, and you in and out of jail, she couldn't continue to care for them by herself."

Those tears that filled Auntie Jo's eyes, finally started to fall. She was getting choke up thinking about how badly she had treated my grandma. "I left my mama hanging out to dry, and not only that, I never went back. Not even to see my little sister."

"It wasn't until 'bout three years later, that I got an unexpected knock at my door. And to my surprise it was a skinny old woman holding a beautiful little girl's hand on my doorstep." Auntie Jo began to weep even harder. "Mama looked different, so different that at first I didn't even recognize her. And she sounded awful too. Now that I think about it, it was the saddest thing hearing her beg me to take care of Jonell for her. Daddy had done left her for that young woman and she was all on her own.

"I didn't have to tell her it wasn't my fault she didn't know how to keep her man...I didn't have to tell her Jonell wasn't my any of my responsibility...And I didn't have to tell her that *my man* probably didn't want any more kids running around the house. But I did. I told her it all and I meant every single word…I didn't want to take Jonell, sister or not, but just so happen, Jose was pulling up from work and heard the commotion. It was the first time mama had ever seen him, and her huge, brown eyes got even biggah when she saw just how old he was. I quickly filled him in on what was going on. Then he took one look at eleven-year-old Jonell and immediately decided to let her stay. Covered up in my own stupidity, I really believed that my man had a good heart. I didn't know that in reality he was thinking about having my little sister."

"The very next day, Jose happily fixed up one of the old storage rooms for Jonell and made her feel real comfortable. Of course she missed mama, but she adjusted well. I mean, she was never the real talkative type, but she'd run her mouth at times. 'Specially with Korey and Keisha, she just loved those two. To me, that was the best part about having her around- the fact that she was a damn good babysitter. Truthfully, deep down inside I envied her. I wasn't half as beautiful as she was at her age."

Slightly drifting away from Auntie Jo's words, I immediately thought about the picture that I had now framed and placed up on a wall in my apartment. Mama was definitely beautiful.

"Sadly," Aunite Jo eyes watered even more, as she continued on with her story, "only a couple months after I took Jonell in, mama died. She was in the house a week before anyone knew. I took it hard, but Jonell took it even harder. It's like she just shut down, because she knew the truth- even though I was letting her stay with me, I really didn't care nothin' 'bout her. Mama was all she had. And after the funeral, Jonell just locked herself up in her room, day after day, sort of like what Charlytte did. She used to get on my nerves because she was demanding way too much attention for me. I was already stressed with Jose losing his job and having to work them long hours at the local meat market. It was just too much to deal with it."

"Then one day- Jonell had to be about thirteen- I come home from work, and Jose, who normally just lets the kids run wild and barely cleaned up anything, had the house spotless and had a nice bubble bath warmed up for me. Unusually, he was in such a good mood. And although I didn't know where all his joy was coming from, I was lovin' it."

"It wasn't until we ate the big dinner he prepared for me, when he brought my excitement down by mentioning that Jonell was having a rough morning. So rough, that he told me he made her stay home from school, and I didn't like that one bit. Furious, I went to grab my belt, but Jose stopped me. 'Don't worry baby, I handled it already. I just had a long talk with her. She's still in a state of shock right now. Give her time to adjust. She'll be fine', was exactly what he told me."

"But she never adjusted. As a matter of fact, she only got worse. She barely ever came out of her room, 'specially when Jose was home. She acted like she couldn't talk. She didn't even play with Korey and Keisha the way she used too. And every day I spent dealing with that, was a day I wished I didn't have to."

"Truthfully, she was starting to do to me, the same things I did to my mama- fightin', stealin', runnin' away and goin' missin' for days. I didn't care though, and never once did I go looking for her. She was just one less person I had to worry about. Hell, Jose seemed to care more about her than I did. If she was gone too long, he would go look for her and every single time, he would find her and bring her back."

Auntie Jo paused again, this time it was much longer than the usual. Everyone was quiet, clinging on her every word, as if we needed them to survive.

"And when she was sixteen," she sighed, "that was the very last time she ran away. She had been gone for over four months, and that definitely wasn't like her. Normally she would just go God-knows-where for a couple of days, and then like a stray dog, find her way back home. Either that, or Jose would go look for her and bring her back. But this time, she didn't come back; and he strangely, he didn't look."

"She just happened to got busted stealin' a candy bar and a bag of chips from out of the corner market. And instead of the police taking her to jail, because she was seven months pregnunt, they decided to just bring her home. Yeah, that's what I said, they brought her home 'cause she was *pregnunt*."

"I couldn't believe that my little sister had gotten knocked up. I didn't even think that she was having sex, but the big lump in her stomach forced me too. And that night, I tore her butt up, pregnunt and all, 'cause I knew that *her* child was going to be *my* responsibility. Worse, I didn't want to accept that my past was catching up to me. I knew it was nothing but karma making its way back around. On top of that, I had just found out that I was six weeks pregnunt with Keyshawn. It was just too much to take in at once."

She looked over at her son's lifeless body and take a slight breather.

"Boy did Jonell and I have it out that night," she said, when she came back to us. I carefully watched her eyes. Life started to form in them again. "Keisha and Korey were so scared that they were hollering and screaming for us to stop… And at 8:14 that afternoon- I could never forget that time- was the very minute she told me that the love of my life, the man that I sold out my mama, my family, and practically my soul for, the only person that I had ever known, and the father of my three children- was the father of her child and had been molestin' her for over three years."

"I JUST COULDN'T BELIEVE IT!" she began to cry hysterically. "I WOULDN'T BELIEVE IT! All I could do was jump on her once more, and if she didn't slip from my reach, I probably would have killed the child."

"*You're nothing to me. You may as well be a dead bitch. I don't ever wanna see you again*!" Those were the last words I said to my baby sister, before she looked back at me with those pretty, almonds eyes and silently cried out for my help. There weren't any tears in them, but the pain in her face clearly showed me that she needed me to believe her. Yet, all my selfishness would allow me to do was let her walk away. And that's actually what I did, I let her walk away."

Everyone seemed to be shaking their heads from left to right, saddened, but interested to hear more about what happened to Jonell. It may have felt like a good audiobook to them, but to me, it was my life.

Auntie Jo went on. "When Jose came home, he kicked off his work boots, put down his toolbox down, and sat on the floor between my legs. The part that he enjoyed best about walking through that front door was getting that nice shoulder massage from me. It gave him a chance to relax and it gave me a chance to bond with my man. Seizing the opportunity, I asked him, 'How was work?' As usual, he said, 'Okay.' Then I asked him, 'What do you want to eat for dinner tonight?' He said, 'Fried chicken and mashed potatoes.' Then I said, 'Baby, da cops brought Joney back here today because she was stealing out the store. Can you believe her lil' fast ass is pregnunt, and the crazy bitch has the nerve to say that *YOU* that baby's daddy. She's really getting outta hand I tell ya."

"Jose looked back at me with the most evil look in his eyes. 'She said that?' he asked me. I told him, 'Yeah.' Then he said, 'Baby, look at me and tell me that you don't believe that.' He was such a good liar, and like the fool I was I said, 'Of course, you don't have to ask me. That lil' heffa is out to ruin my life. Ever since the day she was born. If she's not happy, no one can be. I put her out of the house. I refuse to let her steal my joy."

"Jose smiled, kissed me on my forehead, and then headed for the shower. I don't know what changed in the five minutes time that he washed up, but after he got out, he quickly put on his clothes, grabbed his keys, and said, 'Enough is enough! 'I'm 'bout to go find her and bring her home. This ends tonight!"

"I tried to convince him not to worry about her. I told him I was certain that she was never going to come back. That she would soon be seventeen anyway, almost an adult and almost none of my responsibility. And I remembered being more upset with her then I had ever been because it just pissed me off to see how concerned he was being about her. I hated that every time she acted stupid he had to waste time looking for her. That was time that he could have been spendin' with me. I mean, I wasn't worried about her, so I didn't feel he should have been either."

"Jose ignored my every word. Then he reminded me that Jonell was pregnunt and that she didn't need to be out in the streets like that. He said that we couldn't let her come and go as she pleased, and that we just needed to put our foot down and demand respect. He said the reason why Jonell was so rebellious was because of us."

"Even though I didn't want her back- or anything to do with her for that matter- whatever my man said, went. He stormed out the door, speeding off so quickly that the neighbors had to peek outside to see what was going on. And the entire time I sat on my dinning couch waiting for Jose to bring to the heffa back, never once did I think he would be heading over to the abandoned house that he knew she would be at- the same house he took me to when I was thirteen- and try to cover up what he had done to her."

Auntie Jo could barely speak. Clearly, it took all the strength she had in her to be able to tell us the rest.

"Never once did I think he would beat her senselessly until she passed out…then drag her to the back alley…and slice open her stomach to try to pull her precious little baby out. And I never thought he would have come home and made sweet love to me, knowing that he…he…he… murdered my sister!" She wept indescribably. "I thought many of things that night, but I never thought that!"

Auntie Jo's head dropped in shame. There were a single swipe across her face to dispose of her tears, then she shied away from her the audience and looked to me. "God was on your side. Cause if it wasn't for that homeless man sleeping quietly in that alley, who woke up in the nick of time and startled Jose. And if it wasn't for him running you off to the nearby fire station, Charlytte I hate to say it, but you would have been dead right alongside your mama."

Everyone looked to me. Then I too, looked to the ground. Jeremiah grabbed my hand.

"We didn't have cable, so there was no way for me to see the DEAD GIRL, SURVIVING BABY story that was all over the news. And with Jose constantly making love to me to intentionally keep my head in a bubble, I probably would have known about it way before that detective came to my house and told me that my sister had been killed... and that her baby was in the hospital fighting for her dear little life. For three whole days, I knew nothing."

By now, Johnny had finally turned to her. She was thankful for it.

“Johnny I promise!" she cried out to him. "I may have hated Joney but I didn’t want to see anything bad happen to her. Please believe me! I didn’t know! Jose was with me when I got the news! And the dirty bastard had the nerve to cry with me in my arms! Johnny, he took me to go identify the body and acted perfectly normal! He even went with me to see the baby- *his* baby.”

After she realized that Uncle Johnny still wasn't giving in to her, she turned back to me.

“When we got to the hospital, Charlytte, you were isolated behind a glass bubble. There were tubes going in and coming out of what seemed like every hole in your body. You were so fragile and small- small enough to fit safely in the palm of my hand. And you had this clothe wrapped around your face because the doctor said that when ‘the killer’ tried to cut open your mama’s stomach, he cut you too. You had to get twenty-two stitches across your tiny little face."

I rubbed my scar with two fingers, then continued to listen to her.

"The moment I saw you, I wanted to take you home. Of course, Jose disagreed with it. He said with me already being pregnunt, we wasn’t in a position to take care of another child. He even threatened to leave me if I went through with it. But, for the first time in my life, I made my own decision to sign those custody papers.

Auntie Jo closed her eyes and sighed heavily. “We buried Joney, alongside mama, on a Saturday, and with the baby in the hospital getting better each day, I tried to put the past behind me and focus on how to be a better person and a good mother, not only to my kids, but also to my niece. I couldn't take back how I treated my sister, but I did ask God to forgive me and hoped that I could make up for it in the years to come."

"Jose, sad to say, was still upset about me planning to bring Charlytte home, although he had no choice but to accept it. Ever since Joney had died, he had been acting really angry and irritable. He stayed out drinking night after night, sometimes to the point where I didn't even want him to come home. I just thought it was because he had a hard time adjustin' to the fact that we were going to be havin' two new kids in the house. With him now being the only one workin', I knew it must been a lot of pressure on him. It did hurt me, that for the first time, I wasn't giving him what he wanted, but my family was just more important to me.

"Finally, two months had passed when I got the call from the hospital saying that my niece was well enough to come home. Jose was at work and the kids were at school. I didn't want to tell them because I wanted it to be a surprise. Jose still wasn't proud of it, but the children sure were. All Keisha and Korey kept asking was, when was their little sista' coming home? They loved Joney so much that any part of her was a part of them. And I figured if Jose saw how happy the kids were, then he would just be happy knowing that."

"Charlytte, I was told to pick you up at foe' o'clock that evenin', so I spent all morning cleanin' and doin' laundry. I even went out and bought you a beautiful wall clock. It was white with pink flowers all over it. I wanted to hang it above your crib, but I couldn't find a nail and a hammer no where 'round the house. I didn't panic though. I knew Jose kept an extra toolbox in the shed behind the trailer."

"He kept the trailer door locked and he was the only one who had a key, but I wanted to hang that thing so badly that I climbed through the window to get those tools."

“Once I was in, I grabbed the hammer and the box of nails out Jose’s toolbox, and just as I was about to walk out, I see a plastic bag with a piece of garment falling out of it. My first thought was that Jose had an extra bag of work clothes that needed to be washed, so I carried it with me inside the house. It wasn't until about an hour later, after I finally hung the clock and did a few more extra things, that I emptied the bag, and out came a bloody shirt, bloody pants, and some bloody boots with a knife tucked down inside the sole.”

“Oh Lawd Jesus,” she began to cry. “I fell to my knees right there where I was, and laid on that cold floor in the washroom. I couldn't move. I couldn't feel. I couldn't cry. I couldn’t do anything."

"I had a good feeling whose blood it was, but I just had to find more proof. So, with the little strength I had, I searched his pants’ pockets for any type of hard evidence to back me up. Sure enough, there was a receipt with a cigarette purchase that had the date 5-21 on it, the same day that Jonell had been killed.”

“Lord knows I loved Jose, but he was a killa’. I called the police as soon as I got to the phone, and they didn't even give him a chance to close his car door before about twenty of ‘em rush him when he got home from work.”

“I remember sittin’ on that porch watchin’ the whole thing. I don’t think I blinked once. Jose was looking at me like I had betrayed him, but really, he had betrayed me. I don't know why I thought I was so different. Like I was the only special young girl that he could ever touch or hurt. Why could've I have known that if he did it to me, he would do it to someone else?"

“Everything, and I mean EVERYTHING, I had sacrificed- my body, my family, my sister- all for it just to be a lie. It made me sick to my stomach. I wanted to take my life that day. And if you ask me, I did. I was no mo' good to nobody. Not to Keisha. Not to Korey. Not to my unborn child. Not even to Charlytte- who I never went to pick up from the hospital that day.

"You see, Charlytte," she cried, "I had ever intention on doin' right by you, but after I found out that my husband was yo' father, I just didn't have it in me anymo'. I could barely even look at you. You held the face of both my sista' and my man. It was only because I had already signed those papers, and got some pretty decent donations, that I took you in. And when Keyshawn was born, I definitely didn't want you. Really, if wasn't for Keisha, Charlytte probably would have died from malnutrition 'cause I didn't even care to feed her."

"I can't lie," she continued, "I lost myself in those days. That's why I drink so much. That's why I am so angry. And that's why I'm sittin' in the position that I'm in today saying that I am sorry to my brothers, to my children, but mostly, to you Charlytte. And even if there is just a little bit of your mother living in you, I want you to let her know that I'm sorry too."

"Ya see," she turned back to crowd. "I just can't go on one mo' day living like this. I don't want to lose another one of my family members because of my selfish ways. If you want call me a hypocrite, a devil, a disgrace, that's fine because I deserve all that. I deserved to be punished for what I put my family through, but believe me when I say that I have already suffered greatly for it. I am at the point where I don't care who thinks what of me anymore. All I want is for my family to forgive me."

"Family," she paused and took a deep breath and then extended her arms, "Do you forgive me?"

37: KEEP'N IT REAL

Even though Auntie Jo was standing before an entire congregation begging for our forgiveness, she was only looking to me. I was in such a state of shock that I didn't know what to say. I just couldn't believe my ears, let alone find it in my heart to forgive her. My mama wasn't just some hoe running the streets. She was an innocent young girl murdered by Auntie Jo's perverted husband. And I wasn't just some dreadful curse to the world. I was a survivor, saved and kept here on Earth by God himself for a special purpose. The scar I wore on my face, the strong resemblance I had to Keisha, and the unexplainable hatred Auntie Jo had towards me over the years, was now accounted for, and although it didn't change anything from the past, it did give me some closure. I knew without a doubt that Auntie Jo was really telling the truth and that she really was sympathetic about it all. It was the first time I had ever seen her cry and it was the first time she had ever said the words, 'I'm sorry' to anyone. That's was enough for me.

Despite everything Auntie Jo had just told me, I smiled brightly and ran to hug her. In all my eighteen years, that was also the first time we had ever did that, but the way she embraced me tightly, smothering me inside of her big bosom for as long as she did, made it well worth the wait. Suddenly, I felt Keisha and Korey wrapped themselves around us, and before I knew it, the entire family- including Uncle Johnny and Uncle Joey- were huddled up like a football team, giving off the love and support that we should have many years ago. Everyone in the church was moved. Even the toughest of thugs cried and made their way up to the altar, while they hugged one another and took part in love that was spreading throughout the building.

Pastor Williams signaled for the sound director to bring him the microphone, and then decided to preach just one more sermon.

"If you're able, I'mma need for everyone to step up to the altar," he began. "Step up here and take somebody's, anybody's, hand. This right is living proof that there is a God. And what we just witnessed was by nothing but His *almighty Power."*

"Ya see, the members of this church know that one thing Pastor Williams don't tolerate is foolishness. Church can I get ah Amen?"

"AMEN!" the church said in unison.

"But God spoke to my spirits, and told me to let them go on, let them pour out their hearts and put it ALL on the line. See often times, we tend to wanna put the top on the pot of grits when that water is boiling over, because we're afraid to make a lil' mess on our good stove top. But sometimes...just sometimes....you got let that water come on and flow out of there. Sometimes you gotta let that steam, those boiling bubbles of pain, anger, and ever thing else you got cooking up inside of you, spill on out...AMEN."

"You ever looked back inside that pot once it finished boiling over?...You see how settled and simmered those grits are?

"Well lemme tell you something church family, life's no different. Sometimes we pack ourselves up with all sorts of things, and we think that we are strong enough to just contain them all. We think that we can just lock it up on the inside and pray that it goes away. You don't wanna talk to nobody, 'cause you feel like nobody will understand you. You don't wanna be a burden to nobody, 'cause you feel like everybody has their own problems. Or you just don't want people looking at ya crazy, 'cause you feel like you're the only one who's going through what you're going through. You just keep those things boiled up inside, but eventually, they will come out. And not if, but when, they do, you're gonna explode. Often times, it's in rage. And it's not intentional, it's just that anger is a powerful thing- the bible says it's one of the seven deadliest sins- and once it's released it'll take down everything in its path. That's if you allow it to."

"This young lady, Charlytte, I heard her say to her friend, that this here church was the perfect place for her to speak her mind. She may not have had the right intentions, but she had the right idea. Cause if they had'a been just a few feet off these grounds, this altercation probably would have turned out a whole lot different than it did. GOD... had His hands in what happened here today. And can I tell you what he did? He used the death of this young man, Keyshawn, to bring this broken family back together."

"See, Keyshawn's life was already written before he even came out of his mother's womb. His purpose was already known by the almighty, way before he took that first breath of life. This man's death was nobody fault; it was God's plan. It wasn't about him drug-dealin' or gang-bangin', it was about bringing his family together

and saving more young men who are misled and following the same path as he was."

"We can't sit around and feel sorry for Keyshawn. He's okay. He's with the Lord now. Can't nobody hurt him no mo'. We're the ones who gotta continue to struggle in this madness we call a world and fight daily just to keep our heads above water. Our job isn't to question God. Our job is to not let this young man die in vain by keeping this clearly broken family together and using the mistakes he made as a lesson for you to get yours on the right track, young men especially."

"I gotta be honest with you church...the worst thing you can be in this world is ignorant. Not broke. Not retarded. Not dead- but ignorant. I saw a young man walk in here today wearing a t-shirt with a picture of young Keyshawn holding up a gun, and above it said, 'Rest in Peace.' Y'all young folks don't see nothing wrong with that? The same thing this young man lived by, he died by. When we gone learn people?"

"And I don't know 'bout y'all, but it kills me to see these youngsters walking round with 'bout three or four dead black men on their t-shirts. That just burns me up on the inside. Reminding these prejudging folks of how ignorant we really are. You know how proud them folks out there are to see that another one of us is either dead or locked up? We think we're making statements by putting FREE LIL POOK POOK on our clothes, but the only thing we're making is their day."

"I tell you what, if you really wanna make them mad, when Sharice Albright from our church graduates from OSU, go get a t-shirt with a picture of her in her cap and gown and put 'School of Biology Class of 2013 graduate' on it. On the bulletin board, just on your way out those double doors, Mr. Moses got a picture of him standing in front of his new restaurant he just opened up. I will give

you permission to take that picture up to the mall and get a shirt made in his name. My people, we gotta start glorifying our successes and quit constantly reminding ourselves of our failures. We gotta to do better, not only as black folks, but as people. Can I get an Amen?"

"AMEN!" the members of the church said again.

"I feel some preaching coming on. I think I need to talk to them today. Pastor gotta keep it real with these young folks because I have also been holding stuff in. Holding back from really speaking my mind because I'm afraid of hurting people's feelings. But the spirit is telling me to let it all out. Hurt some feelings, so that maybe I can save some souls. I may be just a Pastor, but I'm from the streets and I know what goes on in them. Y'all youngins think y'all started something, but a lot of this stuff y'all doin' has been going on since before you was born. Believe me, ain't nothin' new under the sun. Can I get an ANOTHER amen?"

"AMEN!" the people went wild. "AMEN!"

"I'm sick of it young folks. Everybody wanna be so real, so down, so gangsta. Fellas, let me tell ya something, being real back in my day, was cutting ya mama and ya grandmama's grass when she needed it done. Keepin' it real was keeping ya grades up in school. Takin' out the trash when it got full. It was fighting with your fist and not with a gun. Either way both men walked off as men: one who was man enough to win and the other who was man enough to accept that he lost."

"Being real was working a nine to five or owning your own, not throwing yo' life away chasing some fantasy rap dream. Now I'm not saying that chasing a dream is wrong, but chasing a dream for the wrong reasons is. I have met so many people who have told me that they've loss the last ten plus years of their lives

chasing silly dreams of being rappers or drug kings because they believed it would bring them fame, money, women, and ultimately, respect. Yeah, it may gain you all those of things, but can't none of them get you into heaven. People, we gotta start expanding our minds to different things, there are other ways to make good money and keep your soul at the same time."

"Young girls, I'm talkin' to y'all too. Prancin' round here takin' pride in being called somebody's bitch. Shaking y'all behinds in the clubs like y'all ain't got no darn sense. Hating y'all own sisters over these sorry men who don't love neither one of you, 'cause if he did, he wouldn't be sleeping with the both of you. Being a real woman is about staying out them clubs and spending family times with your kids. It's about not needing no man to do anything for you that you can't do for yourself.

"And parents... y'all ain't out the way either. Alot of times we judge these kids and forget that we had a past too. We want to point fingers and blame the youth on everything, when a lot of the stuff they do, they learn from us. Every week these young girls in the club and a lot of y'all parents are the ones babysitting. We got parents still taking care of grown kids, washing their clothes, paying their bills, waiting on them hand and foot. I know those yo babies and ya think that ya helping them, but really you're not. You only hurting 'em."

"And quit doing all types of stuff around ya kids. My mama didn't tell me til' I turned thirty-five, that she used to smoke weed and get high. I never knew it cause she didn't do it round me and did a good job of keeping her private life just that- private. Nowadays, kids going to Kindergarten rolling up grass in notebook paper 'cause they seeing their parents do it at home. They smoking round these kids, using the contact from it to try to make 'em sleepy. It just don't make no sense."

Pastor Williams shook his head in disbelief.

"I hate to sound like I'm bashing on y'all because I'm not. There a lot of young folks here today and ain't no telling when y'all will be back. I'm just trying to get y'all to understand that it's more out there in this world then what meets the eye. There are good things waiting for you, but it all depends on the choices you make now, whether or not you will receive them later. If Keyshawn could come back right now, I can bet my life he would say that it's not worth it. That selling drugs and killing your own people just so you can ride on twenty-inch rims, is not worth the sacrifice. See, one thing you need to know about the devil is that he is a big deceiver. He'll have you thinking that material things are what make you who you are. Your mind is controlled, and it has been since the day you were born. Oh, it's get deeps, but that another sermon. As a matter of fact, I talked with a guy last week and he was asking me how did I fell about the 9/11 conspiracies. He asked me did I believe that the government was controlling everything from what we watch on t.v to what we eat. I told him 'no.' I told him that I believe it's God who controls my steps. Don't get me wrong, I do believe that the world is corrupt and that there is a great evil amongst us, but I fear no man and no power but God...But still, all people, young and old, need to be more aware of what's going on in the political world. Educate yourselves, because trust me, there will come a time where we wished we put down the Fakebook, the twitta, the video games, and all those other distractions, and got more involved with what's going on in the world around us. One smart person is stronger than ten ignorant people. I refuse to be a fool, and if you are too, then walk out this door today with a different attitude. Listen to these words and open your minds to a new way of thinking. Don't let this man, or anyone else you've known who left here this way, die in vain. Make a change for the better. Can I get a big Amen one last time church?"

"AAAAAMEN!"

38: DARK BLACK

After the beautiful drama-free burial, everyone met up at the park in my old neighborhood to take part in the repast. People from all over Ordale joined in to show their love for Keyshawn and get their share of the good old barbecue that was being cooked up in his name. It felt very nice being back to the place where I grew up and I especially enjoyed seeing some of the people I hadn't saw in a long time.

Auntie Jo seemed to be having a good time too. She was in much better spirits- laughing, mangling, and talking with some of her family members about the funny things Keyshawn used to say and do. She even played with Power for a little while. But the most surprising part of the evening, was me when she pulled me to the side and handed me a medium-sized cardboard box with about five layers of duct tape wrapped around it.

Auntie Jo told me not to open it until I got home, so when I made it back to my apartment that night- besides getting Power in bed- getting that box open was the only thing on my mind. It was around nine o'clock, Jeremiah was kind enough to walk us inside and even asked me if I needed him to stay the night. Normally I'd say yes and we'd cuddle, talk about the events of the day, and share each other's feelings on them, but I just needed to reflect alone. He was a little disappointed because he really wanted to be there for me, but he had no choice but to respect my wishes.

After a passionate hug and kiss, I saw Jeremiah out, then immediately washed up Power in the sink. He had been drastically tired from all the playing he did at the park, so of course he went straight to bed.

I was also very tired myself, emotionally and physically that is. Anxiously but weary, I grabbed the brown box and rested across my bed with it. Then I tried to tear it open, but it was wrapped so tightly that I had to pry it open with a pair of scissors I kept nearby. And when I finally got it unwrapped, I was surprised to see the many photos of my mother, and the rest of my family, staring back at me. There were hundreds of them.

A smile so graceful appeared on my face as I looked at every one of the images. There were pictures of my grandma, my uncles, all of the children when we were kids, even Auntie Jo when she was younger. I must say, she indeed was a bit on the chunky side. I laughed hard at the one of her devouring a piece of chicken leg.

I was admiring a picture of my mother, when I was interrupted by booming sounds and beautiful colors exploding outside my window. I had forgotten that it was the first Friday of the month, and every first Friday, fireworks would fill up the night sky. The people who lived in the projects had the best view of them. It was the best part about living there. Normally I would take

Power out on the balcony and his eyes would light up as he watched in amazement, but I guess he'd have to miss them.

Although they came faithfully every month, I couldn't help but feel like they were more than just a repeated tradition staged by man. Maybe it was God, alongside my mother and Keyshawn, letting me know that everything in my life would be just as bright as those fireworks. Maybe He was showing me the sign that I had asked Him to show me some time ago. Mrs. Simmons once told me that all I had to do was have faith and believe, and that's actually what I did.

After the last green and pink spark disappeared in the sky, I made my way back to my room. I laughed once more at a couple of the pictures as I put them back inside the box and sat it down carefully on the nightstand.

Then I laid across my bed, said a quick prayer, shut my eyes and began to dream.

LOOK OUT FOR JESSICA GERMAINE'S NEW NOVEL: <u>THE MAN I HELPED GET AWAY</u>

Being the first person in her family to graduate from college, let alone make it out of high school, Sharice Albright is determined not to live the poverty-stricken life that her family has endured for many generations. Landing a job as a certified librarian and using her income from it to move into a nice neighborhood in the suburbs, Sharice finds out that the sophisticated, classy life is not as exciting as she thought it would be.

While her 'ghettofied' struggling family members envy her, she secretly envies them and longs for the hood life that she has known for over twenty-five years. But after a great deal of pure boredom with her new life and finding herself slipping into a mild depressive state, Sharice get an unexpected surprise when she checks her mailbox and finds a jury summon for an upcoming robbery trial.

Bad luck seemed to follow Sharice, so it was no surprise to her when she found herself being picked as one of the Jurors to serve on the case. But what she didn't expect, was to fall in love with the man who is being the accused of committing such crimes- the defendant himself.

As a heap of evidence starts to unfold and the suspect begins to look more and more guilty to all the other jurors- and anyone with a right mind- to Sharice, who is falling deeper and deeper in love with him, he is beginning to look more innocent. Determined to do whatever it takes not to let this man spend the next thirty years of his life in prison, so that maybe they can build a life together, Sharice stands behind her belief of his innocence until the trial is over and he is set-free to go. It isn't until then, when she is now able to talk about the case, visit social sites, news media and such, that she finds out the disturbing truth about' ***the man she helped get away.'***

For more information about Dark Black and other upcoming novels check me out on:

www.facebook.com/jgermaine2

www.twitter.com/darkblackjg

....

For music by Jessica Germaine:

www.youtube.com/jsmit259100

Direct link to the Dark Black The Mixtape is

http://www.datpiff.com/Jessica-Germaine-Dark-Black-mixtape.367122.html

CHECK OUTS SOME OTHER LOCAL AUTHORS IN THE SAVANNAH AREA!!!!

Local Authors

Aundrea Dumas, author of *The House That Cooks Love* and *The House That Cooks Love too*

Natarielle, author of *Diamonds in my Own Backyard*

Shalonda "Coach Treasure" Williams, author of Let's GO! *Get Over to Get On with Life* Great inspirational read! and A Heart's Thought: *Love Walk Mediations Series*

I couldn't end this book without personally thanking those who have influenced me whether directly or indirectly. THANKS………… My beautiful daughter, Alourie, you are my rock. To mother Loretta, I love you more than you can ever know. Quentin 'QD' Smith, that relationship you seek is coming one day…you'll see. Stay determined and you will succeed. Calvin Wallace, pure-spirited. Couldn't ask for a more caring older brother. Theodore Holmes, my father. Thank you for everything. Grandma Emily, the backbone of the family. My aunt, Barbara Fleminig, you have the strength of ten women and you're the reason I don't complain. Tamika Fleming, I've always admired your personality…no offense but I built my character Keisha around you (her better qualities) Carl Fleming, can't wait til you get home. Love u cuz! Betty Brown, another pure-spirited woman and a great aunt. Tiffany Brown…You're a queen. I love you and I can relate to you. Better days are coming. Uncle Jimmy and Uncle Robert, funny uncles, I love them so much! My beautiful Aunt Shirley, and Vaughn Monroe, I've always admired you guys. Love yall! Benjamin and Jessica Monroe, Ben, hopefully I can sell some books so that I can be as successful as you. Cousin Bessie, 99 years of life, what more can I say. JR and Jacob, Lil Robert and Ashton, The Wilson Family, I wish I can go back and change some things. Just know that I love and miss all you guys. Traneka whats up! Auriel Mitchell, down sister doing her thing. Proud of you girl. Much love! Ricky 'Mac' Oneal, Get well. Glad to call you family. Tall Angie, to real for the streets. I love that about u. Grandma Flora, may you rest well. To my bio father, Anthony Brown, thank you and I love you. Bossman, Frankie Gary and Family, Joyce family, Kerry Smith, Will and Ralphie and their little ones, Paulette Watts and family, Weezy, Lori and family, Brandy. Aisha Thomas, I wish you the best in life. Take care of my beautiful nieces Qamyra, Qaelyn, Qayla. They are so special and full of love. To Jazz, Chris, and

Lionel. Thank you Lionel for caring enough to find me. Thanks Jazz for supporting me. Chris, I hope to see more of you really soon. Heather Ferguson, The Hancocks, especially Tracy and Jasmine Hancock, I wrote the majority of Dark Black when you were keeping Lourie. Thanks! Xav, my baby's father, thanks for the years. Good and bad. Much Love! Shoqun Hicks and family, stay up sister. God has a plan for you. No matter what I got love for you. My Philly family, Felicia Milbourne and family, Antonia Singleton, a true supporter. Dushawn Banks, another true supporter, Juanita Walker, Kendra Owens, Kenya from Columbus, Michelle Taylor, gotta shout you out. Virginia Hardy, Michelle, Earl Holt, hehehehe, The Staff of Live Oak Public Libraries: Kaylon Ferris, Lawrence Bradley, Asia Lavant, Latrelle Mobley, Wanda Grandberry, Kemira, Maria, Alex Pinkston, Monifa Gregory, Trenia Brown, Shelby Parsons. Kevin Green. Mrs. Barbara. Mrs. Jernell for letting me use her computer. To Chris Jetter akaI Marcus..lol…and Denise Jetter thanks. Markie Savage…yep I put your full name. One of the first people to believe in my music. Thanks. To LaDrann, Linda, and Kel, true supporters, Mrs. Frieda, thank you for supporting me, other great supports Jay Blaque, Jay Hollands, Gleniece, Camille Kimble, Tiyana Hurst, Summer Bess, Julian Moore. James Locke, My neighbor, Krystal Giles, good neighbors make coming home a lot easier. Love ya like I been knowin ya for a while. Stay up! Marquel Brown, been showin' major love. Angel and family, Craig Baggs, Lisa McCormick, Anthony Mo Phats, thanks for your wisdom and your support. Pastor James Paul Witherspoon and first lady Natalie Witherspoon, Tony "Polo" and Davena Jordan, Thanks for all that you do for the community. DJ Playa, gotta shout you out funny man. Thanks for your support. Lil Mel, stay up! Lil Red, keep grindin'! Ace on the Beat, I see you!

A special thanks to Taz David, you pushed me from the start and motivated me throughout my journey, without you the mixtape nor the book would not have been as great as it was. That's for real. Thanks for your contributions. Alecia "Lucy" Robins, one of the first to believe me, you could have told me no, but you didn't. Thanks girlie! Erick Tyree, another believer. Find me! Paulette Watts, not too many support these days, yours was incredible. Thanks! Mrs. Elisha, my mother from another mother, or should I say 'best friend'. Brittany Johnson, the first person to read Dark Black thoroughly and my editor. Glad to have you and Miss Kennedy as family. Thanks, your help means more than me than you will ever know, Ontreal "Trigg" Bowers, mixed and master the mixtape. Thanks for your encouraging words throughout my journey and thanks for making the music sound A1. To my good friend Mel Graves, thank you, I still believe in our dream. This is just the beginning.

Also thanks to everyone who made the mixtape possible. Punch, Kj, Sie Sie, Turtle, Breeze Baybe, Grizzy Graham Portlife, Dana Bernard, Taz Gutta, and QD

If I took the time to name you guys, I have real love for you all. Please don't get offended in any way. And if you missed you, I truly apologize. But don't worry, they are more novels to come. PEACE!!!

Made in the USA
Columbia, SC
29 May 2017